Andrea Bolter has always been fascinated by matters of the heart. In fact, she's the one her girlfriends turn to for advice with their love-lives. A city mouse, she lives in Los Angeles with her husband and daughter. She loves travel, rock 'n' roll, sitting in cafés and watching romantic comedies she's already seen a hundred times. Say hi at andreabolter.com.

Hana Sheik falls in love every day, reading her favourite romances and writing her own happily-ever-afters. She's worked in various jobs— but never for very long, because she's always wanted to be a romance author. Now, happily, she gets to live that dream. Born in Somalia, she moved to Ottawa, Canada, at a very young age, and still resides there with her family.

GW00361868

JET-SET ESCAPE WITH HER BILLIONAIRE BOSS

ANDREA BOLTER

FALLING FOR HER FORBIDDEN BODYGUARD

HANA SHEIK

MILLS & BOON

First published in Great Britain 2024
by Mills & Boon, an imprint of HarperCollins*Publishers* Ltd,
1 London Bridge Street, London, SE1 9GF

www.harpercollins.co.uk

HarperCollins*Publishers*, Macken House, 39/40 Mayor Street Upper,
Dublin 1, D01 C9W8, Ireland

Jet-Set Escape with Her Billionaire Boss © 2024 Andrea Bolter

Falling for Her Forbidden Bodyguard © 2024 Muna Sheik

ISBN: 978-0-263-32137-1

08/24

MIX
Paper | Supporting
responsible forestry
FSC™ C007454

This book contains FSC™ certified paper
and other controlled sources to ensure responsible forest management.

For more information visit www.harpercollins.co.uk/green.

Printed and Bound in the UK using 100% Renewable Electricity
at CPI Group (UK) Ltd, Croydon, CR0 4YY

JET-SET ESCAPE WITH HER BILLIONAIRE BOSS

ANDREA BOLTER

MILLS & BOON

For my BAND group

CHAPTER ONE

"YOU NEED TO learn to relax, Jackson." Dr. Singh leaned forward in his chair, obviously trying to make his point. "When was the last time you took a vacation? Or walked on the beach, or even played a round of golf?"

"There are only so many hours in a day," Jackson quipped after pausing to reach into his pocket and tilt up his phone screen so he could get a quick check of the time. After his examination, Dr. Singh had asked him to step into his cluttered office, where they sat across each other at his desk. Jackson was already behind schedule, the doctor visit taking longer than he'd anticipated. "I'm swamped." Indeed, running the acquisitions company that became his after his parents died took every moment from him. Who had time for a vacation?

"Being busy doesn't exempt you from taking care of yourself."

With both of his parents dying much younger than average age, Jackson was screened regularly in the hope that any developing heath problem would be caught and treated early. But he'd scheduled a special appointment because the tightness in his neck and shoulders was becoming more frequent.

"I felt that muscle strain you're talking about. You're hard as a rock. You report headaches in addition to the occasional shortness of breath. Those are irregularities in a thirty-three-year-old man. We'll run some tests but I think what you're describing is chronically uncontrolled stress."

Jackson figured plenty of people lived to ripe old ages with lives that didn't leave time for golf. He tried to speed up the conversation with a short "Fine." At least Dr. Singh didn't think he was in immediate danger.

"I'm serious. It's long thought that lifestyle, and mental and spiritual wellness, greatly influence health. You need to rest, eat well, exercise. And take breaks from all of it every once in a while. Did your parents have pursuits other than work?"

"Are you kidding?" Jackson snarked. He thought back to his father and mother when he was growing up, both putting in eighteen-hour days, sometimes seven days a week like he did now. His doctor was stating the obvious, that Jackson was following in their footsteps. Which he knew in his gut to be true.

Still, the Finns weren't people with hobbies or sports or pastimes. They worked a lot and slept a little, plain and simple. That's how empires were built and maintained. Jackson's lean physique was the result of poorly digested meals eaten indifferently at desks and on airplanes more than from following a nutrition strategy.

"I think it's essential that you make some changes.

Carve out the time for yourself. You must find a balance or you're going to get sick. How about starting with a massage? That can be restorative."

Dr. Singh had no idea how ironic his suggestion was.

One, two, three, four, five stories, Jackson counted, eyes ticking upward as he studied the Sherwood Building across the street from where the driver dropped him off after his doctor's appointment. He owned that historic building, or that was to say that Finn Enterprises did. Which, of course, now came to mean Jackson and Jackson alone, as he was an only child. With his mother's untimely death followed by his father's, he was left with full ownership of their many assets. He hadn't seen the landmark Sherwood Building in a year, so long ago that while he knew it was five floors, he wanted to get a good view of the structure from across the street, counting the stories to reconfirm. He'd be spending time here now, remembered agonies notwithstanding. Jackson was on a mission.

New York's busy Tribeca neighborhood surrounded him. A syllabic abbreviation for Triangle Below Canal Street, the Lower Manhattan neighborhood was renowned. In the early eighteen hundreds the area's Washington Market was a central shopping hub for meat and fish, dairy and produce. In fact, upon completion in 1830, the Sherwood Building itself held dry goods merchants. By the end of that century many of the area's original brick buildings were replaced by factories, manufacturers and warehouses. Fortunately, the lovingly nicknamed Sher survived. In the past fifty or so years, Tribeca received a huge boon when film-makers, artists and celebrities began buying up property. Now a mélange of restoration, new construction, green spaces and a few remaining cobblestoned streets, it was one of the city's most unique enclaves.

Even with the typical New York swirl of hurried pedestrians, horns honking and the rattle of subways underground, Jackson's eyes stayed glued to his building. He'd really forgotten how dramatic it was, Italianate architecture with huge arched windows on the street level, and cast-iron front facades that were among the first of their kind in New York. He was proud to be such a grand old dame's owner.

On the street, businesses populated every available space. A boba café stood on one side of the Sher with a pet groomer on the other. The building's ground floor was leased to an art dealer and a couple of colorful abstract paintings hung in those front windows. Offices on the second, third and fourth floors housed longtime tenants. It was the fifth, and top, floor where Jackson had business today.

Some of those memories he dreaded ticked across his mind like a camera roll of still photographs. His awful debacle of a marriage had nearly shut down operations four years ago on the fateful fifth floor, which housed a day spa that had previously made every best-of list around the globe. Until Jackson's disaster. After that, it languished. Operational but underutilized. No longer buzzed about, true spa aficionados having long moved on to newer places. With a swallow, Jackson re-affirmed to himself that he was going to restore Spa at the Sher to the greatness it once held a reputation for. It was the least he could do for his parents. They wouldn't be there to see it, but Jackson would know he did it.

It was actually a paradox that the Finns owned a spa at all, given their all-work-and-no-play mode of operation, as Dr. Singh had just pointed out. It was only one business within their varied portfolio, but obtaining a landmark building in Manhattan was, in and of itself, a crowning triumph for his parents. Starting from an early age, they'd both worked three jobs a day to save up enough money to leave Ohio and start a life in New York. That they made it to the top, to own one of the city's most famous addresses, was truly an American dream. Jackson turned it into a nightmare.

It gnawed him alive that he had let their prized acquisition become irrelevant because of bad decisions. Meanwhile, other luxury spas pressed forward with beautiful designs and features, and both classic and cutting-edge offerings. With no new innovations, the Sher had lost its luster. Jackson himself had been isolating and living in hotels everywhere but New York, as if avoiding the city would make all the history fade away. Now he was finally back, as the spa's group of investors was gathering in a few weeks to vote on the fate of Spa at the Sher.

The spa deserved to be restored to its former glory, and Jackson was going to convince the investors of such. Lest they vote to back out of their shares in the business. He'd get rid of that cute fairy they'd hired as manager who they'd never given any power to. What was her name—Emma, Eden, Elsa? He'd hire a real spa director with a vision and give him or her the budget to implement it. Hopefully then the ache in the back of his neck that represented the past would subside. And perhaps he wouldn't wake up unable to catch his breath in dark hotel rooms alone in the middle of the night anymore.

Maybe he'd even take his doctor's advice and get a massage. After all, that was one of the services spas were best known for. There was a time when Spa at the Sher employed some of the best massage therapists on the planet, who came with their own client rosters and weeks-long waiting lists. He'd return it to those good old days.

He took in the majesty of the Sher one more time before retrieving that pixie girl's name from his phone. Up in the window of the fifth floor, part of the spa, Jackson spotted someone gazing down to the street scene. It looked like a woman. Was it that manager? For some unexplainable reason, a wiggle shot up his spine.

"My six-o'clock glycolic-acid-peel client canceled so I'm going home," Demi, one of the Spa at the Sher's estheticians, said to Esme, who was gazing down to the street from the large fifth-floor windows.

"Okay, see you tomorrow," she answered without turning. She didn't know why she was gazing down from the windows or what she was looking for. Well, actually she did. But she had things to do, so, with great effort, pulled herself away. She returned to her tasks, separating a large vase of colorful flowers into smaller ones so that she could place them on three different tables in the reception area. *He* was expected any minute now and she wanted to make the spa shine as much as it could.

After all, although the spa had no director, and therefore no direction, as manager she was running things with what she had to work with. Right down to repurposing a floral arrangement, or buying some new flavors of tea for clients to enjoy. Anything she could do so that guests had a memorable experience and would return. At that thought, she clicked her tongue against the roof of her mouth. *Not easy.* Not when there were incredible, unforgettable spas all over the world that offered so much more than the stodgy old Sher, which had seen better days.

"The Vichy shower is broken again," Esme's assistant manager, Trevor, announced as he came out from the main corridor and into the reception area. "Do you want me to call for repair?"

"Yeah. Get them to come as soon as they can. I don't want to have to rebook anyone because of it."

Trevor turned and ducked into a treatment room. Esme neatened up the front desk, putting away the sticky notes staff sometimes left for each other reminding them of things that needed doing. She didn't know why she was nervous. Maybe it was because owner Jackson Finn hadn't said why he was coming in as opposed to the typical email or phone call that was his usual method of communication. He rarely even scheduled a video meeting. Appearing after what Esme guessed was close to a year made no sense. Unless he was coming to fire her, having the decency to at least do that in person.

She again peered down to the street, as if she would recognize him in the crowd at this distance. When she'd seen him on video and a few times in person, she did notice how handsome he was, with his thick dark hair, impeccable in tailored business clothes and a devastating smile that made rare appearances. All of that was neither here nor there, merely observation. She reassured herself that he had no grounds to fire her. The spa wasn't losing money; they were afloat. It had lost its charm, though it was a perfectly serviceable establishment. The Wall Street crowd did still make their way up for deep tissue massages, sometimes booked at regular biweekly intervals to fit in with busy schedules. The Tribeca and SoHo art scene still trickled in for the ministrations given to battle the damaging effects of big city life. The Sher was still as much a part of the neighborhood as the dry cleaners and the pizzeria.

Esme remembered years ago reading about it in spa magazines. The historic building. The fifth-floor oasis of pampering and unfathomable luxury in Lower Manhattan. She'd read interviews with the professionals who worked here and had brought leading-edge everything from the online accounting program to the latest in skin rejuvenation. They'd all moved on now. Esme didn't know the full story of why the spa had fallen from its highest peak. When she was brought in four years ago, she'd heard gossip that Jackson's wife had been running things. Or that was to say, ruining things.

Esme was curious about what really transpired but was never privy to anything other than hearsay.

Doing her final walk-through before he was to make his return, she double-checked the side table that displayed those new teas. One large clear cylinder held cool water infused with cucumber and a second one was flavored with lemon slices. There were whole fresh fruits, nuts and dark chocolate to nibble.

With its palate of the palest lavender and sage accents against tan furniture, it was welcoming, pleasant although dated. All of the walls held photos, paintings or drawings of flowers. Again, pretty but not compelling. Likewise, the treatment menu itself was flat, nothing to offer those chasing the next new experience. There was nothing she could do to dazzle Jackson. A spa without a director, a direction and a budget to make it happen was stagnant.

Hearing the elevator doors open outside the spa's glass entrance door and catching sight of tall and formidable Jackson Finn meant that she was about to find out what brought him in. He opened the heavy door and entered, his dark brown eyes quickly scanning the foyer until they landed on her. "Esme Russo, right?"

"Are you okay?" Ooh, that was a bit personal but it popped out of her mouth. His shoulders were practically touching his ears, obvious even under the bulk of his fine wool coat.

"What?"

"Your shoulders are so tense."

"Yeah, I know. Everybody keeps telling me that."

He approached and reached out his hand to shake

hers. Which was strange to her. Spa people didn't shake hands. If you knew someone, you hugged and if you didn't, you weren't sure how they felt about touch so wouldn't want to invade their personal space until that was established. In any case, she'd forgotten that Jackson had a formality about him that was instantly out of place at the spa. Out of propriety she returned the handshake. His was firm and his hand all but wrapped around hers, an unexpectedly pleasant sensation.

"Can I take your coat?"

As he removed the garment topping a formal gray suit and handed it to her, she had this ridiculous impulse to bring it to her nose just to see what his smell was like. Of course, she resisted and quickly shook her head in surprise at herself. She hung the coat on the rack put out in the colder months so that clients weren't encumbered with heavy outerwear they didn't need in the warmth of the spa. When she turned around she saw that his eyes were directed at her, and she had the sense that he'd been watching every move she made. Please, please, please. Don't let him have come to fire her. With her considerable experience, it wouldn't be hard for her to find another job, but being fired never looked good on a résumé.

Jackson then scrutinized the reception area. Two sofas and the registration desk, with the relaxation room in sight to the right. "Was this how the front room was arranged last time I was here?"

Oh, no. She was sure she heard disapproval in his voice. "I believe so. We may have repositioned the sofas with a bit more feng shui."

He raised his eyebrows as if he didn't understand her. Was it possible he didn't know what feng shui was? She supposed, as the CEO of a multi-million-dollar company, he had underlings that handled everything for him including the harmony of environment. "Were you successful?" He caught her eyes so they locked with his. Wow, they were deep and soulful, brown like black coffee. She also saw pain inside them, and not just from the stiffness of the shoulders.

"Successful in what?"

"Improving the feng shui."

"I don't know if that's really measurable. It's just a flow decision."

"A flow decision?" Why did his tone sound like an interrogation?

After all, if he wasn't going to be involved with the spa enough to see it more than once a year, he didn't really get to be critical. Moving a couple of sofas around to create a more welcoming entry didn't seem like a change so big that she even needed to communicate it to her higher-ups. "Do you dislike it?"

He shrugged those stiff, broad shoulders slightly. "I don't have a feeling about it one way or the other." He was so tightly wound. He obviously didn't lead a spa lifestyle. Peering over to the beverage table in the relaxation room, he asked, "Are those cucumber slices in the water?"

"Yes."

"Your clients enjoy that?" Again he sounded like he had either just landed from another planet or thought she had.

Without waiting, she dashed over to pour him a glassful. "Try it. It's very refreshing."

He eyed it skeptically before taking a sip. Again she felt like her entire career now rested in that eight ounces of water as he weighed his decision. "Blech."

Failure! As if she'd just lost a contest.

Surprisingly though, he tried a second time. When he brought his full lips to the rim of the cup, she nervously licked her own. How did he make the act of drinking a beverage seem so…important? He didn't appear to like the water any more on the second sip.

"Would you like to sit down?"

"No."

"Is there something I could do for you, then?" She still had no idea what the true purpose of his visit was, and whether she was to assist him with it in some way.

He pointed to the computer at the reception desk. "Who has access here to your system?"

Wasn't that an obvious answer? "Staff."

"All of them?" What was he fishing for?

"Pardon me, I mean the administrative staff. Myself, my assistant manager, Trevor, and our two front desk supervisors."

"How often do you change access passwords?"

"I believe it's on our schedule every six months."

"It's very important." Esme thought he sounded suspicious. She felt a bit insulted by that. Maybe it was an attitude left over from what she'd heard were some shady dealings at the spa before she'd started working here. "I'd like to refamiliarize myself with the space."

She couldn't ask why. All she could get out was,

"Okay. A couple of the treatment rooms are in use—"
she pointed down the corridor "—but otherwise, I'm
sure you know your way around."

"Actually, I don't really remember the layout."

That was so unexpected she had to collect herself
with a deep inhale through her nose and a slow exhale
through her mouth. She hadn't realized she'd be giving
Jackson Finn a tour of his own property.

CHAPTER TWO

JACKSON DIDN'T DOUBT that there were people in the world, New Yorkers even, who enjoyed a glass of water with mushy chunks of bitter plants in it. He just wasn't one of them and wondered what it would take to get that godawful taste out of his mouth. Perhaps a pastry from the Italian café down the block. Fortunately, there was a bowl of mints on one of the tables so he could grab a couple and pop them into his mouth immediately, which made an instant improvement.

"If you'll follow me, then." Esme pointed to the main corridor. He'd forgotten how pretty she was. She wore brown trousers topped by a sweater that was woven in varying shades of pink. Somehow the pink and brown complemented each other in a most unlikely combo that was unusual and upbeat at the same time. She no longer had what he'd thought of as a short pixie haircut; instead the brown locks had grown into a choppy shag with golden highlights that brushed her shoulders.

The sweater ended at her hip, and when she turned and gestured for him to follow, her most attractive behind swung a bit under the fabric of the trousers. Jackson checked himself. He was hardly in the habit of perusing women's bodies. Since his divorce four years ago he'd had intimate encounters with women, business types he met in bars around the world, when his mortal need for human contact had reached a crucial proportion and he had to have a release. The women were picked by their ability to understand that was all he was available for. He was exactly one and done when it came to relationships after the horror show known as Livia.

It was interesting that even Esme had noticed his shoulders were tight. Apparently, it was that obvious. Tension had become his normal state. Once he got the spa revamp underway, would all that he'd submerged release? He knew Dr. Singh was right that if he didn't manage his stress and modify his lifestyle he was surely on his way to the same early grave as his parents. Though in the past he'd dismissed advice to slow down and find ways to recharge, he acknowledged to himself that it had now become critical.

"This is typical of our massage suites." Esme pushed open a door to let Jackson enter. The room had the same cordial, if drab, decor as the reception area, referencing flowers as decoration. Dried stems in a collection of small vases adorned the side table while black-and-white photos of various blooms were hung four in a row on the wall. Meditation-type music played at a low volume. Regarding the massage table in the center of the room, she informed him, "We use Northstar tables in all of the suites. I think they're the best on the market. Made with a high-density foam that lasts a lot longer than some of the other brands."

"I wouldn't know. I rarely use spa services."

Her eyebrows bunched. "Interesting that you own one, then, isn't it?" He was taken aback—or was it intrigued?—by her bluntness yet it was something he'd asked himself. In his family, self-indulgence was not part of the regime. The Finns toiled; that's what they did. Spa was foreign to them other than profit/loss statements. Esme bringing it up merely added to the ludicrousness of the situation.

"My parents bought the Sher for its status as a landmark building. The spa was already established here so we figured we'd just continue with it. That is to say until my wife, my ex-wife, my then-wife…" Jackson tripped over his words. He still felt pure shame that he'd let any facet of this historic building into the hands of flinty Livia, who not only falsified business records for her own financial gain, but also cheated on Jackson with a man she organized the whole scheme with. His parents were furious at their son's lack of judgment in a partner.

Livia wasn't at all the type they'd have wanted him to couple off with in the first place. They were serious people. Never a couple. Never romantic. Never displaying love. Livia was loud and dramatic and liked the sound of her own voice. Jackson was attracted to the flash and fantasy, if only to offset what felt like an emptiness in the somber life he'd grown up in. His parents couldn't understand any more than Jackson could, really, why he was cut from a different cloth and needed more than the life they had created. He became enraptured, which led him to trust her, and that's how

the trouble began. After the fury from the embezzle-
ment, Jackson sensed a pervasive malaise grow in his
parents, a disappointment in their son that he believed
contributed to their untimely deaths, a stabbing guilt
that he still carried. Which was why he returned. He
couldn't bring them back to life but he could the spa.

Esme was probably completely unaware of the Finn
family's problems when she was hired. He'd put his
human resources team right to work finding a replacement for his cheating ex-wife, who he fired as soon as
her ruse was discovered by a thankfully persistent accountant. They decided to bring in a manager, rather
than a director. Someone who could just keep things
running while they figured out what to do next. His
HR people had picked Esme's résumé from a stack of
others.

Unfortunately, Jackson's interest in the spa languished alongside his parents' weariness and their
deaths. So much time had passed that his investors
recently informed him they were considering pulling
out of the partnership. The news lit a fire in Jackson
he didn't know he could kindle. It was now or never
for him to rebuild the spa's relevance or sell it off. Un-
finished business whose time had come.

"It's an exquisite building."

Esme stopped his ruminating on Livia and those
awful times. "Do you like it here?"

"Um, sure." She seemed thrown by the question and
didn't know how to answer. He wondered if that meant
that she didn't. Not an easy thing to say to the owner,
especially not knowing him well.

She led him into another treatment room set up for facial work. "Here's one of our skin care rooms. We've got a separate sound system in each room—" she pointed to the speakers in each corner "—if the client likes particular music. We also utilize candles and aromatherapy."

"Is that what I'm smelling?" Jackson sniffed.

"That's actually the product we use in our pineapple facial."

"You use pineapple in the treatment?"

"It's the key ingredient in the products we use for the protocol. Pineapple contains a powerful enzyme, bromelain, that's great for the face."

"Pineapple. On someone's face. Not on a fruit plate." He didn't know why he was trying a little humor. Maybe because he was so out of place. All he knew about skin care was that he had to put sunscreen on after he shaved. "Why would anyone want to smell like fruit?"

She smiled, which he was glad for.

"I guess that might seem strange but in this case, it has a purpose. Scent can also be unwinding or stimulating, depending on what we're going for. A favorite smell can be transformative to the client during the fifty minutes or so that they're in the treatment room with us."

Jackson remembered how his doctor told him that he needed to find ways to relax. Although he couldn't imagine mucky cucumber water and sickly sweet smells as getting that done for him. He absentmindedly rubbed the back of his neck.

"May I ask, are you having some distress? I noticed your shoulders were tense when you came in. And just now I saw you self-massaging your neck."

He hadn't realized that he'd brought his hand behind his neck or that the motion had a name. "No. I'm not here for a massage." Despite whether or not he needed one. Esme's spine stiffened at the harshness of his tone. He hadn't meant to offend her. "Carry on."

He followed her farther down the corridor. "This is our wet room." It was as if the entire room she showed him was one gigantic shower, with floor-to-ceiling tiling, a large treatment bed in the center that had some sort of drainage below and a contraption above it that had seven water jets.

He had a vague recollection of receiving a very large plumbing bill to repair some sort of problem in this room. "What is this?"

"It's called a Vichy shower. The jets rain down on the client and we adjust the temperature and the water pressure to create a massage-like experience. Unfortunately, it's on the fritz yet again." Esme certainly knew what she was talking about, unlike him. After getting rid of Livia, he found less emotionally fraught projects to concentrate on. But it ate into his gut as a physical manifestation of letting his parents down. He wasn't born to a happy and demonstratively loving family. But his parents were good people and he discredited them by thinking he had to have the swirl of romance they considered a waste of time.

Esme continued her tour with the men's shower and locker room. "We've got a large whirlpool bathtub, steam room, six showers, two vanity areas and full-length cedar lockers. Another snack lounge, complimentary toiletries, hair dryers, lots of charging stations. I love our guests to stay for a lengthy visit with us, and take as much of a break from the real world as they can spare. And leave rejuvenated."

Rejuvenated. Interesting. Though he'd never thought of a spa that way. That it could become a personal oasis, a fee-paying club of sorts. He'd categorized it as a luxury for people with cash to burn, not unlike money spent on jewelry or expensive restaurants. When his parents bought the spa, there had been a longtime management team who'd spent over twenty years creating a top-notch, highly regarded establishment.

When the Finns bought it, that group took the change of ownership as an opportunity to move on, opening a few spas of their own in the Midwest. Then Livia came along implementing changes that didn't work, and willy-nilly eliminations of services that clients still actually wanted. Plus, in retrospect, even Livia's high-strung, reedy voice and fast, jerky way of moving never matched with what was supposed to be the vibe of the spa. Unlike Esme, whose lush voice sounded like the middle of a cool forest. One that he could walk through and feel a grounding he'd never even imagined. There was something unique about her.

He asked her solely because it popped into his head, "Where did you work before you joined us?" Obviously, he could have gotten that information from a résumé they must have had on file and she probably thought it was ridiculous that he hadn't. Or she might be wondering why he was inquiring after she'd already been working at the Sher for four years.

Nonetheless she responded, giving him the chance to hear her thick, luscious speaking voice again. "I held a supervisory position at a luxury hotel spa in Miami. Prior to that I spent two years at a Mayan spa in Mexico. And before that I did an apprenticeship in Denmark."

"So, you're not a stranger to moving around."

"Actually, I was born and raised in New York. In the Bronx. I can't think of anywhere I'd rather settle. New York is in my blood."

He let a smile tip up. He was raised in New York, too, although far from the Bronx. He grew up on Long Island in the wealthy suburbs. After Livia, New York was nothing but streets of regret so he stayed away. Although lately he'd been thinking otherwise. How long could he run, remaining a nomad of cold hotels and no roots?

The Sher's physical space was terrific; it was the lack of vision and keeping up to date that was needed. Weeks of work, not months, would be all that was required.

A couple of dangling pieces clicked into his mind. How much a spa director and a spa manager were different. He'd want a director who knew spas all over the world, who kept up on marketing, social media, human resources, client relations. Meanwhile, a manager would keep things running smoothly, supervising employees, and making sure what was needed for services was operational. Would he retain Esme as that manager? He supposed it depended if the still-to-be-hired director wanted her. His lips pursed at the idea of never seeing Esme again. Although he had no idea why.

What was Jackson planning? Esme wondered. He surveyed the spa as if he was a potential client inquiring about services, not the owner. Perhaps his online files kept him as informed as he needed to be. After all, he seemed disdainful of everything from cucumber water to enzyme scrubs. Was he on the premises to merely refamiliarize himself with the property and layout for the purpose of shutting the spa down? Would he repurpose the space entirely, into offices, shops, even residences if he had the required zoning? Although someone would have to be bonkers anyway to want to alter this gorgeous monument to the city's architectural history.

His personal questions continued. "What got you started in the industry in the first place?"

That shouldn't have been a loaded question but, in her case, it was. "I like spas, where people get taken care of."

"All right, so you could have become, let's say, a doctor or a nurse."

"True, but…" Did she really want to get candid with someone she barely knew and was unlikely to see much of? Still, she had nothing to hide. "I'm not from a family of means. Something like medical school would have been out of our reach."

"Yes, but there are scholarships and loans."

Why was he cross-examining her? "Is that how *you* went to college?"

"I'm very fortunate that my parents sent me to business school to manage our company someday, of course not knowing how soon someday was going to be." She remembered that both of his parents died, his mother not long after Esme had been working for them a year, and his father soon after that. There had been a lot of obvious strife in the Finn family and they had a black cloud over them, from what little she knew.

"Business. Was that your choice of study?"

"It made sense for our family as I'm an only child. The only one who could take over the company."

"Was that what you would have picked if you'd had a choice?" He glared at her, not actually at her, but into her, those luminous dark eyes suddenly fierce as a warrior.

After the awkward silence that followed, where Esme's fingers rolled on little bits of her sweater and he seemed to watch her do so, she realized she was nervous around this forbidding yet troubled man who held her fate. She'd offended him with her too probing question. She wasn't used to interacting with the boss man.

He broke the moment with defense. "Weren't we talking about *you*?"

"The truth is that there was dysfunction in my family and planning for my future was the last thing on my parents' minds." No, Gia and Matt were far too concerned with themselves to have ever put thought into their only daughter's future. "They'd have as soon had me never leave home, so that I could take care of them."

Jackson's expression flickered at her frank answer. "Oh." It was a lot to tell a total stranger. But she learned long ago that the more she threw past trauma out into the ether, into the universe, the less power it held over her.

An elderly woman emerged from the ladies' locker room frazzled and rifling through her purse. Esme rushed over to pick up a few things that had fallen out. "Sit down, Mrs. Lee. You're not at peace. Was something wrong with your treatment today?" She brought the woman to a couch.

"I lost my phone," Mrs. Lee lamented as they sat. "I can never find the darn thing."

"Let's do some breathing and then we'll figure out the phone. With me now, a deep breath in through your nose." She demonstrated and Mrs. Lee followed. "Then a slow exhale through your mouth. Do it again, in through the nose, out through the mouth. Two more times." She glanced up to see Jackson noting the interaction.

"That's better."

"Okay, now, when was the last time you saw the phone?"

"In the locker room. I was calling my daughter to tell her I was finished here."

"Should we have another check in your purse?" Within seconds, Esme located the phone. "There we go."

"Thank you, Esme." She helped Mrs. Lee to her feet.

"See you next time." As she walked the tiny woman toward the exit, Jackson dashed over to the door to open it for her. Hmm. To add to the enigma that was Jackson Finn, apparently, he was a gentleman as well. In the process, his arm brushed against Esme's, creating a shocking prickle down her arm.

"You were saying," he quickly returned after the woman left, "how you got into the industry." He peered down at his arm where it had touched hers as if he was expecting to find something there. The contact had affected him as well.

After she verified that there was, in fact, nothing on his arm other than her aura she answered, "There was a small spa near where I grew up. I got a part-time job there in high school. I mostly did laundry. You'd be amazed at how many towels a spa goes through in a day. I saw people come in colorless and hunched over, and walk out changed, standing tall, smiles rediscovered, as if their burdens had been lifted, even if only temporarily. And I liked that."

She wouldn't share with him the similarity to what went on at her home. Self-centered people having the attention and intention focused on them. That's what Esme was used to and what came naturally to her. Her father *needed* a pizza from Santini's. Her mother *needed* a hot bath drawn for her. Her parents weren't slave drivers; they were just endlessly helpless. Her father wouldn't have had a clue how to order a pizza or even understand how to walk into a pizzeria and wait for his order to be cooked.

They lived on money inherited from Esme's maternal grandparents, who died before she was born. The payout was dispensed monthly with just enough to meet expenses, so that didn't motivate her parents to go out and get jobs. They spent most of their time watching television. Currently, they did so in the ramshackle house that was left to them in Alabama, all they now had, their move allowing Esme to remain in New York and not have to be responsible for them anymore.

She'd always known that she'd get out from under their cloud of listlessness as soon as she was old enough. Taking care of people was the experience she could bring to the job, something she enjoyed as long as it was by choice. Washing towels, mopping floors and restocking products and tools was a start in a business she seemed born to be a part of. Now, at thirty-two, she'd been at the Sher too long, hoping she'd achieve her ultimate goal of becoming a director so that she could create the spa of her dreams. One that would claim her place in the storied history that dated back to medieval times when people would drink and bathe in mineral-rich waters to promote health and healing.

"The work comes naturally to you," he concluded. For reasons that she couldn't name, she wanted to tell him things she'd never told anyone. She wouldn't, of course, but she had never met anyone she'd ever had the urge to confide in. He'd figured her out right away. For a caretaker, the focus was always outward. What was going on with *her* was of no interest to others. Right? That was her role in the world. Except that Jackson was asking. About her. He was listening.

"I went to school to learn massage. I obtained a license in Western modalities and then later another in Eastern traditions."

"You're comfortable touching people you don't know?"

She chuckled nervously. Okay, so she had a one-second idea about touching *him* further than a hand-shake or a brush of his sleeve. He sure as heck needed to be touched, what with the rigidity in his body that needed loosening up. He was slim but powerfully built; she could see as much under his clothes. "That sort of goes with the territory, doesn't it? We do skin care and bodywork. It involves a lot of touching. And a contract of trust."

"You do the skin care part, too?"

"Yes, over the years I've gotten certified in every-thing in order to run a full-service spa. When I take time off from here, I go to conferences and trade shows and industry events. Though massage was where I started and it's what always had my heart."

"Impressive that you've taken it upon yourself to continue learning and growing."

"Have you ever had a massage?" Crazy that was a question for a spa owner but she was curious as he'd already declared that this was just another business to him and that it was the Sher Building that had inter-ested his parents, not the spa.

He shrugged. "Here and there. Honestly, they're a waste of time for me. I don't relax. That's not on my agenda. Although..." He let his voice drift off. She was dying to know what it was he stopped himself from saying but it wasn't her place to ask.

"I hope you don't mind me saying so but I do see a lot of tightness in your neck and shoulders. Would you like to lie down or even sit in a chair and let me do a few acupuncture needles and see if I can help out?" At that his eyes froze. She knew she had immediately goofed; that had not been an acceptable offer. Okay, a big businessman does not need an employee to offer to heal him.

Taking care of people.

"Sorry, of course not. That was silly of me."

"Needles?" Oh, he was a needle scaredy-cat! So were many people until they tried it.

"Yes, acupuncture can be an immediate and powerful way to rebalance."

"Not in a million years."

"It was just a thought. My apologies."

"You're qualified to stick needles into people as well?"

"Yes. Acupuncture has been a respected discipline for over three thousand years."

"I'll take your word for that." He tried to chuckle it off. "I think I've seen enough today." He gestured toward the treatment rooms farther down, where, in his mind, sinister and painful things happened. He was quite a bit taller than her so she craned her neck back a little to study him further. Wow, was he gorgeous! Visible stiffness aside. He had smooth golden skin against that dark hair, and a jaw that seemed to catch light. She could detect the slightest five-o'clock shadow in his beard line, but she knew skin well enough to know that his stubble wouldn't have been coarse. Which had nothing to do with anything—he was just an attractive man who crossed her path.

She didn't do men, anyway. The last thing she needed was yet someone else to have to look after, to be used by, to take her attention off herself. No, thanks. Single spa professional was just fine. Which brought her back to the matter at hand.

"Jackson," she began, finally deciding to bite the bullet, "why are you here? Are you shutting the spa's doors? Have you come to fire me?"

CHAPTER THREE

JACKSON STOOD SLACK-JAWED at Esme's question as to whether he'd come to the spa to close it down, and to let her go. His inner staff knew of his plans but he hadn't specifically announced them widely or to Esme when he arrived. His agenda was quite the opposite. Her two-part question was a bit tricky, though. He didn't yet know whether she'd be remaining on staff. She'd held her lovely green eyes open and had boldly and bravely inquired about her future. She deserved a response. He had none for her. "To tell you the truth, I don't know."

"You don't know whether you're closing the spa or you don't know if you're firing me?" One hand moved to her hip in a stance of waiting for his next reply. Which was kind of sexy, her straightforwardness.

"I'm definitely not closing the spa. I'm revamping it. I want to take it back to the days when guests came from all over the world."

"What, you're planning to bring in all new people?"

"We want to attract practitioners who have their own client rosters. Each treatment room should be able to generate a lot more revenue than it is now. As to upper management, we're interviewing candidates."

"I see." There was a tinge of sadness in her voice. "When will you know?" Those eyes hooded a bit.

He intended to make the changes and get the new spa up and running quickly. In fact, he'd have to put it to vote with the investors in just a couple of weeks. That deadline was what finally provoked him. As he lay sleepless in bed in a five-star hotel in Croatia, his brainchild began to take shape. That he had to do it for his parents. And, if he was being honest, that he had to do this for himself. Or the stiff neck and shoulders and the chest pains were going to turn into something worse, as his doctor had just confirmed. While he never felt his parents forgave him for the Livia fiasco, they certainly wouldn't have wanted him to die an early death as they had.

He'd do this reimagining with a staff his HR team picked out. He didn't know about Esme's future. She was right to be concerned about her own employment status. "I'll let you know as soon as I can."

She inhaled such a long, slow breath that he could almost see her nostrils fill with air. Then she exhaled like she was blowing up a balloon. Just as she'd done with that older lady who'd gotten upset that she lost her phone. Was it some kind of spa breathing, perhaps meant to steady herself? He'd never dealt with any hirings or firings at the spa; that was left to HR. But he wasn't heartless and didn't need to know how to run a spa to know that people's livelihood was in large measure his responsibility.

"Great," she said, slicing with sarcasm.

She flustered him, a feeling he wasn't used to. *Just*

leave, he told himself. He really had nothing more to say right now. Everything wasn't going to be settled today. Something in him didn't want to go, but logic won out. He moved toward the exit. "We'll talk again soon."

"Great," she snapped again, clearly not saying words that were on the verge of spilling out.

With that, he went out the door and stepped into the elevator that was conveniently waiting. As the doors closed, his neck seized up. He felt bad leaving Esme with such uncertainty but he'd told her all he knew.

For a moment, he wondered what it was like for a client to leave the spa after a transformative treatment. Did they descend from the fifth floor in a euphoria that carried them into the busy, loud and abrasive New York City streets as if they were floating on a cloud? How long did the high last? He wouldn't know from personal experience because he never took a time out. Dr. Singh's words came back to him.

You need to learn to relax.

Maybe he'd get a massage soon, after all. Not from Esme, of course. That would be inappropriately intimate.

As he reached the street, late afternoon was falling to dusk and bustling Tribeca was shrouded by a gray-white sky. He wasn't as eager to leave the area as he thought he was. Instead of returning to his hotel and the many phone calls he had left to accomplish, he spotted the Italian café a few doors down from the Sher. A coffee and perhaps a snack could fortify him until he ordered dinner brought to his suite. The fall chill in the

air was mitigated by the heating lamps that stood between every few tables of the café's patio, which was
so inviting he sat down before talking himself out of
it. He ordered a cappuccino, and then pulled out his
phone to talk to his assistant, Kay, with his first question the most topical. "What sort of applications are
we getting for spa director?"

"We've got a spa employment agency helping us
evaluate. There was a candidate from a hotel spa
in Philadelphia, nothing jazzy. A kinesiologist who
worked in sports massage with a minor league baseball team. Okay, but she doesn't have spa experience."
Jackson thought about Esme telling him that she was
trained in both Western and Eastern massage techniques and had her esthetician's license in skin care.

"Are you finding that these people want to bring
in their own support staff, like a manager or lead positions?" Again he thought of Esme's welfare and
whether she'd be happy working under a spa director.

"Some do, some don't. We got a message from an
entire staff of a spa closing in Brazil and they all want
to come together but none of them have New York li-
censes so it wouldn't be easy. We're vetting everyone
who applies."

"All right, keep me posted."

He tapped off of the call and stared into the middle
distance as he took a sip of the warm cappuccino that
had arrived.

Out of the corner of his eye, he spotted Esme coming
through the Sher's ground-floor doors to the street. He
couldn't help thinking how pretty her hair was, thick,

with those caramel highlights. She was really quite beautiful in an organic way. He could imagine holding hands with her in a meadow of waist-high grass. Or splashing naked together in an ocean cove. Kissing under a waterfall. He could tell she was a woman who could make a man *feel*, something to be avoided at all costs. He'd felt enough for one lifetime already. Esme's attractiveness was of no consequence to him. Although it had been strange, the little jolt between them as they were helping that elderly lady out of the spa. Jackson didn't have much touch of any kind in his life. Yet in that moment he'd wanted more from her.

She stopped to button a violet-hued coat over her clothes and to wrap a multicolored scarf around her neck. For no logical reason he thought of the skin of her throat being protected by woven warmth, and the idea of that gave him a weird contentment.

He hoped she would head down the street in the opposite direction of the café, as they had concluded their discussion for the day. In fact, things had been left on an awkward and uncertain note. Instead, she turned in his direction and wasn't but three steps closer toward him when their eyes met. She nodded in recognition and as she approached the café's outdoor seating area, he felt both compelled and obligated to shout out, "Esme, join me for coffee?"

"Oh. Hi. Okay." She may have felt she had to say yes to the boss but, in any case, she took a seat and ordered a chai latte.

"Do you live around here?" he asked.

"No." She made small talk with, "How long will you be in New York?"

"For as long as this takes. Not letting the spa go to pieces—"

"Excuse me, Jackson," she quickly interrupted, "the spa is not in pieces. In the four years I've been there you haven't given me any upgrading budget or marketing or advertising. I'm doing the best I can with what I have to work with."

Her spunk fired him with energy. "I'm not arguing that, I assure you. What I consider to be our downhill slide began before you were in our employ. And it's my fault for not having corrected that. You've done fine for us."

Her latte arrived and she took a sip as she contemplated what he'd just said. "I just want to be clear that I refuse to be scapegoated for the spa's failings. If you do fire me, I would like to be assured that Finn Enterprises would give me a good recommendation."

Somehow, he already couldn't picture the Sher without Esme, but she was right; she had to think of her own future.

"Absolutely. HR has nothing but respect for you. We wouldn't be taking it lightly if we let anyone go." Respecting employees was something he took seriously.

"Besides bringing on new staff, what are you planning?"

He wasn't prepared to give a presentation although there was no reason to hide his overall plan. In fact, his PR team had already crafted press releases announcing the relaunch of the venerable old spa. Those would go out as soon as the investor group okayed his plans. "I want to know what's out there, what makes the world's best spas *the* best. What we can bring into a city environment. What we can offer that other spas don't."

All of that made sense to him in theory. There was so much to learn. He thought of his parents, who also knew nothing about spas other than that they wanted to own a piece of New York history. Until Livia, with her sleek hair and wandering eyes came along. A master manipulator who sensed that while Jackson was successful and wealthy, he was in need. The medicine he thought she fed him was love but it turned out she only used him, played him like a game. He'd never let that happen again.

"If I may say so," Esme started, then stopped.

"Go on," he urged, interested in what she had to say.

"I think it would be hard for someone who doesn't know spas to reinvent an already existing one."

"I couldn't agree more."

Her attentive eyes got big again. The way the little wisps of her shaggy hair blew this way or that was kind of like watching leaves rustle in the wind, both soothing and majestic. He'd never met anyone who gave off the same essence as she did. Especially while she was facing the possible loss of her job.

"What I'd suggest," Esme told Jackson as they continued sipping their warm drinks, "is that you physically go see some of the world's finest spas. There's only so much you can glean from photos and menus."

He nodded in acknowledgment. After he'd asked her

for any suggestions she might have, she was embold-
ened to share some. Suggestions, ideas, theories, plans,
she had plenty of. What she hadn't had was the chance
to implement them. She never thought she would at the
Sher—her *babysitting* job was clear from the start. Yet
she stayed for four years, having got a bit stuck in the
sameness. Now the tide was turning whether she was
ready for it or not. "I can help provide you with a list if
you'd like. I mean, it's all subjective but there are definitely some obvious choices around the globe."

"The trouble is I only have three weeks until I have
to take the whole prospect to my investors and get
their approval."

"I guess you'd better leave soon, then." She tipped
her mouth in a little grin.

Interesting what almost losing their job could do to
a person. Instead of being intimidated by the powerful CEO she worked for, she figured she had nothing
to lose by showing him how knowledgeable and experienced she actually was. He'd already said that no
staffing decisions had been made. It couldn't hurt to
dazzle him with her grasp of the industry. Besides, she
knew with her contacts and work history, she could
find another job. But she didn't want just another job.
She wanted to step up. To move forward.

As night fell on Tribeca and they talked and talked,
the sky changed from dusk to the indigo of night. Hot
drinks at the café turned into two glasses of the house
red. Which led to a cheese board, several varieties
served on an attractive wooden plank with walnuts
on one side and dried apricots on the other, olives and

small slices of crusty bread. Once they'd polished that off, Jackson flagged the waiter to order a tiramisu with two forks.

She told him about special spas she knew, about everything from decor to equipment to marketing incentives. It was obvious he didn't know what extractions or fascia stretching were, but he did understand when she talked about promotions and loyalty programs.

"I certainly appreciate your thoughts. How is it that you know all the spas?"

In a flash, she wondered if he'd consider... *No, he probably wanted a fresh start... Although she knew she could...*

The conversation, explaining her world to Jackson, jazzed her up. The change at the Sher was a call to action for her. She couldn't stay in the same place anymore, with all new people above and below her, even if Jackson asked her to. It was time for a revamp of her own. As hard as it might be sometimes, like trying to walk through the molasses of her life, she had to take steps ahead now. The universe was shaking her up. It was time. This was good.

What if...? Could she be that bold...?

As to why she knew the best facilities, the answer was simple. "With my previous jobs and apprenticeships I was able to tour around. It's really a wonderful industry, great people who want each other to succeed. Everybody teaches each other."

"If only my ex-wife thought that way."

"There was a problem, which was why I was hired, right?"

"*Problem* would be an understatement," he let out with a bitter snort of a laugh. "She stole and falsified the books. Good heavens, do all of the staff know about that?"

"Nothing specific. I think everyone knew that the director had been fired for misconduct. Did people know you were married and then, subsequently, divorced?"

"Not many. She'd misled me into believing that she knew something about spas, having estranged parents who were hotel owners. Turns out she knew nothing but since I didn't, either, I was pretty easy to fool. I trusted her. Something I deeply regret."

Ah, so that's why the redo. He felt guilty for both believing his ex-wife was honest and for letting his parents' property devaluate. "Uh-huh," she uttered to encourage him to continue. It was interesting, though, to get the real story.

Esme even observed that between sips of the chianti and a lively volley of chat with her, Jackson's square shoulders settled down and were no longer grazing his ears. She studied that sort of thing in people. It's what made her good at her job. Checking in to what the other person was thinking, doing or feeling. Anticipating.

She had zero interest in men for fear that she'd end up with someone else to take care of, to put first, just as it had been since she was a child. Nonetheless, Jackson had awfully nice shoulders and it gave Esme satisfaction to see them release from their tight hold.

"I was preoccupied with other businesses of ours. I maintained total ignorance of the day-to-day running of the spa. But it gets worse."

"Sorry?"

She watched a series of reactions take over his face. First that jaw cut so exquisitely it could slice ice twitched several times on the right side. Then several blinks of his eyes seemed to further darken his pupils, really actually deaden them. And finally, he settled into a huff of stilted breath wherein she knew he was not going to tell her what *gets worse* about his ex-wife. Although, she was too curious not to try a prompt to get him to continue. "Is that why you don't partake in spa services?"

"I don't have time for spas. Finns work, that's all we do."

"Perhaps *relax* isn't a word that resonates with you. Self-care is essential."

"You sound like my doctor."

"Have you really acknowledged the emotional pain your divorce must have caused?"

"Acknowledged my emotional pain," he repeated as he swirled the last of the tiramisu around the plate with a fork, not wanting to leave anything behind. She liked that he enjoyed his dessert enough to finish it. Even though his tone in repeating her words was a little mocking.

"Have you?" she asked again point-blank. Heck, she was possibly about to be fired or quit; there was no reason to hold back. Something in her had an inkling that if she was able to help him see how restorative, how actually life-changing, a spa could be it might end up being both a good deed and a favorable reflection on her.

"Am I over my divorce? Is that what you're asking?"

"In a nutshell. We carry pain in our minds, in our bodies and in our souls. I'd imagine the body retains energy data for a long time after trauma such as divorce."

"Energy data?"

"Yes. Trauma."

"Trauma. Like the battlefield of war or a child's neglect?"

"Yes. Exactly." A child's neglect. Like her, maybe. Oh, yes, she'd consider herself traumatized.

"So you're likening a divorce from a dishonest woman to being in the middle of, say, a bombing?"

She sat back and folded her arms across her chest. Was this going to be his strategy, to challenge and, in fact, denigrate the work that meant everything to her? "I hear you, Jackson. You don't want to take what I'm saying seriously so you're making fun of it. Yes, people experience trauma from many different causes. It's okay to hang on to it if it feeds you in some way."

"I am not traumatized! I'm just divorced." His eyes shot into hers and she knew that while he was trying to shoo away her words, they had actually penetrated. He ran the back of his hand across his cheek in a motion with a certain tenderness that made her want to reach across the table and do it for him. In reality, he was just buying himself a moment to think. Then, he'd abruptly had enough and returned to an earlier topic, back to business. "I had intended to hire a spa consultant to help me redesign our style and our menu."

She could play, too. "And your retail, which could be

a big moneymaker for you, bring people into the spa, and keep them returning. Right now it's doing none of that. The retail shelves are paltry and ordinary, no products a guest couldn't get somewhere else."

"Okay, menu, look, retail, marketing, all of it."

"And I'd say again, you've gone as far as wanting to make all of those big changes, wouldn't you want to go see for yourself what's out there to compare to?"

"Where would you propose I go?"

"Let me think that all through. For certain, one stop would be Bangkok. Warm rain, juicy fruit, fragrant flowers."

"I take it that's a place you like?"

"What's not to like about Thailand?"

"I've seen the views from the thirtieth floor of a hotel."

She nodded. "I defy you not to enjoy an experience at Spa Malee." At this point she could only ponder his seeming refusal to have any fun at all. No wonder he was tense. She contemplated for a moment if his version of his divorce might be very different than that of his ex-wife's. Maybe she needed what he wasn't able to offer. He did mention she embezzled from him, though. There was no way that could come forth from a marriage of compassion and partnership. "What do you say?"

"I'll consider it." A smile spread across his lips as he removed his napkin from his lap and tossed in onto the table in obvious preparation for leaving. She hadn't seen a spontaneous grin from him. Whoa, when he wasn't trying not to, his smile could light up New York.

They stood and bundled back into their coats. She said a quick goodnight, mentally replaying that smile, as she turned away from him and left.

She called Trevor, her assistant manager, on the subway uptown to where she lived in Washington Heights. "If he invited you to dinner, he must like you."

"He definitely doesn't like me. In fact, I think I made him mad."

"How so?"

"Because I pressed him about whether or not he'd come to fire us."

"Please don't scare me. I have two kids." He and his husband, Omari, had just adopted twin babies. She had him to worry about, too.

"I don't know what he's thinking at this point. Let's don't borrow trouble yet."

CHAPTER FOUR

"I CAN'T THINK of a reason not to, can you?" Kay responded to the idea that Jackson just threw at her as they held their daily telephone meeting. An idea that Jackson knew was a little funky because he'd felt a sort of woggle in his stomach—or maybe it was lower on his body—when he'd thought of it last night, and the woggle returned as it crossed his mind several times already today. He wasn't sure that was a reason not to go forward, though. Or maybe it was. His brain was a little bit jumbled after yesterday's moonlight over Tribeca.

He'd spent such an unforeseen and interesting evening with Esme, his employee that he barely knew. He'd really never met anyone like her, someone who'd had so many obstacles to overcome and managed to make it through with a level head. Not to mention the fact that his brain had also lingered all day on thoughts of those almond-shaped green eyes that the golden highlights in her brown hair set off. And about the long, delicate fingers that picked at cheese and olives as they chatted.

"Do we have someone who can run things in her absence?"

"There's the assistant manager, Trevor Ames."

"I would just fly around the world with her for a couple of weeks?"

"If that's what you've decided to do. Like you said, go see some spas."

Jackson's wheels were turning. During dinner last night, Esme had mentioned Thailand, and also spa destinations in Sweden and Mexico that she believed were noteworthy. The thoughts of which made him feel a young man's rush about travel and adventure. Totally unlike him, the weary world trekker, lately burnt out on airports and hotels.

Kay intuited that something was going on. "So do you want me to make trip plans?"

"I haven't asked her yet if she wants to go with me." He sounded like a schoolboy inviting a girl to a dance, which made him giddy inside.

He arrived at the spa just before closing time again, not sure why he didn't just text or call Esme. He wanted to ask her in person. Or maybe it was that he wanted to see her today. In any case, she was surprised when he came through the lobby doors. "Oh, hi, Jackson. I wasn't expecting you."

"I have a proposition I wanted to talk to you about."

"I see. Are you firing me?" She said it with that cute lopsided smile so he thought, hoped, that she was kidding and knew today wouldn't be the day of her demise. Hadn't they already established that he didn't know yet whether her job was secure? A client came out from one of the treatment rooms, a woman in black yoga clothes. Esme turned her attention to her. "How was everything, Gwen?"

"Fine. Namaste."

"Namaste." He knew that was a yoga word. After the woman left, Esme turned back around to Jackson. "A proposition." That word sounded loaded coming out of her mouth.

"Can I buy you dinner again, or a glass of wine and we can talk about it?" If she said yes, they could sit down and have a leisurely discussion and lock down the itinerary.

"I'm sorry, I can't. I have plans."

Tightness clenched his gut. He hadn't even told Esme about Livia's betrayal of their marriage vows in addition to the money books. He met a woman he'd naively dared to have faith in. After two years of marriage an old friend informed Jackson that he'd seen her in a booth at a tony restaurant on the Upper East Side passionately kissing a flashy man. When Jackson confronted her about it, she didn't even try to deny it.

The whole thing set off a sickness in him, an acrid dry smell of jealousy and distrust. It kept him from getting close to people. It made him suspicious and skeptical. Irrationally childish, as a matter of fact.

His gut pulsed again. After Livia, he went back to his old self, the businessman who didn't let emotions direct his life. His parents had a marriage devoid of any romance or passion. Devoid of conflict as well, but it was a home run like factory machinery, the wheels on track and on automatic. Livia was a rebellion against all of that. Jackson thought he needed the fireworks that his parents did not. He got way more than he bargained for.

In any case, he needed to not let his silly disappointment show because Esme had evening plans. She was a coworker, nothing more. Although they'd talked last night about personal things, further than Jackson was used to.

"I wanted to get your feedback on something I'm thinking about. Can we at least sit for a few minutes?" He didn't want to schedule an appointment with her for tomorrow. Partially because he was excited about his idea and wanted to share it with her.

"Oh, so you *have* decided you'll fire me?" she asked in a slightly mocking way.

"Stop that." He grinned, again more open than usual. "I already told you it's too early to determine that."

Her smile matched his. He felt a connection in the merge. Like the smiles were reaching each other, like they were meant to. This woman was affecting him in a powerful way so he'd better keep his armor on. She threw him off balance, like the earth under his feet was shifting. The worst part about it was that he liked it.

"What, then?"

"Let's sit down." He gestured to the reception area couches.

"Oh, wow," was the first thing she said after he explained his plan for her to accompany him on the trip and show him the *what* and *why* of her favorite spas. Without too much more deliberation she jumped in with, "Thank you for the vote of confidence and the lovely offer. However, I'll have to say no."

Jackson's jaw slackened. A wave of defeat swept over him. Why had he been so cocky as to assume she would say yes?

She pulled the beige flowy sweater she'd been wrapped in even closer around her. When she focused on responding to him, she talked directly to him, making eye contact. There was something almost unbearable about that directness, nowhere to hide from it. "It's pretty simple. If we were to revisit spas where I've had the good fortune to know the owners and the operators, and they agreed to let you go behind the scenes if you will, that would be a lot to ask. Spa people are incredibly generous, but I can't abuse their comradery."

"I don't exactly follow."

She leaned back on the sofa and tucked her feet under her legs, like she was settling in to tell him a bedtime story.

"I have to look out for myself. Let's say I cash in on my contacts and they help you build out your menu. And let's say you hire a spa director for the Sher who lets me, and Trevor for that matter, go or I decide to leave. I may need to ask my contacts to help us find work, and to share their own connections with me. I'm going to have to hoard those favors for myself."

Jackson had to admire her foresight. He could see her as a scrappy teenager folding endless carts of towels or refilling massage oil dispensers. How she worked herself up through the ranks to a managerial job in Manhattan.

To the task at hand, though. It would be so valuable to have an industry veteran show him the possibilities. Not to mention the fact that something inside of him was telling him to spend more time with Esme. That she was good for him. Maybe it was his doctor's orders that he learn to replenish his well. Being in the same company as someone who brought that to people for a living could rub off on him. Also, there was something mesmerizing about her. He wanted to know her more. That last bit had nothing to do with the Sher but he acknowledged it, just part of the list of why he didn't seem to want to take no for an answer.

"Esme, there's no circumstance where you could do this with me? I can pay you a huge consulting fee."

"No. Thank you, but that still wouldn't solve my reluctance to overstretch my relationships with people I know in the industry."

They were at an impasse, both playing over things in their minds. "Hmm."

"Hmm."

"Hmm."

"Hmm," she repeated although hers seemed to sound like something was brewing. Then she relented, "Nah."

"What?"

"I do have one scenario in which I'd agree to this."

"What is it?"

"I know it wasn't at all what you were thinking."

"Let's hear it."

"My career goal is to become a director."

"Yes."

"I've been a manager for four years gaining skills and experience. I'm ready for it."

"I don't follow you."

"I'm ready to become a director now." She looked down, then lifted her eyes to meet his again, as if she'd had to summon the courage.

"Uh-huh."

"Are you ready to take a chance on me?"

"What do you mean?"

"If I take you on this trip and we redesign the menu, the style, the way we run the spa, you appoint me as the director and Trevor as manager. You call off your search."

He admired her bravery. "Without interviewing anyone else?" HR had mentioned some other candidates. Shouldn't he at least talk to them?

"I'm qualified. All I need is…opportunity." He wasn't sure why she hesitated for a moment. Maybe her bravado hadn't had a chance to display this much persuasiveness.

"You become the spa director?" He considered it. "I'd have to talk it over with my HR staff."

"You're the boss." That he was. If they'd been sitting in a corner office on the fifty-fifth floor of an office building and she'd just made that pitch to him, he'd hire her on the spot. In his estimation, people who wanted something badly enough did a great job of it. He got the impression she'd make a very fine director. "What do you think?" she asked him patiently.

Esme let herself into her apartment, still lightheaded from replaying the conversation she'd had with Jackson. Even though she'd met her friend Yina for the movie date they'd planned, her mind hadn't stayed on the screen. She'd wasted ticket money on a movie that may have been very good, may have been very bad and may have been just okay. She wouldn't know.

Plopping down on the sofa, she still couldn't believe that she had point-blank given Jackson Finn an ultimatum. That she'd take him on an odyssey to better understand the spa business and in exchange, if and only if, he'd name her director of the new operation. After all, if she advised him on what was feasible and desired by loyal clients, that would be within the purview of a director's duties, for which she was well ready.

She'd been lolling at the Sher. She well knew what a director did and could have been applying for that position at other spas after her first year or so at the Sher. She'd risen all the way up from washing towels, yet she'd stopped growing. Maybe she was just tired after so many years of hard work and keeping on a happy face, her adult personality miraculously mostly positive. Or perhaps she needed a boost of confidence beyond satisfied clients and cordial industry relationships. Beyond therapy sessions and self-care, the childhood slashes still hurt, crippled her. But now opportunity was roping her along. She was not going to let this pass by, which was why she'd surprised not only Jackson but herself with her steely determination. She had to at least try.

Jackson hadn't answered yes but he hadn't said no, either. She thought she did pretty well at pretending to be courageous when she proposed it to him even though her heart was beating so fast she could hear it in her ears. Of course, he left it hanging and didn't answer right away. That was fair enough. He needed to mull it over.

For now, she looked over to the clock and decided

to give herself fifteen minutes of pretending that he'd say yes, letting herself truly experience manifest destiny. Even if it was a fantasy, seeing herself in the role would create something like a memory, making it that much closer to real. She set the timer on her phone and closed her eyes. She saw it, herself welcoming clients to a spa that felt like hers, that she had a stake in, within the walls and under the floorboards.

Lying in bed later, she turned her thoughts from the decision she couldn't control to Jackson himself. His six feet plus of man was warm, strong and inviting with a smell of good soap. Making her feel something inside. Jackson Finn was intense. He made her think about things she'd forbade herself. Denied for her own survival. Even if she was lucky enough to have convinced him to let her have the position and she set off for travel with him, she needed to remember to protect herself first, as surely no one else ever had or ever would. Which meant no personal feelings for a man. That could suck her energy dry.

She and Jackson hadn't made any further plans to meet or talk but she figured the ball was now in his court, as the saying went. Therefore, it was both a surprise and it wasn't when he came through the lobby doors at closing time, as he had for the past two days. His navy blue shirt against his black suit was sexy and stylish.

"Ms. Russo, you drive a hard bargain."

"What?" She didn't want to assume she heard what she thought she heard.

"You drive a hard bargain, but okay. You show me

how you'd make this place something spectacular again and I'll give you the reins to it."

A nervous giggle emitted from her that she wished she'd been cool enough to hide. Instead, her stomach flipped over and then back again, and she was sure her face turned beet red. Luckily, she was able to stop from overdoing words and became überprofessional with, "Thank you. You won't regret your decision."

"I hope not. When can you arrange the trip and be ready to leave?"

Whoa, there was so much to do to make that happen. She had to see if Trevor could fill in and make sure her current duties would be covered. She had to make the arrangements with the spas she'd take him to. But she didn't want Jackson to have any reason to hesitate or change his mind so she quickly blurted, "How about the day after tomorrow?" Somehow, she'd pull it together.

"Good." He stayed to walk out with her, watching her go through the tasks of closing for the night. She turned off equipment, locked doors, set alarms and timers on the way out. As they exited, she fumbled to put on her coat. He reached a long arm to pick up the section of sleeve that was dragging and held it open so she could slip one arm in and then the other with ease. Something about the whole maneuver touched deep into her core. He'd noticed that she was having trouble with her coat. He took action to make sure she didn't go out in the cold without it. Someone caring for her. That was a new one.

First order of business was to impress, dazzle in fact, Jackson with her spa tour. She'd already thought of what she'd consider three representations of how unique and special a spa could be. Places that lingered in people's minds for decades, for a lifetime even. That made them dream of returning again and again, and of telling their friends and family about it. Jackson didn't know what would make a spa like that. She'd show him. After meeting spa professionals she'd been invited to visit, shadow and apprentice, she knew a lot of people. On top of that she kept up to date on spa news and had seen photos and menus for hundreds of establishments. Spa was her meat.

"I can tell you right away that we'll be visiting my friend Freja Olsson, who owns Spa Henrik in Stockholm."

"Right, Swedish massage. Even I've heard of that."

"Which wasn't even developed in Sweden but, yes, that will be our starting point for Western-style bodywork."

"Okay."

The last time she'd seen Freja was at a trade show in Las Vegas. Henrik was definitely a world's top pick. Freja was always very generous in giving back to the industry, so Esme was sure she'd be receptive. When she got home it was time to get cracking. It was the middle of the night in Stockholm so she'd fired off a quick text to Freja saying that she'd call her tomorrow but asking if she would be able to spend some time with her and her spa owner, Jackson. Demonstrations of traditional massage would be a good place to start with him.

Esme's mind spun with details as she lugged her favorite suitcase out of the back of her closet. She began unzipping the compartments when her phone rang. The number was not from her contact list. "Hello."

"It's Jackson." Hmm, she had assumed that their planning had been completed for the day.

"Oh, hi." He hadn't changed his mind about their agreement, had he? That would be devastating. "Can I...help you with something?"

"I was just calling to confirm that I'll have my assistant arrange the flights and book a car to pick you up and take you to the airport." His voice was lower over the phone or perhaps it was just evening. In any case, it was kind of sultry to talk to him over the phone. Seductive.

"Okay."

"You'll arrange everything with the spas?" Again, his voice was so resonant it was blowing through the phone like warm air, filling not only her suitcase but her entire bedroom. In fact, his tone prompted her to take off the sweater she still had on. She doubted he knew how magnetic he was. His charisma was something she needed to watch out for. She was not going to have a crush on the boss. There was too much at stake.

"Yes, I've already left a message for Freja in Stockholm."

"Send me all the travel bills, of course."

"So does your company have, like, a private plane?" She didn't really know much about Finn Enterprises on the whole.

"No, we're not at that level." His response came with

a laugh that was friendly not scolding. "I can promise you the first-class cabin on all the flights, though."

"And I can promise you the best spa services you're ever likely to encounter."

"Wait. I have to receive the treatments myself?"

She smiled to herself. "Well, of course, Jackson. I want you to experience for yourself how good and beneficial these protocols are."

"How about we do them on you and you can sort of narrate for me?"

"No siree," she teased, remembering how resistant he was to let her do acupuncture or even massage on his tense shoulders. And what shoulders they were. She pictured his long, lean body. She wondered if he was calling her from an office or a hotel room. Was he at a desk, or a sofa or…in bed? What was he wearing? She mashed her lips for a minute, hardly believing she was having those thoughts. So unlike her. She forged on with, "Will you have the treatments I choose for you? That's the whole point. Besides, your doctor would approve, wouldn't he?"

She could practically see his thousand-watt smile take over. "Oh, all right. What should I pack?"

That was a valid question as his fine suits and smudgeless dress shoes didn't scream relaxation. "Do you have casual clothes?"

"What kind of question is that?"

"You've said you're all work and no play."

"True, but I do business all over the world with all sorts of people. Of course I have casual clothes."

"Great. Let's put them to proper use, then." And

in quick succession she pictured him in a ski outfit. In loose-fitting yoga pants. In just a towel slung low across his hips. Wicked musings that had no place in her dealings with him. Her tongue made a once-around her lips. She resuscitated herself with, "Stockholm in autumn will be colder than New York so you'll need outerwear, but Mexico and Thailand will be warmer."

"All right, I'll check in with you tomorrow."

"Good night, Jackson."

As she swiped off the phone she thought this could all go well or it could go horribly if Jackson wasn't impressed with the trip. It was a crossroads for her. A person didn't get many of those in their life. A way to turn the corner and cumulate the past into something that served the future. It was possible that Esme Russo had officially, finally, arrived.

CHAPTER FIVE

"GOOD MORNING." Esme greeted Jackson at the airport lounge before the flight as agreed. "Everything good?"

They hadn't talked yesterday after that flirty phone call the night before, just sent a couple of texts.

"Yes."

He gestured for her to accompany him down the jet bridge, onto the plane and into the first-class cabin, him flashing the boarding passes on his phone. He watched her take stock of their surroundings. The appointments were deluxe on this aircraft bound for Stockholm. A table between the two seats was set with a bottle of champagne and two flutes. It was almost, well…romantic. He was suddenly unsure about this strange journey that forty-eight hours ago he would have never imagined himself taking.

Not to mention the promise he'd made to her about the directorship. No sooner had he instructed his HR people to launch a search for the right person than he'd told them to halt the hunt, at least for now. It occurred to him, though, that had Finn Enterprises announced that they were hiring a spa director, perhaps Esme would have formally applied for the position anyway. He may have been saving time even if he'd acted uncharacteristically impulsive in saying yes to her. They'd both better be right as there was no time to lose before the investors meeting.

Once they were in the air, he tipped open his laptop and logged into the plane's Wi-Fi as soon as it was available. He'd work, slip into his cocoon for a while. Hours passed. He noticed Esme watch a movie from start to finish and then do something on her tablet. They chatted briefly about the food and drink they were served and that they'd both been to Stockholm before. However, neither knew the city well and there wouldn't be time for much exploring. At one point, the flight crew passed out hot facecloths, which he disregarded.

"This is always a nice touch," Esme commented. "Flying can be dehydrating to the skin."

"Good to know," he said, glancing over at her. Which there was no denying was a very pleasant activity.

Observing that he didn't pick up his hot towel she asked, "Why aren't you using yours?"

"I wasn't aware my skin was being dehydrated so it wasn't a crisis that needed resolving."

"Very funny. Remember, you're to pay more attention to your wellness."

"I do. It's a policy of distrust and jealousy that I rely on." Wow, that was sharp. Even she seemed taken aback. Who had he become, just a sarcastic and bitter shell with health problems? That was no way to live. Especially not at thirty-three. Esme's basic humanity and lack of pretension made him want to tell her more of what he had stashed inside. She'd told him on the phone that he'd be actually receiving the spa ministrations she thought so highly of. He didn't even know what had propelled him to call her at home. They'd laughed a bit about his aversion to therapies. Talking to her came easy to him. He picked up the hot, wet washcloth and brought it to his face. He wiped in big circles, a few times. He had to admit that it was pleasant. Not necessarily healing, as Esme would say, but nice nonetheless.

"See, not half-bad," she ribbed him sweetly. Her little told-you-so smile was adorable and sent a pang through him. "Distrust and jealousy, huh? Is that a blanket statement? Does that mean you don't trust me? Don't you think that if I was going to steal from you that after four years I would have done it already?"

"Fine. I didn't mean trusted employees, although—" he wasn't ready to share that one with her "—suffice it to say I'll never be in a personal relationship again. It clouds my judgment."

"I'll give you that—neither will I. But actively married to distrust and jealousy, do you know how toxic that is?"

"Toxic."

"Those kinds of emotions fire off your adrenal glands, which weakens your immune system and makes you especially vulnerable to autoimmune disease."

"And it's your position that you can just let go of that with a wet washcloth?"

"No, but finding techniques that give you a respite from all of that really does make a difference. There are thousands of studies on it. You've been working nonstop since takeoff. How about stretching your arms above your head?" She demonstrated and he followed. "Let go, and then arch your back. Rotate your neck. Little changes add up."

"I didn't tell you all about my failed marriage." The words were on the tip of his tongue until they just fell out. Was it the hot towel or the stretching that opened him up a little, like his lungs could take in more air? Or was it her, pulling him along? "Not only did Livia betray me with the spa finances, she didn't honor our marriage vows."

"What do you mean?"

"Forsaking all others. She didn't."

"You mean she cheated on you?"

"All over town." No wonder he'd avoided New York until now.

"Oh, Jackson, that's awful. Was it just once?"

"No, it went on for months until I learned of it." He had no idea what a relief it would be to say all of that out loud to someone. Not anyone, of course. Her.

"How did you find out?"

"A friend spotted her kissing someone at a restaurant."

"In plain sight?" She put her hand over her mouth, taking it all in.

"No regard for the decency of marriage."

"Then what happened?"

"Livia didn't even try to deny it. Although she didn't admit to the spa's bookkeeping irregularities that were uncovered at that time. Because she knew that she and whatever man she'd taken up with, her partner in crime, had committed illegal acts. We could have had her arrested but we didn't want to draw attention to ourselves, which we knew the whole mess would."

"Jackson, how awful." She looked at him with concern, or maybe it was pity. "Then what?"

"Very simple at that point. I had her out of the spa, changed the locking codes, took her off the bank accounts and so on." In his gut he wanted to keep talking to Esme even though he was embarrassed that he'd picked such a crooked person to marry. Esme had that way about her, like she was receptive and she could handle someone else's pain. She'd mentioned the neediness of her own parents shaping her into that caretaker she'd become and that she had parlayed it into a spa career. He hoped, in turn, she had people she could tell her secrets and hurts to. For reasons that made no sense he wondered if he could ever be that person for someone.

Not someone.

Her.

"You're having emotions about it now." Was she looking into his third eye or something?

"Frankly, the whole thing left me with my guard up, which is how I plan to stay." A way he thought was serving to protect him. In a moment of clarity, he realized how instead it was holding him in shackles. "I surely won't make the same mistake twice."

"At the expense of your health and well-being?" He was suddenly aware of her close proximity. He could almost feel her body heat. He'd bet her skin and her hair were as silky as they looked.

"What about *your* internal trauma?" he repeated, employing terminology that she'd used.

"You want to know something?" He surely did, ready to take the focus off himself. "I know all about jealousy. That was a little trick my parents used to play on each other. Fight for my attention and loyalty to make the other one jealous. I don't know what's worse, romantic jealousy or pitting your kid against your spouse." The heavy statement weighed like a brick and he ached for her.

Couldn't they both use a little fun on this trip? Doctor's orders, after all. Strictly professional, of course. Maybe he wasn't going to be as resistant to spa life as he thought he was. Or maybe something else was hammering at his walls, trying to tear them down.

"Ladies and gentlemen," came the pilot's voice over the sound system, "we have begun our descent into Stockholm's Arlanda Airport."

"I take it we're in Stockholm because the term *Swedish massage* is best known to people," Jackson asked as they stepped out of the taxi in front of Spa Henrik, their first destination.

"Yes," Esme acknowledged, "although there are some historical questions as to whether that namesake massage was really developed in Sweden or just popularized here. No matter, though, it's accepted as the traditional Western massage." The snowy and cold weather made their breath visible. The clean air of Stockholm was invigorating.

The spa was housed in a Gustavian building, the

city's classic architectural style, and they buzzed the intercom at the spa's entrance. Once Esme announced them, the door clicked and they entered a long hall of rooms with wooden doorframes and wood floors. She remembered from her visit years ago when she was doing an apprenticeship in Copenhagen that the minute she'd stepped into Spa Henrik, the outside world faded away. Perhaps it was the hush of the high ceilings combined with the thickness of the walls. She and Jackson moved toward the reception lobby. "See how this place just sucks you in. Makes you forget where you are. I'd like for us to be able to create that. Envelop people so they can leave their everyday lives at the door for a while."

Jackson took in the information. What she was ready to show him was her vision of a future for the Sher, something she'd thought about for a long time. He'd either be impressed enough with what she presented to him that he'd agree to implement it and let it rest in her arms or he'd reject everything she suggested and choose another spa director with a different perspective. She'd decided that she wouldn't stay if she wasn't offered the directorship. Not after four years of being the manager. The humiliation of being passed over would be too difficult. It would be her sign to move on. This was the beginning or the end for her.

It was fitting that she was now walking the hallway of Freja's spa. When she'd come to Europe and taken the same footsteps years ago, straight after getting her first license, she was just learning the hierarchy of the industry. And now there was the possibility that a facility would be placed completely in her hands. To nurture like her offspring. Putting those hard-learned caretaking skills to use, with a spa baby of her own.

When they reached the welcome lobby she said to the receptionist, "*Hej*. Freja is expecting us." The young woman pressed a button.

"Esme!" The familiar voice called out as Freja appeared from an inner office.

"Freja! Gorgeous as ever."

Freja Olsson approached. She was a tall, thin reed of a woman in an outfit of dark leggings and a flowing white blouse with sandals despite the outdoor temperature. She moved swiftly with a kind of hips-forward gait that belied her age. Esme estimated she was in her mid-seventies. They embraced, Freja pulling her close and pressing Esme into the narrowness of her bony body. "I want you to meet Jackson Finn."

"A pleasure." Jackson put out his hand for a shake but Freja bypassed it completely and embraced him as well. Esme could tell Jackson was tentative and leaned forward for the hug rather than allowing his entire body to make contact with hers. He'd said he didn't have a lot of touch in his life, one reason he didn't like bodywork. He'd even initially pooh-poohed using a hot washcloth on his face during the flight.

But then, goodness, had he opened up, telling her buried secrets he must have been holding for years. He wouldn't recognize it yet but that was probably as valuable to him as the most penetrating massage. Plus, they had some inherent similarities, minus the cheating spouse for her, but finding those was cathartic to her, too, which was not unwelcome. She'd learned not to dredge up her past too often but, on occasion, the fellowship was reassuring.

"The spa was established by my grandfather in 1928. We've resisted modernizing and made as few changes as possible."

"Oh, I don't think that's so," Esme countered. "What about your cutting-edge skin care regimes?"

Esme's heart was in bodywork, but many spa users came through the doors for skin care. It was a huge source of revenue. "Jackson, Freja and I texted yesterday about giving you a massage and her men's facial."

"You'd be demonstrating the treatments on me?" He pretended to be in shock.

"Yes, darling," Freja answered.

"Wait, did we agree to that?" Esme could tell he was only halfheartedly protesting.

"We talked about it on the phone the other night," she reminded him. During that strange phone call when his voice crawled all over her. He shrugged and put his palms up as if in surrender. The three of them chuckled.

"You're in good hands," Esme promised.

"We'll begin with a massage," Freja instructed. "Do you prefer a male or female therapist?"

"Male," he answered at bullet speed. Esme knew that men were often uncomfortable being treated by women and vice versa. No doubt stemming from the seedy and inappropriate shenanigans that sometimes took place in what was incorrectly called a massage parlor. Esme, Freja and everyone they knew, had ever known, were absolute professionals. In her career Esme had never even heard of any improper behavior. Still, the reputation lingered and she'd had occasion to have to assure clients of their safety. In a spa setting, sometimes the client preferred the smaller, softer hands of a woman or the opposite, the strength and size of a man's.

Freja led them to the dressing room. "Use any of the lockers you want. Please take a robe. Generally, we prefer the access of a nude body, at all times covered with a sheet, but you're more than welcome to leave your underwear on if that makes you feel more comfortable."

"Jackson—" Esme wanted to check in as well "— we were planning to meet you at the massage table so we could talk about the session as it happens. To give you a sense of how we work. Is that okay with you?"

He definitely took a moment to digest it all and she couldn't blame him. He'd be naked under a sheet with an unfamiliar man's hands on him and two women watching. Spa people had a very clinical, medical view of it all but she was sensitive to the fact that he might not. Yet, anyway.

He nodded, "When in Rom— Stockholm."

"Anders will be your therapist today," Freja announced as a big strapping blond man entered the room. He wore a blue uniform shirt not unlike a hospital scrub that bore the insignia of Spa Henrik, a pair of hands joined together to resemble a heart. Underneath, he wore black pants.

Esme had never met Anders but she knew that Freja would have brought in one of her top people for this demonstration. "Nice to meet you," Esme said to him with a polite smile. Jackson watched her every move as she interacted with the man. In fact, he scrutinized Anders from head to toe before extending his own hello.

"If you'll lie face down on the massage table." Anders pointed. He helped Jackson lie down on the padded table and removed his robe at the same time as he covered him with sheets, leaving only his head and the bottoms of his feet exposed. "Are you comfortable?"

Jackson fit his face into the cradle of the headrest, a horseshoe shape that allowed the recipient to breathe fresh air while their head, neck and torso remained aligned. "I'm all right."

Anders brought his oils on a trolley next to the table. "Do you have any allergies?"

"No."

"Anders is asking that," Esme explained, "because he'll be using oils to lubricate your skin and facilitate his hands' movements on you. Some people are very sensitive to certain products or scents."

"I use a sweet almond oil as my base," Freja said. "Then I can add other oils for aroma or skin care properties. Almond is not the cheapest, that's for sure, but it's worth it."

Anders pumped oil from a dispenser and rubbed his hands together to warm it. "Let's begin."

"We start with effleurage," Freja began her narration, "which is the technique of using long gliding strokes along the curves of the body aimed toward the heart. This promotes relaxation and allows the therapist to get to know the client's body and where there might be tension. The oil gives us a way to warm the muscles."

Esme chimed in, "Also, we can learn if the client prefers light or firm pressure. A massage that uses heavy pressure is called deep tissue."

Freja continued, "The idea of calming the muscles manually is part of the Western style of massage, which looks at physiology and understanding of body mechanics. As opposed to the Eastern philosophies, which approach health by analyzing the life force, and flow or blockage of energy." As was proper protocol, Anders worked on a section of Jackson's body at a time, removing and then recovering parts with the sheet and uncovering others. He moved to each arm and leg and then his back to take inventory of Jackson's physique and where he was holding tightness or misalignment. "Next, we'll go to the technique called petrissage. Here we lift and knead the muscles and fascia to draw blood to the area, which promotes all-body release."

"How are you feeling, Jackson?" Esme asked, wanting to check in because he claimed not to see value in massage at all so she hoped this was helping to change his mind.

"It's fine." His voice sounded strained or maybe constricted. Esme hoped he didn't have his mind on work or on his ex-wife and the atrocity he'd told her about. Although he wasn't the easiest person, he certainly seemed honest so it was a shame that he put his faith in the wrong person. Although she understood plenty about not being able to count on people. Her parents took advantage of a child's innate trust.

Eventually, Anders explained the next phase. "We'll move on to tapotement. I'm sure you've experienced this rhythmic tapping. My hands are in what people call karate chop position. I move quickly up and down a large area to awaken the soft tissue after we've increased the blood flow. To create vibration within the body, which is profoundly restorative."

"With massage," Esme said, "we address muscles and tendons and ligaments and joints and connective tissue all at once. And the process reduces constriction to both the body and mind."

It was a lot to take in so after that they stayed quiet while Anders continued until he finished the session.

CHAPTER SIX

"HOW WAS THAT for you?" Freja asked after Jackson's massage demonstration.

Jackson didn't know what to say to these people for whom that question was of the utmost importance. *Fine* was not going to be an acceptable answer. Although, that's what he thought. It was soothing to have his muscles worked on by Anders, obviously a skilled professional who knew exactly what Jackson's body needed. But Jackson didn't feel like he'd had a monumental *aha* about it. That was okay. He found the details very interesting.

What he wished was that he hadn't winced to himself when Anders smiled at Esme for a little too long as they were introduced. He'd had a silly stab of jealousy at that, which was absurd on so many levels. First and foremost, he had no attachment to her other than as coworkers. She was an independent woman responsible for herself. Second, just because Livia had cheated on him didn't mean that every woman he got near was going to hurt or betray or double-cross him. His intellectual mind knew that. His mere acquaintance with Esme shouldn't be unearthing those demons. After all, he had many women in the company's employ. He hadn't exactly figured out what triggered him with Esme. It was a kooky yet instinctive response. Also, Esme had mentioned her parents pitting her against one another to make the other jealous. Which was sick and cruel and something she didn't need any more of in her life. He needed to nip his immature feelings in the bud right here and now.

As Esme had pointed out, he'd trusted her as an employee and that's all that mattered. He could trust her with the spa but not trust her with his heart. This had nothing to do with their personal lives. Which, in turn, had nothing to do with each other. Yet the mere thought of that made him sad.

"Marvelous," he answered Freja's question, not wanting to negate anything that had transpired.

"Would you like to do some inhaling in our salt room?"

Inhaling. Yes, he supposed he'd like to do some inhaling. So as not to die, that was. "What I'd like to do is eat."

"Wonderful. We have our spa café on the lower floor. Let me inform the chef right now that you're on your way down and she'll prepare a sample menu if that's all right." Freja drew her phone from her pocket and punched in.

"Jackson," Esme piped up, "why don't you stay in your robe and have that experience? Often people come to a day spa and spend hours there, keeping it fluid between treatments and their own leisurely pursuits. Many spas have extra features like meditation rooms, steam chambers, whirlpools, saunas and classes. Freja has a juice bar and a full-service restaurant for spa cuisine where it is absolutely acceptable, encouraged even, to eat in your robe and leave your belongings in the locker."

"Does *spa cuisine* mean I will still be hungry afterward?"

She chuckled, which was his intention. "People do tend to eat light and fresh at the spa. You can imagine that a massage might not feel as good on a stomach that was digesting a lot of food."

Freja said, "I promise to fill you with foods that will increase your vitality and be kind to your digestive system."

"Oh, so I'll certainly be hungry afterward," he said forcing his eyes wide open to make Esme giggle again. He couldn't think of the last time he purposely tried to make someone laugh. Maybe that massage had loosened him up some after all.

"Let's go." Freja led them down a flight of stone steps to the lower level, which was hushed with an almost echo. An enormous vase of yellow, gold and white flowers welcomed guests to the restaurant area.

"Beautiful blooms," Esme commented.

Freja pointed to a side door that led to another staircase. "Non-spa clients can enter here from the street. The restaurant provides good cash flow for us because people from the nearby office buildings and shopping districts come to the restaurant for lunch."

"That's not something we'd be able to do," Esme added. "I just wanted to mention what some people are doing to increase profits."

Freja spoke to the chef and then she sat them at a blond wood table with padded chrome chairs.

"Thank you, Freja," Esme said to her friend. Esme had such warmth about her, it seemed to emanate from every inch of her. He'd never been around someone like that. His parents were as cold as ice. Esme touched his heat inside. He wanted to wrap his arms around her as if he was a giant winged bird and could envelop her in his span. When she asked which was worse, being cheated on or being betrayed as a child, his heart clenched. As she'd said, she turned around the childhood of having to care for some selfish people to a vocation of taking care of others. Was she taking good enough care of herself?

At the Sher a couple of days ago, her eyes misted with tears after he'd helped her put on a coat that she'd been struggling with. Was she so unaccustomed to kindness toward her that even such a small gesture was a big deal? He was just being decent in seeing that she could use a hand. It was hardly a heroic act. While his parents were stoic, they were at least well mannered. And the funny thing was, after he helped her get her coat on he wanted to do more for her. He wanted to lay his own coat down on a puddle in the street so she could step over it. Or give her the imaginary gloves he had on to keep her hands warm.

He looked at her across the table. Yes, he'd like to keep her warm.

Then he blinked his eyes open. What kind of crazy fantasy had he just had? He needed lunch.

A waiter brought two glasses of water in goblets.

Jackson downed his in one sip. "Hmm. Room temperature?"

"We can request ice if you'd like. Freja thinks icy drinks are too shocking for the organs."

Next the waiter placed a small plate in front of each of them. "This is our farm-to-table quinoa beet bowl with fresh picked kale." As he'd feared, rabbit food. Kale was supposed to be a garnish on the side of the plate! "With an avocado goddess sauce." He had no idea what that meant but he liked avocado and there was definitely something goddess-like about Esme.

"Thank you." He'd give it a try.

The waiter stepped away and returned with two tall narrow glasses of a milky pink drink. "Our antioxidant berry lassi."

Jackson sipped it, a delicious smoothie that managed to be creamy, tart and sweet all at once. That wasn't as hard to get down as the kale. Wasn't Swedish food heavy and hearty, to combat the cold winter? He'd go get two dozen meatballs later.

Since he was stuck here for the moment, in a robe no less, as Esme gamely chewed her weed salad, he asked, "You and Freja began to explain about the variety of massage techniques. What are some other types besides Swedish?"

"I think we were explaining deep tissue. That's when we'll use more pressure. In doing that, we can better relieve pain or chronic stiffness and concentrate on one area of the body."

The enthusiasm in Esme's voice made him want

to keep her talking. He could listen to her for hours. "What else?"

"Well, there's trigger points where we work on one part of the body to assist another. For example, relieving pressure on the neck can help with the frequency and duration of persistent headaches."

He creaked his head to stretch out his neck in one direction and then the other. He had to admit that he felt more range of motion after that massage than he had in a while. "Interesting."

"I can see that your neck bands are more fluid," she said in response to his stretching.

"It amazes me that you can glean that from across the table."

"You have chronic stress, Jackson. I could tell from the minute you walked into the spa. What are you doing to relieve it?"

"I had been doing nothing. Now my doctor is warning me what could happen if I don't address it."

"What will you do?"

"I'm supposed to do relaxing things. Take more vacations. So, hey, this counts as a vacation, doesn't it?"

"Not based on how much time you spent on your computer during the flight."

"Do you have the magical, mystical work-life balance that everyone is so highly touting?"

"I don't know that it's so idyllic for anyone. But I take yoga and I practice mindful breathing."

"What's that?"

"Slowly breathing in through your nose and just as slowly out through your mouth."

"You were doing that with that elderly lady at the Sher."

"Try it with me. In through the nose." They both inhaled. "And out through the mouth." They exhaled.

"Okay."

"And you do it as many times as you need to. It will transport you, I promise." She took a few bites of her food.

He used his fork to isolate a couple of chunks of avocado and brought them to his mouth. "Tell me about other treatments."

"People have been using heat and cold as body therapies for thousands of years. A simple, non-messy and effective way we can deliver that is with hot stones."

"How do you use them?" He looked at his bowl while visualizing a big plate of bacon and eggs. "Are there twigs in this?" He scrunched up his face and got another smirk out of her.

She pressed on. "We place warmed stones on parts of the body where we want to open soft tissue and increase blood flow."

"Are there particular kinds of stones?" He managed another bite of the bunny food, fascinated by listening to Esme. He thought back to that first night with her in New York when a coffee at the Italian place turned into delicious wine and dinner. They'd shared a tiramisu dessert, a rather familiar act for two people who barely knew each other. Yet he'd relished it, hadn't realized how much he craved simple, honest conversation. A face across the table. He was a boss to many but friend to few.

"Really almost any smooth stone is fine but the industry standard is basalt, which is heavy and volcanic."

She was so truly passionate about her work. He loved that she'd found what she wanted to do with her life at an early age and was doing it. And that she was gutsy enough to stand up to him, to tell him that she'd take him on this trip only with the promise that if he liked her ideas, he'd name her spa director afterward.

"That sounds like it would be a unique sensation."

He sensed she was enjoying sharing her expertise with him. "Let's see," she continued. "Any spa session can be enhanced with aromatherapy." Thankfully, the waiter noticed that Jackson wasn't eating the garden in a bowl and brought another berry lassi and a plate of crackers and nuts. "We use scent to awaken the sense of smell along with everything else we're doing. For example, lavender is known to produce calm whereas citrus is a wake-up call."

"What about you, Esme? What's your favorite kind of massage?"

She looked at him as if no one had ever asked her that question. Which brought back his musings that if she was busy caring for other people, who was caring for her? Was she as complete as she fronted she was? He doubted it. Just like him. They were quite a pair.

"Thanks for asking. Actually, it's the Thai style. Bangkok will be our last stop on this trip so I'll have a chance to show you. It's a guided-movement practice performed on the floor with the recipient in loose clothing."

"What do you like about it?"

"To each his own but for me, the manipulation of my movements is so therapeutic."

He felt a surge of excitement, as if he'd never traveled to the ends of the earth which, in fact, he had. Never with her, though. Her spirit was infectious.

"Please," Freja said and gestured, "get comfortable in the facial chair." After lunch, it was time for Jackson's skin care treatment, which Freja was going to perform herself. He sat down and she used the controls to recline him and elevate his legs.

"This is like being at the dentist," Jackson said, "which, by the way, I hate." He snarled at Esme like a grouch. She gave him a thumbs-up signal.

"Some clients prefer to use earbuds and listen to their choice of music or spoken word, guided meditations," Freja said, "while they're having the treatment. Of course today, we want to talk to you about the protocol."

"Yup."

"We'll start with a thorough cleansing," Freja explained as she began. "I've got half a dozen cleansers here and I'll choose which one to use based on the client's skin type. Jackson, I can see that your skin runs a little dry so I'm going to use a product that I know is moisturizing. I'll blend that in all across your face starting with the neck and working my way upward. We want to completely clean the face and beard area. How does that feel?"

"Strange."

As she moved across his face she continued, "Skin

has a lot of impurities. I can see that you hold some deep grime, as we do in the cities. I also see patches of dehydration, which can be caused by a lot of travel and also from poor sleep."

"Check and check. You can tell that from my skin?"

"Skin works hard. It can become fatigued. It needs attention." She used wet disposable sponges to remove the cleanser. And followed that with a calming toner applied with cotton balls.

"Now she's going to use a polyhydroxy compound, which won't further dry out sensitive skin," Esme narrated. "What we need to do is exfoliate, meaning slough off the dead skin so that we can bring out the healthy cells underneath."

"Are you painting my face?" Jackson reacted to the small brush Freja was using to apply the product.

"As a matter of fact, I am."

"Would you like to see yourself in a mirror?" She didn't wait and grabbed a handheld mirror from the counter. She handed it to Jackson, who shimmied in disbelief that the so-called gentle exfoliator was... bright yellow, covering his face from forehead to clavicle, except around his eyes and mouth.

"I look like a lemon!"

Esme reached over to lay a reassuring hand on his arm. "What happens in the spa stays in the spa." She had to tell herself to take her hand back. It wanted to stay there.

"Now, we'll do the extractions." Freja pulled her wheeled work trolley over and began to position her lighted magnifying lamp correctly to view his face.

"This is often what clients find to be the most uncomfortable part of the facial and so they opt out of it. But there's nothing that replaces removing blackheads and other pollutants one at a time. May I continue?"

"I suppose, although you're scaring me," he answered with trepidation. After covering his eyes with cotton pads so the rays of her lamp didn't bother him, she used the magnifier to locate, and then used her metal extraction tool to scrape off the blackheads and clogged pores she found on his face. "Yikes," he commented immediately on his discomfort.

Esme couldn't disagree. But she wanted Jackson to understand the skin care component to the spa menu. "Very often clients book both facial and bodywork sessions for the same day."

"Are we done yet?" Jackson all but pleaded as Freja picked and picked until she was satisfied.

"Now we'll do a gel mask for hydration. It uses algae to firm, lift and brighten the skin."

"You're putting seaweed on me?"

"It's a nutrient-rich ingredient that yields fabulous results. Another thing I think would benefit your skin is microneedling."

"Does that have the word *needle* in it? I already don't like it." No more than he had liked Esme's suggestion of acupuncture the other day.

She showed him the penlike tool used for that process. "See, it has tiny needles. We brush the skin making minuscule punctures which stimulate the skin to produce collagen to heal them."

"Punctures. I'll take your word for that." He jumped out of the chair.

"Thank you for bearing with us." Esme wanted to hug him but he'd suffered enough, she laughed to herself.

After he showered and dressed, they decided to walk to their hotel despite the cold. They strolled through the Gamla Stan, Stockholm's Old Town, with its cobblestoned alleys and buildings of muted colors and carved wood. The air was filled with brisk flurries of snow.

One minute they were walking forward, continuing to talk about spa operations and then, really not meaning to, he took Esme's hand. Her skin was unspeakably satiny. He shot his eyes over to her for approval. She looked down at their entwined hands, as surprised as he was, like a force in and of itself had made the move, neither of them having anything to do with it. A bit like the energy wave that had passed between them at having brushed against each other at the Sher that first day. The thing was, it felt absolutely natural, normal and right. As if their hands had been searching for each other since the beginning of time. Like they had each been lost and finally found their way home.

A peace came across his face that he could actually feel, another move happening without him consciously instructing it to. He stopped walking, which pulled her a little closer to him. Still holding one hand, he took hold of the other to make their two spheres form a circle. And when his face drew just a few inches from hers, he kissed her. A quick wisp of a kiss, just letting his mouth make contact with the velvet that was her lips. His eyelids fluttered because he liked it so much, the smallness of the action becoming a still photo. His brain told him that the earth had, in fact, shifted. That there would forever be this instant. The timeline in the history of the world would now be divided between having not yet stood on the street in Stockholm in the snow kissing Esme Russo, and then time forever after it occurred.

He kissed her again, let his lips linger a bit longer, to feel the press of their mouths against each other. His tongue flicked a snowflake from her upper lip. One of his hands disentangled from hers in order to cup her cheek, downy, pillowy and cold at the same time. He brought her face closer, this time to kiss deeper, to kiss longer, letting himself swell with the desire to keep kissing her.

As the snowflakes fell, cascading them with powder, they kissed and then kissed some more. Until there was actually no weather, no sky, no Stockholm—there was only their bodies against each other, two as one.

Then, suddenly, after they'd been standing in that one spot for who knows how long, some kind of awareness took over Esme. She pulled her head back, creating an undeniable space between them, a chasm. The moment was over. Definitely and completely over. "Jackson, I don't…" She struggled for words, taking in one of her slow inhales and exhales. "I don't… With men… I don't really…date."

His mouth fell into a circle like a surprised child,

shocked by the kissing he'd instigated and even more shocked by her abrupt end to it. "Oh, was dating what we were doing?"

"And then there's lymphatic drainage, reiki, reflexology, shiatsu…" Esme forced herself to stop babbling as she and Jackson continued their walk.

"Uh-huh."

There weren't many people on the street; it was too cold. She knew she'd been talking a mile a minute as snowflakes whooshed around them. She was doing anything to avoid dealing with what had just happened.

He'd kissed her, with a fire that could have melted the snow around them for a five-foot radius. It had been a long time since Esme had been kissed by anyone. And she'd never been kissed like that, with a force and passion that she'd only seen in a movie or read in a book, nothing she'd ever thought was real.

It wasn't true when she told him that she didn't date. New York married friends always knew a great guy they wanted to introduce her to. The trouble was she never connected with any of them, never found any Venn diagram where their worlds overlapped. She wasn't interested in what they cared about and it appeared to be vice versa. Or worse still, they were needy and once her elemental competence was visible, they'd started wanting her to be their mother or at least their social director. In any case, it had been a long time since she'd even exchanged that with a man.

She decided to bite the bullet with Jackson, stop blathering about spas, and get said what needed to be expressed. After all, they were leaving for Mexico in the morning, and had the rest of the trip to get through and then a possible long-term working relationship. They had to get past what had just transpired. "So hey, you asked me if what we just did was dating? What did you mean by that?"

He glanced over to her as they walked, and then returned to facing forward so he didn't have to make eye contact. "I don't know. I just wanted to be clear with you. What just happened…"

"You kissed me," she jumped in. "Out of the blue."

"Did I? I can't remember how it started."

"What do you mean, you can't remember? We were walking and then we were kissing."

"Did I do something improper?"

"I suppose it could have been. I didn't regard it as such."

"So you were…as receptive as I thought you were."

She'd be lying if she didn't admit that she'd been thinking about him since he arrived in New York to make himself a presence at the Sher. Not only was he beguiling, but also he had a depth and a frankness that she was very attracted to. At this point in her life, she didn't need superficial encounters. And the way he asked her what kind of massage she liked or how he always held the door open were tiny moves that spoke volumes to her. But feeling good from the actions of a man, no matter how engaging and attentive he was, wasn't in her plans. Spontaneous kissing wasn't on the itinerary, either. And, most importantly, not with her boss! Her boss! She needed to be oh so careful that nothing got in the way of her big opportunity. To kiss him was to tempt the fates. "Yes, I was receptive, I just wanted to be clear that I don't think that qualified as dating."

"You don't pull any punches, do you, Esme? You tell it like it is."

"I can't afford not to. Whoever started it... Oh, wait, I mean that was you, which isn't to say that it wasn't lovely."

"And you want to agree that we'll never let anything like that happen again?"

"Right, I mean we're work partners now and maybe just being here in Stockholm in the snow was a little romantic." Well, actually, very romantic.

"Got it. Pact. We're coworkers and that's all we should ever be."

"Good, I just wouldn't want you to misunderstand my willingness to... When you kissed me and..." Then she yanked his hand to stop walking. And turned herself toward him, got up on her tippy toes and kissed him again. Was she crazy? Just after they'd made big proclamations that they weren't going to kiss again? His mouth felt so amazing that she couldn't help herself, kissing him in short presses. Soon followed by a not-so-short one that involved their tongues. That involved his tongue rolling along hers. Their mouths sealing to each other. Kisses that were hypnotizing, making sparks ignite that heated her on the inside. How could she feel so hot in the snow? "Oh, no." She stopped abruptly.

"Okay, that was definitely you, right?"

"I'm sorry. That really, really was the last time." The words came out of her mouth but she didn't mean them. She did want it to happen again. Right there on the street, or in more private quarters. She couldn't be blamed, could she? Those kisses were a kind of wake-up that made a person want more. Like a lifetime's worth, perhaps. Although she wouldn't do it again. She bore her eyes into his and told him so without words. His eyes were glassy as he returned the stare. With desire. His mere gaze sent blood coursing through her. This trip was quickly becoming very complicated.

When they came in from the cold and entered the hotel, a few people sat at the tables and chairs in the lobby as the front desk manager greeted them. "May I send up some champagne?"

Esme didn't ask Jackson before answering, *"Nej, tack."*

Things had become awkward and she just wanted to get away from him at this point to collect herself and regroup.

Jackson argued, "Not so fast. Can you send me up a plate of meatballs and potatoes?" he asked the manager. "What about you, Esme? We only ate leaves at the spa. Aren't you hungry?"

"Nothing for me. I'm ready for bed." Although she certainly took note that he'd asked whether she was hungry. Someone concerned if she'd had enough to eat. Hmm. How nice that was.

They ducked into the elevator. Exiting on their floor, they walked down the quiet and softly lit corridor until they reached their rooms, which were across from each other.

Based on those kisses that they equally participated in, Esme sensed that she'd only need to invite him in as a method of communicating that she wanted to take things further. On one hand, she did. Desperately, as a matter of fact. She was so drawn to him and imagined little snippets of what could be. How his kisses might land on her neck. How his big hands might feel on her bare skin. Would they be rough or gentle? Would they feel hot like his tongue?

She'd been intimate with a few men. A couple of encounters were one-nighters and a few more lasted for a couple of months until it was clear there was nothing going on to warrant continuing to see each other. She knew that she'd never been made love to in a way that stirred her center. That would make her replay the encounters in a dreamy haze for days afterward. The kind that touched all the way down. And the scary thing was, she was certain that would all change if she shared a bed with Jackson. Like he had all of that in him just waiting to burst up. The thought set off screaming red warning signals that taking things any further with him would put her in emotional danger. Not to mention the possible jeopardy of her career.

So, it was in great haste that she tapped the key card to her room, said a quick good-night over her shoulder and dashed through the door, waiting to hear the definitive click of the lock behind her before she could lean back against the wall and let out a sigh that was relief mixed with disappointment. Because maybe, just maybe, she had actually met someone who was showing her that what she thought she had all figured out, that living her life alone was the best solution, might not be so. This was new information. And unwelcome at that.

On the plane to Oaxaca, Esme and Jackson were served a lavish Mexican breakfast of eggs and chorizo topped with red salsa and cheese, accompanied by sweet bread rolls called *conchas* and spice-laden coffee. He'd ordered room service last night yet they both ate heartily. It was so yummy they didn't talk for a few minutes; all they could do was sensually indulge. More sensuality. His kisses at night and great food in the morning. She could hardly decide which was more decadent. Oh, that wasn't true. She knew which. Though she hadn't had much of that deliciousness in her life.

Lying in her Stockholm hotel bed last night, she'd felt everything change. That steely-eyed future she envisioned became not enough. She'd decided long ago against men and coupledom. That she wasn't going to devote all of her resources to someone else. There'd been enough of that. Especially when her journey had taught her that she could expect nothing in return. She was not going to spend her life repeating the same pattern. Of people taking but not giving. As a result, she'd never been in a relationship as she only seemed to attract the wrong sort of man. Until now.

Was it the way Jackson kissed her that was so earthshaking? A give-and-take kind of exchange unlike anything she'd ever felt before? Whatever the provocation, her mental fog lifted and she saw the sky in a whole new way. How honest she and Jackson were with each other about their pasts and about how those pasts colored their lives now. There was something similar about their fear of betrayal, of trust, a trait hardened by their circumstances. She had this strange instinct that she could tell him anything and that he'd understand, and that she wanted to tell him everything. She had friends but she tended to keep things closer to the vest. When a child learns that information from one person can be used against another, it's training to keep their intimacies to themselves.

Now here, on this whirlwind trip with Jackson, she realized, and strangely for the very first time, that she was walking a very lonely road. It was a choice. And that there might be another one. A scarier one. But one that might have untold rewards that she'd never dared to dream of. Where someone wanted to know if she was hungry, and two people shared their ups and downs, hiked through the hills and valleys of a lifetime holding hands. It was overwhelming to consider what she'd never allowed herself before.

Once they finally slowed down on their gigantic plates of food, Jackson said, "I have to admit that I felt pretty good after that massage." His out-of-the-blue comment made her smile from ear to ear. Half in victory that she was getting him to understand the benefits of spa and half because it was so cute that he was admitting it to her as if he couldn't believe it himself. "Maybe my personal methods of self-care could use a makeover just like the Sher."

"Remind me again, what are those?"

"Barriers to ever being close to someone. Then there's living in corporate hotels so as to call no place home, spending as much time alone as possible, burying myself in work, always a screen in front of me, not getting fresh air. I think in your parlance you'd say I was *disconnecting* as best I could."

"Ooh, very good. Disconnecting."

He bowed his head as if accepting the accolade. "Thank you."

He reached over to steal an orange slice from her plate without asking. The familiarity in that made her heart ding though she pretended to protest with, "Hey!"

It was good that they weren't hashing over the snowflakes and hot sparks of last night. They'd talked it through, agreed it was a mistake. Now they were back to getting to know each other as colleagues with some kind of kindred spirits that would enhance their professional relationship. A good decision. No problem. If only she believed that herself. Because her insides were definitely replaying what had transpired.

"I told you," he continued, "my parents didn't value, or even understand, self-care. They worked day and night, coexisting in a world of numbers and flow charts and global predictions."

"And you've followed in their footsteps."

"I thought I needed more. Romance. Rapture. Exaltation. My one attempt to rebel was to marry a sparkly person who turned out to be made of smoke and mirrors. And now that's how I regard most everyone. As if I suspect them of something. In fact, after the whole debacle with Livia I did something I'll always regret."

"What's that?"

He hesitated before he committed to saying, "I fired the accountant who discovered that funds were missing from some accounts."

"He or she was who brought it to your attention?"

"Tom, yeah. I fired him in what I told myself was an abundance of caution. I found out later that he'd only reported on those accounts, he'd never had any access to them like Livia had."

"Couldn't you have hired him back?"

"He rightly didn't want to work for someone who thought that little of him."

"That's a lot to carry. You might want to unload some of this."

"What does that mean?"

"See a therapist, read a book about letting go and forgiving yourself. Hoping for an honest wife wasn't so much to ask for, or expect." Her words hung in the air. "Let's do some breathing. Inhale through your nose…"

He followed along but she could tell he was contemplating what she'd said. Finally he changed the subject to, "What's in store for me in Mexico?"

She shifted. "Cozumel and Luis's spa is very specialized. That's what I have in mind for the Sher."

"Give me a preview."

"I know so many spas with full menus of skin and bodywork. New York is obviously one of the magnets in the world for the finest in skin care. So what if we eliminated that entirely from our menu?"

"Huh?"

"Don't compete with those famed skin care salons. Focus only on certain kinds of bodywork. And build a reputation on that. Let's be the best at specific modalities. I want to show you what Cozumel and Luis are doing. That's what I'd like to model us on."

She could see his wheels turning. He was the boss, after all. That was okay. She wanted them to have a partnership where they both had a vested interest in the Sher's success. She'd need his approval. This was already a victory for her, being heard, allowed to show him her vision. His snow-flurry kisses, buried agonies of his past and her questions about being alone would all fall to the wayside. She hoped.

CHAPTER SEVEN

SECRETLY, JACKSON'S GUT was doing push-ups while he tried to keep his face neutral. He was all but sitting on his hands to resist the temptation to get another taste of what he'd gorged on last night. Esme's lips. He would never recover from those kisses that were the sweetest nectar he'd ever tasted. Not to mention the soft skin of her face and neck that his fingers had the good fortune to have stroked. All of which was very logically discussed and decided against, the same as an ill-advised business decision. Of course, the trouble was that he'd spent the entire night tossing and turning on those pale yellow Swedish sheets in bed alone with very contradictory thoughts.

"*Bienvenidos* to Oaxaca International Airport," the pilot announced over the sound system after they'd touched ground back on the North American continent. Jackson looked out the window at open sky and mountainous terrain, so very different than the Swedish vistas they'd arrived from.

"I hope you find this a special visit," Esme turned to say.

A driver took them a bit outside of Oaxaca City to

reach Spa Bajo el Sol, or Spa under the Sun. When they arrived, Esme couldn't wait and flung the door open to bound out of the car and greet a man and a woman who were seemingly waiting for them outside the entrance in front of a tiled fountain with a bountiful spray of almost blue water. Esme ran toward them calling out, "Cozumel! Luis!" When she reached them, the three exchanged hugs. Esme turned to extend a hand to Jackson and bring him into the circle with the Aguilars. "This is Jackson Finn, who I told you about."

"Hola," Cozumel greeted him. "Thank you for having an interest in the work we do here."

"With Esme's help I'm only just beginning to understand the scope of what spa really means." He brought forward a hand to shake, which Cozumel and Luis ignored, both bringing him into an awkward hug of their own.

After they disentangled, Cozumel said, "Here at Bajo el Sol we focus on ancient work regarding fertility and both male and female reproductive health. What we do is unique. We're blessed that guests have found us and have spread the word about our treatments."

Esme said to Jackson, "See, that's what I'm talking about. Rather than a general spa, they specialize and draw a clientele from all over the world."

"This is a place of love. Our bodies. Our bellies. Our babies."

"You must be hungry and thirsty after your journey," Luis said. "Let me show you to your casita." Esme had told Jackson that while Bajo el Sol wasn't a hotel spa, they did keep some accommodations for friends and family, and guests having sensitive treatments. They'd be staying in one of the small houses that faced out to a view of groves and mountains. The sunny skies and blustery breezes were quite a change from Sweden.

"Remind me, Luis," Esme asked as they walked toward the horizon, "what year did you establish the spa?"

"It's twenty-five years already." They followed him to the casita he pointed to. "The adobe walls of the buildings help keep the interior cool in summer and warm in winter. Come in." The small house was furnished and decorated with traditional Mexican design, bold colors in a rustic setting. Two bedrooms shared a bathroom.

"This is lovely."

"We are closed for the evening and there are no other overnight guests so you have the run of the property. Drop off your bags and then join us in the kitchen. It's the back door in the main house, or did you remember that, Esme?"

She'd told Jackson that she'd worked here for two years, staying in a spare room in the house, and credited Cozumel and Luis with teaching her many valuable lessons about both operations and treatments. "Oh, I remember the kitchen. How could I ever forget your Oaxacan cooking? Jackson, you're going to love Luis's food."

"As long as there's no kale."

They did as Luis suggested and freshened up in the casita, putting on comfortable clothes to suit the mild weather. Jackson had taken Esme's advice during that sexy phone call before they left and had packed light-weight clothes and canvas shoes. Esme looked angelic in a loose white dress.

In the large, open kitchen, Luis was stirring a huge cauldron over a fire, and everywhere Jackson turned there were pots and utensils that looked to be centuries old. "We have some *antojitos* ready," Cozumel said and pointed to the counter where an appetizer was sitting invitingly on a platter painted with the sun and moon around the rim. Beside it was a glass pitcher filled with a pale green drink. "These are *garnachas*," Luis said.

Cozumel jumped in with, "Small tortillas topped with shredded meat."

"And pickled cabbage," Luis added.

"And, to drink." Cozumel gestured to the pitcher.

Luis said, "That's a melon *liquado*."

They helped themselves to a more than ample snack. "Oh, my goodness," Jackson couldn't help but extoll, "these are divine."

After Luis attempted to stuff their faces into oblivion merely on appetizers, Esme wanted to go back to the casita before the main course. She plopped herself down on the couch. "I'm exhausted. I didn't sleep on the flight. I think I have jet lag."

"New York to Sweden to Mexico in just a few days can cause that." He cracked open the cap of a water bottle from the counter and handed it to her. "Drink."

"Maybe I'll take a little nap."

"Nope. The best thing is to get on Mexican time. Let's sit outside in the sun. That helps me sometimes."

"Mr. Finn, do I actually detect some knowledge about taking care of yourself?"

"Don't tell anyone." He put one finger up to his mouth for a shush. "I travel a lot. It's more like self-preservation." He stretched out an arm to pull her off of the couch.

They lay on the patio loungers that were on the patio. Esme lifting her face to the sun was unspeakably beautiful. After a while she said, "Hey, thanks for looking after me. I do feel better."

His mind was everywhere. How connected Cozumel and Luis were, practically finishing each other's sentences. Strange flashbacks about Livia, remembering the giddy feeling he had for a very short time in the beginning when he thought he was in love. How being a couple made him feel part of something he wanted and felt incomplete without. How it wasn't that his parents didn't care for each other, but they just didn't show it. For some reason they didn't think it needed expressing, or kindling, or romancing. In Livia, he was chasing that something different he thought he needed. Instead, all he came away with was hurt. And shame. Esme was right. If he was ever going to let go of the regret he carried in his body, he needed to let the shame go.

When they returned to the main house after it had gotten dark, Luis had finished preparing dinner. It was to be eaten under the stars at a table made from clear blue glass pieces that picked up bits of moonlight here and there. Just as Esme's hair did.

"When everybody thinks about Oaxacan cooking they think of our moles. There are many variations,"

Cozumel explained as she served Jackson a piece of grilled chicken onto which she ladled a dark sauce.

Luis jumped in with, "Mole contains dozens of ingredients and takes days to make. When Cozumel told me you were coming, I began this mole *negro* for you."

"You'll taste the subtle flavor of chocolate balanced with acidic tomatillos, nuts, tortillas, dried fruit, chili peppers. It's both savory and sweet."

Jackson took a bite and the richness and complexity of the sauce delighted his taste buds. "Thank you, Luis, this is beyond delicious."

Esme nodded emphatically in agreement.

Luis carried out a clay pot. "With it, we'll have black beans with epazote, an herb we farm here at the spa. We cook it with some onions and a little bit of bacon so it's herby but rich."

Next came a tray. "My goodness," Esme marveled. "This is enough food to feed New York City."

"*Tlayudas*, which are like our pizzas. We spread a tortilla with beans, *asiento*, which is pork lard, cheese and tasajo. Dried beef."

"And no kale whatsoever," Jackson said to no one.

After dinner Cozumel served them a small glass of mezcal, a spirit made from the agave plant, which had a smoky flavor. And a chocolate sampling on another beautiful plate, this one painted with sunflowers. "Chocolate is very important to us. It's used for all occasions and rituals. You'll see tomorrow we even use it in the spa."

"Cozumel, what treatments will we show Jackson?"

"I have a longtime client, Payaan, who I've seen

through her fertility issues. She's willing to have you observe our work together. Tomorrow, we do demonstrations. Tonight, we rest. Now, go sit by the firepit, take the mezcal and the chocolate with you and just be. Surrender to the moon." It was as if Cozumel knew him, knew that her simple instruction wasn't an easy one for him to follow.

Sitting on one of the circular stone benches that rounded the firepit, they quietly nibbled the chocolate and watched the orange flames tickle the night. It wasn't just the physical connection between them he couldn't stop thinking about. It was that all of his pronouncements and decrees about never getting close to a woman were melting like snowflakes in the firepit. He'd be all business with Esme, like they'd agreed. Yet his heart would know that it was her who had cracked his hard shell, giving him an inkling that being with someone heart, body and soul might be worth the risk of his greatest fear coming true, that he'd be betrayed again.

Eventually, he stood. "After such a wonderful meal, I think I'm the one who is going to fall asleep right here if we don't get to the casita." They got up and strolled under the moonlight and stars to their little house.

"Hard to believe we began our day in Stockholm."

"Let's go to bed." It was strange the way that came out of his mouth. As if they were a longtime married couple who always retired to bed together. It just came out that way. He surely wasn't speaking from personal experience. He and Livia had no bedtime ritual. He often stayed awake much later than she did, communicating with the rest of the world from his computer, some people beginning their workdays, some at the end. Time had no particular meaning to him and he hadn't considered it that much until this moment, when it seemed as if he and Esme and the black night sky were part of something connected, and last night in Stockholm they were part of something else. But perhaps his lofty musings were just those snowy kisses doing the talking.

"Here we are," Esme stated the obvious when they stepped into the casita and headed to the bedrooms.

His best bet would have been to walk straight into his room and close the door. Which he succeeded at. Except for one tiny detour. And that was over to Esme's face to give her lovely cheek just a peck of a goodnight kiss.

Okay, he almost succeeded in that scenario, too. The kiss ended up on her sumptuous lips, which tasted like chocolate. And it was decidedly more than a peck.

"That kiss was your doing, right?" Esme pointed at him and played tough guy, but with a twitch of a smile.

"Yes. Not you. Me."

"Just checking." She entered her bedroom and shut the door, leaving him standing in the divide between the two rooms, frozen, stunned.

"Mayan abdominal massage, which is part of healing practices called *sobada*, has been around since Meso-american times," Cozumel told Jackson the next morning as they walked to the open-air massage plaza with its tentlike roof. A massage table was dressed with clean linens and a wooden cabinet with open doors displayed shelves of towels and products used for treatments. A small woman sat on the table under the shade. "Payaan, these are my friends Esme and Jackson who I told you about."

She made eye contact with them. Esme considered that it was very open of the woman to allow her and Jackson to observe her treatment. As if on cue, Payaan ran her palm across her belly.

Esme asked her, "Can I help you lie down?" She put out her hand and Payaan took it to help herself into position.

"We're being extra careful with Payaan. Although she has one beautiful daughter, six years old if I remember correctly," Cozumel said, to which Payaan nodded, "she's having trouble holding another pregnancy. We're going to try some techniques that have been used for centuries to aid in fertility."

"Gracias," the otherwise quiet Payaan whispered.

Cozumel began with a singsong chant in Spanish, blessing the elements that had joined them for today's journey. While she did that, she gently stroked Payaan's left arm from finger to shoulder and then her right. She did the same up the length of each leg from foot to hip. She rolled Payaan's skirt down from the waist, exposing the smooth brown skin of her abdomen, the soft center of her. "We'll set our intention to pour love into Payaan's belly, to send her the sun and the moon, water and fire."

"I will." Esme closed her eyes and brought those very images to mind, trying to use her own energy to penetrate into Payaan. She imagined her spirit traveling into the woman with every exhale. Afterward, she opened her eyes and shifted her gaze to Jackson. She didn't imagine he'd be spiritually trying to move his life force but nonetheless he was stilled by the uniqueness of the moment. And, after all, that's why they were there, to show him how transformative this specific care could be. Esme had this one chance to affect Payaan's reproductive health because tomorrow they'd be gone, and Cozumel would be on to her next client.

Cozumel washed her hands with the collected rainwater she poured from a pitcher, and dried them on a fluffy towel. She rubbed her palms together to warm them and then placed both down on Payaan's belly.

"Join me, Esme. If that's all right, Payaan." She nodded. Esme followed Cozumel in washing and drying her hands, warming them with friction and then placing them onto Payaan. The four hands moved to gently press into her belly, feeling for information. "Payaan, I sense some movement in you. Perhaps you are ovulating, either today or within the next couple of days." She began gently lifting and gliding along Payaan's stomach, moving with her fingertips in an outward circle. Esme did the same.

To Jackson, Esme explained, "With *sobada* techniques we can sometimes guide the uterus into the optimal position in the lower pelvis."

"How?" he asked simply. Esme was happy that he was taking an interest. She had wondered how he would feel about coming to Oaxaca to a spa that concerned itself mainly with fertility. But he seemed to understand that this was a very specialized practice, and Cozumel a very gifted practitioner.

"We can increase circulation to the area and break up blockage. That brings a better flow of oxygen and relieves stagnation."

"Esme has a beautiful touch," Cozumel said to Jackson. "She always has. She was born with it." Jackson caught Esme's eyes and smiled sweetly with what looked like pride. She all but blushed in return. A moment not lost on Cozumel.

No one but Esme knew the surprising gift of Jackson's touch. When he'd embraced her during those kisses in Stockholm. Even his impromptu palm at the small of her back when going through the airport was hypnotizing. His big hands were sure and powerful, teeming with energy waves. She was trying very hard to pretend that she didn't crave more.

Esme said, "The menu here can help with other ailments and maladies as well such as endometriosis, blocked tubes, fibroids, cysts, painful menstrual cramps, prostate health for men. And prenatal care, to ensure the mother and baby are comfortable and breathing easily."

They were quiet for the rest of the treatment, the rustling breeze their only sound. Upon completion of the session, Cozumel said, "Now we'll bring closure to our work together. That's part of the healing. We'll anoint Payaan's belly with cocoa oil and wrap her in a rebozo, a ceremonial shawl." Esme pulled the needed items from the cabinet.

After the session they reviewed. "I could see Payaan respond to you, Esme. You were a talented novice and you've become skilled in and out of the treatment room. I wish I could bring you back permanently. I'm too busy to take on all of the requests I get. Plus, my spa director, Itza, will herself soon take a maternity leave to birth her own baby and she hasn't decided if and when she'll return."

"My honor." Esme appreciated the praise. It was a transformative two years she'd spent here, learning from Cozumel and gaining the confidence her own parents failed to give her. Poignant that she was back here during this turning point in her life. In more ways than one, as she was here with this extraordinary man who was making her question all that she'd held sacred.

With the demonstration completed, Cozumel suggested Esme show Jackson the mud therapy. They changed into swimsuits and headed to the mud pavilion, another outdoor space on the property. As he walked a few paces ahead of her, Esme couldn't help admiring Jackson's sturdy back, his skin glistening in the late-afternoon glow. When they were in session with Cozumel, it was a thrill that he was so interested in the work that was done here. To understand this was to understand her. She'd never met anyone outside of the spa industry who had.

"Have you ever used a mud pool? We coat ourselves in the wet clay mud and then we sit out in the sun to let it dry. After that we rub it off, and then rinse with geothermal mineral water, which is one of nature's greatest detoxifiers."

Esme used hands full of clay from the well to completely cover one arm in a thin layer to show Jackson, who was quick to follow. "Slimy."

"It's food for your skin. The paste will nourish."

"Does my skin need nourishing?" he asked, getting used to the sensation and applying the clay to his chest.

"Yes, this is incredible restoration for your skin, another natural remedy that's been around for centuries. It stimulates your skin function. Did you know that skin is the body's largest organ?"

"I didn't even know that skin was an organ."

"The mud pulls out the impurities so they don't enter your bloodstream. It balances the skin, which can even have a sedative effect."

"And I didn't know that my skin needed sedation, either."

"Oh, that's a little thick on your chest. Let me." She reached out with a flat palm to spread out the too-heavy layer he had created. He took a quick intake of breath, making her realize that her hands were having an effect on him.

Just as his chest was having an effect on her hands. His solid muscles and skin so warm it was bringing the mud to a perfect temperature.

They looked at each other, a silent conversation that went long past clay. She wondered about being here in Mexico, about Jackson's dark eyes, heated skin and the penetrating feeling that she had been missing out on something central to the meaning of life.

"Do you want me to do your back?"

"Please."

He turned around, and it was almost painful not to

be able to see his face. She dutifully coated his back, whispering in his ear from behind, "It's easier when there's someone to help, isn't it?"

"I can see that now."

Once she'd applied the mud to the curves and planes of his extremely attractive back, he circled around. "My turn." It was a statement not an inquiry. She gave him access and his hands were indeed sent from heaven as they applied the clay to her shoulder blades, vibrating through her. In fact, she had to pull away because she was starting to feel so turned on and needed to put herself in check.

Fully coated, they lay on wooden reclining chairs. After a quiet time breathing the clean air and lost in thought she said, "Thank you for your suggestions yesterday. You really helped me with my jet lag."

"I'm glad to hear." He'd done something for her, and they both valued that more than she could express.

After a while it was time to begin sloughing the mud off. They moved to the cavelike rock formation where the spouts of showers awaited. "It's best if you rub as much as you can while it's still dry so there's less thickness to wash off. See?" She vigorously rubbed one area of her arm, watching the now-powdery clay fall from her skin. He did the same. Then they turned on the showers and let the rest of the mud glide down their bodies and swirl into the drain. "We'll finish washing up at the casita." Their time here was coming to a close. Tonight they were headed out on a late flight to Bangkok, onto the next, and last, spa.

CHAPTER EIGHT

JACKSON TURNED ON the casita's outdoor shower with its privacy and unforgettable mountain view so they could finish getting the mud off. He took a mental snapshot as he would remember this place for the rest of his life. This whole trip had already been an unexpected odyssey. What he was learning about himself as well as spa. He slipped off his still-muddy swim trunks and tossed them into the woven laundry hamper provided. Naked, he turned to Esme, aware that removing the small piece of fabric from his body actually presented a dilemma. He could tell that he'd aroused her by applying the mud, the way they'd talked to each other with their hands instead of words. And he certainly couldn't hide the physical effect she'd had on him. Was she comfortable being nude around him? There was no choice but to find out. She removed her bathing suit and he tried to keep from gawking at the parts of her he hadn't seen bare. Sort of. He was overwhelmed with a desire for the freedom, to take the action that his heart so wanted.

Unable to not, he guided them both under the showerhead and he took her face in his hands. He kissed her lips, lightly, then again until each kiss was slower than the last. He put his arms around her, hands stroking up the length of her back. The more mud that washed off, the softer she felt. He held her to him closely but not tight, just taking in the totality of the moment. Here, with her. It almost didn't seem real, this new life he'd stepped into the moment he returned to the Sher after his long absence. It was only the job of washing the mud off of her body that kept him grounded on earth. Otherwise, he might have floated up into the white clouds that dotted the bright blue sky.

"We're doing it again." He felt it necessary to label the moment, to make sure he wasn't coercing her.

"I want to make love with you, Jackson. Just once. We can handle that, can't we? We know what we're doing."

"I've wanted you every moment of every day since I came into the Sher." He kissed the lips that were glistening wet from the shower. "Yes, once, and only once, then we'll never taste the danger again." He had to have her. A promise of only once made sense. Then, with their itches scratched, they'd go on to a long and prosperous partnership. It would be a matter of will that they were both capable of.

He began wide swipes with his hands across her sides and lower, washing away every speck of mud until impulse had him move to the front of her. His hands held her breasts before his eyes did, round, firm, sized for a precious handful. The hiss of his inhale let her know she had his rapt attention. He'd dare not reach down between her thighs, not yet anyway. They had until late night to board their flight to Bangkok.

He was not going to rush this moment that they promised would be a one-time memory. He knew it would be his greatest treasure, forever.

His lips trailed to her neck and when he moved her wet hair aside to kiss and nip there, she let out a small moan of pleasure that gushed through him. His mouth traveled to kiss those inviting breasts, first with wisps down the outer side of one, then the other. Then his mouth longed for, and found, a nipple which he tickled with the tip of his tongue at least a thousand times. When his teeth returned to her throat, her head fell back to receive him again.

"Jackson," she barely murmured, "that feels so good."

"Thank you for telling me so." He did love making love even though he'd previously compartmentalized it as recreation with no emotional involvement. He'd barely witnessed any physical contact between his parents, who were always walking out the door to a meeting or some such. His father never sat him down and talked to him about anatomy or contraception, leaving that to the little bit of health education that was taught in schools. Nor did anyone ever talk to him about how to treat women. Gentlemanly behavior, yes, but not intimacy matters such as consent and consequences and attachments. He was left on his own with all of that. Perhaps a little more information in that regard might have helped him recognize who not to marry.

But by about age sixteen, when he was expected to participate in the family business, he found himself at functions and charity events where well-to-do women who were twice his age took interest in him and introduced him to sexuality. To some wild escapades, in fact. For example, making love on the rooftop of a forty-story building in Manhattan at two o'clock in the morning. Through being with older women who easily communicated their proclivities and needs better than less experienced younger women, he learned a valuable lesson. That sex was much more pleasurable to him if it was equally pleasurable to the woman he was with. He made up his mind to become a skilled and perceptive lover.

Those women, some married or divorced or career-focused, were as careful as he was not to form any taboo emotional involvements. He broke no hearts nor had his heart broken until Livia, who swindled him into thinking they *had it all*—the business, a passionate love and a genuine connection. How gullible he'd been, perhaps starved after all of those meaningless encounters with other women and the chilly home he grew up in.

Now it was Esme who was presenting him with a test to all of his rules and regulations. He felt something toward her that with Livia was only a facade. The pulling in his soul that told him he might want to actually be with her, to be a melded couple that moved through life together. *Together* together. Which was an unsafe place for him to be. He couldn't have his heart broken again. All of this traveling with Esme, seeing things as if through only one lens, natural partners in every sense of the word, was making him reconsider what he'd resigned to, whether he wanted to or not. He really didn't mean for this closeness to be developing between them, yet it was. Like destiny. Like fate.

His mouth captured hers again to merge under the shower into their fullest, most urgent kisses yet. She wrapped her arms around his neck and he ran his hands along the expanse, from her shoulder to her elbows to her wrists.

"Yes," she moaned. "Oh, heavens, yes."

A smile cracked his lips as his hand trailed down her side and slipped between her legs. She gasped. He held her in the palm of his hand, letting her sex press against it, finding what was good. She buried her face in his neck and her slow train of breath coaxed him to continue. His fingers started a gentle motion and found a groove for her, so he didn't vary it either in speed or in pressure, instead letting her do the moving against his hand, tuning it to her own comfort and pleasure. He himself became rock-hard in the doing. Once she was close to going over the edge, he added kisses to her décolletage until her back arched then she shattered into his hand with a long cry out.

He murmured into her ear, "Magnificent."

After sufficiently washing each other with soapy hands, he shut off the tap and handed her a big fluffy towel in the terra cotta color that was part of the spa's signature logo. "Jackson, I have to tell you something."

"Okay, please do." What did she have on her mind? Even though she'd said she wanted to make love, he wouldn't go any further if she had any hesitations.

"I've never..." Oh, was she going to tell him that she was a virgin? She'd mentioned dating although not having ever been in a serious relationship. He'd imagined that she'd had sex before. Not that he would have minded being her first as she seemed to be enjoying herself so far.

"Yes?" he encouraged her.

"I've never had real lovemaking before. The men I've been with were only interested in their own pleasure, and in achieving it as quickly as possible."

He brushed her hair from her face and smiled with what he hoped was reassurance. "Shall we change that?"

"I think we already have. The way you made my body quake just now was a first for me. I'm sorry I don't have experience pleasing a man, either. Will you tell me what feels arousing to you?"

"I will." He let her lead him into the casita and straight into the bed that had been designated as hers. She laid her naked body in the center of it. "I'll be right back," he said, remembering that he needed to grab protection from his luggage. He dashed into the other bedroom and back as quickly as he could. Then he climbed onto the bed, kissing and caressing her shapely legs along the way.

Hours passed although it seemed like days as he and Esme gave and received. Learning and taking chances. Bringing each other to unimaginable bliss. Finding themselves in positions that were not only unfamiliar to Esme, but were to Jackson as well. While he'd had some profound sexual encounters, ones that he revisited in his mind even years after the fact, those too, were nothing compared to what he shared with Esme in a wooden bed in Mexico with the scent of dirt and flowers wafting in and out of the open windows. Finding out what brought Esme to ecstasy was the most erotic experience he'd ever had. She was more than capable of igniting him without needing instruction. They rose and fell, danced and shook, penetrated, twisted, grasped, held and joined over and over and over again.

After the visit to the heavens and back with Jackson, Esme could see out the bedroom window that dusk was beginning to settle, which meant they only had a few hours left until they departed for Thailand. There was one more thing that she wanted to do before they left Spa Bajo el Sol, a place of such importance to her. Although it wasn't easy, she dislodged herself from Jackson's enveloping embrace and got out of bed. She turned to him. "Come on."

"Where are we going?"

They threw on some clothes and wandered into the main house where, no surprise, Luis was hard at work in the kitchen chopping vegetables. "Do you want to show Jackson where you stayed when you were here?"

"That's exactly where I was headed."

"Take a look at the photos we put up."

Easily remembering her way, she took Jackson's hand and led him through the common areas of the big house to the other side where the bedrooms were. Her old digs were through the farthest door on the left. The room was decorated as all of the house was, with traditional Mexican styling and open windows. A single-sized bed had a colorful blanket and pillows.

"This is it. This is where I slept when I worked here."

Jackson looked around. "Small, but I'm sure you had everything you needed." He noticed a gallery of photos mounted on the far wall and he moved to check them out. He pointed to one and beckoned her over. "Oh, my goodness."

As soon as she spotted the photo he was referring to, she put her hand over her mouth with a giggle. "Yup. Yours truly."

In the photo she was standing behind a seated Luis, her hands on his shoulders giving him a shoulder massage. Cozumel stood beside, squeezing oil from a bottle onto him, the three of them laughing uproariously. Esme even recalled that exact moment. The validation she'd gained here was invaluable to her.

Jackson actually reached out and touched Esme's face in the photo. "What a little beauty you are. How old were you here?"

"Let's see. I'm thirty-two now, so I was twenty-two."

She glanced at the other photos on the wall. They were of other young practitioners the spa had employed over the years, happy faces of every race, creed and color. Cozumel and Luis made it a habit to employ industry workers seeking experience. She used to joke that it was because they had no children of their own.

"You were just a babe." Jackson stayed focused on her picture.

"Yeah, but I was licensed by then."

"Could you teach me a little bit about how to give a massage? I mean, obviously it would take years to develop the skills you have, but would you show me how to do something simple?"

"Why?"

"It would be such a gift to make people feel transformed the way you do."

Oh, he'd made her feel plenty good just a while ago in the casita. What Jackson did to her very being. He lifted her to the spirits, taking her to a celestial high. It was a lifetime's worth of sensual information in only one encounter. Besides him having some sort of mystical skill at knowing her body, they had a desperation for each other that had to be fulfilled. Still, she'd bet he'd have a pretty fine touch for those basic massage strokes.

"Okay. Lie down face down on the bed." He stretched his gorgeous body out and she knelt at his side. "Even though you claimed you weren't that impressed with the massage in Stockholm, what do you remember about it?"

"That massage therapist was intense. I didn't like the way he looked at you."

"What? I mean about the work he did. How did he look at me?"

"Like you were prey."

"I doubt that." She'd barely paid attention to him, she was so busy trying to make sure Jackson had a positive session.

He considered her words, seeming to replay the session in his mind. "Well, in any case, I got a bad vibe from him."

"How about his skills?"

"He had some good moves."

"Name one."

"His palms along the sides of my torso. It was a kind of lengthening that was pleasant."

"Like this?" Esme demonstrated on Jackson's body. "It's called effleurage."

"Yeah. Can I try it on you?" The man who started off saying he didn't value touch wanted to practice some technique. Everything but everything seemed to be changing in the winds.

She had to admit this was fun. And of all places, in the house where she'd spent two years learning and growing. She gave Jackson a gentle push to make room for her on the bed and then he was the one to kneel beside her. He rapidly glided his hands along her torso.

"Okay, first of all you've got to slow that down." He attempted again but this time he was using the tips of his fingers. "Not with your fingers, use your palms."

She let him try a few more times, offering pointers with each attempt.

"This isn't easy."

"You see what we mean if someone has a particularly good touch. It takes hundreds of hours to master a protocol."

He kept trying, genuinely paying attention to her tutorial and improving with every stroke.

"That's nice, Jackson. What you have to do is learn from my body's response. Am I melding into your hand or are my muscles resisting?" He'd certainly gotten that one right at the casita. Was she really never going to have that with him again?

"It's so much more complicated than it looks."

"It is at that." Were they still talking about massage?

Eventually, they ended up lying next to each other on their backs, holding hands and staring at the ceiling, the sky outside now pitch-black. They might have slept there all night.

However, they had a plane to catch.

"Welcome to Thailand," Esme said, peeling her gaze away from the airplane window after she'd watched their descent into Bangkok. It had been a couple of years since she'd been in the country and she was looking forward to showing Jackson about traditions that particularly resonated with her.

She was also glad to be seeing Hathai Sitwat, owner of the world-renowned Spa Malee, which translated as *flower spa*. In fact, as soon as they made their way off the plane and to the baggage claim area, their host was there waiting for them. She was a curvy woman with lush black hair, wearing a vibrant print dress. After all the hellos and introductions Hathai said to Jackson, "I visited the Sher when I was last in New York. It's a magnificent building."

"Thank you. It meant a lot to my parents."

"Precious gifts," she added, "things that were important to family that came before us." Given that most of what Esme remembered from her parents was their selfishness, she could only raise her eyebrows at Jackson. He seemed to understand her with a reassuring single nod. Lack of modeling healthy and caring relationships was, unfortunately, a childhood similarity that they shared at this point.

They took in the sights and sounds as their host

drove them through a very lively and traffic-congested Bangkok. Hathai insisted that they stay at her house while they were in town. After turning down a street here and another there, Hathai entered the gate codes to access the front driveway, which was redolent with many colors of plants and flowers. Her home itself was a natural paradise.

Esme said, "This is incredible."

"I used to live in a high-rise apartment right by the spa," she explained. "It became unsustainable to never have quiet, to not hear a bird chirp. It was important for me to make the best use of my off time as possible."

"Yet you're still in the city."

"The best of both worlds. While I wait for grand-children." Hathai was divorced with two grown sons. Had Jackson thought about children and grandchildren? Esme couldn't help but feel that this trip with him had opened her eyes. That it wasn't just a strategic move to win her the directorship at the Sher. That it was bring-ing her whole self into the light. And she wondered if it might be doing the same for him.

They entered the large house and Hathai showed them to their rooms. While they nibbled some snacks, Esme couldn't take her eyes off Jackson. She'd watched him sleep on the plane, taking her time to indulge in studying his face. In repose he looked different than when they'd made passionate love, the feral, urgent burn in his hungry eyes so untamed she thought she'd orgasm from just gazing into them. As exquisite as his big dark eyes were, there was art in them asleep as well. His face took on a calm that she didn't see while he was awake. With his lips slightly parted and the tiny whoosh of air that accompanied every exhale, he was a sight not unlike one of the world's wonders.

She hadn't slept on the flight again, and was moving forward on fumes. That and the memory of the love-making she'd never forget. Esme had had sex with a few men, slipping out of bed when they were done, out the door before morning as she let her actions speak for her. That she was done. Although that kind of con-duct would now forever be in question should she ever again think to have unsatisfying relations with anyone else, so mind-altering was her interlude with Jackson.

Her body quivered just thinking about it now as she picked one of the slices of mango laid out on a plate. She slid a slippery, ripe and fragrant piece through her lips. How she wished she could slip half of the mango slice into Jackson's mouth while keeping the other side in hers and let them take slurpy bites of the juicy fruit until their mouths met in the middle.

Fantasy aside, she was well aware that she'd been walking on a dangerous wild side when she'd told Jack-son that she wanted to make love with him. Once. Of course, in fairness to her, she had no way of knowing that doing so would be so spectacular it would send her into a daze she might never return from. How was she going to keep her vow that she was allowed a one-time exploration and nothing more? Her second bite of mango was more of a frustrated chomp.

The car ride was quick to Spa Malee. "Oh, this is so much like the Sher," Jackson noted to Hathai right away, given that the facility was located upstairs in a commercial building in a tony part of town. Also like the Sher, the spa had a separate entrance, an unassuming front door that was either opened by code or through a phone app. There was a small elevator, same as the Sher.

"Well, here's where the similarity ends," he said when the elevator door opened.

They exited to a small foyer, just big enough to hold a wooden bench topped with a couple of colorful cushions. Ambient sound of rainfall made the space seem farther from the street than it was. It was a perfect nook for someone who needed to sit for a moment as a transition. A side table had a pitcher of water with a stack of small metal cups. Art on the wall was traditional.

Esme said, "That's what I was saying about the Sher. The elevator opens to a sleek and exclusive New York property. Instead, I'd like clients to have a total magical paradise as soon as they arrive."

"Agreed," Jackson said.

After they stepped inside that door, Hathai gestured for them to remove their shoes and place them in the cubbies provided. Jackson's eyes began a three-hundred-and-sixty-degree survey of the lobby. "My, my," he uttered. Long panels of intricately carved wood adorned some of the walls. Others displayed paintings of the sun, the moon and stars. There were clusters of teakwood furniture with pillows covered in brilliant-colored silk fabrics, deep blues and bright yellows. Succulent green plants and fresh flowers were everywhere, creating the most delightful scent.

"The bare floor with all the wood and greenery gives it such an open look," he said.

Esme was glad Jackson could appreciate what a stunner this spa was.

Hathai said, "Let me take you in. When a guest enters, we always greet them with tea or water." She discreetly pointed to a group of four women who were enjoying tea and laughter. "We have soundproof glazing on the windows so that in here we can disassociate from everything outside. And focus on being in a healing oasis."

"Hathai," Jackson asked, "when we were driving here through the city streets, and just like in New York, you see Thai massage businesses everywhere. With a sign outside listing prices, often much lower than for a spa. What is different about Spa Malee? I looked at your menu and of course you have high-end prices, appropriate for a luxury establishment like this."

"I think you answered your own question, Jackson." Hathai brought them to a semicirclular area of treatment rooms with more woods and silks. "In a street corner business, there are many people receiving massage in the same room. One next to the other. It's not at all private and it's not personalized for each guest. You could almost think of it as an assisted-movement class, comparable to yoga. Which isn't to say there's anything wrong with that. It shows us that this is medicine in Thailand, as it has been for thousands of years. It's part of a health care system for physical and energetic well-being. We advocate for those small studios. In fact, I own a dozen of them throughout the country where people who don't have the funds can receive treatment for free."

"What Hathai has established here," Esme added, "is the lavish secluded world of the day spa combined with a wellness center. That's what I want us to do at the Sher."

Ideas were solidifying in Esme's mind. Her concept for the spa she wanted. Something she'd mulled over for a long time but hadn't been in a position to execute. Bringing together all of these traditions from across the globe and creating a unique place like none other in New York. And the vision had now come to include Jackson, who had suddenly become her partner, her friend and one time, therefore, former lover. Everything seemed possible.

Hathai said, "We have chosen the finest of materials and furnishings for this spa, our flagship, and we hire only extensively experienced practitioners. Please," she invited and gestured with her arm to usher them into a treatment room.

"Welcome to utopia," Jackson said as he again took in the palatial surroundings.

"Please meet Aroon." A small man entered holding a big wooden bowl filled with flower petals and water. Esme knew right away that Hathai had called in this practitioner over another because he was small in stature, so that if he deemed to give Jackson the pressure technique of standing on his back, his weight wouldn't be a burden to bear.

Aroon put the flower bowl down on a small table that held a stack of white towels. He invited Jackson to take a seat in a cushioned throne-like chair. "At Spa

Malee we have a special welcoming ritual to let you know how glad we are that you are here."

Again, Esme thought of what saying those words to a client in New York might mean, that level of welcome to someone who was sick or had an ongoing health issue, or to someone who didn't have a lot of touch in their life, or even to someone who was just burnt-out and needed personal attention.

Aroon set the bowl of water and flower petals down on the floor in front of Jackson, and dropped to his knees. Gently lifting one of Jackson's feet, he placed it in the water and began to use his fingers back and forth to brush one foot with the water, and then the other. Esme and Jackson smiled at each other, her knowing he was as grateful as she was to be sharing this together.

CHAPTER NINE

JACKSON WAS DEFINITELY in unfamiliar territory. Esme's world of the healing arts wasn't anything he'd ever contemplated. The people he'd met in the past few days were truly remarkable. While Aroon rubbed his feet with flower petals, strange as both a sensation and the unfamiliar setup of this tiny man kneeling at his feet, he couldn't take his eyes off Esme, who was observing the proceedings as if she was judging the accuracy. Making sure he was being attended to correctly. More of her caretaking instinct again.

In Oaxaca he'd had a chance to show her that she could be the one taken care of sometimes. He was still elated to reflect back on the satisfaction he felt from her cries of pleasure and her tight grip that begged him to continue whatever he was doing, a request he was only too delighted to oblige. He tried to close his eyes for a moment just to take in the sensation of the water at his feet, but it was too agonizing to take his gaze off her. Something was rising in him that he didn't ask for but had arrived nonetheless.

His feelings for her were long past employee and employer, no matter how many times he proclaimed that, and even past two single people who'd decided to give themselves to each other for one coupling. No, Jackson was starting to settle in to Esme being a permanent presence in his life. One he wanted to have around him all the time. He could see them as both business and life partners, could visualize a life in New York where he stayed put and they moved forward step after step after step into a reality he'd never expected, especially after his divorce. He blinked his eyes a few times to try to come back to the moment.

He was so glad that before they'd left Oaxaca, he'd asked her to teach him a tiny bit of her considerable repertoire. It would be useful for him to think about the work from the practitioner's point of view as well as the client's.

"We work holistically," Hathai said from where she stood back to avoid interfering. "Some people know it as part of the Indian system of Ayurvedic health, or as traditional Chinese medicine, in which the energy lines in the body become blocked or diseased as opposed to having a healthy flow. It has also to do with acupressure points."

Esme added, "Aroon will move and stretch you in a way that is also known as assisted yoga."

With that, Aroon had Jackson lie face down on the mat on the floor. "Thai massage is done on the floor and with the recipient wearing loose and comfortable clothing. And we use no oils. Very unlike Western massage," Hathai said. Aroon began pressing Jackson's feet with his open palms. And then his legs and arms, which was to awaken his energy.

"It's thought that this type of bodywork might have originated with Buddha's own physician twenty-five hundred years ago, who learned from Indian medicine and integrated it into a regime for good health. The process helps with circulation, mobility, strengthening the immune system, even anxiety and headaches."

As they spoke, Aroon began pulling on Jackson's legs, grasping him with remarkable strength for a man his size. "The giver and the receiver become very connected during the treatment. Jackson, I can see your muscles releasing, perhaps because your body is following Aroon's instincts."

He stretched, then compressed, then rocked each limb, indeed putting Jackson's body into yoga-like positions. And there was more surrender involved when Aroon did walk on Jackson's back, steadying himself by holding on to an apparatus hung from the ceiling for specifically that purpose. Eventually, Aroon ended the session by pulling on Jackson's toes and fingers and ears. It was an unforgettable experience. No wonder it was Esme's favorite type of massage.

For someone who had little regard for massage, he'd undergone a metamorphosis. He hadn't had as much tightness as he had when he'd been to Dr. Singh's office. Although they'd been busy, it had indeed been a much-needed vacation from his usual grind. He suspected it had more to do with Esme's company than anything else. Nonetheless, his respect for these serious disciplines was profound.

"Okay, you sold me. That was incredible."

They decided to go out and enjoy some of Bangkok. Neither knew the city well.

Esme said, "I've never gone to the floating markets."

"Me, either. I know they've become more tourist attraction than anything else but I'd like to go."

Hathai recommended a famous one. Jackson knew that the floating markets used to be the main method by which food and other goods were transported along the country's rivers and canals. Because people settled near them, the culture of riverside shopping was essential to the city's livelihood. Nowadays, shoppers would find fruits and vegetables and a myriad of cooked food and sweets, also clothes, crafts and souvenirs. He quickly arranged for a private boat and driver, and they got to the riverfront and set sail.

"Wow, look at how many boats are on the river."

Indeed, dozens of vessels navigated their way in and around each other. "What do you want to eat? That was my ulterior motive," he said with a wink.

"They say Thailand has the best fruit in the world." She pointed to merchants on the riverbank selling fresh fruit. There was more of the ubiquitous mango, looking as inviting as it had on the platter Hathai served them earlier. Also on display were unusual fruits like mangosteen, with its dark shell and tender white segments inside. Rambutan, with its red spiky rind. The beautiful dragon fruit, white fleshed with black seeds inside surrounded by a vivid purple outer skin. And the famous durian, which was to be a love-it-or-hate-it item because of its extreme smell.

"What do you want to start with?"

"We'll have fruit after. Let's start with something spicy."

"Like you." He didn't necessarily mean to say that but it tripped from his mouth. The sun-kissed highlights of her hair glistened and her lips looked as juicy as the fruits vendors cut and sold in clear bags at the riverbanks. He followed his impromptu comment with an impromptu kiss, something he'd been working on holding back from all day at the spa as he didn't want to make Esme uncomfortable. Among the chatter and commerce of people in the boats and along the banks, conversing, bargaining, yelling out to each other, he kissed her succulent lips again and again, not able to pull away, as if his very life depended on it.

His hands lifted to hold her smooth cheeks, both their faces moist from the natural humidity. He wanted to find a way to join their bodies together, to become not two but one entity, the sum most definitely more potent than its parts. He glued his mouth to hers until they had to break away to catch their breaths and return to a stasis. Jackson noticed the boat driver had his head slightly bowed, which he was sure was in politeness to not watch the two of them kiss and to try to conceal the sweet smile that their display brought to his lips. Even a couple of vendors in boats alongside them giggled in approval.

"So. Spicy. Food, that is."

"I want to try boat noodles," she stated decisively. They saw the boats where pots of noodles were being prepared right on board. Their driver brought them close enough to one of the vendors to make a purchase and they could hardly wait to dig in.

"Oh, my gosh, these are scrumptious," he exclaimed after two bites.

"The broth is so flavorful with both the beef and the pork meats, the dark soy and the chilis."

"I want this every day. We'll have to find a place in New York that makes them well." *We'll* have to. Hmm, he was referring to that as if it was the most obvious thing in the world. *We*. Like they were a typical foodie couple who might travel throughout the New York boroughs in search of new tastes. Was that what was happening? He could no longer imagine a different reality. A New York without Esme. Kissing anyone else on the streets of Stockholm. Of making passionate, rapturous love after the mud bath in Oaxaca. Eating these very noodles on this very boat with someone other than her. Unthinkable.

"Okay, but we have to find somewhere authentic in Queens or somewhere. No fancy-schmancy."

Esme had opened up a door he thought was closed. He felt her in his bones. His priorities had changed. Her. It was her. Sharing boat noodles wasn't supposed to fill his heart. It was noodles, for heaven's sake. But everything with her made him stand up and take heed. He wasn't just pushing through anymore. He was awake and alive. A boat came by and the merchant was selling mango with sticky rice and coconut milk, a most perfect dessert after the strong flavors they'd just eaten. Esme bought a bowl and with her fingers, she fed him a piece of the ripe and luscious fruit. It was the sweetest thing he'd ever tasted.

* * *

Esme was sure she was in a dream, or watching a movie. This couldn't be fact. That she was kissing Jackson in a riverboat in Bangkok. Jetting around the world, visiting spas and kissing and now fitting in some tourist pleasures. Pleasures. After fantasizing about it, had she literally picked up a piece of mango and fed it into Jackson's lips? Her fingers tingled from the contact with his mouth, making her want to feed him all the mango in the world and lick the juice that remained on his lips.

He ran the tip of his tongue around his mouth after another bite of fruit. Was that just cruel, forcing her to witness that? Could a person be jealous of a mango? It got to touch his lips and tongue. Well, that was just it, she thought. She had no claim on those powerful lips, a mouth that had made her body shudder for hours. The mango didn't have to ask her permission for his lips. Still, she looked at the glistening orange slices and scowled at them. How dare they?

"Why don't we do an event for the investors when they're in New York for the meeting?" she said quickly, nudging her mind off of lucky mango slices. "We can do it big with some nice food and decorations and give them some mini-treatments. I can do a presentation about benefits and ancient treatments. It'll be great."

"I love how confident you are about this."

"I've been honing this concept for a while. I just didn't think my opportunity was actually coming right now. It's all presenting itself in my mind. I want to focus on women's wellness." She was more used to disappointment, so she didn't get her hopes up about things. Parents in the throes of a fight with each other had tried to bribe her loyalty with promises of a special gift or shopping money. Then once the argument was over and they were back to short-lived bursts of basic decency toward each other, the promises to Esme were forgotten. So she didn't know when her specific scheme for running a spa was going to come to fruition but now she knew it would be someday. Maybe simply saying that good things come to those who wait was real?

"An event is a great plan. The investors love razzle-dazzle."

Wasn't it okay if she gave him another kiss? Yes, she'd vowed to avoid a personal life and the potential hurt it could bring. But that thinking had become ridiculous and limiting. Was it possible that life had made a seismic shift for her? That by spending all of this time with Jackson she could understand just how good it could be to be a *we* under the right circumstances. That what she needed was someone to believe in her, who wouldn't drag her down and take more than they gave. Maybe she needed Jackson. To get her out of her rut and see herself through his eyes and with that, she could conquer the world. Jackson had enriched her life beyond measure, not stolen from it. Maybe *alone* had been a defensive mechanism that she didn't need to hang on to anymore.

She hadn't forgotten that when she was a young child her mother had told her that she'd once wanted to have a career, perhaps go to college. Then she'd met Esme's father and because there was just enough family money to live on, he talked her out of it. They soon had Esme and became nonfunctional, rarely leaving their apartment and teaching Esme to manage their needs as soon as she was old enough. Her mother never took even the smallest step to encourage Esme to pursue the dreams that she herself hadn't.

Could it be that history didn't repeat itself? Couldn't Esme make the jump? Break the mold?

She'd be lying if she didn't admit that spectacular lovemaking was part of the picture. Jackson had coaxed more sensation, awareness and sensitivity than her body had ever known. And she wasn't afraid to be impulsive with him, to do what felt natural and spontaneous, with her own lips, her hands, every part of her. Even though she said they'd satisfied their urge to explore each other and wouldn't do it again, she mentally tossed that rule over the boat and watched it float down the river in between merchants selling pad thai and T-shirts. Yes, she could let him in a little closer. Maybe she'd never devote herself to someone and the risk and obligations that might entail. But she could do this. Have this time with an accomplished and sensual man. She deserved the progress of it. She could keep that separate from long-term worries.

She leaned over and took one of his earlobes between her teeth. The sumptuous dark rumble that came out of him was electrifying. She opened her mouth to let her tongue trace his ear, enjoying that one small move to its fullest. "Jackson," she whispered.

"Yes."

"I have an idea of what I want to do with the rest of this mango." She gestured to the bowl she'd set down on the boat's bench.

"Is that right?"

"Mmm-hmm," she said with a kiss to the private spot behind his ear. "But I'm going to have to show it to you back at the house." Hathai had evening plans and wouldn't return home until late.

CHAPTER TEN

"Do you want to stop?" Jackson asked while taking off Esme's shirt when they got back to the house. They had dropped their belongings and purchases on the table and then crashed into an embrace, grabbing for each other tightly, as if their lives depended on it. Did they?

"No." She appreciated his little verification of her consent, but stopping was not an option. Not while his bites, one after the other, were making a line from her jaw down to where her throat met her shoulders. Her back arched at the sensation. His mouth was both commanding and questioning at the same time, wanting her to tell him more and more. She crooked her neck in the opposite direction to allow him wider access and a moan escaped her vocal cords when he took it. "I definitely don't want to stop."

He continued with his slow, erotic mouth for as long as she wanted him to. She remembered a time with a guy named Rob she'd been with for a few dates. It had actually been the first and one of the only times she'd really experienced sexual pleasure with someone. However, as soon as he noticed her responding to what his hands were doing to her, he pulled away, as if her enjoying it meant she was finished. With Jackson, it was a green light to keep going, and he seemed to relish doing so.

"Esme," he exhaled with a desperate gratification when she unbuttoned his shirt in return. It was equally exciting to know that she was arousing him, also not something she'd ever had validation of before.

And then their motions became like two flowers in bloom, her throat, his shirt buttons, opening, releasing, bending toward each other.

"We said we wouldn't do this again."

"Yup."

"Yup."

They issued their one-syllable protective thought but didn't halt what they were doing even for a second. After the kiss in Stockholm, they'd decided. In Oaxaca they changed that to a one-time license to be intimate. Now here they were, defying that rule, unable to keep away from each other.

How was it that, instead, she felt liberated by Jackson? Perhaps because of all the respect he'd shown her, relying on her professionally, making all that she'd been through to get to this point worthwhile. The quick trip around the world with him was the stuff of fantasy. They'd both had a rebirth and both were still forming, finding their new shapes. That fit into each other. She hadn't even realized how much she needed the affirmation he'd given her.

At the moment, though, after she'd peeled his shirt off his body, her mind was on a quick dash to the table to get the sliced mango they'd bought on the market boat that she'd brazenly promised to continue employing in a private way.

"Oh, yeah, you said there was more about that mango."

She took a piece of the fruit from its bag and held it between her teeth. She approached him and wrapped her arms around his neck to bring him closer. Then she used the piece of mango to draw a line with its juices starting from his Adam's apple and heading downward. The journey was such a turn-on to her, painting him with the mango, marking him, if only for the moment, as hers. She moved slowly down his solid chest, still gripping the fruit with her teeth. When she'd painted that line all the way down to the top of his pants, the task was complete. She coaxed him down into the chair behind him.

"Now what?" His smoldering stare asked the question.

"It seems to be true that Thailand grows the sweetest fruit in the world." She could hardly believe the words coming out of her mouth, so sexual with a courage that she was half faking but somehow believing that if she acted that way it would become so. She leaned over him in the chair using her hands to bolster herself on the armrests so she could hover over him.

"Delicious. Yes," he graveled out, his voice husky and sounding like three in the morning. She brushed her mouth against his but then lowered herself to begin to taste the sweet juice she'd just painted on him. She sunk to the top of his pants and took her first lick there. Indeed, the fruit mixed with the musk that was him was an absolutely intoxicating combination that made her body undulate this way and that, moving to the music his body made her hear. She used the flat of her tongue to work up his torso. A groan forced its way out of him, a sound he didn't seem to have much control over. "Mmm, that feels ridiculously good."

"I want it to." The charge rattled through her again, him acknowledging that what she was doing was favorable to him. The more he gave back to her in that way, the more she wanted to keep doing it. A focused, long, thin lick up his very center made his head roll back, and his lips parted as his even louder groan filled the room. As did the sheer sensuality. The confidence did become real, her body swaying above him, a full-grown woman aware of her wiles. She felt a whole different person inside when she was with him. She didn't understand such magical powers but they were true.

Then as she covered his mouth with hers, she took the thoughts even further. That she was willing to risk for this. For him. That's what it came down to, wasn't it? Risk? She didn't have a crystal ball to look into the future. Maybe embarking on this partnership with Jackson, the personal one and the professional one, would be a total disaster. Maybe she'd give her all and end up jobless and brokenhearted. At least she would have done something. She'd opened up enough to try. Her heart knew it would be worth it and that if she didn't do it she'd regret it for the rest of her days.

Jackson placed his hands under her arms and pulled them up, kissing them into a lip lock. What was there in life without taking a chance? She, who'd thought it out so carefully, how to avoid being anyone's pawn, evading trust, never planning to relent. She'd grown a hard shell. She thought of it as her protection. But with armor, she wouldn't let things in and she would keep things out. Funny how that had seemed the right thing to do in the past, and now it made no sense at all. It wasn't who she was anymore.

He led them to his guest bed and pulled back the silk coverings. His gaze seared through, almost burning holes in her. But then he changed his expression to a majestic smile. Which said he was present, which might have been saying he needed to take a chance, too.

After they'd showered off the mango and all it entailed, Esme and Jackson were ready to go back out and have an evening before they boarded a flight home to New York the next day. Hathai had recommended a bar where they might want to get a drink.

"It's the famous ex-pat bar," Jackson said as they approached the entrance that was made up of six shutter doors, all open to let in the evening breeze. "The Federal."

"Hathai said it was where the Westerners who live in Bangkok met. Businessmen, volunteers, writers and so on."

"As long as I don't see one more mini-Buddha statue." They'd been bombarded with enough cheesy souvenirs at the floating markets earlier.

They entered and, indeed, they were all Westerners sitting apart from one another. Most of the men were dressed in white shirts and khaki pants as Jackson was, presumably the uniform for the humid weather. There were distinctly more men than women there. All eyes turned to Jackson and Esme when they entered.

"Toronto," one of the men called out to them.

"London," yelled another.

"Perhaps. Too well-heeled for the US West Coast," added another still.

"Or Chicago. But they don't look European." This was obviously a game of Guess the Strangers' Origin being played at their expense.

"Certainly not Aussie," the only man with an out-back hat voted in.

"Good evening." Jackson called out, deciding that in good manners they should participate. "What are you basing your guesses on?"

"Nothing whatsoever, mate," said the man who had tagged them as not Australian but his accent suggested that *he* was. "We used to be better at it. We've been in Thailand for too long. The heat has made us stupid." That comment gained a couple of sniggers from around the room.

"We were always stupid, Callum," someone disagreed.

"New York," Jackson answered flatly. One of the men in back began singing about making a brand-new start of it.

"What are you drinking?" asked the bartender, an Asian man who spoke with a British accent.

"Whiskey," Esme called out.

"The lady dabbles in the dark spirits." The man with the Australian accent, Callum, leered at her as he said that. Which ruffled Jackson right away. Was that some sort of flirt? Jackson thought it was rude to comment when a woman walked into a bar with a man. Even more so if she was alone but, nonetheless, he bristled at the unexpected focus on Esme.

He lightly took her elbow, not wanting to seem too possessive, as they made their way in between some empty tables to get to the bar and retrieve their drinks. He sensed this was a pub full of regulars who drank together and were gruff but well intentioned.

"To the Sher." Esme tipped her glass to clink his, seemingly less aware of the vibes in the room than he was.

"To the Sher indeed," he toasted. That she so genuinely cared about the spa moved him.

After they finished their drink, Callum approached Esme, adjusting his hat on his head. Jackson wondered why he wore a hat indoors at all. "Buy you another? Or are you and Mr. New York together? In marital bliss even?" he rasped into Esme's ear, perhaps thinking he was whispering but the volume was well within Jackson's range.

This was getting ridiculous. Was this guy trying to provoke a fight? Maybe that's what drunk ex-pats did when they were bored. The equally boring habit of his jealousy and pessimism crept in. Between the parents that were so icy they'd never even notice the other one's interactions, to the wife that cheated on him with mind, body, soul and wallet, he didn't have much of an example of ethical relationships. He'd made a decision to never need that education, which was how he'd been living for years. Until Esme.

He looked at Callum as if from a distance, in an objective view. Sure, lots of men were going to be attracted to Esme. Why wouldn't they be? She was gorgeous but in a friendly way, wholly approachable. No wonder she was so well suited to the needs of clients. She was also smart and kind. Then he thought of *her* objectively. Even if he was to strip off those bandages that kept his hurt hidden from the sun, was she? After a childhood full of manipulation, she said she'd never take a chance on love. He had no reason to disbelieve her. Well, other than the last few days where they'd been as exposed as they possibly could. Something given openheartedly to each other. Somehow their barricades had been toppled over, despite their best efforts. Did they want to leave them demolished, or build them up again?

Was it only temporary? Were they going to zip up their coats along with their hearts when they got back to New York? Jackson didn't want to. While Livia had destroyed his hope, Esme brought its promise back. Esme was nothing like his ex-wife. He was sure that if she was ever in any kind of liaison with a man she'd be trustworthy and faithful to him, unless they had agreed otherwise. Without even answering the drunk stranger Callum's question as to whether Esme was together with Jackson, he said to her, "Let's go get dinner. Night, all." He laid some money down on the bar. Most of the men growled indifferently.

Jackson ushered them out because he surely didn't

want to spend their last night in Thailand, their last night on this globetrot, dealing with this Callum fellow or his own overreaction. While they'd been inside, it had started to rain. As they walked, he kept checking the expression on her face to see if she was appreciating the walk as much as he was. "Do you want to keep walking in the rain or should we seek cover?"

"I love it. It's refreshing. It's almost sticky on your skin." He wanted to touch her arm, or kiss it even, but they were walking.

"I hope I wasn't wrong in my assumption that you weren't interested in that man's attention?"

"No, but I'm not sure that was a battle I needed fought for me." Obviously, Esme was a very strong person. If she ever was to be with someone, she'd never be the little woman being overpowered by the big possessive male. Her fierce self-sufficiency, born of necessity, was something that was so compelling about her.

"Well, he bothered *me* so I wanted to get away before I provoked him."

In addition to learning about all of the amazing techniques and skills involved in the healing arts of spa, he'd never spent this much time with a woman. Full stop.

"What happens when we get back to New York?" He blurted what he only intended to answer in his mind.

"We put together a quick investor event. I've been texting and emailing with Trevor, and he's already got an event manager and caterer on call."

"I meant us."

"Are *we* an *us*?" They both chuckled at the pronouns.

He reached for her hand to hold as they turned a street corner and said hard things. He needed her palm in his to center himself. Motor scooters, bicycles and cars all fought for territory in the busy evening. "This time with you has completely caught me by surprise. I've told you all the things I had firmly believed were not for me."

"And now?"

He shrugged. "Now, it's a new dawn. This trip made it different. You made it different."

She focused her eyes forward; she needed a minute. He felt unwrapped, even though he hadn't made any declarations. In fact, his thoughts were a jumble as she asked the very thing he didn't know the answer to. "What does happen now?"

"Is that entirely my decision?" His answer was a bit short and he chided himself after he'd said it. But he was confused about what he should dream of. And what would never be.

"Fair point."

It seemed like neither of them were saying what had to be said. What did he really want? "I never imagined that I would care about someone the way I've come to care about you." He saw a flicker in her eyes. "I see now that I'm cutting myself off from too much if I keep myself closed and locked. Which would all just be a bunch of theoretical musings if I hadn't met you. You've changed everything for me. Now I want to explore my heart. I can't see going back to New York to a work-only situation."

"Meeting you has shaken all the pillars that I held

to be true, too. Nobody has ever made me feel so valued. That's a bigger deal than I'd ever thought it was. I assumed I'd be my only cheerleader."

And then he kissed her. In the rain. Their clothes soaking wet and clinging to their bodies. It had only been a few nights since Stockholm but it felt like a lifetime. He and Esme under the sun or the moon or the snow or the stars. Together.

CHAPTER ELEVEN

THERE WERE A million things to do as soon as Jackson and Esme got back to New York. It was good to be busy because everything that happened on the trip had her walking on unsteady ground. The Sher and her managerial duties, and planning the investor event, would keep her mind occupied. Elation propelled her every step but she still wasn't sure what was going to be with Jackson. During the plane ride home they'd committed to a sort of a let's-see policy as neither knew whether they could truly open themselves to the other in the long term.

They'd arrived in the evening and paid a quick visit to the closed spa just to make sure everything was okay. Which, naturally, it was in Trevor's capable hands. Once they turned off all of the lights, set the alarm and went out the door, Jackson voiced a dilemma.

"You know I don't actually keep an apartment in New York. Can I book us a hotel suite or...?" His voice trailed off, not sure how to finish, obviously inviting her to. They hadn't talked about the nuts and bolts of that we'll-see arrangement. Was he going to stay with her? As in day and night, work and...not work?

Instead of overthinking it, she was decisive. Terri-
fied, but putting one foot in front of the next. "Why
don't you stay with me? My place is tiny but we're
going to be spending a lot of time at the spa."

The most charming grin came across his face, as if
she'd given him a gift he'd really wanted. "I would love
that." On the little landing outside the spa door, under
the safety light that cast a wide glow across their faces,
he reached over and wound her scarf around her neck.

"Here we are." The driver dropped them off at the
curb in front of her apartment building and they took
the staircase to the second floor. "I'm sure it's the size
of some people's closet."

"I don't have a home so yours is, by definition, bigger than mine," he said as she opened her front door.
He glanced around, at what she thought were taste-
ful, budget-friendly furnishings. On the wall she had
hung two poster-sized photographs, one of rain falling
in a forest and another of sunset over a beach. A small
smile crossed his lips.

"What?"

"Nothing. These are just so you." He pointed to the
posters. "Something to meditate on right up on your
walls."

"Don't knock it until you've tried it," she mock-
snipped.

They kissed softly and quietly. She rarely had anyone in her apartment, most certainly not a man. She
thought his energy might feel oppressive but it was like
he belonged. His essence filled the apartment, a kind
of fragrance she could never get enough of. Was he a

tree that could grow roots? Would he be able to stop chasing himself and settle into her? Would she, him?

She said as she shook her scattered head, "I'm whacked out again from the time change. How about I order a pizza and we can make some quick notes about what we need to do in the next few days so we can get right to it in the morning?"

"Sounds like a good idea."

After they ate and, in fact, outlined an action plan, she went into the small bedroom to put fresh sheets on the bed and lay out some clean towels for Jackson to use. By the time they collapsed into bed, it was the wee hours. Esme was unused to sleeping on one side of the bed rather than in the middle. At first it bothered her and her body tensed. It didn't need to be said that they wouldn't do anything other than sleep tonight, as they were exhausted. But while Jackson fell right to sleep, she kept her eyes glued to the ceiling for as long as she could stand it, and then rolled over to admire him. His gorgeous face was a work of art she could stare at endlessly, the way his features were so perfectly arranged. The long eyelashes, the elegantly sloped nose, the plump lips.

Was she going to play house with this man, and was it really playing after all? If so, it was a dangerous game. If she lost, she could lose big. If Jackson was to further break what was already broken, she didn't know if she'd be able to put herself back together. That's why she'd vowed never to let someone this close. And yet every fiber in her being told her that this would be worth it. *He* was worth it.

Although her musings kept her up most of the night, they had to hit the ground running if they were going to pull off this event before the investors voted on whether to stay involved in the Sher. Prior to their arrival, Esme had asked Trevor to rearrange her office and put a computer and desk in for Jackson so they could work.

"Will this do?" Trevor asked when they came in.

"Perfect, thanks. How are the twins?"

"Exhausting. Every second of it precious." He showed her a photo on his phone of the babies and Omari, whose smile said it all.

Esme and Jackson settled themselves in and began ironing out the details. The board president of the investors group was to come by in a couple of hours so they wanted to give him a mini-presentation of what they were planning.

"We're doing the cacao theme. Like in Oaxaca, everyone likes those tastes and aromas, and it has medicinal value. I can weave it into the food and use it in the treatments. I can even get some scented lotions and lip balms so we can do a gift bag they can take home."

A smile spread across his face. "In a million years I wouldn't have thought of something like that."

"I guess you're pretty lucky to have me around," she joked. She wasn't really joking but she voiced it with a laugh so that she wouldn't sound arrogant.

"In more ways than one," he replied in a flat voice that slid down her sternum. Although, there wasn't time for her to melt into goo.

"Continuing with the theme, of course we'll do a mole with lunch. Tamales would be good but they require a fork and sitting down. Let me think of something easier. I'll text Luis at Bajo el Sol. He'll have some ideas for me." Her mind filled with their time in Oaxaca, the *sobada* protocol, the mud therapy after which they made love for the first time. What a magical place that was. She wondered if Bajo el Sol would always be a touchstone place for her, the smell of the mountains, the almost supernatural treatments. It was perhaps the most unique spa she'd ever been to. She looked forward to the next time she could visit.

"Luis and Cozumel." Jackson smiled to himself, perhaps having a nice memory of his own.

"And we'll do a *tejate*."

"What's that?"

"It's a drink made from cacao and maize. It's high in antioxidants and tastes really rich. And we'll finish with a bittersweet brownie made with coffee and cinnamon or something like that to end on a heavily chocolate note."

"I have to concentrate on the financial prospectus I had my accountant put together. If you don't stop talking about chocolate, we may not have a spa soon."

Trevor's voice came through the intercom, "Brent Lloyd is here."

"Have you met the board president, Brent?" Jackson looked up from his computer screen to ask Esme.

"No, would I have had any reason to?" After all, she was previously only the spa's manager, responsible for things like schedules and supplies. She wasn't involved with investors or long-term planning decisions. Until now. She took a breath so long it started down in her toes and ended above her head. She was at the big table now.

"I'm just printing something. I'll be there in a minute."

"Hello, I'm Esme Russo, the spa director," she said as she approached Brent Lloyd in the reception area. Wow, that was the first time she'd identified herself out loud as director. The sound of it gave her a thrill. Proof that hard work and perseverance paid off. She was an unlikely success story. Who couldn't wait to pay it forward, to give someone else the break they needed to grasp their goals. She intended to start with Trevor. And then maybe her own children someday? Hers and Jackson's?

As to Brent Lloyd, did she perceive the tiniest wince on his face when he shifted his weight from one hip to the other? He was a salt-and-pepper-haired man, nice looking with aging skin, wearing a fine leather jacket atop his dress pants.

"Brent, if you don't mind me asking, are you in pain?" His body language all but announced that something wasn't right. She always pointed out observations like that and would continue to whether to prince or pauper or board president.

"How did you know?" he asked in surprise.

"I can see it in your stance."

"Can you? I have lower back pain. It's been worse lately."

"Do you spend a lot of time on a computer?"

"Yeah, hours upon hours. Seven days a week."

"Is it a stabbing pain or a dull ache?"

"Ache."

"I may be able to relieve the pressure a bit. Do you want me to give it a try?"

He rubbed his lower back, which caused him enough discomfort that his jaw clenched. "Sure. Anything would help."

She invited him to take his jacket off and sat him down in one of the chairs. She began some long strokes the heel of her palm to his lower back, the lumbar section, then used the tips of her thumbs to add more pressure.

"Tell me if I'm creating pain because that's the last thing we want to do." She pressed in but kept it gentle and could feel each small area she worked on loosen up. "There we go. Do you do physical therapy or get massages?"

"I used to. Then once I get busy, things like that just fall by the wayside."

She concentrated on a particularly tensed-up spot.

"Thank you, I can feel the difference already."

"So can I talk you into booking some treatments at somewhere convenient for you?"

"I live upstate but I'll have my wife make some appointments for me. I don't know why I stopped doing the thing that was helping." He let out a chuckle and she joined him.

"We all think we're too busy. Believe me, I hear that from a lot of people. Do you do any stretching?"

"Another thing I've let lag."

"Or applying heat or ice, or both?"

"Now you're making me look bad."

She smiled and glanced up from Brent to see Jackson standing in the office doorway as if frozen. His eyes bore into her but not in the sensual way they had been for the past couple of days. No, his look was equal parts fury and shock.

"Jackson, what's wrong?"

After a long day's work, Jackson and Esme decided to go for a walk. They ambled without talking through Tribeca up to Greenwich Village, passing shops, restaurants, galleries and all Manhattan had to offer. Jackson was agitated, not from the excitement of the city but because he hadn't gotten over what he witnessed earlier at the spa.

"Are you going to tell me what's bothering you so much?" Obviously, his mood was palpable.

"It's madness."

"So, it's madness. If it's real to you, it matters."

He loved that she said that but was he going to tell her things that he considered shameful? If he was ever going to change and be able to commit to her, he'd have to. And he wanted to. He did want to.

"You've been off the whole afternoon."

Did anything escape this woman? It didn't seem so! "When Brent Lloyd came in and you were touching him, I felt that jealousy I can't seem to control. Which I know is destructive."

"Are you kidding me, Jackson?" He could hear the annoyance in her voice. "I could see he was having some pain. I offered to help him out."

"That's what I assumed." His face became hot. He

was embarrassed. His ire had risen in Bangkok with the pushy Australian man at that pub. He'd even had a twinge in Stockholm when he felt that massage therapist Anders's eyes had lingered on Esme for too long. "Brent is a good guy, president of the board, I've known him for years. But when I saw the two of you…my mind just spiraled back to… I know it makes no sense."

"To what, specifically?"

"To my ex-wife. Not only that she had cheated on me both in business and with other men. The whole idea of trust. When I saw you with Brent it was like you had been deceiving me or doing something behind my back."

"Because I was touching a man in a professional capacity?"

"I told you. My suspiciousness is sometimes so fierce it feels like it could eat me alive."

He could tell by the set of her face that she was troubled, maybe even angry. This was really his moment of reckoning. The time had come. He knew he'd stay alone and bitter unless he broke free of the past. They walked at least three blocks again without a word.

Esme broke the silence with, "After my parents used me in their war games, I'm not playing anymore."

"You shouldn't have to."

Washington Square Park came into view, with its famous arch. NYU students gathered in pairs and groups, exuberantly talking and gesturing. Others sat alone, studying or typing furiously into their phones. People walked dogs. Older men played chess. Tourists posed for photos with the arch in the background. Jackson wanted to be part of this pulsing New York. To make a life in a truly great city with this magnificent woman. Could he possibly get out of his own way?

"Jackson," she began and turned her head to look at his face while they walked, "I want to move forward with my life. Going on the trip with you, our arrangement about me becoming spa director, the positivity heading me in the right direction. There's something I haven't told you."

"What's that?"

"I didn't need to stay at the Sher for four years before applying for directorships. After a year or two and all of my previous experience, I'd learned enough and I had the right ideas."

"Why did you stay?"

"Because while I project myself as confident, I got lost in doubt. I let myself loll. I was tired after thirty-two years of serving others. Even though I wanted to, I didn't really know if I could go further."

"What changed your mind?"

"I needed my confidence boosted. The old days were pulling me back down again. You gave me what I needed."

"Which you deserve."

"That's right, I do. If you care about me, don't hold me back, or let me hold myself back."

"That's the last thing I want to do." He had to do better. He owed it to Esme. He owed it to himself.

A group of young women rushed by, a cloud of squeals and perfume and colorful beanies.

"I'm willing to go further with you than I ever imagined I would with anyone," she said. "But I'm still frag-ile, and I always will be. I could shatter if injured. So if you can't do this, decide that now. Don't make me put myself in so much danger."

"Of course, I want to. I wish it was as simple as that. Just to have courage and faith."

"You want to start from a place of total *distrust*?"

They both laughed. "Because it's only up from there. Be patient with me." Two dogs barked at each other in greeting. Jackson gave Esme a kiss on her forehead. Horns honked and people walked by. He teased her with an overly dramatic raise of one eyebrow. "What, so you like that Brent Lloyd?"

She pretended to slap his shoulder. "Yeah, I gotta go. I have dinner plans with him."

"You rascal," he said as he pulled her in for a hug. "Seriously, what do you want to do for dinner?"

"Spend it with you being threatened by every move I make."

"That's a great idea. No wonder I named you spa director."

They walked the perimeter of Washington Square Park like tourists, pointing out buildings and trees. Students holding hands while lugging backpacks heavy enough to topple them. Two older men arm in arm as they slowly strolled. A pregnant woman walking alongside a man pushing a stroller with a sleeping toddler in it. Love was in the air in New York. Maybe it had always been, maybe not just in New York but everywhere. She just never thought it would apply to her.

"What do you feel like eating?" he asked as they ambled.

Even that, even him asking a simple question, made the world different. Growing up, she was never asked what she wanted to eat. She was lucky if her parents gave her enough money to get groceries for the three of them, always sending her with a shopping list to adhere to.

"Weren't we going to try to find good boat noodles here, like the ones we had at the floating market in Thailand?"

"Ooh, that sounds great. Let me look it up." He pulled his phone out of his pocket and began swiping a search.

It wasn't going to be an easy task, creating something solid and long-lasting with him. The business with Brent Lloyd earlier was almost more than she could handle. Jackson could see himself in action and explain his rationale yet he couldn't stop those old feelings from resurfacing. He felt some kind of certainty that she'd betray him in some way, trick him, further tarnish his dead parents' disappointment. She couldn't make his problems hers. Although, perhaps that was what a true partnership was, helping to hold each other's monsters.

If she let herself go down a certain path of thinking, it was actually touching that she arose jealousy in him. It was because he wanted her only to himself. Albeit unhealthy and unworkable, it was a measure of devotion. She'd surely never been protected before, which she had to admit was welcome in that bar in Bangkok with that aggressive Australian man. Maybe they could reframe Jackson's behavior into something positive while he hopefully *grew out of it* as time went on and he saw her as loyal. Or maybe that was asking too much of herself. Yet she knew she'd regret it for the rest of her life if she didn't try.

"I've got a couple of places in Queens." He showed her his phone. "Let's try this one tonight and we'll compare it with these others until we find the best one. I'll call a car."

They slid into the small wooden booth in the window of the restaurant. The smells alone were making her hungry. They ordered two different flavors of boat noodles. The server, who was also the owner, nodded approvingly at their ability to dig into the spicy cauldrons of noodles and broth without a flinch. They also ordered Isan chicken.

"We'll take the rest home and have it for lunch."

"What makes you think there will be leftovers?" He smiled and dug into a piece of chicken marinated and coated in spices, grilled to charred perfection.

They sat and shot the breeze, as the saying went. After all that hard stuff with Brent Lloyd earlier, they needed the casual quiet of a window seat and some comforting food in a low-key neighborhood. He'd been right that while their ravenous hunger was satiated, they still managed to pick at the savory chicken until there was none left to take home.

Home. Did he live with her now? It was only their second night back in New York but there had been no further talk of him going to a hotel. Nor did she want there to be. She wanted him wrapped around her. All night long. When they got *home* she washed her face and brushed her teeth. While he was in the bathroom, she turned down the bedsheets and put on some soft music. When he stepped out, she was there to greet him, standing on tiptoe to wrap her arms around his neck. They were finally relaxed, warm, with full bellies and a good workday behind them. She led him to the bed and guided him down. *He* was her new home.

If she could go the distance. As she lay in bed practicing her deep breathing before going to sleep, she made some decisions on her boundaries.

CHAPTER TWELVE

"I WAS GOING to put these out on the front tables," Trevor said as he put the finishing touches on the gift bags for the investor event. "But I think it's too easy for people to forget. I'm having someone taking and returning coats at the door. We could give one to each person when they're leaving."

Esme approved. "Good thinking."

Jackson stepped away from the tech setup he was working on with his marketing people. He came up behind Esme and wrapped his arms around her. "You okay?" he asked. She leaned back into him, knowing she had time for about a twenty-second hug and that was all.

"Yeah." She turned her head back toward him. "You?"

"Ready."

"Go." Lovey time was up. In fact, the first guest arrived, an older woman with white-blond hair.

"Yes, that's a longtime investor." He turned to her. "Millie Abernathy, please meet the spa director and visionary for what we want to do with the Sher, Esme Russo."

Millie's handshake was bony but firm. The woman moved on as someone else came through the door, another woman, this one probably in her forties, with dark hair and skin lacquered with a little too much makeup, in Esme's opinion.

Jackson made introductions. "This is Pia Bravo."

Before Esme could blink, a lively din filled the spa. Guests were served *tejate*, the famous old drink from Oaxaca that had been a refreshment for centuries. People who knew each other reunited while others met for the first time. Out of the corner of her eye she saw Brent Lloyd come in, the man with the lumbar issue that turned out to be a trigger for Jackson. Esme would try her best not to provoke Jackson, but after mulling it over, she wasn't going to be babysitting, or condoning, his behavior. That could only lead to resentment in the end.

"And that's why we invited you to join us today so we can give you a sense of how we see the Sher moving into a highly specialized place of healing that we hope will be cherished by New Yorkers and visitors alike for decades to come," Jackson spoke to the crowd.

Next it was Esme's turn. "Let's gather together and get centered with a simple breathing technique to ground us. Breathe in slowly through your nose," she said to the attentive audience, "and slowly out through your mouth. Concentrate on making it smooth and seamless. In. And out. Today I'm going to explain a bit about the Mayan traditions of *sobada* that we want to become foremost practitioners of." She gave her multimedia presentation, finishing with, "What we're going to do now is give everyone who would like a mini-treatment to get a hands-on sense of what we're doing."

The freelance massage therapists Esme had brought in who knew how to do the Mexican Mayan massages fanned out in the room and invited the investors into treatment rooms and a few makeshift areas they'd created in the common spaces. Of course, it would take years before a therapist could become an expert on a certain technique. This was merely a quick way to introduce the intention and spirit, plus the luxury of the rich and high-quality products used. She'd taught the staff to do a closing ceremony with each person, to wrap them in a makeshift rebozo shawl that they were able to approximate with some scarves Trevor picked up in East Harlem, an area called Little Mexico that had a large population of Mexican residents. They also concluded with a cup of raw cacao, which was thought to have highly medicinal properties.

As she surveyed the event, board president, Brent Lloyd, caught her eye and beckoned her over.

"I want to thank you for your therapeutic touch last time I was here."

"How's your lower back?"

"I wish I could say it was consistently better but it's not with my overuse."

"Can I have a feel?"

"Would you? I'd so appreciate it." She let her hands roam over Brent's lumbar area and inform her of his condition today. Indeed, his muscles were seized up, his body like stone.

"If you could even get one of those hot and cold packs from a local pharmacy, that might help."

He nodded.

Then, she felt it even before she looked up. From in between people mulling about, she sensed Jackson's eyes piercing into her. A lump in her stomach grew so big it almost burst. Because after all of their talk about recognizing negative patterns, where they came from and the relevance they did and didn't have, none of it amounted to anything when actions spoke louder than words.

The look she returned to him was one of anguish. Had all they'd said to each other just been drivel? She should have known that, in the end, they were like children playing dress-up. Despite them sincerely wanting to, the clothes didn't fit. She knew in an instant that they would both lose the match.

"Esme, is something the matter?" Brent noticed that her hands had gone slack, had stopped concentrating on his muscle pain. Jackson's face, contorted, threw daggers at her. The realization sent devastation coursing through her. But she had to keep herself together, with as much will as that took. That's what professionals did.

Yet she couldn't. All she could do was stare back at Jackson while he glared at her through arms holding colorful Mexican shawls. Perhaps both of them coming to the same conclusion. That nothing could work between them if she wasn't free to be herself. She'd thought maybe she cared enough about him to accept him, damage and all. Maybe someone who had her-

self come from a firmer base could have done it. In the
end, though, she was too weak for him.

There was only so much she could do for him while
still respecting the promises she'd made to herself.
Which let anger slowly bubble up in her body. Because she'd thought they'd found a way to each other.
But those seething glares of his were too much, not
in their menace but in their sadness, both hurtful and
hurt. Her anger quickly blended with sorrow. The notion that she could see his emotional issues clinically,
and therefore not have them affect her this much, vanished. She was only human. He drained her. It could
only get worse.

"Excuse me," she said to Brent as she stepped away,
finding a quiet alcove down the corridor. There, one
lone tear dripped out of her eye, which she quickly
brushed away with the back of her hand. Two more fell
from the other eye. She grabbed a tissue and mopped
those with the same vigor, making sure none of the investors could see her.

Jackson knew in his gut. He couldn't put himself or
anyone else through this again. Despite how much
he wanted to, he couldn't pull himself out of his own
wreckage. He'd vowed to never risk again and apparently, he was right to do so. As he'd stood watching
Esme talk to Brent Lloyd, the same old thoughts took
him over, a speeding train with him tied down on the
tracks.

He supposed he'd made some progress. He knew
enough not to think there was something untoward

going on between Esme and Brent. Although that was
only when he could force his rational mind to take the
forefront. Because the child's mind, and the young husband's mind, remembered every shard of heartbreak
and guilt as if it freshly cracked in him today. If it happened once, it could happen again. Esme would never
be able to trust him to trust her. So there was nothing
to fight for. It was about more than other men's attention. Their future would be him waiting for her to de-
ceive him as Livia had. She could never tolerate that.
Nor should she have to. His ears rang loud and clear to
him the simple message that he was alone in the world
and that's how he would remain. He was too volatile.
He carried too much baggage.

He'd seen Esme slip down the corridor and he moved
to find her. A passerby would just assume they were
conversing about spa matters.

"I'm sorry," he said as the truth gushed through him
like boiling blood through his veins. "I can't do this. I
thought I could but I can't."

"I see."

Those sweet green eyes of hers hooded. He wouldn't
subject her to him. To deny himself was better than to
squelch her. That's how much she meant to him. She
didn't need him, suspicious and prying, keeping tabs
and not letting her fly free. No one needed that in their
life, but especially not Esme, who'd already borne the
brunt of other people's misconduct.

He'd let her think it was simple jealousy. That was
easier for both of them. Neither having to face that
those demons were a disease, a terminal illness. Never

again make a bad decision that would let his parents' memory down. Never be taken on an emotional roller coaster where he'd end up feeling used. He wouldn't survive it again. He'd take the safer route. He might have been able to trust her with the spa. But not with his heart.

"It's better for you. And what's best for you is what matters the most to me now."

CHAPTER THIRTEEN

WHILE SOOTHING THE arthritic left hand of Mrs. Abernathy, Esme was determined not to lose her cool. As she worked the woman's joints, she gazed across the room and observed Jackson standing in a little conversational huddle with three other guests.

"Reducing inflammation can have a big impact," she said, her voice airy, not even sounding like herself.

"It feels better." The older woman's voice floated away.

Jackson looked wound up like a rubber band. His shoulders were up to his ears as they were when he'd first come to visit the spa a few weeks ago. She didn't wish him harm but if he'd just said to her in the corridor what he did and he wasn't affected by it, she'd be even more destroyed. If that was actually possible.

Yet he waved her over. She finished with Mrs. Abernathy's hand and joined him at his circle.

"Esme plans to also incorporate some ancient Eastern medicine techniques into our offerings," he told the group, gesturing for her to turn on the spa talk.

"Energy work has been practiced in the Eastern traditions for centuries and can be so powerful for overall health and wellness," she explained for probably the tenth time today. That voice that didn't seem to even belong to her came out as if she was in a trance.

Really, she was holding back the ocean of tears that wanted to burst forth from her eyes, drenching the room, drenching the building, maybe drenching all of New York. The words coming out of Jackson's mouth spoke to the investors of the Spa at the Sher's future. Esme was no longer certain if those plans still included her. Would she even want them to?

"We like what we see so far," one of the investors told Jackson.

Her zombie voice said to someone, "Thank you for coming."

"I'm so sorry," Jackson whispered in her ear as they ushered out the last of the guests.

Was he apologizing for what he'd said to her in the corridor or that he wasn't able to control himself for saying it during the event? She supposed his knee-jerk reaction to seeing her with Brent Lloyd again got the best of him and he lost his decorum. "Believe me, I came to the same conclusion when you again glared at me like I'd committed a crime. Because I tried to help Brent with his lumbar issue. Your board president, who is a nice man and who it might be beneficial to impress with the work we do here. You're right, Jackson, I can't go on like this."

"I know it seems twisted that not wanting to subject you to me is an act of devotion on my part."

"So you keep saying. Are you congratulating yourself?" All of it was riling her up and now that the guests were gone, she saw no reason to hold back. "Have you ever heard that expression about cutting your nose off to spite your face?"

"Esme." He reached for her hand. She pulled it away. "Esme."

"You're just going to be tortured for the rest of your life? You're so concerned with history repeating itself that you're going to bury what could have been a re-birth. Take the less risky road even though it might not be the one that could give you joy and fulfilment. And end up alone and with health conditions, just like how you started."

"I thought I could do it. I can't."

What would she do now? She wanted the spa directorship. And she'd known this was a possibility, that things wouldn't work out with him personally and that it could cost her the job. In fact, after all of this, could she work with him? Could he work with her? Either way, she'd forever live inside a shell of rumination, of what might have been with him. That she opened her heart once and it was swiftly trampled on. This shift was monumental. The world was suddenly a darker place, a lonely terrain. "You made me rethink every-thing, Jackson. I will forever regret that I wasn't able to do the same for you."

"No, it's not you. You are the finest person I've ever met."

"I know," she snapped.

"It's my albatross that I'll have to continue to live with."

"If that's what you choose."

The conversation was going around in circles. She absentmindedly began throwing out drinks and food that had been left behind. She wanted to go home. Jackson could book a room at the best hotel in the city. She needed to remove herself from this situation. While she had her hands full of plates, she felt her phone vibrate in her pocket. Once she put her armload down, she pulled it out to see the call she'd missed. It was Cozumel in Oaxaca, her familiar voice saying, "Esme, give me a call as soon as you have a chance. I have a question for you."

Jackson tapped his key card to open the heavy steel door of yet another hotel suite, as he'd done hundreds of times, one door indistinguishable from the next. Just a five-block walk ago, he'd locked up at the Sher and stopped to appreciate the dedication plaque on the door.

In memory of Beatrice and Wesley Finn

Today had been the launch of the newly revamped spa. All of the publicity his staff worked so hard on had paid off. Trevor kept everything running smoothly. It should have been a terrific day. The *New York Times* and the *Village Voice* came, as well as the spa industry trade publications. It was the signal of a new phase for Jackson. Although there was a gaping hole in the proceedings, one about five and a half feet tall with golden highlights in her hair.

He kicked off his shoes and moved to the thirty-fifth-floor window to look out at the city lights. What could have been one of the most transformative days of his life was dampened by the missing component. The piece that was the only thing that could complete him morning, noon or midnight, special days and ordinary ones, too. Instead, this day would have a different history. Of all that wasn't.

Good luck. Those were the last words she'd said to him. After he'd broken up with her, to use a common parlance. It occurred to him for the first time how powerful the word *broke* was. Because he indeed felt broken without Esme. Broken into shards, in fact. Too many to even count. Too numerous to ever put back together as one. *Broken up.*

Good luck. He was going to need it. Luck, or something. To survive losing her. She, who'd made him want to try again. She, who'd reminded him of what he was searching for all those years ago when he mistakenly found Livia. Esme seemed like she could fill the hole inside of him that was desperate for demonstrative love and excitement and passion. Someone to gush over. He thought he was in big, fireworks, trombone-salute love. One that energized him inside and made life worth living.

Good luck. That was three weeks ago. The investors had approved the launch. Esme had worked remotely with Trevor tirelessly helping get everything in order. They named Trevor as spa manager, which was a promotion Esme wanted for him all along. And Jackson returned to hotel life. Room service food that was never quite warm enough. Uniformed housekeepers tracking his packages of laundry.

Oh, how he missed the coziness of Esme's little apartment where he felt like a man at the start of his adulthood whose life was unfolding a little bit at a time. He missed Esme's mismatched coffee mugs. The one shaped like an apple, symbol of the city, had become his favorite. He missed her towels, always fresh and stacked high in the bathroom cupboard, encouraging an indulgent shower. Mostly, he missed being around her. She'd become his touchstone, his talisman, his password into the world. Nonetheless, despite her physical absence, the reopening came together. She'd been away from him for twenty-one days, each of which he counted with a check mark on his calendar. That was a lie because he really counted the time away from her by the hours. No, the minute. The second, if that was possible.

"Cozumel called me," Esme had explained to him over the phone the day after the investors event. "Remember she was telling us that their spa director, Itza, was going to take maternity time off and that she wasn't sure she'd return. She let Cozumel and Luis know that she wanted substantial time with her family and that they should look for a replacement."

"And of course, they thought of you."

"Yeah, I mean, we've always had a great working relationship."

"When we were there, Cozumel complimented your work with that woman who was having trouble with fertility. She said she'd love to have you back. Why wouldn't she?"

"By the way, the woman, Payaan, did get pregnant."

"That's beautiful." For some reason, a lump formed in his throat thinking about pregnancy and the desire for family. The continuum of life. What an amazing place Cozumel and Luis had created.

"They want you back. You are both a consummate professional and a true healer."

"It'll give me a start at that directorship I've always wanted. Luis plans to expand, open a second location. It's a great opportunity for me."

He knew her well enough to know that she wasn't saying everything she was thinking. "That's great." His lack of sincerity was audible.

"I'm doing us both a favor." She stopped. It sounded like she was slowing herself down, choosing difficult words. "We couldn't make something personal work. Why have the torture of running a business together? Let's cut each other loose, take the gains with the losses and walk away."

Why did she have to be so smart and logical? On the other hand, if she was swept with emotion and begging for them to keep trying, what would he do? No matter. Of course, she wasn't going to do that even if that was her impulse, after she'd been thoroughly rejected. She wasn't going to sign up for more.

"You'll find someone chomping at the bit to lead the Sher," she continued. "And Trevor is a gem. We did a great thing, you and I. We gave your parents' spa a direction forward."

"No, you did that. I bankrolled a quick trip around the world." Maybe she didn't realize that she'd also brought a dead man back to life. Changed his mental outlook in ways that would inform the rest of his life. *We gave the spa a direction forward*, he silently repeated the words into the recirculated air of the hotel room.

If he loved her, he'd let her go cleanly and completely. Wait. *L.O.V.E.* A word that might have been casually tossed around when he was with Livia but it wasn't until he'd met Esme that he began to even have a cursory understanding of its meaning. Yet he wasn't able to do what love demanded, to be fearless with no promises. It showed someone what was possible. If they believed in the best, giving what they took. He loved Esme. He was in love with her. Which was why she was telling him she was leaving and he was wishing her well. It was the greatest wish he'd ever have. For her to be well. In every way. Thousands of miles in another country or five blocks away. Self-love in action. She was taking care of herself, finally. She had to go, to fly with steel wings and make sure no one ever rusted her again.

"Good luck to you, too," his gravelly voice had creaked out.

He stared at himself in a mirror on the wall for a long while. Indeed, his shoulders were up as high as his ears. He didn't want to die. He inhaled deeply through his nose and exhaled slowly through his mouth as Esme had taught him to.

Finally, he picked up his phone and returned to the

website he had been lurking at for a couple of weeks now. A recommendation he'd gotten from Dr. Singh.

On the home page was a photo of tall trees and dirt trails. The graphic read, "Kendrick Washington, Psychologist. Is your past holding you back from what you want?"

CHAPTER FOURTEEN

THE MOON WAS so bright it provided light to what Esme knew were the wee hours. She didn't have her phone with her so didn't know the correct time. After tossing and turning in bed she'd stepped out of the casita and breathed in the cool air of night. She lay down on one of the lounge chairs by the firepit where just a few weeks ago she and Jackson had slowly sipped a mezcal in the mild evening. There were no sounds to be heard at this hour, just a maddening quiet that made her ask the moon a question. How would she clean off her wounds and move on yet again?

She'd spent most of her life fixing things. Placating her parents and compensating for their shortcomings. What would have become of her if she hadn't found her way to that local spa and all those towels to wash? Would she have ended up taking care of a man, repeating her childhood role? Or stuck at a job where she'd never found a passion or calling. Or, for that matter, she could have ended up homeless and destitute. Taking stock under the Mexican sky, it seemed, though, that she had let a man throw her off her balance. In spite of her better instincts.

Earlier this evening, she'd talked to Trevor, who

said the opening was a big hit although some of the guests wanted to know where the director with the good breathing techniques was. That made Esme smile, although with a double edge. Maybe she should have been strong enough to stay in New York and run the spa with Jackson, driven enough to put the romantic past behind them. The minute he pushed her away because his own scars hurt too much, she turned her back on him. She didn't stay to fight for the man she'd fallen in love with. The one who she'd never thought she'd meet.

Cozumel gave her a once-over when she came into the kitchen after falling asleep on the lounger. Luis was stirring pots on the stove and looked over. She said, "My, Esme, you don't look happy."

"I'll be okay," Esme said. "I won't let you down."

"I know that. It's you I'm concerned about."

How grateful she was that Cozumel and Luis had become friends, not just colleagues. She'd called Esme three weeks ago, on the day that happened to be the investors event, one of the best and worst days of her life. Taking over the Sher, and she and Jackson together in a way that really felt *together*. A dream she'd never dared before. Until he woke up and turned it into a nightmare.

"Does that handsome Jackson have something to do with it?" Luis asked while putting a mug of *café con leche* in front of Esme. "He was more than just your boss, am I right?"

Esme took a sip of Luis's creamy brew. "I thought he was. It turns out we're not a match."

"No," Cozumel jumped in, "I could feel it in my

bones. And see it in the way you looked at each other. You are each other's safe haven." Cozumel's words entered Esme's ears and she kept hearing them over and over in her head. *Haven.* She and Jackson were each other's haven. That was the truth. He wouldn't allow it, though, couldn't let her eyes guide him home no matter how hard she tried.

Had she tried hard enough? He knew what was imprisoning him. That self-awareness itself held promise. With her love, could he break free?

"I made a mistake in falling for someone in the first place. My first real relationship and I managed to choose the wrong person."

"You didn't choose him any more than he chose you." Cozumel shook her head. "Your destinies found you. Are you going to turn your back on fate?"

"That's exactly what I've spent my adult life doing." Anything to not become a statistic. Protecting herself. By denying herself. Never needing anyone no matter how much she was needed.

"You accepted our offer because it was an easy way out, is that it? We whisked you away from New York," Cozumel said. "And from seeing it through with Jackson?"

"Mi amor," Luis said to Cozumel, "maybe I think we made the wrong decision to keep Esme for ourselves. We're not going to stand in the way of Cupid."

"Wait a minute here. I didn't leave him. He's the one who cut it off." As always, she was the reed that had to bend with the wind. Always the teacher, always the forgiver. She'd had enough of that.

Yet she did need him. He gave her herself. He was the missing piece for her to become whole. By his side, she could soar. They'd be there to catch each other if the flight wasn't smooth.

Luis came away from the stove to give Cozumel a hug and kissed her face a dozen times. "When Cozumel and I found out we weren't able to become pregnant, we decided to share all the wisdom we'd gained in our own struggles by making the spa our baby that we created together."

"I predict you and Jackson will have many babies besides the Sher, although that's a good place to start," Cozumel said. "I have a few other people I can talk to about Itza's job. Go back to New York."

"It's too late."

"It's never too late."

"We don't need you hanging around like a sad yard dog," Luis added. The three of them smiled.

Cozumel was right to feel it in her bones. Esme did, too. Her body didn't align without Jackson; she was off kilter. Hiding from him was not the solution. And Cozumel and Luis had seen their vision come to fruition here. Esme couldn't be happy tagging on to their dream. She was finally ready to see her own. She'd gratefully take all Jackson had to give her.

Within hours, she was standing in front of the spa's tiled fountain with a suitcase by her side, just as she'd arrived. She gave Cozumel and Luis a final wave as she got into the car that would take her to the airport. The couple put their arms around each other as they watched her go.

Love conquers all was only a phrase Esme had heard. She needed that promise to be good to its words.

Once Jackson stepped off of the airplane and inhaled that fresh smell, he felt better. It was as if the flight took one hundred hours, so desperate was he to get back to Mexico and claim what was his. He didn't mean that to sound like a caveman but he wanted to try the image on for size. He liked the fit very much. His and hers.

Ah, Oaxaca. Where bliss had taken flight. The frozen kisses of Stockholm started it and Thailand's beautiful journey was the end but the warm skies of Oaxaca were unimaginably romantic. It was here he'd started to believe that everything was possible. Until he let the monsters wreck it. Just a few weeks ago, in the quiet night with Esme, he'd started to think he could throw his past into the firepit and watch it burn to ash. Turned out, he wasn't able to. That was then. This was now. With no chance of not getting it right. Esme was his. He was hers. End of story, or should he say beginning.

The airport was just as he remembered it, as was a particular smell of the terrain. He could recognize it with his eyes closed. He fantasized returning to visit here with Esme. That was if Cozumel and Luis forgave him for the tumult he was about to cause. Maybe this could become a special hideaway for him and Esme. Maybe they'd bring their children. Maybe their grandchildren. He enjoyed that thought. He wanted all of that old and gray stuff with her.

He carried his small bag through the terminal. He

hadn't packed much because they weren't staying long this time. He got a partial view of a woman walking toward him, her face obscured by other people. He craned his neck to see more. About her height and the same bouncy brown hair with golden highlights. Was he hallucinating?

Some people veered left or right so much that a space opened and they caught sight of each other.

"Jackson?" she exclaimed once he came into focus.

A rosy wash softly poured over him to hear her say his name. All was not lost. He hoped. "It is, my love." My love.

"What are you doing at the airport?"

"I came for you."

"You what?" She stopped a few feet before reaching him. Maybe to stake her own ground before entering his.

"I made a horrible mistake. I came to correct it." He advanced a few steps. "I can't live without you. And I won't."

"How was the Sher's reopening?" Oh, she needed to divert the topic. Okay, he had plenty of time to get everything said.

"The dedication plaque turned out beautiful. I can't wait for you to see it. I did what I intended to do. In my small way I made a peace offering for all the disappointment I caused my parents."

Then Esme took steps toward him, closing the gap. "You didn't disappoint them. Livia did. We've got to get you to forgive yourself."

"In any case, the Sher is ours now. We're going to

grow it from seed like two gardeners in the field." Her face lit up. "What did that make you think of?"

"Oh, just something Cozumel said about the Sher being our baby."

"Esme, in almost losing you I realized how much I am ready for you. If you'll have me, stumbles and wobbles and all." Finally, she stepped close enough that he could almost feel her. His breath quickened. "Wait a minute, though. Where are you going? Why are you at the airport?"

People passed by them, coming and going in every direction. A man walked through an exit gate and what looked to be his family rushed to hug him, the four of them running into a tight embrace. A couple deplaned holding hands, the woman wearing a sash that read Bride, both with big smiles on their faces. One young woman dropped her purse and its contents spilled onto the floor. A man about her age dropped to his knees to help her gather up her things and she smiled up at him. Jackson flashed back to the first day he'd returned to the Sher and Esme had been so kind with an elderly woman whose belongings had fallen out of her purse the same way. Lovers parted, after kissing until one had to hurry through the boarding gate. Tour groups and sports teams juggled carry-ons along with their coffees and electronics. Esme and Jackson were two people in the middle of the world, making rotations around the sun, most everyone doing their best.

"I was heading back to you, Jackson."

"I'm capable of evolving."

"We already decided…our starting place is total distrust." They both smirked.

"I'm further than that now."

"Are you?"

"You'll love the new version of me." He touched his own face with his fingers. "Look how I have a skin care regime now. I'm deep breathing. Kenji on our staff is fabulous at shiatsu massage. And I'm seeing a psychologist."

She brought her hand over his on his cheek. Explosions of joy went off inside of him. "I love you."

He wrapped his arms around her, lifted her up and spun her in a circle. "I love you."

When he put her down, she looped her arm through his. "Come on." They headed in the same direction, like they always would. "I heard about this job in New York I just have to have."

* * * * *

If you enjoyed this story,
check out these other great reads
from Andrea Bolter

Pretend Honeymoon with the Best Man
Adventure with a Secret Prince

Available now!

FALLING FOR
HER FORBIDDEN
BODYGUARD

HANA SHEIK

MILLS & BOON

To Soraya,

For taking the messy first draft of this story,
seeing what it could become and making it sparkle.

CHAPTER ONE

Take care of yourself.

ANISA ABDULLAHI READ the text from her older brother, Ara, as she had several times throughout her long flight from Canada to Madagascar, yet it still elicited the same shock from her.

A shock she had every right to feel.

Ara hadn't spoken to her in four years, cutting off all communication when Anisa had decided to leave their family home in Berbera, Somaliland, to pursue an education and a career in Toronto. It was petty of him, but he'd wanted her to know that he was displeased with her choice. At first Anisa had met his cold shoulder with her own childish behavior. Blocking him on all social media had been a way to push him out of her life. She knew that nothing would aggravate him more than not being able to immediately access what she was up to. After all, Ara had shunned her in the first place because he had lost his precious control over her.

A control he'd exerted to protect her...or so he would have her believe. Anisa only went along with his obsessive helicoptering for the sake of their long-dead parents. She'd told herself so many times that Ara *needed* to do what he had to do to save the family he had left: her. Losing their mother and father had changed him, and it took her a long while to realize that his change wasn't for the better.

And that was why she refused to be the one to break their silence.

At least, that was how she felt. Over time, Anisa's embittered heart stirred with a longing. For family. For her brother. Not the man who imprisoned her in their home and tracked her every innocent movement with eagle-eyed precision. Rather, the boy who after pranking her would laugh so hard he'd get a bellyache, but who would then just as easily chase off her school bullies.

She wanted that version of her brother.

Almost as much as she'd just wished for some sign, *any* sign that he wasn't gravely upset with her anymore.

Though admittedly the long-awaited message from Ara wasn't exactly as she'd pictured.

"'Take care of yourself'… What does that even mean, and how am I supposed to reply back?" she muttered under her breath before dropping her phone in her lap and massaging her throbbing temples. Her hands stilled suddenly when she considered that maybe Ara had messaged her accidentally.

He meant to text someone else, not me.

She sighed, supposing that the universe was having some good fun at her expense.

She'd only waited for most of four insufferably long years to hear from her brother—

"And now I need cipher to decode his message. Great." Anisa groaned, biting back her sarcastic moaning halfway when two businessmen sitting in chairs nearest to her stopped chatting and eyed her funnily.

With a blush, and a softer groan of embarrassment, Anisa sank into the comfortable armchair in the hotel's foyer. Before she could hope to disappear, she caught the eyes of another person.

A man standing before the revolving glass doors of the hotel's entrance and exit.

Anisa's breath whooshed out, not remembering when she held in the gulp of air. She must have, after noticing the handsome stranger who seemed to be watching her. He was dressed in business attire like the men who had looked at her strangely, but unlike them, his suit molded seamlessly to unmistakable muscle, hinting at the exquisite work of a tailor handling expensive material for his creation. The result was a jacket and pants of obsidian, with a pale gray dress shirt and a gleaming white tie. He was a monochromatic emblem. One that had her discreetly wiping at her mouth after picking her jaw up off the floor.

In fairness, it was the only appropriate reaction to a man who looked that good.

A man who really, truly *did* appear to be boring holes into her skull from the short distance that separated them.

Instinctively Anisa slid up the chair, sitting straighter, with her hands fastening on the supple leather of the armrests and her sneakers pressed flat to the soft rug carpeting the waiting area. She looked around, certain there was a perfectly logical explanation.

Someone's standing behind me, that's it. Probably a gorgeous bikini-clad woman heading toward the hotel's crystal-blue outdoor pool.

Only she had seen the sign pointing to the pool, and it was in the opposite direction from the foyer, nearer the back of the hotel for privacy.

Yet because it was far more plausible to believe than thinking this hot dude was checking her out, she clung to the woman-in-a-bikini theory.

But no one conveniently stood behind her to explain who he'd been looking at. No half-dressed woman sauntered along the foyer. There was no one but her. And that unleashed a torrent of heat through her blood, her skin flushing readily, her limbs weakening just as her heart strengthened its beats. It wasn't an entirely awful feeling. Strange, unexpected…

Not terrible, icky, or ugly and unwanted.

But she suddenly experienced a vulnerability she wanted to outrun. That explained her physical reaction.

She wanted to get out of there.

When she tried to move, get up from the chair and rush back to the sanctuary of her hotel room, Anisa couldn't budge. Couldn't bring herself to do anything but gawk at the devastatingly handsome man staring her down from across the brightly lit foyer.

So Anisa studied his heart-stopping features. And she missed nothing, her eyes tracking almost hungrily over his short, curly black hair and the low fade that started right around his ears. From there her gaze traveled over his big shoulders, his strong, distinct jawline, up to his well-cut cheekbones, broad-tipped nose, and thick black eyebrows that lowered subtly now that she was noticing. His lushly round lips, dusky in color, curled with the beginnings of a frown under her observation.

But it was his eyes that arrested her mind completely. Fathomlessly dark pupils beheld her as though no one else existed…despite there being several people in the entrance hall with them.

I'm imagining things. Any minute now he's going to raise his hand, and somebody else will pop up. Any moment he'll look away. Any second—

If Anisa held another thought in her head, it flew away the instant he suddenly moved in her direction, and along with it any hope to sneak off.

She froze, a doe trapped in a hunter's snare.

In college she'd worked as a paid student assistant on a nature documentary at a Florida wild cat sanctuary. Right now she was having flashbacks of the big cats she had met. Specifically the rare black panther. Only this man wasn't prowling toward her on all fours. Rather, his steps were unhurried in polished brown cap-toe oxfords. And it seemed to her that, like an apex predator's, his stare intensified upon approach.

Another few strides and he'd be right by her side.

What am I going to say?

Anisa's heart rate quickened as her mind flailed. The worst part was she knew that she wouldn't be able to utter the first word, not with the way her jaw slackened and her tongue grew stiff in her mouth.

It didn't stop her from trying. She pried her drying lips apart—

"Anisa! There you are!"

Anisa jerked her head to see her coworker and friend Darya hurrying toward her from the elevator. She blinked in surprise, once, twice, before finally shaking off the stupor clouding her head and discovering she could move her limbs again.

She stood as Darya touched her arm, concern painting her friend's pale, round face.

"I've been calling you," Darya said. "Weren't we supposed to meet up in your room first before heading out?"

Because they'd only landed a couple hours ago, and it was well into the evening in Madagascar's capital, Antananarivo, their film crew wouldn't officially begin work until tomorrow morning. Once production started, there was very little chance they would have time to themselves outside the long hours that awaited them, especially as they had one day allotted in Antananarivo for their filming schedule. That meant she and Darya had the best chance to do a little city exploring tonight and tonight only.

"Sorry, I got bored and decided to come down for a little people-watching." Anisa cast her friend a sheepish smile.

"Well, if you're done scoping out the other hotel guests,

may we please go catch our rideshare before it decides to leave us?" Darya batted her long fake lashes for comical effect.

Anisa snorted a laugh.

Darya grinned before hooking her arm through Anisa's and pulling her toward the exit.

Anisa's humor dried up on recalling that there was one hotel guest in particular who had consumed most of her attention. She spotted him at Reception, speaking to the staff behind the large circular bronze and white marble desk. Looking back to the armchair she'd vacated, she figured it was possible that he'd been aiming for the hotel's front desk all along, and that she'd let her imagination get the better of her.

There was no way he was coming for me.

The thought carried some relief and a smidgen of dismay.

Even when she'd wanted to run, she wouldn't have minded a guy *that* incredibly hot focusing all his attention on her.

Allowing Darya to tug her through the revolving doors out into the city, Anisa flung a final look back at him before losing sight of him altogether, then forced herself to release her strange bout of disappointment.

Surely there were other attractive men in the world. Maybe even some who were actually interested in her.

So why couldn't she get this one out of her head?

Anisa couldn't figure out if she was losing her mind or not. But she didn't know how else she could explain seeing her stranger from the hotel all over the Analakely Market, a popular outdoor marketplace in Antananarivo, or Tana, as the locals called the city. At first, it was just glimpses from the corner of her eye.

In the narrow paths snaking between vendor stalls. Behind her in the sea of bodies flooding the market space.

He seemed to be everywhere—and nowhere at the same time.

Even when she paused to right her hijab, using her phone's

camera as an impromptu mirror, her hands froze at the sight of those dark eyes searing her. Yet when Anisa whirled around…no one was there.

But when she saw him striding past the large front window of the small restaurant she and Darya had chosen to dine at, Anisa began to question her sanity.

He can't be stalking me…

Anisa wished her confidence backed her thinking. She continued to feel out of sorts after she and Darya split their dinner bill and left the restaurant, strolling back through the expansive market.

Spread over several blocks, Analakely Market had almost everything, from produce, seafood and meat to clothing, shoes, household items and bootleg films. In that way, it was not unlike most outdoor marketplaces. But it also had unique perks like pop-up nail salons served solely by young men, and grilled lizard meat among other traditional street foods.

Anisa sniffed the air laced with the tantalizing smells, though luckily her stomach was immune to the scents. The big Malagasy-style dinner she'd shared with Darya had saved her from shelling out more money sampling the foods from the market vendors.

Walking past the delectable, deep-fried temptations on display, Anisa trailed her friend to a stall selling hats of all kinds.

The stall owner, an elderly woman with brown skin lined with age, smiled widely in recognition of them. Like most of the market vendors, she was eager to make a sale. Happy to oblige, Darya zeroed in on a fedora.

She popped the hat on and modeled it for Anisa. "Does it make my head look big?"

Anisa disagreed with a laugh.

Smiling her approval, Darya started haggling over the price with the stall owner.

Free to look around the nearby stalls, Anisa paused at a table full of sparkly trinkets, never thinking she would see so many hair clips and ties, ribbons, and bedazzled broaches all in one place. She was looming over the rhinestone-embellished silver pins when the vendor encouraged her to try some on. Eagerly Anisa clipped a bow-shaped pin to her hijab and studied her reflection in the hand mirror the vendor offered her.

Even with the small cracks in the smudged mirror, she couldn't deny the attractiveness of the accessory.

Parting with a few Malagasy ariary, the local currency, wasn't an issue.

As she strolled away with her new purchase pinned to her hijab, Anisa hoped Darya was done with her price negotiation so that they could finally leave the market and head for their hotel.

Between Ara's enigmatic text and believing that she had a handsome stalker, her day could be summed up as a wild roller-coaster ride, and she couldn't wait for it to end. Pulling her phone up by its long, pearly cross-body chain, Anisa scrolled past Ara's message and thumbed a quick text for Darya to meet up with her at one of the three long stone stairways that led in and out of the market. Her thighs and calves already burned in anticipation of the workout she'd be getting from climbing all those steps up to La Ville Moyenne, the city's Middle Town, where they could hail a cab easier. She wasn't looking forward to it, yet if it meant that she could lock herself in her hotel suite and pretend she had no worries, then Anisa was up for the exercise.

After she sent Darya the message, she bobbed and weaved through the crowds back to where she'd left her friend and wondered how she'd managed to wander away so far, then came to an abrupt halt.

Anisa did a double take, gawking ahead of her, the crowds

milling around blocking her view. Springing up on her toes, she searched avidly for some sort of confirmation this time.

Because she saw him again. The stranger from the hotel.

Only just as before, when she searched hard for him, he vanished. No trace or indication that he'd ever been there.

A tug on her shirt from behind startled her. Anisa whirled on a young boy in an old, faded shirt and shorts, his oversized and overly worn sandals caked with grime and dust. He looked up at her with large, dark eyes, held out both hands and said something pleadingly in French.

Anisa didn't need a translation app to understand what he was asking for. She rooted for some change and passed it to him. No sooner than she did, more children and even some adults approached her with outstretched hands. She didn't have spare change for them all and knew that she would have to back out of the situation she'd created. But they circled her, and she saw no direct path to slip away.

They crowded closer.

Someone stepped on her foot, an elbow dug into her side, and her phone chain was yanked roughly from behind.

If claustrophobia wasn't an issue before, she feared it would be after this.

"I don't have any more money. I'm sorry—*désolée*," she pleaded, barely recalling how to say *sorry* in French. True fear pricked her heart when the beggars, not heeding her plea, pushed in closer, crowding her personal space.

Not knowing what else to do, Anisa kept backing away helplessly. Right into a solid wall...of unyieldingly hard and very warm muscle.

She lurched forward away from the person she'd bumped into and turned to face them with a ready apology.

An apology that never fully formed as her jaw dropped open.

"It's you!"

Those *weren't* the words she'd pictured coming from her, but they seemed appropriate enough when she came face to face with the stranger from the hotel.

Just as appropriately, she followed that surprised observation with, "Are you stalking me?"

Of all the terrible things Nasser Dirir had been called—a rebel, a criminal, a heartless monster—he'd never expected to add *stalker* to the list.

"Well, are you? Stalking me?" Hurling the query at him, Anisa shuffled away, just as she had when the beggars flocked to her. As though he posed a real threat.

Her defensive posture shouldn't have bothered him, but it did, and somehow that irked him even more than her downright rude accusation.

It took everything in him to rise above his steaming annoyance and ignore her question. He skipped to the part where he dangled her phone in front of her face, clutching it by its gaudily bejeweled chain. Of course he had to hold the ends of the now broken chain together or else risk the phone dropping and possibly breaking.

"This is yours, is it not?"

Anisa shifted her narrowed gaze from him to the phone swinging between them. He raised it higher so there would be no doubt who it belonged to. Her eyes widened with recognition, the light of a nearby lamppost reflecting off the dark of her irises.

And before she could open that mouth and sting him with her tongue again, he explained, "You should be careful. This pretty string might as well be a sparkling target for pickpockets." He emphasized his point when the streetlight glinted off the milky-white pearls on the phone chain.

She grabbed at the phone, and Nasser let her have it without a fight.

After checking it over, she looked up at him, her accusatory glare gone. "I didn't think someone stole my phone."

"They didn't get far."

"You caught them," she breathed, looking behind him, as though he had the petty thief in cuffs.

"Yes, and then I let the child go."

"Child?"

"A boy. No more than ten. It was enough that he was scared. I didn't see a need to drag him before the *gendarmerie*." That and the local police would only further traumatize the child thief. Nasser clenched his jaw, leaving out the part that would reveal his…unresolved issues with police officials and other authority figures.

He hadn't realized he'd been holding a breath until Anisa nodded, silently agreeing with his decision to let her pickpocket go free.

"Well, thank you for recovering my phone." She pursed her lips, her body language shifting again, and he should've seen what was coming. "Though that doesn't explain why you followed me from the hotel."

So much for getting through to her.

Allah give me strength.

How was it that she still believed him to be a stalker? Nasser curbed a frustrated growl that managed to roll like ominous thunder through his gritted teeth. "Your brother sent me."

Anisa blinked, her face an open book conveying her shock.

"He didn't tell you," Nasser commented briskly, knowing it to be true and not needing her to confirm it. Her expression was answer enough. Barely containing his irritation, he said, "Ara hired me to watch over you, and he gave me the impression that he'd be informing you of that fact." The contract was signed and sealed, the price of his hire paid in full and nonrefundable.

"What do you mean, he sent you to watch over me?" Anisa asked.

"He feels you could benefit from some protection."

"Protection."

She said the word slowly as if to let its meaning sink in. Then she shook her head, muttering so quietly he almost missed what she said. "So that's why he messaged." He detected a flicker of sadness.

"Anisa? Anisa!"

Nasser watched the petite, pale-haired, pale-faced woman who had been with Anisa since the hotel break through the market crowds and come to a breathless stop beside her. If it hadn't been for her friend's interference, Nasser would've approached Anisa in the hotel lobby and introduced himself far earlier, sparing them both from the embarrassing debacle of having Anisa believe him to be a stalker.

"I got your message, but when I tried calling, you didn't pick up." Her friend trailed off, pushing up the fedora on her head before flicking a glance at him. "Who's he?"

Anisa looked over at him, the frown unbudging on her face.

"No one," she said quickly. Taking her friend's arm, she pulled her along, away from him and toward the steep stairway that marked the market's entrance and exit.

She might believe she'd shaken him off, but Nasser knew better.

He would see her again. Tomorrow, in fact, and the day after, and the day after that, because her brother had paid him handsomely to do his job.

And unfortunately for her, she *happens to be that job.*

CHAPTER TWO

"OKAY, SO YOUR brother sent a hot bodyguard—and why are we angry about that?"

Anisa huffed humorlessly and rolled her eyes at Darya's comment. It was simple for her friend to jest and make light of the situation, but she wasn't standing in her shoes, feeling betrayed. Her brother had gone behind her back and sent a stranger to shadow her. Ara didn't have to say he didn't trust her; his actions spoke for him clearly. His distrust of her was why Anisa had ultimately chosen to leave his side and chance being frozen out of his life.

Does he really believe that I can't take care of myself?

Sadly, she knew the answer to that question. But what cut the deepest and stung the most was that Ara had finally messaged her *only* out of some clear need to step in as her overprotective older brother once more.

I let him get to me...

She had herself to blame, yet it didn't mean that her hands were tied. Anisa didn't have to suffer a bodyguard, attractive or otherwise.

"I'm going to tell him I don't want a bodyguard," Anisa said. The idea had come to her after she'd tossed and turned and pounded her pillow one too many times last night. It was the most sensible thing to do. And since she had no need of a bodyguard, surely her stranger from the hotel wouldn't force the matter. "He'll probably be relieved that he doesn't have to do his tedious job."

Her searching gaze landed on her unwanted bodyguard standing poised under the shade of a large tree several meters from her.

They were filming on the grounds of the Rova of Antananarivo, a royal palace complex atop the second tallest hills in the capital city. Formerly the seat of major political decisions and a home to the Merina monarchs who once ruled the southeast African island nation, in modern times the Rova was a tourist attraction. The film crew had set up in the front yard of the Queen's Palace, one of a dozen structures that remained standing in the former royal complex.

An impressive building, the palace had been gutted by a fire decades ago. It awaited completion of restoration work to regain its glory.

Scaffolding from the ongoing renovation wrapped the building, and tarps hanging in some of the palace's windows flapped in the easy wind. Anisa saw beyond the construction equipment to the palace's architectural beauty and the riches of its history. But with the day still so early, and the yard outside the palace looking so empty, its grandeur wouldn't be admired by anyone else right then except her fellow crewmates.

And though emptier for the lack of tourists, the buzz of activity in the yard was still loud. Soon they would begin filming, and Anisa would miss her window of opportunity to dismiss her brother's hired man.

She set aside the gaffer tape she was using to connect set equipment wires and marched for her target.

He didn't step out from the tree's dappled shade on her approach. Anisa stopped in front of him, her head tilting back and compensating for their significant height difference. But she didn't need an extra six or so inches to make herself feel taller. Her confidence came from her unflappable determination to get him to leave her alone.

"I'm not sure exactly what my brother has said to you, but I'm not in need of protection of any sort." She jutted her chin higher to punctuate her point.

His lips appeared to hike on one side, until she blinked and any evidence of a smile vanished.

"I'm sure my brother paid you already."

"*Oui.* He did, and quite generously," he confirmed, his voice as meltingly smooth as his French.

He was wearing business attire again, minus his suit jacket this time. The slate-gray suit vest and dark gray tie popped against the pristine white of his button-down shirt, whose sleeves he'd rolled up. He had his legs crossed at the ankles, a shoulder pressed to the tree, and his arms crossed over his chest. Designer aviator sunglasses obfuscated his eyes, yet she couldn't deny feeling the weight of his stare.

"Great!" She clapped her hands together and forced a smile. "Then you can take that advance payment and leave me."

Anisa basked in the glow of her good idea, anticipating that he'd be glad to be rid of the duty imposed on him by her brother. But the longer she waited for his agreement, the more aware she became that it wasn't coming.

"If you're worried I'll say something to my brother, don't be." It wasn't like she was close to Ara anymore, and she doubted he told a random bodyguard he hired all about his strained relationship with his sister. "He doesn't need to know, and you can let him believe you performed your job."

He was still unmoved. His shoulder remained leaning on the broad tree trunk.

She quieted the urge to fidget from frustration. What did she have to say to get a reaction from him?

To get him to go away!

"I don't even know your name," Anisa blurted, not sure why she was so curious suddenly.

"Nasser," he said, his accent rolling the end of his name. "Being on a first-name basis isn't of import though."

Anisa put her hands on her hips. "Let me guess. My safety's more important."

"It matters to your brother."

"And because he hired you, it's now your concern too." She shifted her glare off to the side, where the production crew was wrapping up. Soon the assistant director would be calling both crew and cast to their posts for filming. Any time she had left for persuading Nasser to abandon his guard duty was coming to a fast close.

Biting her lip to prevent herself from letting out a shout of frustration, she presented a calm front she wasn't feeling at all.

"Fine. Then tell me *why* my brother's hired you now. Why suddenly send protection?"

"Isn't that a question better posed to your brother?"

Anisa breathed sharply through her nose, feeling her nostrils flare with her indignation.

It was a mistake she regretted the instant her lungs were saturated with the scent of him. A blend of freshest mint and earthy notes she couldn't quite name, Nasser's cologne swarmed into her twitching nose on the balmy October morning breeze. She fought against closing her eyes and inhaling him unabashedly.

Nasser looked just as enticing as he smelled. Golden streams of dawn sunlight dappled his deep, rich brown skin.

Before she got too swept up in his attractive physical qualities, she realized just how physically close they were.

When did that happen?

Though startled, Anisa rectified that immediately. Once she established a polite distance between them, she retrained her glare on him, reminding herself that he wasn't there to be ogled. That as he ignored her demands, he was quickly making himself her enemy.

With that firmly in mind, she tried reasoning with him again, mindful of breathing in any more of his aromatic scent. "If you're not going to leave, the least you could do is tell me what he's up to that requires my protection. You both owe me that much if you insist on disrupting my life."

"It's not my place to speak for your brother. I insist you direct your inquiries to him."

I can't! Because then I'd have to talk to Ara, and I won't give him that satisfaction—not now, not after this, she wanted to holler.

Behind her, she heard the call from the assistant director for crew members to get into their places for filming to commence.

She was out of time.

She could see it from the way Nasser looked at her, his immovable expression and relaxed posture reading almost smug to her.

Annoyed beyond comprehension, and also too flustered for comfort, Anisa huffed and whirled away from Nasser, storming back to where she had been working before drifting over to chat with him.

Not long after, Darya appeared at her side.

"Is he leaving?" her friend asked.

Anisa glowered at Nasser watching her and grumbled, "No, and it was like getting a great big lump of a stone to budge. I might as well have been talking to a wall."

"You're going to have to tell the director about your bodyguard hanging around."

Anisa glared harder at Nasser, not happy that she had to report her personal affairs to her boss. "I'll tell him."

"Why not just text your brother and let him know how you feel?"

"At first, I wanted to. I just didn't know how to reply to his message. Then I started telling myself that maybe he'd accidentally messaged me when he meant to actually text someone else." She gave Darya a tight smile. "And now, after this bodyguard stuff, I don't want to give him the satisfaction of messaging."

"Are you giving up, then?" Darya wondered.

"No," she said resolutely. Her words might not have gotten through to Nasser, but her defeat only motivated her that much more.

One way or another, Anisa would make him leave.

Nasser wasn't oblivious to the fact that Anisa didn't want him near her. In fact, he'd anticipated some pushback from her. She wouldn't be the first obstinate client he'd had to handle in his line of work. Not everyone required the comprehensive physical and cybersecurity services his company, Sango Securities, provided, and those who did weren't always open to it. Part of his job was to ensure those resistant clients didn't wiggle away and come to harm under his watch. It was a burden Nasser could do without, and yet one he bore for the success of his business and the hundreds of employees who relied on him for their livelihoods.

So, no. Nasser wasn't surprised by Anisa's reaction to the news that her brother had hired him. It was even to be expected considering his arrival had come as a shock to her.

What did intrigue him was how she confronted him about it, getting up in his face…or as close as she could to his face given their notable height difference. That gave him pause in planning how to approach her. For every stubborn client who didn't believe his services were needed, Nasser strategized on how to appeal to their sensibilities. Whether it be

stroking an ego or ingratiating himself to them, he did what
he had to for his career and company. And in the six years
since Sango Securities' inception, Nasser hadn't found a client he couldn't sway into becoming cooperative.

But his intuition warned him Anisa would be different.
She wouldn't be like the philandering politicians, playboy
millionaire heirs and other glitterati that made up the largest
sum of his company's profit margin. Although an heiress to
her family's shipping empire, and likely quite wealthy herself, Anisa proved markedly different the instant she squared
up to him.

Normally Nasser wouldn't have taken the bait, but Anisa's
defiance sparked a fire in him and provoked a response. The
thrill of that clash unleashed something deep within him.
Whatever it was hungered for another encounter like it, and
that disturbed Nasser greatly. Particularly because despite
seeming to have won their little argument, he couldn't shake
the feeling that the battle was far from over.

She's going to try again.

Of that Nasser had no doubt. He saw it in the baleful way
she would glance at him—*when* she deigned to look at him,
that is.

He could see her mind puzzling out a scheme to wiggle
free of his protection detail. It was truly impressive considering she worked nonstop while plotting against him simultaneously. Before meeting her, Nasser had done enough
research to understand her job was film-industry-related.
And though he hadn't seen a need to dig further into what
she did for a living as it didn't seem to endanger her, from
simple observation Nasser deduced she was an indispens-
able member of her team. With a headset glued to ears and
a walkie-talkie clipped to her belt, Anisa was called on to do
a number of tasks, running all over the grounds of the Rova.
As the sun climbed higher and the dewy coolness of dawn

yielded to a hotter late morning, Nasser marveled more at Anisa's endurance.

She never seemed to stop for very long, her sneakers burning rubber over the pavement as she accomplished one task and moved to the next. The only time she came to a rest was when she paused to cool off with a long pull from her water bottle. Yet juggling all that she was, Anisa still managed to carve out time to look daggers at him.

She's definitely plotting something...

Nasser sketched a mental note to beware her crafty mind *and* her surprising beauty.

The photos he'd seen of her, both the ones her brother had provided and the ones Nasser had collected from her social media accounts, didn't hold a candle to her in the flesh.

Anisa was very pretty, with her adorably small, turned-up nose, heart-shaped face, and soft, alluring mouth. It was wide and full, its heavier lower lip caught between her teeth whenever she was focusing on a task. Which was far too often.

Like yesterday, she was dressed simply in blue jeans and a plain long-sleeved shirt. But yesterday her hijab had been wrapped more classically over her head and neck. Today Anisa had styled it differently. The headscarf wound around her head in a simple turban, her slender brown neck left bare. He surmised that it was a way to keep herself cooler while she was rushed around.

He knew Anisa could easily have relied on her family's wealth and never had to work a day in her life, certainly not as hard as she was right then. Nasser commended her industrious spirit.

Admittedly, he was also relieved that Anisa was preoccupied as it gave him a chance to consider his strategy to win her over.

A stratagem he was confident would make her accept that

it was pointless to fight him. That one way or another, Nasser would see through his protective detail until Anisa finished with her work in Madagascar and left for her home in Canada.

CHAPTER THREE

SEVERAL HOURS LATER, and Nasser's confidence had taken a hit.

Waiting for Anisa to finish working for the day so they could finally speak without interruptions had resulted in him following her around the city. Had Nasser known she would be working long hours, he might have reconsidered a better wardrobe and footwear.

He might even have rethought agreeing to this job.

Nasser sighed, knowing his decision to accept Ara's request to protect his younger sister had more to do with his own personal affairs than the big payday it offered. Money wasn't an issue in his life. He had millions to his name. But he was being paid with peace of mind.

Protect my sister, Ara had instructed him, promising, *In return, I'll help you find the men who killed your brother, Nuruddin.*

Nuruddin...

Nasser hadn't heard his brother's name mentioned in so very long. He knew that it was sadly the way things went when one passed away. Time eroded memories, names, faces. He hadn't expected to hear about Nuruddin from Ara. Anisa's brother was affording him a chance to finally track Nuruddin's killers. Because in spite of Nasser's wealth and powerful connections these days, vengeance was still one thing that eluded him. Vengeance for his brother. For their bro-kenhearted parents, who'd had to bury a son far too young.

And for myself. For the peace that could be mine, Nasser thought, the pain in his heart mingled with guilt.

He hadn't been able to save his brother—but this...re-venge he could do.

Nasser lifted his head, closed his eyes and breathed in the city air, cooler at this late hour. When he opened his eyes again, he trained them on the expansive water before him.

Lake Anosy, with its jacaranda-lined shores, was a few miles away from Antananarivo's Upper Town, or La Haute Ville. Though still a frequented part of the city, it was far more peaceful a place to visit after a bustling day in the urban center of the capital. Of course, like most places, certain times of the day were less crowded. Right then, for instance, the setting sun cast long black shadows on the tree-lined trail along the shore. An isthmus connected the mainland to a small island in the manmade lake's center. The area boasted a tranquility that could quiet even the most anxious of minds.

He let that serenity in to clear his head until only a single thought remained: Anisa.

He hadn't forgotten that they still needed to chat. For him to do his job smoothly, he wanted her compliant. Her safety required a combined effort from them both. After all, if she insisted on placing herself in danger, Nasser could only do so much to protect her.

And if he couldn't protect her, then he could consider his job forfeit now.

Nasser frowned at the mere thought of defeat. He scowled more when he imagined the fight Anisa would put up.

So much for peace.

He spotted her easily amid a group of her coworkers, not far from where he stood under a fully blooming jacaranda tree. Her posture and expression were more relaxed now that she was officially off the clock. Though he couldn't hear what she or her crew members were saying, he watched a brilliant smile lift her cheeks, her mouth opening with laughter, her hand immediately flying over to catch the sound. He couldn't discern her mirth from the chatter of the group, and yet somehow he imagined the sound of her laugh would be something worth hearing and experiencing.

Why not right now? They were overdue a chat, and he hadn't endured twelve hours of her job to be deterred.

Fixing that to his mind, he made his move.

When he was within earshot, he caught another wave of laughter swelling from the group and dispersing into the evening air.

Aside from Anisa, who stood out to him the way an insect ventured to light even to the detriment of its well-being, the only other face he recognized was her little blonde friend. Darya, he believed she was called. He was still looking into her. The others, four males and one other female, were new to him. But since they were working alongside Anisa, Nasser would make it his business to search their backgrounds and ensure they posed no threats to her.

He tensed when one of the men flung an arm around Anisa's shoulders, pressed her to his side and lowered his head to angle his lips close to her ear.

Nasser narrowed his eyes at the point of contact, images of him ripping that arm off Anisa flashing into his mind unbidden.

And he might have succumbed to his baser urges if Anisa hadn't chosen that moment to roll her eyes at whatever he whispered into her ear. She drawled, "Hands off, Lucas," before elbowing him off her. She did it far more gently than he would have, but the elbow in the ribs did the trick in pushing away the unwanted advance.

With one final dark look at this Lucas who dared touch

her, Nasser scrawled a mental instruction to have his diligent staff take extra time researching him especially.

Anisa looked past her circle of friends then, right at him.

Her eyes rounded in open surprise before she appeared to catch herself, furrowed her brows and pruned her lips.

Seeing no point in lurking in the umbrage of trees, Nasser stepped into the orange glow of the streetlights that illuminated Anisa and her coworkers.

"We need to talk," he stated, the announcement catching the attention of her friends. Unlike her, they hadn't noticed him yet.

Now that they did, their curiosity was flung from him to Anisa and back again.

Anisa visibly stiffened and crossed her arms, but she broke away from her group and walked up to him.

"After we talk, I will see you to your hotel," Nasser said and held his car keys up between them, hoping that his no-nonsense tone persuaded her.

"Fine."

She turned back and pulled her friend Darya aside. "I'm going to catch a ride with him." She pulled out her phone and added as if to goad him, "I'll send you a live location, you know, in case I go missing."

When she retraced her steps back to him, Nasser stepped in closer to her, and she took one sharp inhale in reaction.

"Good. I'm satisfied that you're endeavoring to protect yourself as well."

With her hijab styled as a turban, he could see her throat ripple in response to his words. Backdropped by the purple blooms of the jacaranda—a tree whose flowers only bloomed in October and November—Anisa made for a mesmerizing portrait. It was one he cataloged for memory as his stare roved over the rosy-brown flush painting the tip of her nose and the swell of her cheeks. The longer he studied her, the louder her breathing became in the silence, her lips parting for her quicker intakes of air. Fighting not to close his eyes, he subtly pulled in her natural scent mingling with the blooming trees all around them. *Ya Allah.* But how could anyone smell so good? Feeling the same kind of breathlessness, he stepped off to the side, discreetly giving them the space they both seemed to need to concentrate.

As soon as he did, Anisa tightened her lips and flared her nostrils, huffing, "Your satisfaction wasn't my goal."

Masking his amusement at her comment, Nasser jerked his chin toward his vehicle. "Follow me to my car."

Soon they were merged onto the road and driving back to the city's Upper Town, where her hotel was situated.

A direct route to her hotel would be about ten minutes, fifteen if nighttime traffic delayed them. Nasser expected their conversation needed no more than half an hour. So he would have to find more traffic than usual...

Beside him, Anisa tapped her shoes impatiently on the car floor. When he glanced at her, she speared him with an expectant look and crossed her arms.

"So, are you going to talk?" she asked briskly, all business.

Seeing no point in prolonging their inevitable conversation, at the next red light, Nasser fished for his wallet and retrieved a business card from it.

He set the card down on the center console between them. "Contact the number on the card to verify my credentials and identity. I wouldn't expect you to trust my word alone, even though you seem to already." His cheeky insinuation that she had trusted him without confirming that he was who he said he was didn't go unchecked. Anisa's glare came at him fast and fierce.

In hindsight, he could have worded that better, even if it bothered him that she'd let her guard down. As much as he would have liked to drill cautiousness into her, now wasn't the time or place. The objective was to get her to trust him enough to let him do his job of protecting her—

Not alienate her.

"You have my card now," he carried on, continuing as if her glower didn't have him on edge.

Holding out his card before her, she read, "Sango Securities."

"We're a private security firm."

"You're the boss?"

"I'm the founder and president."

Anisa sucking her teeth wasn't a good sign. "So, who's to say that your staff won't just lie about who you are?"

Once again she nearly pulled laughter out of him, the humor he fought to suppress twitching his lips and threatening to break his concentration. "You're right," he agreed hoarsely, still battling to regain control of his runaway mirth. "The reference from my staff won't be unbiased. There is another option, however: you could also always call your brother and ask him."

It wasn't the first time he'd proposed that she speak to Ara. Earlier when Nasser had suggested that she contact her brother, Anisa looked ready to strangle him with her bare hands. She had that same murderous slit to her eyes now.

"Why?" she asked frostily. "So you and my brother can team up against me?"

She might have said more, but her stomach chose that moment to grumble.

"You're hungry," he observed. "We can talk more over dinner—"

Anisa cut him off with an angry sniff. "No, I don't want dinner. What I *want* is for you to tell me what Ara is doing, and why whatever it is suddenly requires I need a bodyguard."

He could tell her, of course. About how he'd lost his older

brother, Nuruddin, at an antigovernment rally over fifteen years ago, and that his life had never been the same since. Or perhaps he should be honest and come clean about knowing Anisa and her brother had lost their parents in a tragic boating accident—an accident that was no accident, but rather a staged double homicide targeting her mother and father. Ara hadn't spoken much on it, only that he suspected the same crooked government officials were behind the deaths of his parents and Nuruddin.

And that if Nasser were willing, he and Ara could join forces to avenge their lost family members.

He had been more than willing. It was why he was by Anisa's side now. Why looking her in the face, and knowing they were sharing a similar pain of losing people they loved, made it hard for him to utter lies.

She deserves to know, doesn't she?

Wavering, Nasser contemplated telling her the truth of the quid pro quo deal he'd struck with her brother.

And what if telling her places her in danger?

It was the very reason why Ara had sworn him to secrecy.

My sister can't know anything about this deal of ours. I won't endanger her unnecessarily. Just make sure she gets home safely, and you'll have your names. You'll have your revenge.

Ara's vow ended Nasser's indecision.

"Well?" Anisa prompted him.

Nasser hated seeing the hope peeping out from her eyes. He watched the light fade when he shook his head. "Ask your brother. He simply hired my services. What he does isn't my business." Not an outright lie, but not also the truth. It was a middle ground he could live with.

Anisa's dark look could've fried him.

Unsurprisingly, she demanded, "Drop me off at my hotel, then, or I'll get out here and grab a cab."

Refusing to let her take a taxi, Nasser silently obeyed her first order, his jaws painfully clenched as he navigated traffic to her hotel. Once he parked in front of the hotel's entrance, Anisa hightailed it out of his vehicle.

Nasser moved quickly, exiting the car and catching her before she stomped away.

"You'll be here tomorrow, won't you? Because we can talk then."

For a split second, Anisa's anger blinked into confusion. But by the time he noticed the shift in her mood, her features had flickered back to stone, and she jerked her head in what he presumed to be a nod. She didn't stick around after that, marching away into the hotel and leaving Nasser more drained than he'd felt in a long while.

Anisa couldn't immediately recall feeling that angry before.

She vibrated with rage all through the silent drive, half-relieved that Nasser hadn't tried again to speak to her. But the other half was annoyed that he had managed to maintain his composure while she felt seconds away from fracturing.

She resisted slamming his car door when he came to a halt at her hotel's entrance.

His car wasn't the true source of her crossness.

He is.

Still, not wanting to bite his head off, she tried to storm away. But Nasser waylaid her briefly, questioning her work schedule. And she was too furious with him to do much else but nod. Fuming in her hotel suite now, she finally gave herself license to shout into the first pillow she could grab, but even that did little to dull her irritable mood.

This is just as much my fault.

Anisa had allowed him to get under her skin, and now she felt all out of sorts because of it.

Pushing away the pillow she'd screamed into, she flopped

back onto the bed, glared up at the ceiling and racked her brain for a memory of when she'd been so riled by someone. The only other time she remembered being that upset was when Ara had reacted coldly to her desire to study and live abroad alone.

"Of course he's as annoying as Ara," Anisa groused. All of this circled back to her brother, and that just infuriated her more. What was with the men in her life and their all-consuming need for control? She couldn't see it any other way than Ara and Nasser not trusting her with their trifling secrets.

And she wouldn't be so bothered—

But they're disrupting my life!

Was she just supposed to sit there and accept it? That was a hard no, but what more could she do? Nasser's advice was for her to ask Ara…

Anisa's eyes nearly rolled right out of her skull.

If she thought she could ask Ara, she'd have never badgered Nasser in the first place. Not that he'd ever seemed flustered. Unlike her…

The memory of Nasser moving in closer to her at Lake Anosy less than an hour ago replayed in her mind. He'd filled her vision, the beautiful blossoming jacaranda and the lake-side view forgotten in lieu of him. Her brain then recreated the scene of their first showdown atop the Rova. Again, they stood so close that the encounter left an imprint on her. Every time, he had appeared unfazed to her, and that was almost as unfair as Nasser holding on to her brother's secrets along with his own.

Even so, her anger started waning. The void it left behind filled with something curiously new…

She pressed her hands to her clenching belly, her insides churning more violently all of a sudden. Dismissing it as hunger would've been too easy. That wouldn't explain the heat wafting from her face or the delightful shivers rolling over her body. Chilled and overheated, she sat up in a daze, Nasser's stony yet darkly gorgeous face branded in her mind.

Was she feeling this way because of him?

With trepidation, Anisa tested her theory by closing her eyes and letting her imagination wander and wend its way back to him.

Opening her eyes, she moved her hands from her stomach up to her rabbiting heart.

Great. She had a crush on him. That didn't bode well for her willpower if she wanted to shake him loose.

Especially when Anisa sprang up to her feet at the sound of a knock on her front door, and her first thought was, *It can't be him.*

Seeing Darya brought equal measures of consolation and disappointment.

I'm only disappointed because he should have come to apologize.

"Hey," her friend greeted her, tilting her head in confusion. "You got back to the hotel before me. I was surprised to see the live location pinning you here, of all places. I'm guessing it didn't go well with your studly bodyguard?"

"Yeah, we didn't have much to talk about after all. Also, he's not *my* anything." Anisa emphasized the last part with a glare at Darya.

"Easy," Darya laughed, but when her humor abated, she asked, "All right. Tell me. What happened to put you in a bad mood?"

Anisa heaved a sigh. "Where do I start?"

She walked her friend through everything that had transpired with Nasser, starting with the business card he'd given her and ending on his poorly timed offer of dinner. At the end of her complaining, she anticipated a sympathetic ear.

Instead Darya looked his business card over and passed

it back with a shrug. "Honestly, it just sounds like he's trying to do his job."

"A job I *don't want* him to do!" Anisa threw up her hands and groaned loudly. "I don't need to be babysat. What I really want is for my brother and Nasser to accept that."

"Right, but I can understand why they might think it's necessary."

"Please, enlighten me."

Darya snorted in disbelief. "Um, could it be the millions in your family?"

Not many people in her life knew about her family's wealth. Money her parents earned from their import-export business when they were alive, and now the money that her brother had successfully tripled—no, *quadrupled* since inheriting the shipping company their father and mother had begun years ago. When she'd first told Darya, Anisa had fully expected her friend to treat her differently. After all, they had initially bonded over their mutual love of film and being young immigrant women in their chosen industry. Darya had come from a poor background, migrating from eastern Europe to Canada all on her own in her late teens to provide for herself and her family back home. Although she was always careful not to show it, she must have been shocked to learn that Anisa was an heiress. Even if she was a reluctant one...

"All right, I can see your point," Anisa assented grudgingly. And before Darya could gloat, she hastened to add, "But I don't think that's why my brother hired Nasser. Don't ask me how I know. I just do."

Whatever Ara and Nasser were up to, her gut churned nauseously with a warning that their secrets were dangerous.

With that dark certainty in mind, she murmured, "If I didn't see or hear from either of them anytime soon, I'd be happy."

A sharp knock on the door interrupted them.

"Were you expecting a certain someone?" Darya eyed the door with a slow grin.

Anisa frowned, but her heart rate picked up as she answered her second caller. It wasn't Nasser this time either, but one of the hotel's waitstaff. The young woman garbed in a maroon pantsuit held out a large white plastic bag and smilingly informed her, "A visitor left this for you at Reception." She passed Anisa the bag and along with it a folded note before strolling away.

Closing the door slowly, Anisa turned with her gaze trained on the note in her hand.

"Did someone leave you takeout?" Darya leaned closer and took a big whiff. "Mmm, smells heavenly."

Anisa had to agree that the divine smell coming from the bag revved up her hunger. But it was hard to concentrate on anything but the note that came with the takeaway meal. She set the bag down on the entryway table and dropped into the soft cushions of the sofa in the sitting area. Grabbing the spot next to her, Darya said nothing. Nevertheless, Anisa felt her impatience.

Overly anxious herself, she flipped open the note and saw the short message was written on the hotel's memo paper, but she quickly looked past the business letterhead to the few words inked neatly on the page in startlingly beautiful cursive:

I'm a man of my word, and I promised you dinner. I will see you tomorrow. Nasser.

She should have known—she suspected it was him, but though unsigned, the note was confirmation.

He did come back.

And he brought her dinner, apparently. A dinner he hadn't,

in fact, promised her. A dinner she'd walked away from in anger...

"It's Mr. Hot Bodyguard, isn't it?" Darya's soft voice broke the silence.

Anisa didn't even have the strength to argue that he wasn't hers.

She let Darya read the note then, getting up off the sofa to plate the takeaway dinner Nasser thoughtfully sent her. Anisa stopped when Darya walked over with the note.

"Wait. Doesn't he know that we're leaving Antananarivo tomorrow morning?"

Anisa bit her lip and looked down at the plate she'd filled with a steaming hot meat stew with fresh greens and accompanied by a side of white rice.

"You didn't tell him," Darya guessed.

"He seemed to think we'd still be here, and I didn't correct him." She shrugged. Their film crew was set to travel to different locations throughout Madagascar. That had always been the plan. "It's not an outright lie."

Just a lie of omission, she thought with a twinge of remorse not helped when Darya answered with a slow, disappointed shake of her head.

"Anisa, you have to tell him."

"Why should I?" She snapped her head up, a fire catching in her, the flames stoked by her ire at Nasser and Ara for leaving her in the dark over why she required protection. If they could have their secrets, why couldn't she do the same?

The guilt that momentarily had a hold on her melted.

It wasn't her fault that Nasser believed she would remain in Antananarivo tomorrow.

If he doesn't know I'm leaving, then he's just not that good of a bodyguard, Anisa reasoned.

And if he wasn't that good of a bodyguard, then Nasser had no business following her around, let alone protecting her.

CHAPTER FOUR

ANISA WOULDN'T EVER label herself a morning person, yet when her alarm woke her, she bounded out of bed with a smile and drew open the hotel's thick curtains to let in the golden beginnings of dawn brightening the dark sky.

After basking in the light of day, she showered and dressed, styled her hijab, prayed Fajr, and even had time to eat a proper breakfast—something she often forgot to do on her busiest workdays. Anisa didn't think too hard about her unusual burst of energy. She simply attributed it to a good night's sleep, which was rare for her when she was used to working twelve-to sixteen-hour shifts.

Her sunny mood stuck with her until she set foot outside her hotel, where she couldn't overlook the familiar black four-by-four in the circular drive or miss its very handsome driver leaning with his back pressed against the passenger door. His position gave him a straight view to the revolving entrance she stepped through.

Freezing in her tracks, she stared, disbelieving her eyes.

But Nasser didn't vanish.

Which means he's really standing there.

With that realization, all her good humor leaked away like a pricked balloon.

Anisa sucked in her lips, her mouth suddenly dry and her heart sounding in her ears. Squeezing her hand around the handle of her compact suitcase, she rolled it forward slowly, her steps echoing the hesitance that assailed her.

Drawing his sunglasses off when she came to a standstill a foot from him, Nasser fastened her with a searing look.

"Sightseeing early, or are we going someplace else?"

Anisa opened her mouth, then closed it, before opening it again in the hope that an appropriate excuse would come to her. Instead, grumbling car engines pierced the awkward quiet, and a minibus crawled up the drive. Closely following the bus was a mud-stained white four-by-four, older-looking than Nasser's vehicle. Both the minibus and four-wheel drive came to a stop behind Nasser's ride, and the driver's door of the minibus swung open.

"Anisa! Ready to go?" Lucas called to her, climbing out of the vehicle.

Acknowledging Lucas with a fearsome scowl, Nasser asked, "Where are you going, Anisa?"

He knows! How could he know?

Panic setting in, Anisa left her luggage standing on the drive and walked a little closer to Nasser.

"We're leaving Antananarivo. Our filming scheduling is tight, so we have to be on the road very soon." She swallowed hard, her gulp embarrassingly audible before she continued squeakily, "I...must have forgotten to mention it."

"I'm glad you told me now."

Anisa heard the smugness in his response and didn't even need proof of it from his unchanging, shuttered expression. He had known she lied, and he'd wanted her to confess to it. And she had... *Allah*, how could she be so oblivious? She walked right into that one! Now not only would she have to deal with the fact that he would follow her once again, but he'd caught her in a lie of her own making, a lie she couldn't even manage to conceal.

She glared at him to her own detriment, her temples pulsing warningly with a headache. Gritting her teeth against the dull pain, she closed her eyes and touched her fingers to the side of her forehead.

"Are you not feeling well?" Nasser's voice, though still notably deep and irritatingly unruffled in tone, sounded sharper than it had seconds ago.

Opening her eyes, Anisa blinked in wonder. Because it sounded like he actually cared…

Duh! Of course he does.

He was likely just worried for the sake of his job. Ara wouldn't be too happy if the bodyguard he hired had failed in protecting his precious little sister—even if it was only from a big, bad headache. Outside of that, she couldn't delude herself into thinking Nasser truly cared. And she had to be sure not to confuse concern that came with a price tag with real emotion.

"I'm fine," she said from between clenched teeth. Then she called to Lucas, "Make room for me."

She turned away from Nasser to grab her suitcase. Anisa hadn't made it two steps before she heard a commotion from the hotel's entrance and Darya calling to her.

"Anisa! Wait for me!"

Darya hurried toward Anisa and the idling minibus full of their crew members. She crowded closer to Anisa and dropped her voice while nudging her head sharply at Nasser, the fedora she'd purchased from the market nearly falling off from her obvious gesturing. "I thought you said you weren't going to tell him. Changed your mind?"

"He was here when I walked out," Anisa hissed. "He just knew. I don't know how, but he did."

Darya smiled blithely at him while murmuring, "Guess he's that good at his job." When Anisa groaned softly, her friend patted her arm reassuringly. "Well, you could ask him on the road."

Anisa shook her head slowly, letting those words sink in. "Wait. What do you mean, 'on the road'? I'm riding the minibus like everyone else."

"Yeah, about that…" Darya smiled sheepishly and pointed to the bellhop rolling a heavily laden luggage cart in their direction. There was a lot more there than when she and Darya had checked in two days ago. "After you left last night, Lucas drove the rest of us to the market again, and I *might* have gone a little overboard with purchases."

"A little?" Anisa's eyes bugged.

"I mean, I would go with your bodyguard—"

"He's not *mine*," Anisa interjected.

"But it's not like we know each other. That's why it would be better if you go." She chirped the last part happily, like the idea solved their problem.

Anisa watched hopelessly as Lucas and another crew member helped the bellhop haul Darya's belongings into the back of the minibus. She could see there was hardly any room left once Darya climbed in, mouthed *sorry*, and waved back at her. In desperation, she looked around at the four-by-four, but quickly saw that there would be no room for her there with the director and assistant director and their driver.

She heard Nasser before she felt him standing by her and saw his tall, imposing form in her peripheral.

He didn't say anything.

And it forced her to break their silence first. Though it killed her to ask him, she said, "May I please have a ride?" She bit her tongue when she wanted to add, "Since you're going to follow me anyways."

Anisa waited for him to drag this part out. Milk this moment for all it was worth. He hadn't only caught her in a lie; he was now her only option to follow her crew and continue to do her job. It was what she'd have done if their roles were reversed.

"I'll place your luggage in the trunk," he informed her.

Anisa craned her neck up and goggled at him, unclear if she heard him correctly.

"Or would you like to do it yourself?" He looked pointedly down at where her hand clasped her suitcase, her fingers practically glued to the handle from the way her knuckle bones protruded. She peeled her fingers loose. The instant she did, he grasped where her hand had been a heartbeat earlier.

Wordlessly, he pushed in the suitcase handle, hauled the hardcase roller up and forged a path to his vehicle.

No gloating followed.

That didn't mean her defenses weren't on alert. Anisa shadowed him slowly and cautiously, slid into the passenger seat beside him and looked for any signs that he was about to rub this in her face. Because surely, *surely* he wasn't doing any of this for sheer kindness's sake.

He's doing his job, so no. Not out of the kindness of his heart.

But Anisa couldn't figure out what angle he would come at her from. Would he annoy her throughout this long journey ahead, maybe make her wish that she hadn't omitted the truth of the trip? The only thing she could be certain of was that he wouldn't hurt her. Not if he was really working for Ara. Her brother wouldn't have sent anyone who lacked his implicit trust. And yet that didn't mean she trusted him not to be petty with her now.

She looked him over, his expensive suits traded in for a linen blazer, a buttoned oxford shirt and dark wash straight jeans. He hooked his sunglasses into the pocket of his blazer, his sleeves rolled up and the corded muscles of his forearm coming between them as he fiddled with the console screen.

"Would you like the radio on? Music, perhaps."

When she didn't respond, Nasser met her stare head-on. Having his full attention on her in the hush of his car and with no one else to witness whatever went down had a funny effect on her. First, her stomach flopped on her. And her headache was alive and well, but now her limbs were feeling quivery. If she hadn't known better, Anisa would've thought she was sicker than she actually was.

She had to be sick if she was noticing how soft and lush his lips looked, the way his jaw gleamed from what had to be a recent shave, and the decadent scent of his aftershave and cologne interspersed with the new leather smell coming from the car.

"Anisa."

Her name in his low, assertive voice had her sucking in a long breath, snapping to attention, and reminding herself that her little crush on him had no legs. Certainly not if he intended to force his company on her.

"Do what you want," she said with an indignant huff, then stared out the passenger window. "It's what you've been doing all along."

Nasser counted four hours since Anisa spoke to him last.

She hadn't said a word, not one, since they left Antananarivo on the freeway that would take them down south to where her film crew were scheduled to work next. Rather she sulked quietly, refusing to make eye contact or even acknowledge that he was sharing a tightly confined space with her, for better or worse.

He almost wished she would yell at him. Shout to her heart's content, get it out of her system and spare him the cold shoulder.

This is why you're not married—why you've given up on family.

Nasser knew that wasn't the entire truth of why he'd chosen celibacy over so-called wedded bliss. Being in a relationship meant that he provided for his intended life partner in every way. Caring for, loving, and protecting...

He had a problem with the protecting part most of all.

He hadn't been able to protect Nuruddin. Worse, he'd held his brother in his last moments and felt the life ebb from his body. Nasser shuddered at the memory, his heart a block of ice in his chest as he relived the worst day of his life.

If only we hadn't gone to that protest rally...

And if only Nasser hadn't left his brother's side when things had gotten dangerous and the local police and military hadn't used force to chase off protestors.

Breathing deeply, he wrung his hands on the steering wheel and forced himself back to the present, in the car with Anisa, as they drove down the long stretch of freeway. When he thought of Nuruddin, and of all the life experiences his brother would never get, Nasser knew the only thing that could make it right for him was abstaining from some of those experiences himself.

Hence his celibacy.

As excessive as it seemed, even if he were interested in a romantic relationship, he wouldn't be any good at it. Not if he couldn't protect those he loved.

So marriage just wasn't in his cards.

It's not my fate.

For some reason, as he thought this, he flung a glance at Anisa.

She had her back to him, her body angled toward the passenger door as though she intended to pop the lock and spring out of the car at a moment's notice. If that wasn't worrying, she also sat so still that he might have thought she was sleeping. Nasser frowned, not fooled. It was a tactic to avoid speaking to him.

He convinced himself that his annoyance was born sim-

ply out of frustration that came from the oppressive pall of
silence that had befallen them.

He was relieved then when they finally reached a pit stop.
The city of Antsirabe.

Following the lead of her crew ahead of them, Nasser finally pulled in to park in front of a large, picturesque colonial
building, the architectural touches a nod to the bygone Belle
Epoque. Just as fascinating, the city teemed with colorful
rickshaws. Nasser had dodged several of the man-powered
vehicles as he navigated into the central part of the town.

As soon as he cut the engine, Anisa unfurled from her seat,
unlocked her seat belt and opened her door first.

She can't wait to run from me.

Nasser silenced that mental poison before the line of thinking bought him trouble. What Anisa did wasn't his problem
unless it risked her safety. Like when she waved to her friend
Darya from across the street and bolted into the road after
looking both ways only once.

She missed the motorbike that careened around the corner. Nasser acted fast, caught her arm and hauled her back
into him. The propulsion jerked her to his chest. He immediately and instinctively wrapped his arms around her. He
breathed heavily, watching the bike roar past the spot Anisa
had just been standing, and fought back the tragic image of
what could have been her broken body lying on the street.

It might have explained why he held on to her longer than
was necessary.

Why it had gotten to the point where he felt her physically
stiffen in his hold and then press her hands to his chest and
push back against him.

But she didn't step away when he lowered his arms and she
dropped her hands off him. Anisa peered up at him, just as
she had every other time they stood nearly toe-to-toe, standing off against each other.

It's different this time...

Nasser had breached her personal space—and yes, it started because he'd wanted to save her, *protect* her from herself if need be. But what happened after, his panicked visual of her dying on him, and then holding her past the point of rationality, that would be tougher to explain.

Rather than demanding he do just that, Anisa stared at him, in no hurry, it seemed, to order answers from him.

"Are you all right?" he asked gruffly.

She hummed as if agreeing, but the dazed look on her face didn't give him confidence that she had heard him, let alone comprehended what he'd asked her.

Who knew how long they stood there? It had to be a while for her friend to have reached them and yank Anisa away from him into a fierce hug.

"Oh, my God! Did you see that maniac driver? You almost got run over."

"I'm fine, Darya. Really." Anisa soothed her friend and patted her back, but her gaze remained wholly his.

She didn't break eye contact with him until Darya forced her to repeat the assurance that she hadn't come to harm.

Nasser quietly freed the breath he'd held the instant she left the safety of his car.

He itched to get her back there, where he could be assured no harm could come to her, but he knew that it would have to wait until her crew members were finished taking their break in the city.

"Come on." Pulling on Anisa's hands, Darya gestured to their crew and cast across the street, everyone having piled out of the minibus and the dusty white four-by-four. "We're all heading to lunch together."

Anisa's eyes locked on Nasser again, an indecisiveness to the way she looked at him.

A car horn blared.

The man Anisa had called Lucas tapped the horn of the minibus again and waved his arm at them.

"Are you beautiful ladies coming or what?" he hollered, getting the crew laughing at his antics.

Nasser twisted his mouth, aggravated at the recall of Lucas touching Anisa, and the fact that if she walked away now he wouldn't be able to follow her to lunch. He wasn't a member of her crew or cast. And so he'd be forced to remain outside whatever restaurant they chose, where he'd be prowling like a caged beast marking the boundaries of its prison, searching desperately for escape.

That image wrested a memory from the gloomiest recesses of his mind.

It was of him in a lightless, constricted hole of a place, the cold gust of night whistling through the bars and knifing through the thin, worn material of his shirt and pants, and the sole source of heat from the other bodies crammed into the jail cell.

He never, ever wished to feel that weak and powerless again.

If that meant Nasser had to choke down the fiery helplessness creeping up his throat at the thought of watching from the outside while Anisa lunched with her friends and coworkers, then so be it.

But his ears perked up when Anisa said, "Go without me." She didn't look back after Darya shrugged, said her temporary farewell and crossed the street. Before long, Anisa's crew and the cast members strolled off down the street in search of a meal.

It left them alone once more.

"You stayed," he observed, not permitting himself to dwell on the buoyant turn of his mood now that Anisa remained by his side.

She gave him an eye roll. "I *stayed*, yes, but don't get it twisted."

"Twisted?"

"Confused," she explained.

"Why would I be confused?"

For a moment she simply stared. Then, shaking her head as if clearing her mind, she said, "We should try talking again."

Try as he might to quiet it, that odd effervescence only jangled louder in Nasser. Giving up, he nodded. They hadn't gotten the chance to speak last time. Anisa had hurried off on him—

That's after I didn't give her the answers to secrets she wanted.

Nasser silently vowed to be gentler in his refusal this time. Though he wasn't willing to tell her the reasons he'd entered her life, he also wouldn't offer Anisa a chance to get upset with him. Somehow, he'd find a way to keep her happy without burdening her with problems that were his and Ara's.

"Lunch is on you though." Anisa raised her voice to be heard over the busy city noises as she marched ahead.

With her back to him, Nasser indulged in a smile and murmured, "Lunch should be interesting, then…"

CHAPTER FIVE

"ÇA VA?"

It was the second time Nasser had asked after her health, and Anisa couldn't be annoyed, not after he'd saved her from being plowed over by that reckless motorbike driver. To think she'd been a heartbeat away from becoming one big stain on the pavement—

She squeezed her eyes at the horrid image that last thought conjured.

If Nasser hadn't been there…

She still felt his arms around her, his hands poised at her back, holding her to him while the imminent danger passed them by. Because of his quick actions, he'd rescued her from grave injury.

Possibly death.

A shudder raked through her. Now that the adrenaline had ebbed from her system, residual fear left her shaken up, and anxiety pressed down on her chest. Her next few breaths sawed out fast and almost painfully.

They were walking together, Nasser placing himself between her and the street. And yet every car passing had her nearly jumping out of her bones.

Funny. She'd thought she was doing fine enough, but it seemed that the initial shock had held her real fright at bay. Suddenly she couldn't think of anything else except that she'd almost just died.

Ears ringing and heart drumming, Anisa hadn't realized she'd been walking faster until Nasser's hand came out of nowhere and alighted on her arm. Startled by his sudden touch, she stopped dead in her tracks and looked up at him wide-eyed.

Meeting his gaze only reminded her of the close brush with fatality she'd just had.

"Anisa, you didn't answer me. Are you all right? Because if you're not doing well, I would like to know." He spoke with such authority. It should have rubbed her wrong, but the unconcealed concern in his voice and the strain of it in his expression dispelled her irritation.

"I'm fine," she murmured, not sounding at all like she was fine.

"Can you walk a little further? Otherwise, use my arm and lean on me."

Anisa's snort and eye roll had her feeling more like herself. Shrugging his hand off her arm, and ignoring the tingling heat his touch had left behind on her, she said, "I think I can make it, thanks," and forced herself to walk away from him.

He wasn't far behind her when he gestured across the street and instructed her to switch directions.

"We'll ride *le pousse-pousse* from here. It will be quicker."

Anisa wanted to ask what a *pousse-pousse* was, but she had her answer when Nasser crossed the street with her and stopped in front of a rickshaw, its gleaming red body, blue roof, wheel spokes and rims all looking freshly painted.

The rickshaw driver awaited them, his smile stretched wide as he flagged them over to take a seat.

Nasser spoke in rapid French to him. Anisa didn't even bother to follow whatever was being said, simply interpreting that they must have come to some deal in the end. Nasser then offered her a hand she didn't refuse and helped her to a seat on the hard but sturdy black bench of the rickshaw. He climbed in beside her. The driver crouched low, gripped the handles of the carriage and lifted them with an ease that belied his thin, wiry build and ashy bare feet.

As interesting an experience as it was, it wasn't the mode of travel that she would have chosen right then with her stomach in knots and her head lightly pounding with an impending headache. Anisa held on to the side of the rickshaw, her fingers taut and her body tensing in preparation to be rocked back and forth.

Surprisingly, the ride was smooth.

Pleasant, she thought with a faint smile, tilting her head to the breeze that now stirred over her face.

Nasser didn't miss it, not with the way he kept his eyes on her. But he didn't broach the subject of her well-being for a third time, and Anisa was grateful for it, not really wanting to relive having nearly been flattened by a motorbike. She just wanted to forget it ever happened.

She shut her eyes for what felt like a second before rousing at the feel of warmth on her shoulder. She saw Nasser retracting his hand, so she figured he had woken her after she'd accidentally fallen asleep. The rickshaw had come to a stop. He wasn't sitting by her anymore either. Standing outside the rickshaw on her side, he proffered his hand for her to climb out.

They stood before what she presumed was their intended destination, a restaurant with a lovely terrace view.

Nasser found them a table on the elevated terrace, pleasing her with his choice. The instant she saw the outdoor seating, she'd wanted nothing more than to sit down, enjoy a meal and soak in the postcard-pretty vista. She didn't even mind that Nasser helped her order. He had the decency to let her point out what she wanted from the menu and translated whatever French on the laminated pages stumped her.

Their drinks arrived, and she heeded him when he passed her a glass and commanded, "Drink. You had a shock."

Anisa expected the creamy beige concoction to taste sweet, but she was unprepared for the tangy punch to her taste buds. She pulled a face, and Nasser set a second glass by her. This one was plain ice-cold water.

"What did I just drink?" She pointed to the glass, the beverage still thick on her tongue. Though it was cool, and not terrible in taste, her pounding head and empty stomach hadn't appreciated the saccharine kick to her mouth.

"Baobab juice. It's milled from the seed of the baobab trees that are local to this area and along the island. It's a quick fix to elevate your sugar levels, but if it's not to your taste, I could send for the menu and you could pick something else."

Anisa regarded the baobab juice with renewed interest. She wouldn't mind having another sip, but she needed something in her stomach before she was willing to try again.

"Maybe I should have a real meal first."

Nasser smiled. A genuine smile that didn't disappear when she blinked and looked closer to see if she imagined it. As he called a waiter over, it stayed put on his handsome face, adding an extra layer of attractiveness. Now she had to sit across from him and endure the detrimental effect his dashing good looks had on her.

Anisa's stomach swished nervously at that.

But she didn't let it stop her from blurting, "Why are you being so nice to me?"

It wasn't just that he saved her from being roadkill. He hadn't once tried to hold her earlier lie over her head, and now all this concern for her well-being. She didn't know what to make of it.

"You know I lied to you about leaving Antananarivo, right?" she continued, her word vomit not seeming to have an end. If she weren't so bewildered by his displays of kindness, Anisa might have had the sense to be embarrassed. "I didn't want you to follow me."

"I figured as much." Nasser's smile was gone, but there was a humor and ease to his tone.

"And that doesn't piss you off?"

"Piss me off?" he echoed, looking lost in translation.

"*Angry.* Doesn't what I did—*how* I've been acting upset you?"

Nasser tipped his head slightly. "You already made it obvious that my presence isn't wanted, and your behavior is consistent with that fact. So, what reason would I have to be angry?"

"I would be," she muttered.

"Upset or not, my duty is to protect you."

"Is that why you won't tell me the reason I need protection?"

The long, heavy breath he heaved could have rattled their table and the tableware along with it. Nostrils still flared with his exasperated sigh, Nasser said, "Not all danger comes in the form of a careless driver on the road. Sometimes knowledge can be just as threatening. The difference is that at least if you're run over, you might stand a chance of being put back together. But what you learn is harder to undo."

"So," she drawled, "that's your way of saying that I'm better off not knowing anything."

"I only say it because it's true." His face grew harder with his warning.

Anisa expected to be disappointed and irritated by his non-answer. Strangely though, she didn't mind that he stonewalled her again.

At least he actually spoke to me this time.

It was progress—and progress equaled hope that she was a bit closer to uncovering how her safety was connected to Ara's and Nasser's secrets.

* * *

She's safe.

If he repeated it enough times, it was possible Nasser might finally believe it to be true.

But then he grimly thought, *For now, she's safe.*

The question that eluded him was, for how long? And despite convincing evidence that Anisa was not in harm's way, he couldn't rise above the blame holding him down, shackling him in emotional fetters.

Couldn't let it pass that she'd almost gotten mortally wounded, killed even, and on his watch.

See your worthlessness? an insidious little voice hissed from somewhere inside his head. *You can't protect the things that matter. The* people *that matter. You don't deserve happiness.*

Nasser shook his head—and still the voice attacked, chipped at him, echoed the sentiment that he held no value, no true worth if he couldn't protect what was his.

And right now, whether she wanted to get rid of his protection services or not, Anisa was *his.*

His to safeguard. *His* until his job ended.

Mine for now. Mine.

He considered her with that possessiveness coursing through him. Anisa looked and sounded better. That was the important thing. After they left the restaurant, she even insisted on riding back in a *pousse-pousse* to reunite with her crew before they left Antsirabe. Crushed together in the rickshaw, Nasser held still to avoid touching her any more than they were forced to in the restricted space. Anisa didn't seem to care, because she was shifting in her seat and craning her head out from under the rickshaw's roof to take in the passing sights.

"I wish we could stay here and explore," she muttered to herself, but loud enough for him to pick up on.

"Why doesn't your crew film in this city? It's supposed to be quite the tourist trap. A spa town set in the sublime highlands of Madagascar."

Anisa's sigh drifted over to him. "We're on a schedule, that's why. We won't finish filming if we stop every other place."

"And what is it that you do exactly?" He hadn't missed how hard she worked. Surely she must be a crucial member of her team.

"I'm a production assistant," she said, surprising him with that reply.

He wasn't going to judge her skill or merit based on her job title, but a production assistant was an entry-level position. Intrigued, Nasser asked, "Is this a job you wanted to do?"

"Honestly? Not really. It pays the bills, and I get to work with film, but it's not what I finished school to accomplish."

"What do you want to do?"

Anisa pierced him with a look and harrumphed, the sound adorably ruffled. "What's with the interrogation?" She straightened her posture and turned her body to confront him, and he saw where her thinking had headed. "Are you sending this information back to my brother? Is that why you're so curious about what I'm doing?"

Nasser fought to keep his face straight. He didn't think she would appreciate him laughing at her, even though her accusation was laughable.

"I swear that your brother isn't in my ear. Just because he hired me doesn't mean he's privy to a conversation with my client."

"And I'm now a client?"

"In a way, you are."

"Even if I don't want to be," she grumbled, folding her arms and drawing her legs back to her side of the rickshaw.

They had just spoken about this in the restaurant, and

Nasser had fervently hoped that he'd finally gotten through to her that some secrets were better off remaining secrets. Before he could worry that she would try to pelt him with more questions that would weaken his defenses against her, Anisa blew a long breath and rolled her shoulders as if to rid herself of tension.

"Okay, so you're a bodyguard for a living. What does that entail? You know, besides forcing your protection on people who don't want or need it."

Nasser's lips hitched up. He rarely found occasion to smile, but with Anisa he'd done it frequently.

"You have my business card, but essentially I run a corporate security company. Everything from physical security and cyber to natural disasters, we provide our clientele with the means to protect what matters to them most."

Anisa's snort could be heard from a mile away. "That can't be right."

"It's our company motto."

"Doesn't make it right," she quipped, her humor laced with bitterness. "Because there's no possible way that applies to *my* brother."

It was how she said it that had him sitting up straighter, his jaw hardening and his brows slamming down. "What do you mean?"

"I don't know what my brother has led you to believe, but I don't matter to him."

"Why would you say that?"

Anisa whipped her head to him, her eyes ablaze and her voice quavering angrily. "If I really was so important to him, if my safety was truly his only worry, he wouldn't have sent you. He'd be here himself."

Nasser sat back, the force of her words and the emotional pain behind them slamming into him. He had sensed there was some undefined strain in Ara and Anisa's relationship.

Although her brother hadn't mentioned it specifically, when Ara had requested this protection detail from Nasser—the last time they'd spoken—he had hinted at some tension with Anisa.

Wouldn't it be easier and far less costly for you to go yourself? Nasser had asked.

Ara had given him a tired look. *She won't want to see me.*

It didn't seem that way to Nasser. In spite of whatever might have caused the rift between the siblings, it was obvious to him that Anisa would have welcomed Ara. Perhaps not warmly at first, but she wouldn't have turned him away.

"You must have a reason to think that way," he said.

Anisa sniffed and shifted, as if she couldn't look him in the eye while she spoke.

"Again, I'm not sure what Ara's told you about us, but we haven't spoken for years."

Years?

Nasser brooded on her confession, wondering what had transpired for them to not speak for so long.

"Four years almost, next month. No texts, no calls. He just completely cut me out of his life, and for what?" She scoffed. "To assert his control, prove that I somehow need him more than he could ever need me. He was always smarter, more adaptable, and far more reliable than me. What use could I be to him?"

Rather than insisting it couldn't be true, knowing that was probably the last thing she wanted to hear, Nasser instead said, "If you haven't spoken for four years, how does he know so much about you?"

Anisa barked a short, bitter laugh. "Are you sure you've met Ara? I wouldn't be surprised if he had people following me." Continuing on a softer, sadder note, she told him, "I might not have the resources that he does, but I've tried to be a part of his life too. A family friend keeps me updated.

Adeero Sharmarke is my only connection to my brother and our home."

Having done his own research on Anisa's and Ara's backgrounds, Nasser knew this Sharmarke.

A statesman in the Somaliland government and a tribal leader or *suldaan* of a larger local clan, this man she called her *adeero* wasn't truly her uncle by blood. On top of sharing the same tribal bloodline, Sharmarke had been schoolmates and work colleagues with Anisa and Ara's late father, Abdulwahab.

Though they had been friends, unlike Anisa's father, Sharmarke was of a nationalistic mindset. Which meant he hadn't been a supporter of Abdulwahab's idea to expand his homegrown shipping business through a partnership with interested foreign parties from China to Turkey. The Indian Ocean had long held the interest of many international investors. If Nasser were in the business of import-export, he'd have considered international trade contracts and building new ports.

Yet there were some like Sharmarke who didn't see it that way. Who instead worried that inviting outsiders to a piece of the Somali coastline was a sure way to losing nationalistic independence. And Sharmarke was a powerful man, with money and connections he wasn't shy to use to further his political values and goals.

He hadn't ever asked, but Nasser often wondered how Sharmarke and Ara saw eye to eye, especially since Ara had taken up his father's legacy and actively sought to open their waters to a wider global market.

I can't imagine they do see eye to eye.

But Ara and Sharmarke weren't his concern. Anisa was. And she sat with her hands folded in her lap, her melancholy a living, breathing entity that shared the rickshaw ride with them. Without needing her to clarify, he could see the weight this strife with Ara dealt her. And for some reason, that inspired unfriendly thoughts from him toward Ara. Why was he making his sister suffer needlessly when one word of true acknowledgment from him could spell a world of peace for her?

Nasser clenched his fists and locked his jaw tighter as he silently questioned, *Why put her through this pain?*

Feeling the rickshaw slowing compelled him to speak while they were still alone together.

"Whatever you may think, your brother doesn't wish harm to befall you. Otherwise he wouldn't have hired me."

"We'll have to disagree on that," she said with a weary glance at him.

And with inconvenient timing, their rickshaw came to a standstill right behind his four-wheel drive. Their driver lowered the vehicle so they could exit safely. Anisa alighted and returned a wave to her friend Darya. The crew were gathered across the street, back where they started when they first entered Antsirabe.

Intent on finishing their conversation, Nasser descended from the rickshaw beside Anisa and gazed down at her growing frown.

"We disagree then. But never doubt that your welfare matters to me."

There. He'd made his sentiment known. Expecting her to leave now, Nasser waited for her to hurry off to Darya and the crew members loading back into their vehicles. He was even prepared for her to find room on the minibus and ride along with them rather than continue the final leg of their journey to their destination with him.

After what seemed like a moment of vacillation, she veered for his car. Dumbfounded, Nasser followed her jeans molded tightly to her swishing hips, his bemusement quickly devolving into a crackling whip of heat that lashed him out of the blue. And he didn't have to wonder what she would feel like, having held her curves himself not too long ago, his palms re-living the pleasant sensation of that too-brief contact and his body feverish from yearning for another chance to hold her.

No. He gave his head a good, solid shake to right his bro-ken concentration. Anisa was off-limits, for so many reasons he couldn't begin to number them.

Meeting her there, Nasser unlocked the car doors and joined her inside.

"I thought you would have gone with your coworkers," he remarked coolly, still unclear why she had chosen his com-pany again, like she had for lunch.

"It's still a possibility."

He scowled.

Her teasing smirk indicated that she saw his displeasure. "I might be persuaded to stay. Do I get to choose the music this time?" They'd listened to his songs from Antananarivo. It was a small price to pay to fulfill her request and appease her. But had she asked for more, Nasser admitted to himself that he would have been tempted to give Anisa whatever she asked of him, including his secrets.

He should be thankful it was only the music she desired for now…

For the second time in a day, Anisa awoke to Nasser's touch, only this time his face hovered close to hers.

He pulled back from the open passenger window once her eyes fully focused on him, the haze of slumber clearing from her vision.

"You asked me to wake you when we arrived."

"And we did?" Anisa yawned, covering her mouth and stretching her arms. She unfastened her seat belt and mum-bled her gratitude when he opened the car door for her. He was looking at her with that single-minded intensity again, and her skin prickled with goose bumps, a tantalizing shiver trembling over her limbs.

When Nasser didn't stop staring, she wiped at her face, fretting that there was eye goop from sleep crusted on her eyes and drool dried on her chin.

"Is there something on my face?" she blurted, her cheeks warming.

"Non."

"Then why are you looking at me like I've grown two heads?"

A look of understanding chased over his face before he turned from her.

Like he didn't realize he was staring...

Anisa didn't know what to make of that. To her it appeared as if his actions surprised even him—but that didn't seem possible, not when Nasser presented himself as a man in control of everything in his world, with his emotions under wrap.

Lucky for him, she soon forgot all about what she had witnessed in lieu of the natural beauty surrounding them.

"Oh! It's so beautiful," Anisa breathed, her awe racing out of her.

All the pictures of the Alley of the Baobabs hadn't done the place justice, for it was far more magical in person. The dark silhouettes of the baobab trees, their root-like branches blotting out the glittering stars winking awake in the sky, created a hauntingly beautiful portrait. She pulled her phone out, glad she'd recently treated herself to a hardware upgrade, and snapped some photos. Of the light leaching from the sky, of dusk sweeping over the long baobab-lined road, and then the lens of her phone camera trained on Nasser.

He stood as still as the tall, ancient trees rooted around them, a pensiveness in his side profile as he cast his eyes over the horizon, guarding against the troubles that might be lurking in the oncoming night.

The natural lighting worked well for him, and she couldn't resist taking a photo. She didn't have the flash on and managed to sneak the shot. Then another. She grabbed two more photos of him before he suddenly swiveled his head to her, his chiseled features emotionless and yet calling to her so that she nearly dropped her phone, her trembling hands lowering before she did.

"Did you take a picture of me?"

"I might have." She waited for him to ask her to delete it, and when he didn't, she offered, "I could send it to you. You looked good."

Nasser muttered something in French and then glanced away, his head tipping back and his eyes searching the skies.

"I didn't take you for a stargazer," she said, fascinated by this other side to him.

"I'm not. My brother was."

Stunned into silence by that small but significant reveal, Anisa's shock morphed into sadness when realization struck her.

Was. Rather than *is.*

He'd used the past tense. It only meant one thing: his brother was no longer with them.

Grief for him constricted her heart and had her eyes welling up. Nasser didn't even seem aware of what he'd told her, his focus on the stars. Concerned, she recognized that faraway look in his eyes more intimately than she wished she had. It was the look that preceded the spiral of emotions that sometimes followed whenever she thought of her lost parents. Nothing good ever came of it. And leaving him to be dragged deeper into his misery wasn't an option.

So she said the first thing that came to mind. "Earlier you asked me what I really want to do for a living."

When Nasser didn't look at her, she babbled, "A writer. I want to be a screenwriter. Tell stories that others want to bring to life on a big screen, or heck, even a theater's grand stage."

He angled his head down to her finally, his face unreadable but his eyes clearing of any lingering gloom.

Somewhere behind them, the general crew call sounded.

"I should go to work before they notice I'm missing," she said with a timid smile.

Nasser inclined his head.

Anisa took a few steps from him before whirling back. "Thank you."

"For?" he wondered hoarsely.

"For saving me." She hadn't given him his due gratitude yet, though she'd been meaning to. He had protected her when she needed it, not only from the motorbike, but from the despair that arose when Anisa had discussed her tense relationship with Ara. Nasser had made for a surprisingly good sounding board. Ironic, because he was determined to ignore the fact that she didn't *want* a bodyguard.

I might not want one...

But maybe, aside from all her complaining, *maybe* she could use one.

CHAPTER SIX

"IF WE'D WRAPPED a second later, I would have fallen over," Anisa griped to Darya the next morning, another early one. The only upside was that they'd filmed a sunrise in the Avenue of the Baobabs. Watching the starry sky dull and the nighttime fog lift as daybreak bathed the landscape was as much a pleasure as it had been to watch the sun set on that mystical corridor of baobab trees.

Yawning loudly and blinking away the tears of fatigue from her eyes, Anisa followed her crew to the minibus with the last of their set equipment. Their director and assistant director climbed into their four-by-four rental. She freed herself of her walkie-talkie last and then stretched, another powerful yawn raking through her body and curling her toes.

What she wouldn't give to find the closest bed so she could shut out the world for a few hours.

Her nose twitched. She lowered her arms from her stretch, straightening her blouse and sniffing the air. She turned and discovered Nasser holding out a paper cup to her, the aroma of strong black coffee wafting from the cup. It was a welcome scent after a series of early mornings and long workdays.

"Thank you," she moaned after that first sip transported her to nirvana.

A few more sips grounded her, and she had the sense to notice he also offered her a small plastic bag. The last time he'd sent her a bag, it was full of a tasty dinner she had shared with Darya.

She juggled her coffee and peeked into the bag, her eyes closing at the mouthwatering fried scent that teased her nose.

"The shopkeep called them *mokary*," Nasser told her.

"They look like tiny pancakes." She plucked one of the fried cakes from the bag and popped it into her mouth, chewing and delighting in the light sweetness coming from a creamy coconut flavoring.

They walked their makeshift breakfast to his car, where he showed her how to dip the delicate *mokary* into the bitter coffee and savor the robust fusion of textures, flavors and tastes. She might have been embarrassed to be moaning so much, but her hunger didn't have the sense to be humiliated. And it was hunger talking when she polished off the last *mokary*, looked into the empty bag sadly and reported, "There's no more left."

"We can get more when we head back into town," promised Nasser, starting his engine and gearing the car into Drive.

Anisa shook her head, her moan now full of dread. "Don't remind me. We'll barely have enough time to eat before we're back on the road again."

"Where are you all headed now?"

"Are you asking because you don't know, or because you want to confirm what you know already?" Anisa grinned when Nasser's gaze strayed from the road to regard her. "I'm only teasing. We're going to Nosy Be. It's supposed to be this island paradise, a real touristy spot. The pictures online looked heavenly…"

"That's far north," Nasser reported with one of his many frowns. "How is your crew planning to get up to Nosy Be?"

"Let me check our call sheet." She flipped through her phone for the all-important file. "The notes from the assistant director say that we're traveling up the west coast before we go back on the highway to Antananarivo again."

"The backroads up the west coast won't be safer."

"But we save an hour or two on the road," Anisa said, tapping her phone screen when she compared the routes on her map app. Then she snapped her head up. "How do you know the roads won't be safe?"

"The shopkeep who made the coffee and *mokary* explained as much. Some of these rural areas are unpoliced, and banditry is sometimes an issue."

Well, that proved what she suspected. He already knew what route they would be taking.

"I'm sure we'll be fine," she said.

He grunted something in French. It sounded like he replied, "We'll see."

Nasser used every second after they left L'Allée des Baobabs and stopped in at the small coastal town of Morondava once more to plan a safer route of travel for Anisa and her crew.

He made calls and got the ball rolling on the solution he'd formulated in that time. It included pulling the director and assistant director aside and making them an offer they couldn't refuse.

And once everyone was ready to go a couple hours later, Nasser listened in as the new plan—his plan—was announced.

He didn't even mind that the director and assistant director took credit when the crew and cast oohed and aahed their way through the announcement that they would be taking a private jet from Morondava Airport to Antananarivo before flying out from Tana to their island destination.

"Did you have something to do with this?" Anisa said with her hands poised on her hips once the rest of her crew was out of earshot on the tarmac. Then she kissed her teeth and dropped her hands. "Actually, don't tell me. I don't want to know." He followed her to his plane, smiling and greeting the pilot, copilot and two flight attendants at the base of the airstairs.

The tour of the plane cabin kept the cast and crew busy. Anisa joined in, but she kept glancing at him, looking away whenever their eyes clashed.

Eventually she claimed the seat beside him, making it easier for Nasser to watch over her. Anisa turned to face him, her elbow perched on the armrest between them, hand curled under her chin, an inquisitiveness furrowing her brow. "Tell me, what does a man do with so much space?"

"Mostly? Business meetings on the go. Rarely, we use them to transport clients out of…difficult situations."

"Hostage negotiations?"

His lips quirked at her imagination, even though it wasn't far from that really.

"Do you know how bad these big jets are for the environment?"

"I'm aware. Our company incorporates and employs environmentally conscious practices, and we partner with a company that specializes in sustainable aviation fuel. We also only use the plane in special cases."

"Of course you do," she said. "But do you really need glass room dividers—" she pointed to the divider separating a dining space "—the crystal chandeliers, a massive bed, and—is this real gold?" She rubbed her hand over the gold accent lining the buttery cream-colored leather of her armrest.

"I believe it is," Nasser murmured, pretending to be unaffected as her breath hitched and her fingers carefully grazed over the sleek gold touches. It reminded him of when he'd made his first million several years ago. The disbelief at having that much money to call his own had floored him. Now that he had it several times over, the novelty had long worn off, and yet he still counted his blessings every day. He was lucky—

Nasser wished he could say the same for his brother. Nuruddin's death seemed more than unfair. It sometimes felt like a mistake. He should have been taken, not Nuruddin.

Why did he die and I live? Not only had he lived, but he'd thrived. *Why me?*

He often posed that question to the universe, and he hadn't gotten an answer back yet. Wearying of those thoughts, he concentrated harder on Anisa and amused himself with her soft gasp of awe as she tipped her seat to lie back. He bit back a laugh when she sighed happily, closed her eyes and exclaimed, "Okay, I think I like this part the best."

A primal pride thumped in his chest in time with his heart. He'd put that blissful smile on her face.

And she put one on his when she cracked open an eye. "Don't get me wrong. I still think the jet is absurdly big."

"You should see your brother's yacht."

"His *what*?"

Nasser heard the bristling anger in her voice and knew he'd stuck his foot in his mouth. It wasn't often that he spoke without thinking, but now that it had happened, he saw the negative effect of it unfold on Anisa's lovely face. Shock and fury warred with hurt. The latter struck him the hardest, pained him the most.

You fool, he berated himself.

He had worked hard over the past couple days to get in her good graces, and in a few words he'd undone all that effort.

Anisa pushed the button to raise her seat, then glared at him. The power of her fierce stare demolished any excuses he could to evade her curiosity.

"Of *course* he has a yacht! Let me guess, it's a floating manor," she hissed.

Nasser hazarded a look back at her crewmates. As he'd

requested earlier, the flight attendants served freshly prepared snacks from the full kitchen to Nasser's guests before they completed the preflight checks. Though everyone seemed preoccupied, he would've preferred having his chat with Anisa someplace else. And he knew such a place.

"Come with me," he said low and bluntly. Not waiting for her response, Nasser drew himself to a stand and headed for the business lounge.

Behind a solid partition, the lounge was comprised of a long conference table that could comfortably seat twelve. A large, ultra-high-definition flat screen television floated behind the head of the table, and there was a built-in credenza for refreshments if business meetings stretched long.

The partition would give them some privacy from the chatter and laughter floating in from the main cabin area.

As Anisa stalked closer to him, Nasser could see what she was thinking, and so he cut ahead of her.

"I apologize for being so brusque, but I thought we'd be more comfortable here." He sensed the privacy was something they both could use right then.

"A yacht!" Anisa threw her hands up, her scoff loud and high and quaking with emotion. "I can't believe I'm finding out about it from…from you. No offense." She said the last part quickly, and with an extra pinch between her thin furrowed brows.

"None taken," he replied.

Anisa grabbed the back of one of the office chairs lined against the conference table, her fingers denting the dark leather. "I—I'm speechless, really. How could he?" She laughed hollowly. "Why am I even surprised? Did you know that I had no idea he'd gotten married two months ago?

"Yeah," she continued. "Far more shocking, right? My brother—my *only* sibling—gets married, and I'm learning of it from our Adeero Sharmarke. But that's because he wanted to let me know the good news that Ara had married his daughter, and we're technically family now."

Nasser clenched his fists in disbelief. How could Ara do that to her? Not speaking to her was one thing, but totally isolating a family member from such happy news was an unusual cruelty. He didn't need to know Anisa all that well to understand she didn't deserve such treatment.

After everything he'd heard, her angry display made sense. Naturally, Nasser expected for her to continue to vent. He certainly believed she was entitled to her bitter emotions.

But just as quickly as she'd gotten incensed, Anisa's fury vanished.

She pulled out one of the chairs at the conference table and dropped into it with a long-suffering sigh.

"I don't even know why I bother." Her shoulders slumped, and the last of the fire in her extinguished. Staring blankly in front of her, she said, "I'm not sure if Ara told you, but our parents died in a boating accident. Since their deaths, a lot in our lives has changed. I was young, and Ara stepped up to take care of me, even though he was only eighteen himself.

"Because of it, I keep thinking that he's my brother, and that I owe it to our parents to try." She paused, taking a breath before she added, "But it's hard to be kind and understanding when he keeps pushing me away and locking me out."

Anisa bowed her head and wrapped her arms around her middle. In the silence that followed, Nasser considered leaving her to her grief. But as he started moving, his feet carried him to her rather than away from her. Before he knew it, he had grabbed the chair beside her.

Looking at Anisa, he saw himself.

They'd both lost family members, and their trauma had affected their relationships with other family. Anisa with her brother, Nasser with his mother and father. And he'd just discovered another shared attribute: Anisa believed her parents to have been killed in a tragic accident, and similarly Nasser's parents didn't know the truth of how their eldest son died. They thought Nuruddin's death had been accidental and were only ever grateful that Nasser had survived the protest rally that took his brother's life.

He hadn't corrected his parents, sparing them the pain of the reality that Nuruddin had been murdered.

"Are you close with your family?" she asked and looked over at him.

The small, sad smile on her face gripped his heart more tightly than he was prepared for. Perhaps that was why he indulged her with a response when he often avoided talking about his family. "It's just my parents, and no, I'm not in contact with them as much I probably should be."

"Is it because of your brother?"

Nasser tensed every muscle, his confusion clearing quickly once he recalled that *he* had been the one to tell her about Nuruddin. Back in the Avenue of the Baobabs, he'd gazed up at the stars and had thought of how his brother had often loved pointing out the different constellations. Then Nasser had let it slip. Though he hadn't gone into detail and hadn't even told her Nuruddin's name, he'd spoken of his brother in the past tense.

And that was enough for her to piece together that Nuruddin wasn't alive.

If he weren't so worried about where their conversation was headed, he would have applauded her deductive reasoning.

"I'm being nosy, sorry," Anisa said. "Feel free to ignore me."

He should have taken her up on the offer, but instead his mouth opened, and Nasser did the last thing he expected. He answered her.

"My brother's death is a factor, yes. It was hard on my family." Far harder because Nuruddin shouldn't have died.

He wouldn't have if cold-blooded killers hadn't taken his life.

Beneath the conference table, Nasser balled his fists, and as he often did when he considered his brother's senseless death, he quietly swore that he'd avenge Nuruddin.

Somehow, some way—

And with Ara's help, he would find those responsible of Nuruddin's murder and mete out justice.

Nasser wasn't sure how long he was gripped by his feverish thirst for vengeance, only that by the time he shook off his vindictive line of thinking, Anisa was on her feet and looking down at him, her eyes large and filled with sorrow for them both.

"I understand how you feel far better than I wish I did," she whispered.

They seemed to have something else in common, because he wished for the exact same thing.

Anisa wouldn't have ever thought depression was contagious, but it had to be. How else could she explain why Nasser looked as unhappy as she felt through the duration of their flight aboard his private jet?

As miserable as she was, she wouldn't have ever vented to him about Ara if she'd known that he'd end up suffering for it too.

I reminded him of his brother, so why wouldn't he be unhappy?

She should have known not to ask about his family, especially since she understood what it felt like to lose someone.

The worst part was that airing out her turmoil hadn't turned her mood for the better.

And now, on top of her misery, guilt lumped in her throat, making every breath harder.

It hadn't gotten easier when they landed in Nosy Be and Nasser arranged a transport from the island airport to a five-star luxury resort. He didn't take credit for it either, but she knew it was him, and it only made her heart sting that much more from the humiliation.

Here he was, treating them so kindly, and all she'd done was dump her problems onto him.

He must now be wishing that he never took me on as a job.

She hoped that the change in scenery would uplift her spirits, but the emerald-green waters, blue skies and endless white beaches pinged off the cloud of doom that trailed her.

Working was the last thing she wanted to do, but once the crew were settled, filming resumed on a new schedule shortly after.

As trying as her job could be, Anisa did like the creative energy on set and the sense of accomplishment at the end of a long workday. It was the upside to what she did. But today she couldn't even rely on that. After dragging herself through work, she dropped into her bed at the end of the day, which at that point was past midnight, and closed her eyes and nodded off.

It felt like only a few seconds later when Anisa's eyes ripped open, her ears flooded by the harsh, grating sound of heavy breathing. Her own, she realized in surprise. She pushed to a sitting position, the collar of her blouse drenched in sweat and the comforter rumpled beneath her. The air-conditioning was off. It explained why she was soaked, but she couldn't as easily settle the matter of her thundering heart.

She hadn't had a night terror in years.

And since she was out of practice, Anisa drew a blank on how to handle her panicked state. Her narrowed gaze darted around her darkened resort room, and her skin itched with her sudden unease. It was the scene of her nightmare. But was it her imagination, or did it seem like the space was getting smaller?

She gulped and scurried out of bed.

Before the walls could fully close on her, Anisa fled from her room—*and* narrowly avoided colliding with Nasser. She needn't have asked what he was doing outside her room.

Too bad he can't protect me from bad dreams.

He took one look at her and stepped aside, letting her pass without a word but falling in behind her.

With Nasser as her shadow, Anisa trudged through quiet, well-lit corridors and across the many wooden bridges that connected the different buildings comprising the expansive resort. They didn't run into anyone except a couple of staff members who gave them polite smiles on passing.

Walking over one of those bridges, she slowed and faced the cool ocean breeze wafting from the beach and the silver moon hanging in the sky.

Even in the dark, Nosy Be was idyllic.

Closing her eyes, she tipped her overheated face to the air and breathed slowly. Though the sweat slicking her body and dampening her hair under her hijab was cooling, Anisa still buzzed from the adrenaline rush she hadn't asked for. Her hands seemed to have been hit worst, the trembling in them forcing her to grip the wood railing of the bridge to ground herself.

"Before you ask, it was only a nightmare." She looked over at him, confirming that he was staring at her intently.

"Is that common?" he asked.

Those were the first words they'd traded since their last conversation on his plane. Riddled by guilt for making him think of his deceased brother, Anisa had avoided Nasser, mostly because she didn't know what to say to him.

Unable to evade him now, she nodded slowly and said,

"Ever since my parents' death, I've had some variant of a similar dream. But I haven't had it in a while. The only thing that helped back then was teaching myself to dream lucidly. That is, control my dreams."

"Does controlling your dreams no longer help?"

"It always used to. But this…this dream was different."

"How so?"

She flattened her palms against the wood railing. "I couldn't wake up. No matter what I did, I was just stuck in there." Nasser hadn't asked her to go into detail, but now that she was talking, she couldn't stop replaying the vivid sensations the dream imprinted on her. "I'm floating on my back in the middle of the ocean, the sun on my face, and the weightlessness is so relaxing I almost never want to leave. Someone keeps calling my name. Over and over, like they're warning me."

Even now she could hear the echo of her name in the recesses of her mind.

Shaking her head clearer, she continued, "The next thing I know, a motorboat's heading right for me, and I can't move a muscle. Even though my eyes are closed, I somehow know that the driver wants to run me over with the boat."

"Earlier you were telling me about your parents. Perhaps that's why you had the dream," Nasser suggested.

It was a sensible thought, but Anisa knew that wasn't why she was suddenly dreaming of boats.

"Actually, I… I was on the boat with my parents."

She looked up when the quiet had stretched on long enough. Nasser hadn't moved from where he stood facing her, his elbow perched on the wood railing. In the dim lighting, his eyes were as black as the ocean spread before them, but the ocean wasn't weighing what she'd just said, whereas Nasser seemed clearly to be processing her words.

Finally, after another lengthy pause, he said, "Ara did mention how your parents died. He never told me you were there."

"He doesn't like talking about it, and I think it's because he might have lost me too. But that could also just be my wishful thinking that he cares about me." She flashed a tremulous smile and looked away. "I wonder if it's because I'm closer to home than I've been in a long while. Maybe that explains why I'm dreaming of murderous boats and thinking of Ara and my parents more lately."

When a new quiet settled over them, Anisa didn't allow it to stretch as long as before.

"I did it again, didn't I?" she murmured with a grimace. She'd regretted piling her problems onto Nasser once, and now here she was repeating her mistake.

It's just easy to talk to him.

Shocking, really, considering that Anisa didn't want him hanging around. At least, she hadn't...

That's changed now, hasn't it?

Anisa had to admit that she wasn't opposed to his company any longer. Nasser certainly wasn't the person she'd imagined when they had first met. Sure, he still seemed to prefer controlling the situation, and he reminded her of Ara in that way—but unlike her brother, Nasser listened to her rather than shutting her down. He also stuck by her side even though she had tried to push him away. And *yes*, he might have just been doing his job, yet Anisa couldn't help appreciating his iron-willed commitment to protect her.

Which was why she had to tell him, "Listen. I get you're just trying to do your job, and I can't fault you for that. Even though I didn't ask for any of this, I think I owe you an apology. So, I'm sorry."

He sighed, his chest rising and falling from the force of it.

She looked up at him. "For what it's worth, I won't make these last couple days of your job more difficult."

Nasser's lips kicked up at the corners. He hadn't said much since he'd followed her, and Anisa didn't need him to, understanding him perfectly.

Still, he said, "For what it's worth, I appreciate it."

CHAPTER SEVEN

"THAT'S A WRAP!"

The call from the assistant director was met by a chorus of cheers, laughter and loud clapping. Anisa giggled when Darya hugged her and jumped up and down with her in place. They only stopped after Lucas joined them, throwing his arms around them both and interrupting their private celebration.

"Ew! Lucas, no," Darya laughed and pushed him back.

He conceded and stepped back but tossed up his hands. "What? Can't blame me for trying when I thought I saw room to squeeze in between you pretty women." He winked, laughingly dodging Darya's attempt to swat at him.

Anisa rolled her eyes at Lucas's stunt, but her celebratory mood couldn't be quashed.

After another two days in Nosy Be, two days that Anisa felt every hour of by the time she crawled under her bedcovers at the end of the workday, their crew and cast had officially wrapped filming. Which meant that in less than twenty-four hours, they would be flying out of Madagascar and heading for home in Canada.

Anisa expected to be happier about that news. She was not as elated as she imagined she should be.

And she wasn't the only one who noticed.

"It feels so good to be free!" Darya exclaimed with a stretch of her arms. She paused and pushed her face in closer to Anisa's. "Or…maybe not. Is there a reason you look like you'd rather be working another fourteen-hour shift?"

Anisa gave a snort at that. If there was one thing she wouldn't miss, it was the work hours that stretched from dawn until well past dusk.

"Seriously, what's up?" Darya took her by the arm and steered her away from the ruckus their jubilant crew members were making.

Everyone was chatting loudly and more freely as they deconstructed and cleared the area of lighting and sound equipment, and sets and props were packed and stored for their long journey home.

Anisa knew she and Darya should be helping, but now that her friend had noticed her mood, she couldn't think of anything else.

"It's not that I'm unhappy. I'm more than ready to go home." She was due a break before her next gig started, whatever that was and wherever it took her. "It's just that I feel *off*. Like my brain's too tired to fully comprehend that we're done."

Darya nodded sympathetically, only to look around Anisa and narrow her eyes.

"He wouldn't happen to be the problem, would he?"

Anisa glanced over her shoulder to see what she meant and noticed Nasser entering the area. He had stepped away near the end of shooting with a phone glued to his ear. It was the first time in a while that he'd been away from her side during her waking hours. Strangely, it had worried her a bit when he had walked out of sight. After his call stretched to half an hour, she didn't know what to think.

Grinning, Darya clucked. "I guess now we know what's been bothering you."

"I don't understand what you mean," Anisa said evasively. All the while, her face felt like she had placed it near a furnace. And her cheeks only grew hotter when Nasser's voice sounded from behind her.

"Bonjour."

His French greeting, rumbled in his smooth, deep timbre, raised the fine hairs on her arms and inspired a little skitter of thrill through her.

"Bonjour," she replied breathily. Anisa felt the silly smile on her face, but she was powerless to stop it. If Darya hadn't cleared her throat, she might have stood there basking in Nasser's undivided attention for the remainder of the day.

"Are you finished working?" Nasser asked.

"Yeah, we just filmed the last scene."

"Which means we have the whole day to ourselves," Darya added with a teasing nudge to Anisa from behind.

Darya's push brought Anisa that much closer to Nasser. So close she couldn't find air to breathe that wasn't perfumed by his aromatic cologne. Flustered, she tipped her head further back and stared helplessly up at him.

Unfazed by Darya's humor, he gave her friend the curtest of nods. "Then if you don't mind, would you join me for lunch?"

She got the feeling from the way Nasser asked and looked at her—*and only her*—that the invitation had initially been meant for her alone. Yet the fact that he didn't wish Darya to feel left out had raised his esteem that much higher for her.

Anisa didn't get the chance to reply immediately. Lucas had come jogging back. Before she and Darya could go on the defensive, he held up his hands to show he had none of his usual lascivious intent. "Easy. I was just wondering if you two are down to go out with everyone and properly celebrate."

"Why not?" Darya didn't even push Lucas off when he dropped his arm over her shoulders with a wide grin.

"Are you in, Anisa?" he asked her, pinning her with a puppy dog look. "It won't feel the same if you're not there."

Anisa stood frozen in indecision. She looked forward to the gatherings at the end of a wrap. But she was certain this time she wasn't bound for their film wrap party but something else.

Someone else, she thought, looking at Nasser.

"Earth to Anisa—are you in there?" Lucas called.

Anisa startled back when Lucas then reached between her and Nasser and snapped his fingers in front of her face.

Nasser shot out his hand and ensnared Lucas's wrist. Everything after that happened in a blur, Nasser's movements so fast and fluid that Anisa blinked in shock by the end. One second Lucas had been snapping his fingers to grab her attention. The next, Nasser had him subdued with his arm pinned in a painful position behind his back.

"Hey, man, let go!" Lucas tried to shake Nasser off him, whining in pain when he couldn't free himself.

Nasser responded by raising Lucas's wrist higher up between his shoulder blades.

That had Lucas shouting for mercy.

"Mind your behavior," Nasser warned before releasing him.

Lucas cradled his arm and, giving Nasser a wide berth, grumbled, "That wasn't cool."

"Let's go." Darya hauled him off, careful to pull the arm that hadn't been pinned by Nasser.

Anisa watched them go, feeling awful for Lucas, but also curious about where Nasser learned self-defensive tactics. "Lucas can be goofy, but he's harmless."

"If he were truly harmless, he wouldn't have touched you."

"But he didn't," she retorted, baffled.

Nasser seemed to believe he had though. A tic in his lower jaw revealed as much. "Before, in Antananarivo, he put his arm around you."

Anisa racked her brain for the memory, and when it

clicked, she laughed. "Lake Anosy! I forgot he did that. Like I said, he's handsy but harmless."

Nasser's face hardened to her laughter.

Seeing that he didn't appreciate her humor leeched at her cheery spirits. Though she hadn't wanted to think it, a niggling doubt hatched in her mind. It came with sirens and warning bells, and it cautioned that he wanted to control her. Why else was he acting with such overprotectiveness? It would make sense that her brother would hire a man to protect her who thought like him.

He's no different than Ara, the doubt hissed at her. *He's just trying to find a way to control you.*

Then another part of her cried, *But he saved me! Listened to me! He cares...and how could someone who cares like that want to hurt me by controlling me?*

Anisa didn't know what to think.

"You do believe me when I say that Lucas means me no harm. And that if he did, *if* he really was bothering me, I could handle it myself."

Nasser palmed the lower half of his face, his eyes inscrutable even in the bright light of day.

"Because if you don't, then I think it might be better if you just leave now."

His eyes briefly widened before his brows swooped down and his facial expression intensified in broodiness. For a second, she really thought he would leave, but then he flared his nostrils and gave her a jerky nod.

Quietly she breathed easier, masking just how invested she'd been in him responding favorably.

And she hadn't expected any more from him, happy enough that he hadn't tried to diminish her in an argument. So it was to her profound astonishment that he looked her in the eye and apologized.

"I shouldn't have interfered with your…coworker. It won't happen again."

"That's fine," she said quickly and meekly, surprised that he'd done that much. And she'd thought he was like her brother?

Pfft. Ara would never *apologize to me.*

It was sad, but considering her brother rarely conceded that he was wrong, she was inclined to believe it to be true.

But Nasser was different.

Her heart thumping a lot faster now and her smile brightening, Anisa floated on a cloud once more, her happiness restored.

Nasser didn't see any of the changes in her. He nudged that steely chin of his at her boisterous coworkers and said, "You're free to go with your friends. I won't take offense if you do."

"I know that."

But when she didn't move, she figured they both understood what her choice was.

"Are you certain?" Nasser asked.

Was she? She could go with her friends, and she didn't doubt that she would like spending the day with them, but Anisa knew in her heart she wouldn't fully be present. The last thing she dreamed of doing was lowering everyone else's joyous mood.

So, with a certainty that slotted in perfectly with her desires, she bobbed her head. "I'm positive."

It wasn't the first time Anisa picked Nasser over her friends. And yet every time, a sense of wonder overcame him.

She chose me.

Not because she had been compelled to, but of her own volition.

He didn't know what he'd done to deserve her attention.

Sure, Nasser had wanted this very outcome. Without a doubt it simplified his job of guarding her, but when all was said and done, he hadn't cared about that as much as he thought he did. Because it was the furthest thing from his mind after she had accepted his lunch invitation.

And it was even further when they finished their meal and Nasser suggested, "There's a lemur park close by, if you would like to walk off the food."

"Are you saying I overate?" she quipped.

Nasser began shaking his head before stopping at the sight of Anisa's mischievous smile. A chuckle burst out of him, low and rumbling, catching him by surprise.

"You should laugh more," she said softly.

His humor ebbed when Anisa's stare captivated him into silence.

She really is a vision.

It was not the first time her beauty bewitched him, and he figured between now and when she boarded her flight for her home tomorrow, it wouldn't be the last.

Rather than fight it, he basked in her loveliness. The sunlight painted a red flush over her beautiful brown skin, added a sparkle to her glossy lips, and forced her eyes to become more squinty from the brightness of the world as she tilted her head up to him. But in the light of day, she looked ready to take on the world in her blush-pink hijab, long-sleeved untucked blouse with an eyelet collar, and high-rise jeans. He hadn't seen her wearing jewelry yet, but today she had on a pair of rose-shaped earrings, the pink in the simple accessory pairing with her headscarf.

She looked good in anything, but there was something in that moment, with her gazing up at him, a soft smile that was meant for him lighting up her face and making his heart do somersaults in his chest. Nasser knew he wouldn't forget it for as long as he lived.

I won't forget her.

It was a dangerous thought, considering she would be leaving soon and he had her brother to answer to. Besides, he had no interest in a relationship and wouldn't curse her with one with him.

They weren't destined for anything more.

And it's better that way.

After Anisa stopped by her room in the resort for a baseball cap and a water bottle, they struck out for their afternoon adventure. The lemur park was a short taxi drive away.

Nasser hadn't planned for it, so he didn't have a rental car prepared as he had on the mainland, but Anisa hadn't minded the canary-yellow tuk-tuk that ferried them to the park. She happily sat through the ride, her eyes glued to the natural landscape of the island and the small, quaint villages they passed through on the quick drive to their destination.

Like everything about this job and even Anisa herself, the trek through the jungle-like park was an experience carved in his long-term memory bank. Mostly because he'd stepped on animal leavings several times, and with thousand-dollar sneakers, no less. He could already envision himself scrubbing the soles, and it wasn't an image he relished.

But Anisa's little cries of joy made up for his despair.

She thrilled at the sight of the lemurs leaping from the tree branches. Once she discovered that the park allowed guests to feed ripened bananas to the overly friendly lemurs, she stood by a low-hanging branch and held a banana over her shoulder, her eyes rounding in delight when a lemur alighted on her shoulder. Anisa giggled as the nimble, long-tailed creature nibbled the piece of banana from her fingertips. No sooner had she finished than she begged him to try.

That was how Nasser ended up with a lemur on him. He had to admit, he could see the appeal when the lemur dug its five-fingered paws into his shoulder, and once it found a good place to perch, it shoved its small, dark face with large round eyes into Nasser's. As he fed the animal, Nasser felt his worries disappear.

An inner peace settled over him for a while, and he embraced it all too readily.

He might have stayed in that mental state for a while longer, but he looked over at Anisa just as she snapped a photo of him with her phone, the flash temporarily blinding him sending the lemur leaping off him and back safely on the tree branch he stood below.

But not before a wetness on his shoulder became apparent. In horror, Nasser realized he didn't only have crap staining his shoes anymore.

"I'm sorry!"

Anisa dabbed a napkin at the stain on his shoulder. She rubbed harder, discouraged when her efforts only made the stain that much bigger. A noise of frustration rose up from the back of her throat, and he must have heard it, because he gently grasped her wrist and drew it down from his big, hard shoulder.

He gave her a squeeze and stilled her attempt to salvage his shirt.

Not for the first time, she apologized profusely.

Nasser shook his head. "It's not your fault. I should have known better."

"But I was the one that pushed you to feed the lemur."

"I didn't refuse, did I?" When she tried to argue, he stood, offered his hand and helped her to her feet. "Had I not wanted to do it, I would've said no. No one holds the blame but me." With a final squeeze of her hand, he released her and found a trash can to dump the soiled napkins in.

Even though his logic was sound, Anisa carried her guilt with her until they came across the park's gift shop and an idea struck her.

A few minutes later, she passed him a plastic bag. In it was a forest-green T-shirt with a large print of the island of Nosy Be.

"It's not much, but I couldn't just let you walk around like that."

Nasser studied the shirt with a curious look. She could have called it gratitude, but his face returned to its impassive state as he left her to find a restroom to change in. She waited for him on pins and needles, worried that she might have chosen the wrong size shirt.

When he finally returned, Anisa almost missed sight of him as he walked right up to her. The shirt molded to his chest and arms perfectly.

Too perfectly.

She was ogling him openly, knew it and was helpless to stop herself.

He raised a brow. "Have I worn it the wrong way?"

Shaking her head, Anisa licked her dry lips and willed her heart rate to slow its wildly drumming tempo.

"I think…"

I think my crush on you is becoming an issue.

"I could use a refreshment."

Several minutes later, with cool lemonade in hand, Anisa and Nasser were strolling down one of the footpaths of the lemur reserve and outdoor park. She was still having a hard time regulating her body temperature around him, but Anisa wasn't feeling as feverish as she had been earlier. And even though silence hung over them, it was peaceful for once.

She sighed happily, closing her eyes and absorbing her surroundings. It was just the thing she needed after finishing up with work. Just the moment to clear her head of Ara, their lack of a relationship, her worry for him…

And Nasser.

Suddenly, the distinct sound of ice being crushed rose above the noise of the small park animals skittering through the thick green tropical foliage and the chatter of tourists milling about.

Anisa opened her eyes and smiled. "Are you munching on an ice cube?"

He stopped chewing the instant she asked, appearing adorably abashed.

"Old habit," he mumbled once he swallowed and cleared his mouth of the evidence.

"Darya chews on ice, too. She usually does it when she's nervous." Anisa was only teasing when she asked, "You're not nervous, are you?"

"Not nervous. Confused."

She hadn't expected his response and wasn't prepared when he stared down at her with an intensity that left her quietly breathless.

"Why did you choose to come with me and not go along with your friends?"

Anisa shook her head slowly with a shrug. "Truthfully? I don't know. But I guess you looked like you could use the excitement of company more."

It was Nasser's turn to be surprised.

"You don't look like the type that has fun," she explained, chuckling. "I mean, I get that you're working right now, guarding me and all, but how do you unwind after work?"

His brow creased. "My career choice doesn't spare much room for 'fun,' not when my clients are typically at the most vulnerable points of their lives."

Undaunted by his change of expression, Anisa said, "Okay, I'll give you that. And yet you've only proven my point that you could use some more downtime." She spied a bench up ahead on their path and steered him to it. Then, dropping to the seat, she patted the space beside her. "A little R & R never hurt anyone."

"R & R?"

She smiled. "Rest and relaxation."

"I see. And what exactly do you do for…downtime?"

Smiling more sheepishly, she admitted, "I try to squeeze in some rest between jobs, but sometimes it doesn't always work. Lately I've been picking up more gigs to make ends meet, since rent isn't going to pay itself." She frowned then, thinking about what she'd rather be doing for a living, her screenwriting, but knowing that it wasn't paying her bills right now. "I'll probably take a few days off after I fly out tomorrow, let the jet lag run its course, and then hop back into another job. Only maybe this time it won't be a sad romance. I don't think I could handle another tear-jerker."

"Is that what you and your crew were filming? A romance?"

"Yeah," she said. "Two star-crossed lovers, one of them dying, and the other one going through a contentious divorce, fated to reunite on a tour of Madagascar. At least that's the short, logline version."

"Are those the kind of stories you want to write?"

"Maybe one day, but it'd have to be less tragic. Who wants to cry when they're watching people fall in love?" Anisa blew a long sigh. "Until then, PA gigs are all I got."

"So what you're saying is that you could use this R & R too," he drawled.

Anisa laughed and swatted his arm—or she aimed to, missing and landing on his chest instead. Her laughter cut off abruptly on a breathy hitch, her eyes widening and jaw slackening. Time seemed to slow as Nasser looked down to her hand lying flat and unmoving against his pec. He raised his head just as unhurriedly, his gaze finding hers, and his unaffected expression making it hard for her to tell what he was thinking. Despite that, desire unspooled anew in her, its tendrils winding around her every nerve, fiber, muscle, and bone, before finally ensnaring her heart.

Pulling back as though she'd scalded her palm, she rubbed her hands together and, in a hurry to deflect from her social gaffe, stammered, "Wh-what were we talking about?"

"Having fun," he said, his voice low and deliciously gruff.

"Right," she croaked nervously. *"Fun."*

I'm soft for her.

In and of itself, that revelation was innocuous. And unless he chose to pursue it, *pursue her*, his attraction for her and any feelings of attachment would pose no problem for them. He was optimistic that he could control himself. But that optimism faltered when she stopped to pull her shoes and socks off, bared her slim brown ankles and wriggled cute toes before she treaded the beach barefoot. Nasser pulled a long, audible swallow, the sweat on his brow having less to do with the heat wafting off the beach sands.

Anisa drew her baseball cap off her head to fan her face. Her hijab still covered her hair, but now he could see her face more clearly, see the way her eyes slanted up at him coyly.

"Where did you learn what you did to Lucas?" She pretzeled her arms in a crude mime of how he'd subdued her handsy coworker.

"The army." He replied without thinking, her beautiful face the only thing he could focus on until he heard himself speak. He watched the way her eyes rounded and her lips parted with her surprise.

"You were in the military."

"Years ago, yes."

Nasser didn't like to speak of it, mostly because it made him think of what he'd done to end up an instrument of the army.

"So, why the military?"

Nasser could tell her the truth: he'd been given an ultimatum to rot in jail for crimes he was being accused of perpetrating, or save himself and serve the government that was trying to silence him.

And this only after he had been locked up for one horrendously long week and given a taste of criminal sanction.

His choice after that was obvious. Not only hadn't he wanted to spend another second in that overcrowded cell with *real* convicts who had committed *real* crimes, but for his parents' sake, he wished to spare them the humiliation on top of the sorrow of losing Nuruddin. They'd lost one son; Nasser hadn't wanted them to mourn another.

But most of all, he'd been a scared young boy, barely fifteen and freshly grieving his brother's murder.

When the timeline flashed in front of him, he gritted his teeth and abandoned telling her the whole truth.

What would it serve to reopen old wounds?

"I joined the military for my family." Spying Anisa's brows fly up in response, he explained, "My older brother had been in the military, and he was an outstanding officer." Nuruddin had been young, bright, and eager to serve his country. "He loved what he did, and he was studying to be a politician someday."

"I'm guessing you two were close," Anisa said, her kind voice in one way soothing the pain in his heart that arose whenever he mentioned his brother, but in another way, her sweetness made it all the harder because he didn't want her pity.

"We were very close." He aimed his stare ahead, at the point where the alien green jungle of the island bordered the white smoothness of its shore. Risking any chance of seeing the all-too-familiar look of distress on Anisa was not something he wanted to do, not when he knew it would unlock the emotions restlessly rattling within him. Free them for the first time in years—

And not since Nuruddin's death had he cried. He had no idea what chaos his long-bottled-up feelings would unleash. So he thought better of looking at her while he continued, for both their sakes.

"After he died, I decided to go into the military. My brother's salary wouldn't be discontinued, and I could help my parents.

"It wasn't easy, but my time there brought its lessons and growth, and I'm not sure if I would change my experience," he lied.

His military life had been one long tirade of verbal abuse from his superiors and grueling training regimes. While honing his body and polishing his war skills, they'd also beaten out any emotional vulnerability. He'd quickly learned sharing his thoughts and feelings was the surest way to punishment and gave him the furthest chance of surviving his ordeal.

And yet, though his time in the military hadn't been kinder than prison, Nasser had more freedom than he would have from behind prison bars. More importantly, without his military background, he wouldn't have discovered the private security sector.

"After nearly a decade in the military, I was discharged honorably and found work in private security. I loved the job, and eventually realized I could begin my own company doing the same work. That was six years ago," he said with a small smile full of self-pride. He'd been young when he became his own boss and when, for the first time in his life, he felt in control of his own destiny.

"I'm glad something good came of it then, but I'm still sorry for your personal loss."

Anisa's kindness nearly pried the truth from him. He pressed his lips together, forcing his secrets back in. Aside from founding his company, nothing truly good had happened to him since Nuruddin passed away. Losing his brother upended Nasser's whole life. Before Nuruddin's death, he used to laugh freely, voice his opinions and talk of his emotions, but like his brother, that was taken from him.

Gleaming fiery gold above the calm ocean waters, the sun dipped lower toward the horizon, the sky changing from clearest blue to vibrant pinks and purples.

They grabbed another tuk-tuk back into town, where Anisa answered an alert from her phone and reported that her coworkers were at a local jazz festival. The festivities weren't hard to spot when they poured from the homes and buildings into the town streets. People were dancing to the live music, families strolled among the many vendors displaying their wares, and couples held fast onto each other through over-exuberant crowds.

Nasser found the noise in Nosy Be to be peaceful, and just the balm he needed to reset his restless heart and mind.

"Darya messaged that they were over by the main stage indoors." Anisa looked up from her phone and around, her face scrunching in puzzlement. "But I don't see any directions."

The mention of her friends wasn't the most appealing thought after a day greedily spent with her alone, but Nasser helped her by asking a friendly-faced shopkeeper for the way to the main event. Once he had what he needed, he purchased an item in gratitude and relayed what was said to Anisa. Then they were off in search of her coworkers.

"What did you buy?" Anisa wondered as they were walking.

"Something that was needed."

Aside from casting him the most curious of looks, Anisa quietly let his cryptic response stand.

The smile playing at his lips froze as the loudest crack erupted from the streets somewhere behind them. The startling noise rose above the din of the crowds and awakened his adrenaline. Running purely in fight-or-flight mode, Nasser herded Anisa down a narrow alley. There, sandwiched by two squat buildings, he secured her against him, his back caging her behind him, his body between her and whatever danger was close by.

Nasser slowed his breathing, knowing that he couldn't lose his head when the muscles in his arms and legs were taut for action. The feel of her hand latching onto the back of his gift shop T-shirt reminded him that Anisa was relying on him. Even though she'd been fighting this protection detail from the start, her fear was palpable now.

"What's wrong?" she asked hoarsely, her nails pinching at his flesh as the thin material of his shirt yielded to her powerful, fear-induced grip.

"I'm not sure," he reported back, but he wasn't going to stand there and wait for any threat to find them first.

Peeking out of the alley, Nasser faced a scene of normalcy. People were chatting and laughing, and some were still dancing in the streets to the bumping beats of jazz strumming out of stereos. He relaxed once there weren't other signs of peril.

A group of gangly-limbed teenagers streaked past, one of the kids holding a string of firecrackers.

"A firecracker," she breathed, her eyes rolling back in relief and her hand falling away from his shirt. "I thought..."

She didn't need to finish what she was saying. Because he had been thinking the exact same thing.

As relieved as he was that it was merely firecrackers that raised the alarm, he was embarrassed for overreacting and frightening her for no reason.

"I should have figured it was fireworks," he grumbled down at her.

"Festivals and fireworks do go hand in hand," she agreed softly before angling her head back to rest on the stone wall behind her. Trapped between him and that wall at her back, Anisa had nowhere to go, unless she sidled away from him. Judging by the way she leaned back, she was in no hurry to leave.

Not even when a giggling young man and woman, their arms wrapped around each other, lips locked passionately, tumbled into the mouth of the alley. Sensing them, they came up for air and stopped a few feet shy of them. They then laughed as if they thought it the funniest coincidence that another couple would have considered the alley for the same purposes.

The young lovey-dovey couple scurried away together after that, vanishing as quickly as they had come.

Their precarious position dawned on Nasser then.

He only imagined what it must have appeared they were doing. With Anisa looking up at him, her lips soft and glistening, her skin dewy from their action-packed day, and her body so close to his that he could see the pulse at the base of her neck. And with him leaning as close to her as possible without actually touching her, his arms held tensely at his sides and thumbs pressed to the seams of his pants as though he were standing at attention for an army drill. It was the only thing he could do to stop himself from touching her. Cupping her cheek and holding her head still for when he claimed her sweet-looking mouth.

A kiss.

He wanted it so desperately that his muscles strained and his body vibrated from denying himself.

And what trouble could one little buss on the mouth cause them?

Besides everything?

Nasser pressed a hand against the wall by her head. Using his other hand, he cradled her chin with his thumb and forefinger and turned her face up to him even more.

"Anisa."

He said her name with low, guttural intent. If he didn't have the power to stop himself, he needed her to do it. Because right then, he didn't care that she was forbidden to him, or that her brother might do him serious damage for touching her, and he wasn't of the mind to consider how she might misconstrue his actions. All that mattered to him was satisfying this driving, damning need for her.

Stop me, he begged her silently.

He nearly roared in frustration when she didn't. "Nasser," she keened, her back arching up off the wall, the space between their bodies close to sealed.

His brain warned that they shouldn't, but his heart…?

His heart was about ready to fly out of his chest and into her hands, where it would be putty for her to mold into whatever shape she deemed fit.

This was going to happen.

He would throw caution away and kiss her, hard and fast—or possibly soft and slow. He only knew he required it, like he needed the next breath of air.

"Yes," Anisa breathed as his head swooped down, their faces pushing in tantalizingly closer.

His phone ringing saved them both from what would certainly have been a grave slip of judgment.

The caller identified himself as Daniel, the team lead of the security personnel he'd tasked to work on Ara's shipping business. Since Ara first hired the services of Nasser's company ten months ago, Daniel and his capable team had been on the ground at Ara's headquarters in self-declared Somaliland's capital, Hargeisa, and were responsible for updating cyber and physical security, among other things like breach prevention and security training for Ara's staff.

Daniel's call was the last thing he expected, though.

They'd primarily communicated via email, aside from their brief quarterly updates via teleconference. And those calls didn't involve just him and Daniel but the whole company, his board of directors included.

"What is it?" Nasser cut to the chase, his eyes never moving off Anisa.

Daniel didn't prolong the suspense. "It's Mr. Abdullahi—Ara, sir. He's missing."

CHAPTER EIGHT

No! ANISA WANTED to cry out when Nasser hadn't ignored his ringing phone.

She dug her nails into her palms to stop herself from reaching for him. Her body coursed with desire, her chest heaving with her yearning, her every thought replaying the delicious seconds before Nasser was pulled from her. And every second he had the phone glued to his ear was a second more that she burned uselessly for what could have been between them.

But when his searing looks turned to ice, Anisa sensed something was wrong.

Seriously so. What else could explain the steely set to Nasser's jaw? His face was void of emotion, but his hands were clenched and his movements sharp and jerky, his voice curt with the caller.

It sounded as if he knew whoever it was. From the brusque manner of his speech, she would guess that it was someone who worked for him.

She relaxed at the thought that it was a work-related call. He'd told her about his company. Running a business couldn't be easy, and his attention must be in demand. And it wouldn't be the first time that day he had answered a call. He had been on his phone earlier, while she'd been doing her own work with her film crew. It was possible that the two calls were related to the same issue.

Yeah, that's it. Just a work call. Nothing more.

She was further reassured when Nasser said, "And you've begun protocol measures for this? Good. Yes, keep me updated."

Expecting him to come closer to her, even take her in his arms this time and resume what they'd begun, Anisa was disappointed by his retreat to the alley's opening.

"We're heading back to the resort."

The last lingering threads of her longing sloughed off at his command.

"No," she refused, confused and irritated. "We're supposed to meet with my coworkers. Darya is waiting for me."

"Message her to meet you at the resort."

"Why are you in a rush to head back?" She didn't voice her suspicion any more than that, not wanting to feed the anxiety now scratching and clawing around her insides.

His dreadful scowl wasn't helping allay her unease.

"I will answer your questions in your room at the resort. It would be far more appropriate, trust me."

"*Trust* you?" She stepped closer to him, her heart jackhammering in her chest. "How can I trust you when all you do is give me orders and expect me to jump? Besides, trust is a two-way street, and you've given me no reason to believe that you'll ever answer any of my questions."

In a gravelly voice, he grumbled, *"Ah vraiment,"* and she didn't need translation because it sounded like he sarcastically challenged what she'd accused him of.

But what set her off was the way he swiped a hand down his face and heaved a sigh replete with exasperation. Like she was a chore he was ready to be rid of at last. Gawking at him, Anisa couldn't believe he was the same person who'd just had her pinned to an alley wall, ready to ravish her seconds before he took the call that had totally shut him down.

She didn't recognize him.

What hurt most was that she'd thought they were getting

closer. Felt the signs of mutual interest and attraction from him. After all, he had told her about his brother and his background in the military, and weren't they sure signs that he was opening up to her and letting her in?

I don't think he ever intended to let me in.

"Anisa, please." The fear that was circling her like sharks in chum-infested waters tightened at the plea softening his voice. She might have weakened had he not stepped closer a moment later and said, "This is not the place and time to fight me when all I'm trying to do is protect you."

Freshly incensed, Anisa raised her chin and huffed, "First, I *never* asked for your protection. And, as you already know, I'm not going anywhere. Not until you explain why you're acting so weird suddenly."

Nasser leveled one of his intense stares on her, but other than the usual fluttering in her belly, she was impervious to it. Whether he finally realized it had no effect, or that she wouldn't be budged on this, he sighed heavily again and dipped his chin passively.

"Very well. I would have preferred to do this elsewhere."

"Noted," she rejoined, her sarcasm thick. She normally wouldn't have been so petty, but Anisa couldn't forget how quickly he'd gone from hot to cold on her—or how easily he'd believed she would jump to his command.

"I just spoke with my team lead, who's been stationed with your brother's company in Hargeisa."

So it was exactly what she suspected: Nasser had taken a work call. Yet Anisa wasn't following what her brother had to do with it. She nodded for him to continue.

"He's been working closely with Ara."

Anisa muttered, "I'm not surprised. Ara likes having everything done his way." Her brother wouldn't trust anyone's work unless he was double-if not *triple*-checking the process and results himself.

"He and I are alike in that way, yes."

Yes. Yes, you two are.

Anisa snapped, "Just tell me what you're not saying."

"Ara's missing."

Somewhere close to the alley, Anisa heard the familiar popping of firecrackers go off once more, followed by an eruption of applause and laughter, but the noise might as well have come down a long tunnel at her over the sudden shrill ringing in her ears.

"What do you mean he's missing?" she asked on a croak, her mouth running dry, her head spinning with a flurry of questions.

"It seems your brother has been involved in an attack, but it's too early to tell whether he was the intended target."

"Attack?" she gasped.

"From what I understand, your brother hadn't informed my team that he'd be traveling to Mogadishu. A car bomb detonated outside the hotel he was staying at, and he hasn't been counted among the injured living. Or the dead."

The dead.

Those words circled through Anisa's mind until she shook her head in bewilderment. "A bomb? In Mogadishu? I don't understand. Why was he so far south?"

"That's what I intend to find out." But not even Nasser's determined tone and firm expression alleviated her distress at the terrible news.

"He's really missing?" Anisa whispered, her voice breaking. At Nasser's solemn nod, a streak of hot bile surged a fiery trail from her chest up her esophagus and flooded her mouth. She cupped her mouth and gagged, slapping a hand on the cool stone wall of the building to ground her unsteady legs. Squeezing her eyes shut, she cried.

She couldn't wrap her mind around the fact that her brother—the *only* family she had left—was missing. She

hadn't spoken to Ara in years, and for what? A childish dis-
agreement.

Allah, please! Don't let him leave me alone.

Her breaths dragged raggedly from her lungs now, like
she was drowning.

I know what that's like.

Closing her eyes tighter and biting her lip, she tumbled
headfirst into a vision of a crying little girl wading deeper
into the ocean, fighting the tide to get to something she
wanted so desperately that her body propelled her against
the tallest of white waves the ocean could throw at her. Anisa
sobbed as she realized she was the little girl, limbs thrash-
ing in the waters, her head dipping under the surface and
her lungs filling up with the ocean. She'd never thought she
would feel like she was drowning again, but here she was.

Sinking.

Slipping under.

Unable to keep her head above water.

Only now it's not the ocean that's killing me...

It was the reality she might lose her brother that was slowly
suffocating her.

The only thing that saved her from going completely under
was the recognizable scent of Nasser, his body heat in front
of her and his voice calling her back.

"Look at me, Anisa," he urged, panic underlying his voice.

Pitiful whimpering sounded from somewhere in the
alley with them... Anisa recognized it was coming from
her. Shocked by herself, she opened her eyes slowly, her lids
fluttering and her vision swimming with her sorrow. The
open concern on Nasser's face blurred anew. She blinked
rapidly, feeling more tears splash her cheeks and drip down
from her chin. Broken, that was what she was. She felt like
a leaking faucet that could never be repaired.

"I'm taking you to the resort. Now." His brusque tone suggested that she'd best not think of arguing with him.

The fight having gone from her, Anisa let him do what he'd wanted from the start. It was easier to allow him to have his way.

Far easier than it was to face a world her brother might not be in anymore. A world where she was left well and truly alone.

If Anisa were asked how she'd ended up back at her room in the resort, she wouldn't be able to say exactly. The ride from town to their beachside resort was one big blur. All she knew was that one second she was crying in an alley with Nasser staring down at her in abject concern, and the next he was guiding her into her room, pointing out things she shouldn't trip over rather than touching her. She wasn't too far gone emotionally and mentally to miss noticing that he avoided contact with her. Anisa should've been relieved he was being so kind and gentlemanly, but right then, she could have seriously used a hug.

Knowing there was no chance that Nasser would give that much-needed physical comfort to her, she wrapped her own arms around herself, squeezing until a sense of wholeness came over her.

Still, feeling fragile and staring anxiously at the four walls that now surrounded her, Anisa's gaze landed on the sliding patio doors.

"Careful," he cautioned gently when she bumped the corner of the coffee table on her way out to the patio.

She needed fresh air. Being confined in her resort when her brother was out there somewhere had her skin crawling.

Because now that her head was clearing, and she wasn't drowning from the grief of learning that Ara was missing, Anisa refused to believe that her brother was gone.

He's alive.

She didn't know how she knew, only that her gut and heart wouldn't let go of that strong conviction.

She looked out over the expansive green separating her from the gleaming white beach and deep blue ocean beyond. A breeze waved the drooping branches of the palm trees scattered over the lawn and teased goose bumps from her overheated body. Surrounded by such natural and manmade beauty, but Anisa couldn't dredge up the emotion to care about anything other than the tightly coiled ball of anxiety pressurizing her chest.

She didn't care about her legs hurting from standing there until the sky darkened and the last of the sun's rays faded below the ocean's horizon.

She was barely cognizant of the night ferrying in chillier temperatures, the nip of the breeze slipping under her clothing and wrapping itself around her jittery bones. Or how her stomach clenched and twisted, not only from the omnipresent fear for Ara, but out of simple hunger now.

Anisa even missed the sliding door opening until Nasser spoke to her.

"Anisa, come in. I ordered room service."

Not facing him, she shook her head.

She heard his sigh drift to her, the frustration in his voice tempered when he said, "You have to eat."

"Why?" she sniped, forcing back a sniffle. "Ara's out there, alone, maybe with no shelter or food."

"You don't know if he's alone."

Anisa turned stiffly to him, her eyes wide and her lips trembling. "If I know my brother, he's probably alone. He's always done everything *alone*. Even when he's surrounded in a room full of people, he's always by himself."

Nasser leaned against the sliding door, filling the doorway but not making a move to cross the threshold. For a moment he just returned her stare with the same blankness she projected, only he wore his poker face far better. She felt the cracks forming in hers.

Feeling an urge to cry swell over her, she sharply whipped her head away and sucked in her lips to trap the sob that would've emerged.

She wished, in a way, that she could be as stoic as Nasser. Then maybe she wouldn't feel misplaced guilt that this was all her fault somehow. Perhaps she could have talked her brother out of whatever he'd done that had gotten him into this mess. She didn't need to know his secrets or Nasser's to sense that they both had something to do with what had happened to Ara.

"Anisa…" Nasser spoke her name quietly, like he was using it to substitute reaching out to her physically. "If you won't eat for yourself, then eat for him. You'll need energy to stay strong until he returns."

Her bottom lip wobbled, his soft voice breaking through her stubborn shell.

"Come in. Eat," he coaxed her, promising, "and I swear that I will do whatever is in my ability to find out what has happened to Ara and track him down."

She lowered her arms and faced him again, her eyes stinging but the tears held at bay for now.

Nasser extended a hand to her. It wasn't the first time he'd done it, but having longed for that form of connection with him since they left the alley after learning of Ara's disappearance, Anisa latched onto it greedily without another word. Staring down at his larger hand engulfing hers, she calmed, not feeling left alone anymore.

"He'll be okay, won't he?"

Nasser kept his emotions locked and guarded from her, but when he jerked his chin in affirmation, she knew that he would do exactly as he vowed and then some. She released the last doubts assailing her and allowed him to ease her back inside, where not only a warm dinner awaited, but the company of a man who in that moment earned the right to be called her protector.

"Merde."

Nasser uttered the curse, not normally resorting to profanity, but also not in the right state of mind to be polite and poised right then. It was taking every ounce of his willpower to maintain his composure around Anisa, knowing that she needed the brave front more than anything else, but also aware that now wasn't the time for him to have a breakdown.

He had calls to make, and a window to make them alone when Anisa started drifting asleep. She'd started yawning after she managed to clean half of her plate. As much as he would have liked her to finish eating, he couldn't entirely blame her for not having an appetite.

It had been hard for Nasser to do much of anything after Nuruddin died. Sleeping, eating, and even taking his spot in the army had fired up his remorse for having lived when Nuruddin hadn't.

No matter what he said, Anisa's concern for Ara would persist until she heard news of him, one way or another.

And now he'd promised to be the bearer of the news— whether it was good or bad. The thought of giving her news she didn't want to hear heaped additional hurdles on the already daunting task of searching for Ara.

He left Anisa where she lay on the sofa, her head on the armrest and her legs drawn up under a white quilt.

Phone pressed to his ear, he stepped outside, closed the sliding door behind himself and took position where Anisa had stood not too long ago. And there he remained until the blue hour before dawn. Nasser ended what had to be the twentieth call and headed indoors, where he discovered Anisa crying in her sleep.

Pained at the sight of the tears beading out of the corners of her eyes, Nasser crouched beside her and gently shook her awake. He watched as she opened her eyes and blinked blearily up at him, her drowsiness melting away and a look of alarm compressing her brows.

"Is it Ara?" She sat up. "Did you hear from him?"

Nasser had hoped to have some time to gather his thoughts before she woke up, but he'd had time to confirm the news, and he knew it was far more of a torture for Anisa to imagine the worst happening to Ara than it was for him to tell her what he had learned.

"Your brother's been found, and he's alive," he reported, moving from his haunches to a seat on the coffee table in front of her.

She expelled a loud *whoosh* of breath replete with her relief. "But he's been injured."

Anisa shot up to her feet, her eyes wild with fear.

"He'd been traveling down south, intending to conduct business there." From what Nasser had understood, Ara had briefly left Hargeisa and Somaliland and was pursuing a government contract that would allow him to build a port in Somalia's capital, Mogadishu, that would expand the opportunity for international trade.

Since Ara still owed him the names of the true culprits behind Nuruddin's murder, Nasser presumed that her brother's business travel disguised another motive. But he wouldn't be able to verify it with anyone other than Ara himself.

"He's been admitted to an international hospital in Mogadishu. During emergency surgery—"

"Surgery?" Gasping the word, Anisa swayed in place with her hands pressed to her chest.

In response to her distress, Nasser clenched his fists, but without any real specter to fight, he could do nothing for her but relay the information that would be of most use to her.

"Doctors induced a medical coma because of some head trauma, and he's still under from what I understand."

"Coma? He's not conscious."

"I hear the surgery's been successful."

"But what if he…he doesn't…" A shudder rocked her body, her lips pinching together as if the words pained her physically. He knew what she was thinking, knew what she'd been about to say.

What if Ara never wakes up?

And what if his death stole any chance that Nasser might have had at learning the identities of and punishing his brother's killers?

As real as that fear was for him, it was a selfish thought to entertain when Anisa was mourning her brother's mishap. Shame swiftly blanketed him, and with it guilt that prompted him to comfort her.

"He will," Nasser said.

She bobbed her head heavily, all her movements sluggish, weighed down by her concern for Ara.

Glancing at his dress watch, Nasser frowned at the time.

"Have you finished packing? Your flight is soon, isn't it?"

"My flight?" Anisa raised her head from staring blankly at the floor.

"For Antananarivo." Along with her film crew and the cast, Anisa was flying out of tropical Nosy Be to Madagascar's capital. From there they would be heading back to their homes. The moment she was safely boarded spelled the end of Nasser's protection detail of her.

In a few short hours, there would no longer be a purpose to speak to or see one another.

No reason to stop us from becoming strangers once more.

His gut flexed uncomfortably at that. Not exploring what it could mean, he concentrated on Anisa's pinging phone.

"It's Adeero Sharmarke," she said after observing the

screen, her eyes growing saucer-wide again. "Nasser, he's with Ara." She looked to him in shock.

Nasser nodded, his head feeling heavier by the moment. "I know. My team told me. Apparently Ara had taken his wife along to Mogadishu as well."

"He's texting again, asking if I'm coming to Mogadishu."

Nasser's heart thudded, piecing together where she was going with this.

"I can't leave," she said quietly.

Damn.

He hadn't bargained on Ara being injured—and then he hadn't factored in Anisa wanting to stay, though it made perfect sense that she would. Anyone in her place would feel the same.

But where did that leave him and the issue of him protecting her?

She must have read his mind, because Anisa walked away from him into the bedroom. Nasser trailed after her, finding her dropping her suitcase on her bed and opening it, her jerky movements as she stuffed her clothes into her luggage smacking of desperation to be by her brother's side.

"I have to go to him," she announced.

Nasser pinched the bridge of his nose, breathing deeply to generate a calm he wasn't feeling.

"That's not possible."

Anisa whirled on him. "Why? Because you won't allow me."

Yes, he wanted to say, but knowing it would add oil to the fire blazing in her eyes, he said, "No, because there's nothing you can do for him now."

"He'll want to see me when he wakes. He *should* see me. I'm family. He needs his family right now."

"And he does have family with him. There's his wife and your *adeero*."

"I have to do something!" she cried, pressing her hands over her mouth and bowing her head before dropping down onto the bed by her suitcase, now half-filled and temporarily forgotten.

Nasser reacted on pure instinct, and it drove him to her side.

Sitting by her on the bed, and leaving an appropriate amount of space between them, he slid forward, perched his elbows over his legs and nervously clenched and unclenched his hands. He had stood in front of dour-faced directors from his board, led business panels in front of thousands of professionals, and handled clients from powerful oligarchs to well-heeled politicians. Yet somehow, despite his experiences, he was gripped by the fear that he wouldn't be enough. That he was too inept to offer her the solace she needed.

I have to try, though.

After she'd told him about having survived the accident that took her parents' lives, being terrorized by her nightmares, and now this fear for her brother's well-being, he would be a coward if he ignored her pain. So before he broke out in a sweat, Nasser dispelled the quiet oppressing them in the darkened bedroom.

"Anisa, the best thing you can do for him is take care of yourself. He wouldn't want to see you like this when he wakes and recovers."

She was silent for a long while. He measured the time by the way the room brightened with the first rays of dawn.

Finally, she softly asked, "What if he thinks I don't care?"

Nasser could see why she would imagine that. What with her not having spoken to her brother for years, the fear she voiced was natural. Not for the first time, he silently cursed Ara, swearing that if he had the chance, he'd give him a good dressing-down on Anisa's behalf.

"What if he thinks I've abandoned him?"

"Anisa, if he truly thinks that way about you, then that's more his problem than yours." He sat up, planting his hands on the bed by his thighs and meeting her wary expression. "But from what I have seen, that's not the kind of man your brother is." For all his faults, Ara could be generous. Nasser knew he was quite philanthropic and did what he could to give back. Just like his father, his efforts to expand Somalia and Somaliland's exports and imports were all for the good of the citizens. More international trade would help uplift the economy and generate the funds required for public infrastructure.

Ara was a man of his country and people.

The two men weren't different there. No matter the wealth he attained, Nasser never forgot his roots, his past forming his present and paving the way for his future. That fueled his current quest to avenge Nuruddin.

"Ara wouldn't want you to put yourself in harm's way for him. You can doubt anything else, but that much you shouldn't. It's why he sent me, after all."

He didn't know if he got through to her until she spoke up again.

"What should I do then?" she wondered.

Nasser was more than a little taken aback. Since he'd met Anisa, she had made it a point to do what she wanted, including being open about her emotions. He envied her for being so free with her feelings, but right then, he didn't even mask his befuddlement.

Adding to the rattle in his head, in the space between their bodies, Anisa's pinkie finger brushed the side of his hand atop the bed. He froze, holding still as her finger caressed him again. The simple touch unlocked a fissure of heat that steadily burned in him from that point on.

Speaking around it was difficult, his voice noticeably husky even to his ears. "I'm not sure."

"What would you do in my position?"

What would he do? Nasser struggled to make sense of his thoughts, hyperaware that her hand was still touching his. He finally replied, "I would want to be close by, in case of any change of news."

"So, if I asked you to take me home?"

Again, not hiding his surprise, his brows snapped up. "You wish for me to take you back to Canada?" It wasn't part of the deal with Ara, but if Anisa wanted his company, he wouldn't deny her.

A shake of her head dropped his mood. Aside from his disappointment, he remained confused. He opened his mouth to ask her what she meant, only to snap his jaws together the instant it clicked in his mind.

"You mean..."

He didn't finish the thought as she shyly nodded.

She wanted to go home to Somaliland. Berbera, specifically. He hadn't considered it an option, only knowing that he wouldn't send her to Mogadishu where terrorist attacks, banditry, and other dangers could find her. The quaint coastal city of Berbera wasn't exactly a hotbed of crime. The most he could look forward to was more beaches.

Decision made, he said, "I'll take you home then."

She placed her hand over his in what he supposed was wordless gratitude. It lasted only a moment before she took her hand away, smiled beautifully, pushed onto her feet and resumed gathering her things from her bedroom.

Nasser left her to it, promising he'd meet back with her once he cleared his own room of his few belongings, and catching himself flexing the hand she'd touched, the heated longing she'd stirred up in him still alive and simmering.

CHAPTER NINE

"THAT CAN'T BE the house." Anisa's jaw slackened at the sight of her childhood home, unable to recognize the exterior even though it was still on the same plot of land overlooking the beach that neighbored it. Ara's changes to their home were significant. The most obvious were the stories he'd added to the original build. She counted a total of three as they approached, the sun glinting off the many windows, forcing her to squint her eyes and roll her window back up. Nasser steered his black truck up the well-paved private drive, the smooth asphalt bringing them much faster to the steel driveway fence gate and the tall stone enclosure barricading the house and its grounds.

The gates rolled open almost on command, and Nasser didn't stop driving until they were past the front line of security measures and rolling into the wide, stone-paved front yard of the home. Before they even stopped, they were surrounded by half a dozen men, earpieces plugged in, moving in unison to canvass all sides of the truck. They would have made for a menacing sight all on their own, but to make matters more distressing, Anisa spied thigh holsters.

She was used to Ara having a couple of bodyguards on him, but this level of protection was excessively cautious. Tearing her eyes off the small army of security personnel, Anisa climbed out of the truck, shielded the sunlight from her eyes and peered up. "Is that a terrace on the roof?"

"It is."

Her head whipped to him. "You've been up there?"

"I've had the pleasure of being up there a couple of times. Your brother seems to enjoy the rooftop addition immensely."

Anisa gave it another considering look, and it could've been the shock of seeing all the changes to the home, but she didn't see what the hype was about. She dropped her head and forced her feet forward to the front door. Pulling in a deep breath, she grabbed the handle and pushed her way inside. Expecting the interior to be just as disconcertingly unfamiliar to her, she shielded herself for the reveal.

She breathed easier when everything inside appeared almost as it had when she lived there. Of course the details that were unrecognizable jumped out at her, but it wasn't as alien as she imagined it would be. The entryway was wider and the ceilings higher than she recalled. A skylight washed the light of day over her and brightened up the area. A curved staircase with dark wood treads and a bright white banister wound to the upper floors, and a pretty black birdcage chandelier hung above the stairway, beckoning her with its warm, inviting light.

Anisa took a step off the entrance mat onto the gleaming white-and-black patterned tiles beneath her scuffed-up sneakers. Looking down, she heard the memory of her mother's voice gently scolding her to take her shoes off.

As she pulled off her shoes, Nasser caught up with her. He rolled her luggage in, followed her lead and left his footwear by the entrance, and climbed the stairs, stopping only when he noticed she wasn't shadowing him.

"I know the floor layout," he said by way of explanation. "Your brother didn't only hire my company to secure his company headquarters, but his home as well."

After seeing the extra measures of security outside, Anisa could see Ara had used Nasser's expertise well. Did she think it was necessary still? No, but as they headed up to the second floor, Anisa listened aptly while Nasser gave her a tour of the home security features.

"Certain areas of the home, mostly all entrance points, have a footstep detector. It'll send an alert to the control room and flag a security team to any movement."

He pointed to the vents they passed in the hallway. "There is a fogger system embedded into the ventilation of the home. When triggered, it blasts cold fog laced with a nonlethal compound at the intruder."

"What if it isn't an intruder?"

"The system can only be initiated with a series of authorizations and has remote activation capability."

"Seems excessive," she said with a shake of her head. "Next you'll tell me there's a remote weapons system embedded in the house."

Nasser was suspiciously quiet at that.

"There's a weapons system in the house!" Anisa didn't mask her shock, her voice loud and echoing in the hall.

"Behind the walls and embedded in the entrance hall ceiling and your brother's study, but again, access and activation would be near impossible without authorizations from both my company and Ara. You're safe from any perceived danger."

Safe?

She would feel far safer without knowing that the house was equipped to kill her.

Nasser paused and turned to her, his face a mask of severity. "No harm will come to you, not from the house or from anywhere else."

It was like a switch flipped, and her fear had been the trigger for the intensity in him that she hadn't yet grown used to. Her heart pitter-pattered, her stomach swooped, and her body warmed quickly and pleasantly. At the mercy of her physical reactions to Nasser, Anisa only breathed again when he resumed their tour.

"The walls, windows and doors are bulletproof and blast-proof. All the washrooms are equipped with biological washing systems."

"Why?" Anisa snapped her head away from admiring the beautiful tiling and luxurious bathroom amenities of one of the many bathrooms in one of the many bedrooms on that floor alone.

"Biochemical threats are still threats. Better prepared and vigilant than caught unaware and vulnerable."

She thought that nothing could top the extra feature in the bathrooms, at least not until Nasser said, "There's also a panic room on each floor."

"Of course there is," she muttered.

Right as Anisa began to think the surprises along the tour wouldn't cease, he walked her to the end of the long hall and opened the double doors at the end. Inside, the room was spacious and decorated in dark, muted tones. The flooring was a polished obsidian tile, the chairs a deep brown leather. A white area rug lay under a coffee table. On one side there was a sideboard, and on the other, a massive bookshelf that took up nearly the entire wall. But it was the far end of the room that caught her attention most. A grand executive desk of ebony wood, stainless steel, exquisite glass detailing, and touches of white leather panels and inserts.

She didn't need Nasser to confirm that this room belonged to Ara. Anisa could close her eyes and feel his presence permeating every surface of every piece of furniture, each crook and cranny, and even the walls.

"Your brother's study and office." Nasser strode over to the wide, floor-to-ceiling bookshelf, stepping off to the side. He brought Anisa's focus to a panel. "A thumb sensor—" he pressed his thumb to the digital reader "—and a passcode—"

he punched in a series of digits "—protect this part of the full home security system."

The bookshelf she'd believed had been built into the wall suddenly parted down the middle, rolling in each direction before the shelves revealed a steel door with another security panel. Nasser went through the motions and revealed what lay beyond the impenetrable-looking door.

Anisa gaped at the high-tech monitors and paneling inside. "This main control unit is the gateway to every security feature in the home. Aside from your brother, my company personnel are the only ones with access to this area, in person and remotely."

She saw that he was waiting for her to come in closer, but Anisa backed away, suddenly overwhelmed. The shock of everything that had happened in the day was catching up to her. All of this, learning of Ara's hospitalization, returning home, discovering that her brother had spiraled into a paranoia—because how else could she explain the over-the-top security measures that seemed as much a threat to his person?—was too much to take in at once.

So she left.

Ran out of Ara's office and headed for the end of the hall, where, grasping the stairway railing, she peered down at the entrance hall and tried to slow her reeling mind.

What had her brother so fearful that he created a fortress out of their parents' home? In his quest to protect whatever it was Ara felt needed protection, he'd destroyed the memories and sentimental value this place held for her. When she looked around, she didn't see the faces of her *hooyo* and *aabo* anywhere.

Did he get rid of their belongings too?

With a clawing desperation, Anisa had to know.

"My parents' room, where is it?"

She expected Nasser to tell her that no such room existed, but he turned on his heel and had her follow him to one of the closed rooms. He tried the handle with no success. After leaving her briefly to fetch a key, he returned and unlocked the room. Anisa's throat bobbed from her nerves, her socked feet dragging over the threshold, and her body trembling at the thought of what she would see.

Nasser flicked the light on. Besides a trace mustiness coming from the room, it looked exactly as she recalled it should.

The queen-sized bed with the old, scarred headboard, a mirror dresser still holding her mom's perfumes and jewelry boxes, the patterned Turkish rug that took up most of the floor, and so many other touches that swept her back to a time when her parents frequented this space.

"It looks the same," she sighed.

"He doesn't speak of this room often," Nasser said from behind her, his deep voice calm and even-toned, "but from what I've learned, he asked for it to be set up this way after the remodeling was completed and the interior decoration was happening."

Her relief at that was cut off shortly by fatigue.

Reading her mind, he gestured for her to follow him again. "Your room is this way."

Anisa stopped short at the threshold. It appeared that Ara hadn't only left their parents' personal belongings and furniture intact, but he'd enshrined her bedroom too. She walked in tentatively, taking in the familiar sights of her fuzzy baby blanket, her stuffed animals, the journals stacked on her small reading desk, and the DVDs and VHS tapes from her childhood neatly tucked in a media shelf beside the desk. On her bedside table was the heart-shaped trinket box her mother had bought for her ninth birthday.

My last birthday with them.

Anisa walked over to it, knowing that when she opened it, nothing would be inside. She hadn't had the heart to use it after her parents died. She'd tried to throw it away in an angry, grief-stricken state, but it had reappeared the very next day, rescued from being lost forever by Ara. He hadn't even scolded her about it.

She set the box down unopened, turning to Nasser and seeing that he had already placed her suitcase inside the room. Then he stood in the doorframe, watching her, as faithful and diligent in his duty to guard her as always.

Anisa appreciated that he'd been so understanding of her all through this journey. And now she knew that if she were to spill her guts to him, he wouldn't push her away. He'd seen her cry, shown her compassion and sympathy, and though he guarded his own secrets well, Anisa now felt that had more to do with personal issues he had to work through than any deficiency on her part.

But as much as she believed that speaking about her overwhelming emotions would make her feel better, she couldn't bring herself to do it. There was still so much for her to sort through on her own before she unloaded it on someone else.

"Do you need anything?"

His question pained her, mostly because she'd asked him to come along with her, and though Anisa didn't regret it, right in that moment she could have used time to herself. Nasser was trying to be helpful in his own way, but she hadn't signed up for him to hover over her.

"I just… I need to be alone."

Nasser didn't blink, nodding and making a move to leave her. Before he did, he reminded her, "I'll be downstairs if you need me."

Of that she had no doubt. But right then, and more than Ara, their parents, and Nasser, she just needed herself.

* * *

"Let me know if his condition changes in the slightest." Nasser ended the call with the hospital director personally handling Ara's care.

Feeling a crick in his neck, he stood for a stretch. He'd been seated behind Ara's desk, his laptop, tablet and phone all having been put through the wringer for the past twenty-four hours. Since having brought Anisa to her brother's home, and hearing that she hadn't wanted his company, Nasser had sealed himself in the office study and pored over his numerous work tasks. On top of all that, he'd answered several updates on Ara's welfare. He'd hoped to have better news for Anisa by now, but it was looking like time would be working against them.

For now, all he could do was to see that she stayed put in her childhood home.

And what of her comfort? a little voice chimed at him.

Nasser tensed at the memory of Anisa sending him away. She'd asked to be left alone, and he gave her the space she requested, barricading himself in the office to keep his mind off what felt like her rejection. He had only stepped out for mealtimes, always dropping in on Anisa to ensure that she joined him. Although he knew he could just as easily show her to the kitchen, or have Ara's personal chef whip up something for her and fetch a household staff member to deliver it to her room, it gave him additional peace of mind to have Anisa where he could see her.

*And maybe to touch her again...*that sneaky little voice taunted him.

Nasser shut it down before he cleared the office and headed out to pick Anisa up for breakfast.

She opened her bedroom door on the third sharp rap of his knuckles when he'd been one knock away from barging in.

"Join me for breakfast." He never framed it as a question, knowing that there could be a possibility for her to refuse him.

Stepping out wordlessly, and giving him a whiff of her sweet, floral perfume while she was at it, Anisa led him down to the cozy corner of the kitchen where a breakfast table with two seats and a tufted creamy white banquette sat beneath two small casement windows. The bright, airy light shone off the kitchen's warm neutral tones and added an enticing glow to her brown skin. She wore her lightweight, pale blue hijab in a more traditional style that circled her face.

But it was the thin, gold-wired, hexagonal-shaped glasses amplifying her shining dark eyes that had his heart kicking faster.

"You're wearing glasses," he commented lamely, too swept up in this change and in her general beauty to articulate himself any better. Nasser supposed it also wasn't a help that he hadn't slept last night. Worry that Anisa might need him, combined with a rattling longing to be by her side that had nothing to do with his guard duty, kept him up. The result was that his eyes itched and burned for sleep, and his body and mind were pushing the bounds of exhaustion. His answer to that was to pour himself a large mug full of black coffee, the dark, robust taste as rich and refreshing the first sip as it was when he refilled his mug for a second cup.

"I usually wear contacts, but they were hurting my eyes this morning." She shrugged. "Hence the glasses."

He didn't know what else to say, and she was lifting up the lids from the platters of their breakfast spread.

Nasser was displeased to see that her plate wasn't as full as he'd hoped it would be, but Anisa was eating what was in front of her, so he couldn't complain. He still worried when she sat back, apparently done eating her meal, and sipped gingerly at her coffee.

He hadn't seen her since dinner last night, and he was curious what kept her preoccupied in her room. As long as she wasn't crying in there…

"Any plans today?"

She gave another nonchalant shrug, her face eerily blank for her. "Nothing. Maybe I'll get some writing done."

"You're working?"

"No, I haven't picked up another gig yet. I just have time and figure I might as well work on my screenplay." She placed her mug down then, the first real emotion breaking through as she inquired softly, "Have you heard from Ara?"

"I spoke with the hospital's chief director. So far, all his preliminary tests have offered optimistic results. The director assures me that she'll continue to personally see to his care on top of your brother receiving round-the-clock attention from staff."

"But he hasn't woken up," deadpanned Anisa.

When he didn't respond, she excused herself and scooted out from the banquette seating.

Nasser gave her a few seconds' head start only because he was busy grinding his molars and berating himself on his poor handling of the situation. Then he scraped his chair back from the breakfast table and chased after her.

Anisa was halfway up the staircase when he called her back.

"Ara's still in a medical coma, but the director reports that his prognosis is good." Not taking his eyes off her, he rooted his feet at the base of the stairs and fastened his hand on the railing to ease the urge to close the short distance to her. "He's going to be all right."

"You don't know that."

"No, you're right, nothing in health can be fully assured. And yet the tests all point towards an eventual recovery."

Anisa's soft sigh floated down to him. "I know you're trying to be helpful, and I do appreciate it, but I'll rest easier when he's woken from the coma." Then, without waiting for his response, she climbed the stairs and flitted off in the direction of her bedroom.

Nasser could have followed, though it'd be in vain. It was obvious she not only wished to be alone, but that his attempts at comfort weren't wanted either.

After breakfast, he went back to her brother's office and worked from there until noon, when a need for nourishment lured him outside the double doors of the study. He passed her room, slowed and faced her door. Funny how that slab of glossy, dark cherrywood had become an impenetrable fortress of its own.

Nasser forced himself to move on.

She wants to be all alone.

And that was fine by him.

He had to look at the bright side: as long as she stayed indoors, he didn't have to work twice as hard as he'd done in Madagascar to protect her. This way, half his work was being done by the security features his company integrated into the house.

Yet despite his resolve to leave her be, Nasser returned from a quick, lonely lunch only to hover in front of her door again.

There he had a debate with himself on whether he should knock and try to rouse her from her room, or walk on and continue pretending he wasn't immensely perturbed by her decision to lock herself up.

What if she's crying again?

And he wouldn't know, because he was standing outside instead of being with her. Nasser clenched his fists, wishing he could see through the door, if only to ensure she wasn't wrapped up in abject misery. He flexed his hands and tensed his muscles, battling these opposing sides of him to ignore her wishes and act, or do as she requested and remain still.

Finally, and with his feet feeling as though they were encased in cement shoes, he walked away from her bedroom door. Nasser had taken two heavy steps when a lock unlatching sounded from behind him. He spun back just as Anisa stepped out, her head rising and her eyes finding him.

For several heartbeats, neither of them said a word.

Nasser could've contented himself by merely gazing at her and confirming that—at least on the outside—she looked all right. More than all right, it appeared as though she were headed outdoors, a sun hat in her hand, sunglasses perched on her head, and a large, floppy purse strapped over her shoulder.

"Where are you going?" He kept his face smooth of the nervousness now pinging through him.

It was true that he hadn't liked it when she confined herself in her room, but Nasser hadn't wanted her to go out, where protecting her would be that much more challenging. Worse, the thought that she might not want him to go with her struck him.

How will I keep her safe then?

Normally, he'd have pushed past her protests as he had in Madagascar. The biggest difference between then and now was that they weren't the same people they'd been when they first met. At least not to each other. Now he was more familiar with her. It felt downright rotten of him to ignore her wishes and force his protection on her.

Even if it's for her own good?

Nasser's jaw hardened, knowing that despite what was good for her, he would still probably cave to her desires.

He knew that if she asked to be alone again this time, he would do his best to allow it, maybe order security personnel to trail her from afar in his stead. But Nasser delivered a quiet prayer that it wouldn't come to that.

"The beach," Anisa said after a short silence.

He was fully expecting her to then tell him that she'd like to be by herself.

"Did you want to come with me?" she asked.

He couldn't have heard her invitation correctly, yet when she stood there staring at him expectantly, he realized with a jolt that, *yes*, not only had she invited him on her day excursion, but Anisa was waiting on his answer.

Not that she has to ask...

"Oui." And Nasser didn't think he relished saying a word more.

CHAPTER TEN

THERE WAS SOMETHING about being in the sunlight with her feet squishing in the wet sand and the ocean lapping her wriggling toes that put a smile on her face.

"That feels so good," Anisa moaned as she lifted her face to the sun and the heat penetrated her bones and thawed some of the chill that had been clinging to her over the past few days. She stretched her arms up over her head and arched back, the tension unwinding from her muscles as slowly and gently as the tide rushing up over the sand before scurrying back off the shore. "I could stand here all day."

"It is peaceful here," Nasser said.

At the sound of his voice, Anisa lowered her arms and peered up at him from behind her sunglasses. He wouldn't be able to see her eyes fully, and somehow that made it easier to face him and hide from her guilty conscience. She'd been rudely brushing off his kind gestures since they arrived at her home.

Is it really still my *home, though?*

Anisa couldn't completely rid herself of the idea that, despite Ara having preserved her parents' belongings and hers as well, she no longer belonged here with him. The fear that she didn't fit in in the one place where she should have—that's what kept her locked away in her room. She'd barely slept because of it too. It was only here, on this quiet sprawl of shore, that she'd finally felt her overactive thoughts drop from a shout to the softest of whispers.

She wasn't in a hurry to give up the rare peace so quickly. Yet…she had to.

Though she didn't owe Nasser anything, when Anisa had asked him for some space, he had given it to her. Sure, he would pull her out of her room for meals. But that only showed he cared enough to not let her starve. And because he'd been hired to watch over her, it couldn't have been easy for him to stand back. She was grateful to him for overriding his natural protective instinct and respecting her request to be left alone.

It was the reason she'd invited Nasser to the beach with her.

I had time to myself.

Now she was ready to talk.

"Nasser," she began to say, just as he said, "Anisa."

They stopped and stared at each other.

Anisa brushed off her surprise and laughed lightly. "We must have been thinking the same thing."

"I suppose we were," he concurred with a small smile. "You can speak first."

Anisa nodded, her good humor stifled now that the spotlight was on her. Her hands only slightly trembling, she pulled the sunglasses off her face, feeling like she needed to look him in the eye for what she had to say—even if losing the shades left her more vulnerable than ever.

"I'm sorry."

He blinked slowly at her apology, his non-reaction exacerbating her nerves.

"I knew coming home would be hard in some ways. I just didn't anticipate just how difficult it would be." Anisa knew nothing she could've done would have prepared her for her homecoming. True, it might have been easier had her return not been prompted by Ara's injury, but the same doubts and concerns would have followed her around.

"You have to understand Ara hasn't spoken to me in years, yet he still kept my bedroom the same for me. What am I supposed to think?"

Nasser remained silent up until that point, but now he said, "You don't need to apologize for the way you feel, Anisa. Although I can't speak for your brother or explain his logic, perhaps it's his way of showing he cares."

"If he truly cared, he would have picked up his phone and sent a text or called, or heck, done *both*," she argued, scoffing. It was already painful to think about Ara snubbing her these past four years, but to have Nasser defend him added salt to the wound.

"Maybe he was afraid."

She raised her brows. "Of?"

"You might not have answered his calls or messages."

Anisa pondered that, and her anger flowed away as quickly as it filled her up. Staring down at her feet, her curling toes squelching in the sand, she recalled the fury she'd first felt when she had moved away and Ara had cut off communication with her in retaliation. If he had tried talking to her while she'd been that angry, then Anisa knew she wouldn't have been very kind to him. Of course her irritation had cooled as the years passed, and she began to miss Ara more than loathe his choice to push her away.

But he doesn't know that.

How could he when they hadn't spoken for all this time?

"Okay, I see what you mean," she said, looking up from her feet and smiling at him. Nasser made a solid argument, and though she didn't know if he intended to soften her heart toward Ara, he succeeded. "I only hope my brother's paying you well enough," she teased.

Nasser's husky laughter was worth it.

Like his smiles, his mirth seemed a rare treasure to cherish. And Anisa did just that, quietly.

"Did you want to go for a walk?" he asked, tipping his head toward the lonely stretch of beach. It was quiet this time of day when the sun was hottest and most people were at home having *asariya*—their afternoon tea.

Anisa had chosen that hour for a specific reason.

Grinning, she sifted through the open top of her oversized tote bag and pulled out what she was searching for: a spool of fishing line already equipped with a hook. Lowering her tote bag by her sandals and wading into the ocean with the fishing line in hand, she glanced back at Nasser and almost laughed at the frown on his face. "How about we fish for our lunch instead?" she asked him.

For the next half hour, Anisa reeled in a couple fish and collected them in a small bucket she had pulled out of her tote. Standing still at the edge of the water, Nasser appeared content to keep an eye on her from the shore. He didn't make a move to join her or even ask her questions.

Tiring of the silence, she stopped beside him and held out the fishing line.

"Why do I feel like I'm the only one working for our meal?" she joked. "Come on, let's see you try. Unless you're scared to get wet." Anisa eyed his perfect-looking suit and polished shoes.

He looked so good, Anisa understood why he wasn't jumping into the cold grip of the ocean. When he didn't accept the line from her, she shrugged off her disappointment and waded back into the water.

She was tugging at the line, slowly reeling it in, when Nasser stepped up beside her, his hand outstretched.

Anisa gawked at him, her eyes trailing down to where he'd rolled the cuff of his pants up to the middle of his calves. It did little good—the ocean still drenched him. Shaking off her stupor, she passed him the fishing line and focused on showing him where his hands should be. She wasn't going to be distracted by the feel of his fingers as she pried them just loose enough for the line to slip through when he reeled in his catch. Or his hard bicep as she showed him how to hold his arm up and pull the reel in with sharp tugs. And she certainly wasn't going to lean into the fluttery heat when his body bumped hers, his eyes flicking down to her face and flashing with awareness at their dangerously close proximity.

Blushing, Anisa shied back from him and stammered, "Y-you're holding it right. Now just let the fish come to you."

She was still caught up in her attraction to him, but not as strongly by the time Nasser snagged his first fish. Anisa cheered for him, guiding him back to the beach and showing him how to pull the fish off the hook before adding his catch to hers.

They made two more trips with only one other catch before Anisa called it a day. Sitting down on the beach blanket she spread out for them, she checked on the fish in the bucket and beamed proudly at him. "We caught way more than I thought we would."

Nasser smiled back. "I had a good instructor."

"I was pretty good, wasn't I?"

He chuckled at her boast, and then surprised her when he asked, "Did your brother teach you to fish?"

"No, Ara and I both learned to fish from our parents." Anisa wiped wet sand off fish scales, reminiscing about the last time she'd gone fishing with her whole family, so many years ago now. "There's a nine-year age gap between Ara and me, so he learned to fish first. Most of the time I was too young to join him and my father in the ocean, so I would wait on the shore with my mom. Then I'd help her clean the fish before we hauled our catch of the day home."

She smiled to herself, the memories now coming back to

her. "When we weren't fishing, I used to walk this beach with my mother and father. Ara and I were always running after each other, making up games, playing in the sand or ocean, sometimes both.

"I thought it would be hard coming back here, too, but it isn't," she confessed, lowering the fish she'd been holding, her bottom lip trembling as she looked out at the ocean. "I thought I'd be scared of the ocean after what it took from me, but I'm not."

"Is this where it happened?"

Anisa sucked in her lips and managed to nod once, slow. After she admitted to the hardest part, the rest of the events leading up to that awful day came tumbling from her mouth.

"Ara was away on a school field trip, and I couldn't wait for him to get home to play with me, so I begged my parents to take us boating.

"Even though they were both busy, they stopped what they were doing and took us out on the small fishing boat my dad owned."

Anisa felt a smile, small and fragile, lift her lips. "I loved touching the ocean." She could feel her dad's arms around her middle as he helped her reach for the waves, and she could see her mother's beautiful smile and hear her sparkling laughter as Anisa and her dad flicked water at her. "But even more than that, I loved spending time with them.

"We were so busy laughing, it seemed that my parents missed the boat careening straight toward us. My dad tried to wave for their attention, but it happened so fast. They clipped us, and our boat upended." Anisa touched a hand to her middle, swearing that she felt the phantom press of her mother's arm tightly winding around her as they went under together. She never saw her dad again, but she had clung to her mom for as long as she could.

"I was found on the beach alone. When I couldn't find my

mom or dad, I remember running out into the ocean, crying for them. The people who found me stopped me from going in any deeper.

"Later, when Ara finally arrived at the hospital, I learned my mom had washed up only a little further down the beach. She was gone, but the rescue team thought that she'd saved me." Anisa's eyes watered, and no matter how fast she blinked, she felt the tears burgeoning. "My dad washed up later. I can't stop thinking that he died alone, and that she died to rescue me."

Anisa cried quietly, her cheeks growing wetter by the second. And when it became too much, she turned away, her hands too dirty to cover her face, but her pain too ready for her to look into Nasser's eyes anymore.

That was why she was unprepared when his hand covered hers on the beach mat, his fingers squeezing and coaxing warmth into her. Shocked and blinking back tears, she saw that he had moved closer to comfort her. Without thinking, she leaned into him, pressed her face into his chest and cried on him. To his credit, Nasser's hands settled over her shoulders. He held her gently, letting her work out the pain deep inside that she'd unburied. He hugged her back, and Anisa couldn't put into words how good it felt in her moment of grieving.

It felt like ages had passed when she finally stirred against his hard chest and peered up, her eyes sore and her vision still misty, but her heart no longer hurting as badly. She must have looked a mess, but she didn't feel it, not with the way Nasser was gazing at her. His eyes lowered to her mouth. She licked her lips instinctively, dragging her tongue across her lower lip, and watching his eyebrows furrow and his own mouth harden into a scowl.

They were pressed scandalously close, chancing the possibility of someone seeing them.

She was going to point out that they needed to separate, but her hands clung to the front of his shirt, his chest warm and solid under her palms, and her body buzzing with the knowledge that he wanted this too. Anisa could see it in the way he stared at her like he was starved and she was the only one who could feed the hunger.

If she had any doubt that he desired her, it was eliminated when he inched his face lower and closer to hers.

Anisa's breath hitched in sweetest expectation.

The last time they had a moment like this, Nasser had pulled away from her and left her with a heavy disappointment that still pressed down on her. What made it doubly worse was that he'd only stopped to answer the call relaying the news of her brother's injury and hospitalization.

After that experience, she felt shakier that it might happen all over again.

So she couldn't be blamed when her fingers dug into his shirtfront to keep him from running off on her again. Anisa then counted the seconds, her eyelids fluttering lower and her face angling up to his. She didn't have to wait long to finally feel him the way she'd yearned to since Madagascar.

Nasser's mouth pressed down on hers, tentatively at first, almost as though he wouldn't risk harming her, but that changed quickly.

Making a noise that was a cross between a growl and a groan, Nasser dropped his hands down her arching back and hauled her against him. Anisa's gasp was swallowed up in their passionate kiss. Shutting off her mind, she closed her eyes and gave back as good as he was giving her. She had kissed only one person before, and that had been years ago when she'd been a young teenager innocently exploring her feelings. Nothing had come of it, and that kiss would never compare to the maturity and expertise behind Nasser's mastery of her mouth.

Within moments he had her melting into a goopy puddle in his arms.

"Anisa," he rasped against her, his warm breath heating her jawline as he scored her with his hot lips.

Needing him higher up, she framed his face with her hands, the bristly shadow of a beard on his jaw tickling her palms and heightening her pleasure. She lifted him to her and locked lips with him again. The way this kiss curled her toes had Anisa realizing how much more this meant to her than the simple satisfaction of a desire.

I like him.

She liked Nasser a lot, and Anisa knew she'd have to do something about it later, but right then all she wanted and needed was for him to hold her tighter and kiss her breathless.

Kissing Anisa wasn't a mistake in and of itself...

No, I don't think I'll ever regret it.

But now Nasser wasn't sure what to do about the feelings their intimate moment unlocked.

Because she was everywhere for him after their passionate display on the beach. Under his skin, in each and every tug of his heart, and in the heat coiling below his belt. No matter how many times he told himself it shouldn't happen again if he valued what was best for her, he would look down to where her head rested on his shoulder, and he'd forget everything except the achingly sweet memory of his mouth slotted perfectly over hers.

It hadn't surprised him that they fit so well together. In a way, they'd been dancing around this attraction of theirs for some time.

That doesn't mean we had to act on it.

He must have sighed. He couldn't think of another reason why Anisa would lift her head off his shoulder and look up at him, her eyes roaming over his face, curiosity creasing her brow.

"Are you having second thoughts?" she asked, discerning where his mind had gone.

"Are you?"

"I don't really know what to say."

Nasser tensed at the indecisiveness threading her words, and he only relaxed when Anisa continued, "But I do know that I can't regret what happened."

Relieved, he nodded in agreement. "Then we share that sentiment."

"I'm glad..." Anisa trailed off, picking up after a quick sigh. "It's hard talking about my parents. Thinking of their deaths is painful. Sometimes I wonder why I didn't die with them. Why them and not me?" She drew her legs up closer to her body, her arms wrapped over her knees and her gaze pointed at the ocean spread out before them.

Why Nuruddin and not him?

How often had he wondered that?

Knowing the guilt she was living through quite intimately, he needn't have imagined what she was thinking or feeling, because he experienced it every time he thought of his brother. No amount of logic had ever been able to spare him the grief and burden of being the one left behind.

The one who was saved.

Maybe that was why, without any comforting words at the ready, he pried his pinched lips apart and cracked open the steel doors on his well-guarded past.

"When my brother, Nuruddin, passed away, I often questioned why it hadn't been me in his place. He was better to our parents, good at his studies, a *hafiz*, and he had a dream of using his good heart and smart brain to help the world.

"He was everything I wasn't at the time. And it never made sense to me why he died and why I was spared."

"Spared?" Anisa's brows pinched closer together, and the ocean lost her attention as she focused on him. "What do you mean?"

Nasser unclenched his jaws and said, "He died at a protest rally against the corruption within the government."

He'd never be able to scrub that day clean from his mind, and now he was reliving it as he played the events back for Anisa.

"Along with a group of his friends, they marched in Hargeisa and faced off against a hostile military force in the city for the protests. I had gone with him, not thinking that I'd leave without him."

Anisa's face crumpled at that part, and he paused, gathering his own emotions in the face of her sadness for him.

In a thicker voice, he said, "The military officials weren't supposed to do anything more than supervise, but less than an hour into the peaceful demonstrations, they started brutalizing protestors. A fight broke out, and it was us versus them. Everyone was either charging headfirst into the fray or running in the opposite direction.

"When the situation turned for the worse, Nuruddin grabbed my hand and was pulling me away, but I—"

He had to break off, a bilious swell of emotion sticking fast in his throat. Waiting while it worked itself down gradually, Nasser responded to Anisa's searching fingers touching his fisted hand over the small space between them on her beach mat. She caressed his knuckles, her eyes on his face, concern for his emotional welfare etching frown lines around her mouth and between her fine dark eyebrows. When he didn't move away from her, she placed her hand on his, blanketing his fist and calming the prickly feelings needling his insides.

With that touch, she gave him the strength to say what troubled him most. "I feel responsible for his death."

Nasser could see it as though he were living through it all

over again. Nuruddin's hand in his own, his brother's panicked features filling his vision...

"We have to go, Nasser!"

*His brother pulled sharply on his hand, dragging him
away from the clash of protestors against the armored body
shields of the military officers.*

*Fire erupted from a car nearby, glass crunched beneath
his feet, and some of the boards scrawled with protest slo-
gans nearly tripped him.*

*He would have fallen if Nuruddin hadn't helped right him
quickly.*

*"Why can't we stay?" Nasser cried. "They aren't really
going to hurt us, are they?"*

*"Even if they don't, we can't be here anymore. It's not
safe," his brother shouted over the noise.*

In the present, Nasser continued his tale, unable to stop
the floodgates he'd opened. "He tried to get us away, but I
didn't want to leave. Not yet."

"Look, Nuruddin! They're hurting those people."

*Nasser pointed out two men holding boards in front of
their bodies protectively as the military advanced with
batons, battering anyone who stood in their path. One of
the men toppled backwards, and as soon as he was on the
ground, the board was ripped out of his hand. He was bat-
tered by half a dozen military officers' solid batons.*

*They beat him relentlessly, his cries echoing down the
streets.*

Nasser shuddered in real time, his body growing cold and
hot simultaneously as the nightmarish memory haunted him
once more.

"My brother," he continued hoarsely, "he wanted to protect me, but I couldn't leave well enough alone. He followed
me into the fray, and we fought off the officers with boards
we'd picked up from the ground. We weren't alone. Before

we knew it, we were at the epicenter of a battle between protestors and so-called officers of the peace." He spat the word,
his hatred revitalized for the cruel-faced men brandishing
their batons, big shields, and bigger guns. If he could round
every one of them up today and wreak his vengeance on
them, he would. Because what happened after changed his
life irrevocably...

*"Nasser!" Nuruddin cried out his name as Nasser was
ripped away from his side by some of the military officials.
"Nasser!" he yelled one last time.*

*Then there was a series of ear-shattering bangs followed
by an eerie silence that could've stopped Nasser's heart.*

*In an out-of-body moment, and still gripped tightly by the
officers who had grabbed hold of him and hauled them over
onto their side, Nasser watched his brother slacken and col-
lapse to the ground.*

"They shot him. I tried to save him. Tried, but I knew." He
swallowed hard, the memory of cradling his brother's life-
less body after he'd managed to wrench free of his captors
paining him physically. "I knew he was gone.

"After Nuruddin died, crowd control was swift. The protestors either were subdued or ran away." Those who hadn't
managed to escape were caught and carted off to jail, and
he was one of the unlucky dozen or so. "Nuruddin was the
only one who'd died. Many more were injured.

"And it wouldn't have happened if I had listened to him.
He would still be here."

With me.

And with their parents, who still grieved their eldest son,
a son Nasser couldn't ever replace.

He was finished, and he sat in silence after that, drained
emotionally and feeling hollow. He didn't know if he liked
the emptiness left behind, but Nasser supposed it was better
than having memories choke him up any longer. And if he

hadn't said anything, Anisa wouldn't have had a reason to comfort him with her touch. He stared at their point of contact, right now the only thing tethering him in reality. He'd worried that if he trudged through his unpleasant memories, he would get mired down by them. But he hadn't.

Through it all, Anisa hadn't said anything. Now he was done, she said, "I'm sorry for your brother. Sorry for you, too. You must have been young, because I don't remember a violent protest happening in Hargeisa."

"I was fifteen." Seeing by the way her brows puckered and her lips pooched adorably that she was doing the math of their ages, he helped her out. "You would've been nine, I believe."

"The same age my parents died... It wasn't a good year for either of us then."

He couldn't disagree.

The sad look on Anisa's face matched the sorrow darkening his mind. He blamed himself for upsetting her after she'd already cried not too long ago. He then recalled the reason why he'd even opened up, remembering that he had tried to share in her sympathy and return the trust she'd offered him in speaking about her parents. It had hurt telling her of his brother's final moments, but Nasser couldn't deny that he wasn't as burdened anymore.

Oddly, he felt better now that she knew.

He didn't understand what that meant, only that his heart didn't feel as cold and unreachable when Anisa pressed their palms together and laced her fingers through his. In fact, for the first time since losing Nuruddin, talking about his brother didn't inflict him with the usual grief and guilt.

CHAPTER ELEVEN

NASSER DIDN'T THINK Anisa could surprise him after the unexpected fishing trip, but when they left the beach, she led him to a restaurant where they handed their fish to staff and had their catch of the day prepared for lunch.

It was a unique experience made all the sweeter by Anisa's smiles and laughter. Seeing her happier did his heart a world of good. She hadn't had much reason to be lighthearted these past few days, with her brother being hospitalized and then having to confront the ghosts she'd left behind in Berbera. Nasser knew it couldn't have been easy.

If it were, I would have done it myself.

Going home was a sore topic for him too. He loved his parents, and it wasn't their fault that he couldn't stand to be home for very long, not with the memories of Nuruddin haunting the rooms and corridors of their house.

That was why he was proud of Anisa. In facing her grief, she did something that he couldn't.

They had come a long way from her fighting his protection. She might have only graced his life for a little more than a week, yet in that short time she'd made a big impact on him. The kind that he'd never be able to forget.

The kind he didn't *want* to forget.

After lunch, aiming to take her home, he slowed his truck when Anisa stopped pointing out the places she used to frequent regularly while growing up in that city. She simply stared out the car window. He followed the line of her vision to a small but seemingly popular supermarket, if the crowd in line out the door was anything to go by.

"Our parents would take Ara and me to this market all the time for ice cream bars after a long, hot day of fishing together."

He didn't have to ask, but he did. "Would you like ice cream?" He left out that they'd had a long, hot day of their own on the beach.

It got pretty hot near the end too, didn't it?

Unwilling to follow where that thought led him, Nasser instructed her to wait in the car for him. "I won't be long," he promised.

In the end, he baked outdoors under the sun and at the very end of the line into the supermarket for a solid ten minutes. When he was finally able to navigate the store, there was little choice of ice creams. He had to settle for what was left: two mint chocolate chip sandwich bars. Not his most favorite flavor, but he prayed Anisa was satisfied since she'd requested a chocolate ice cream. Another line slowed him down at the checkout lane. Though he was antsy to get back to her, he kept a grip on his patience by anticipating the joy on Anisa's pretty face once he passed her the sweet treat.

He had just reached the cashier when a commotion outside drifted in. Peering out the front glass of the store, he saw a crowd gathering on the street.

Frowning, he left behind his change in his hurry to pay for the ice cream, his instincts telling him that he needed to be outside.

And his gut didn't fail him, because he immediately saw that Anisa and his truck were surrounded by strangers. Someone had thrown a large stone onto the hood of his vehicle.

Nasser halted, a mix of shock and adrenaline locking his muscles before his blood heated and he unfroze. The first thing he did once he was free was to run toward Anisa and assess the situation, clocking all the relevant details. The stone had cratered the windshield and part of the hood. But the damage wasn't the foremost item on his mind. Intercepting any more threats to her leaped to the top of his priority list. If he had to whisk her away to keep her safe, then so be it.

Glowering at the curious onlookers, he ushered Anisa into the truck and passed her the ice creams he'd managed not to crush in his angry fright. He hauled the stone off the truck and onto the sidewalk before he slipped into the driver's seat and got them out of there as fast as possible.

He drove out of the city and to the outskirts where her home was in record time. All during the drive, out of the corner of his eye, he noticed Anisa holding on tightly to the handlebar. She slowly let it go when he finally parked the truck behind the well-guarded enclosure of her family property.

Unbuckling his seat belt, he opened the car door and waited for her to do the same.

When she didn't move a muscle and stared unblinkingly out the cracked windshield, he faced her. "Let's go inside and decompress."

She followed him slowly into the house, shock seeming to have totally numbed her into silence.

Up to that point, he'd placed her safety before his curiosity, but now that he had her secured in her home, Nasser asked for details.

"What happened?"

She shook her head as if rousing from a reverie before whipping her head to him. "A young boy threw the stone and started shouting at me. He said that Ara sent his father to prison. When I said that couldn't be true, he told me that Ara had his father falsely accused of embezzling public funds from his office."

Nasser folded his arms, furious that he'd left her alone and exposed to danger but tabling his anger to ask, "How did he know Ara was your brother?"

"His mother was there, too. I…recognized her. She was one of my mother's friends, and she used to visit often back in the day." Anisa bit her lip, her anguish palpable in her voice when she asked, "What they said can't be true, right? Ara couldn't have sent an innocent man away."

"If he sent him away, he likely wasn't innocent."

Anisa's mouth dropped open. "Okay, but why would Ara even get involved?"

"Your brother's sense of justice is strong. That and he has the wealth and power to stand up to corruption. Of course that means he's made enemies."

"Enemies?" Anisa spoke the word slowly, like she was tasting the syllables in her mouth and then pruning her lips at the distaste.

"It might seem like exaggeration, but these enemies of his could pose a threat to you simply by association." As she surely had just witnessed herself. "In the meantime, we should remain indoors, out of sight—"

"You mean *I* should remain indoors and out of sight," she interjected.

Nasser quelled a sigh. He had thought they'd moved past this. Her distrust cut deeper now though.

Because I kissed her.

And because of it, he had a pain in his heart that was projected in his sharp tone. "If it means safeguarding your well-being, then yes. Indoors and out of sight."

"And if I refuse?"

"You'd be foolish," he snapped, already irritated at the incident in the city. Her unwillingness to protect herself was the last straw.

Anisa's shock at his comment wore off rapidly, her anger

storming over her face. "Then let me be foolish. Why do you care?"

"Your brother hired me to do a job—"

"A job that ended when I decided to come home."

She was technically right, but also wrong. "The job was for me to protect you until you left for Canada, and since you have yet to do that…" He let the rest of his explanation stand, seeing no way for her to argue against the logic he'd placed before her.

"What's the point of protecting me if you're going to lock me up instead? You did a fine enough job in Madagascar. Why does it have to be different here?"

Her confidence in him was touching, but the truth was that he hadn't done a very good job at protecting her just now. And she must have sensed his self-doubt in his silence because she gentled her voice.

"I just don't understand why you're being so cautious. You saved me. Isn't that enough?"

Okay, so he saved her this time, only because he was able to intercept the danger to her.

But what about next time?

What if he couldn't get to her in time to rescue her? Then what? Nasser would've failed her. Failed himself.

Just like I failed Nuruddin.

Another person lost to his inability to protect those who mattered to him. Those he loved—

Love? Where had that come from? He didn't love Anisa. He *couldn't* love her.

He had no right to it, not if he couldn't protect her.

Anisa approached him, sealing the gap between them, and infiltrating his senses with the sweet sultriness of her perfume. He took in her full, glossy lips, small, pointed chin, upturned nose and round, dark eyes that reflected his uncertainty back at him. He wavered between taking her in his arms and walking away from the temptation—*no*, the promise that she presented him.

"Nasser, you can protect me. You have. There's nothing to worry about."

"Anisa, I…can't."

What happened on the beach had to stay on the beach. The only other place it could exist was in their memories. She thought she knew him simply because he shared the last moments of his brother with her, but she had no clue of the depth of anger, the hunger for revenge her brother promised him, or the real reason why fate had crossed and then tied their paths.

If she only knew…

She wouldn't be looking at him with that clueless softness of hers.

The anger he kept bottled really was no different than the young man who had come at his truck with a stone. The kind of rage that started young only built on itself, calcifying to a point of no return, and turning one's heart as hard as the stone that cracked his windshield and dented his truck's hood. He could have easily done that if he were facing the culprits who had killed his brother. Not the military officials who had been ordered to violently disrupt the protest, but the true puppeteers behind the cruel carnage that stole Nuruddin's life.

That's what I have to focus on.

With that firmly in mind, Nasser turned away from her. "Since we don't seem to be getting along or seeing eye to eye, I'll leave you." Then, having never taken off his shoes, he grabbed the handle, opened the front door, and walked out of the house before he decided walking away from Anisa was a mistake.

The coward.

The low-down, no-good coward.

Anisa quietly stewed for days after discovering that Nasser

had called it quits on her and passed her protection detail to one of his employees.

Like a hot potato, she observed sourly.

She might have accepted that he hadn't wanted to deal with her anymore *if* he'd had the common decency to tell her that much.

Instead, he'd relegated some other guy to do his job for him. The new guy, Daniel, was nice and seemed capable enough, and he'd told her that he had the pleasure of working closely with her brother. Anisa was admittedly intrigued by that, but it didn't let Nasser off the hook.

She was cross with him.

At first she'd wanted to hunt him down and shout his ears off, but then she realized that no one would allow her off the property on Nasser's explicit orders. Even if she could manage to sneak off, Anisa didn't have a clue where Nasser had gone. A quick, simple internet search mentioned that he had homes in several places all over the world. She wouldn't know where to begin to look.

Why am I chasing after him?

It was so apparent that he didn't care about her at all. Not in the way she imagined and hoped he would.

Lying in her bed, flat on her back, she touched her lips, the soft pads of her fingers sadly not a comparison to the immense pleasure his mouth had given her. Anisa sighed and dropped her hand away, resting it on her chest over her thumping heart. She sat up when her thoughts wouldn't let her relax. Moving over to her small writing desk, she picked up the empty notebook she'd found and begun writing in. It was a first draft of an idea that she had started kicking around in her head.

She hadn't attempted a screenplay in over a year now. Her work, paying off her student loans, and the rent on her apartment had become her priority. But now, with all the free time she had after Nasser basically ran off on her, Anisa had drifted back to the haven her creativity once offered her.

And it was looking like it would be a good distraction for her again. Sitting down, she picked up her pen.

She poured her emotions onto the page. Letting out the frustration, anguish, pining and every other tumultuous feeling she couldn't name while she created her world, characters, and plot in a frenzied daze.

By the time she lifted her head, it was nearly midnight. Her body ached, her brain shutting down for the day, the thoughts of Ara's well-being, Nasser's sudden abandonment, and what the future held for all of them no longer tormenting her. It was only then that Anisa pulled herself away from her desk and all the words she'd written and crawled into her bed with nothing on her mind but a wish for a good night's sleep.

She lived in isolation like that for three days and nights after Nasser handed his protection duty over to his staff.

Anisa anticipated nothing would change on the fourth day.

And nothing had in the beginning, her day unfolding the same. But sometime in the late evening, she was distracted from her writing when noises in the hallway dragged her over to her closed bedroom door. Tiptoeing over as the unmistakable sound of heavy foot treads passed, she placed her ear to the door, stilled her heavy breathing and listened.

The footfalls receded down the corridor in the direction of her brother's study. This was followed by the faint click of a door latch being unlocked.

Anisa pulled back, staring hard at the door.

Who had the keys to her brother's study besides Nasser? And if that was him, why was he skulking around the house so late like a thief in the night?

Duh. He's trying to avoid me.

Anisa seethed at that.

She'd done nothing to him to deserve this treatment. And who kissed someone and just up and pretended like nothing happened?

Heartless jerk.

Bristling, Anisa flung open her bedroom door, determined to corner him and tell him exactly how awful he was making her feel.

The house was incredibly still—the kind of stillness that carried its own kind of noise. She could hear her heartbeats clearer, as well as her breathing, and the creak of the hardwood floorboards beneath the carpet runner spanning the long corridor.

What if isn't Nasser but an intruder?

She hadn't really considered that, and it gave her pause. But she realized it would be a next to impossible feat for any intruder, what with all the guards, and all the cameras stationed outside and inside the home and equipped with fancy heat vision, not to mention the sensor wires that Nasser had told her were running along the property so no one could walk in without being detected.

Feeling that the likelihood of it being a burglar or some other nefarious character was slim, Anisa snapped her shoulders back and steeled her spine as she closed in on the double doors to her brother's study. Her heart rate picked up when she heard footfalls inside, like someone was in there pacing. A shadow slid past the crack of light streaming from under the doors. She grasped the door handle. Before she could talk herself out of barging in, she flung open the door.

It was just as Anisa expected, her eyes finding and landing on Nasser the instant she stepped into the room. She recognized him even with the darker stubble masking his jaw. Triumph drummed in her chest when he appeared taken aback by the sight of her, his eyes doubling in size.

She opened her mouth, ready to count all the ways he'd

hurt her with his sudden departure, but ended up swallow-ing her words as she heard her name.

"Anisa?"

That voice—she would've recognized it blindfolded de-spite not hearing it for four years now.

Ara.

Anisa hadn't looked the whole room over when she marched in. Now that she did, she could easily see her brother sitting behind his big, opulent desk, bathed in the golden glow of his desk lamp. "You're awake," he said, proving that he was there. In the flesh. Alive and whole and looking like himself despite sitting in a wheelchair, a bandage wound around his head and neck and another one plastered to his left cheek.

The bandage covering his face didn't hinder him from smiling.

It was a slight upward tilt of his lips, but Anisa would take it. Whenever she dreamed of this encounter, it was al-ways with the worry that he would look at her in the same cold way he'd done when she had chosen to move out of their family home.

He's here. He's really here, and he's smiling at me.

Anisa couldn't express the jolt of emotions that seized her all at once. Her overflowing joy seemed to have no end.

"Ara." Her voice broke as she said his name. Anisa swiped at her cheeks and felt the wetness on them. She took a jerky step forward, and then another one.

Looking like he intended to meet her halfway, Ara rolled toward her, grunting as he did, not able to entirely mask the pain tightening his hard-planed face. He stopped in front of her, locked the wheels and slowly pulled himself to a stand. Anisa fought the urge to help him. Not knowing if her touch would awaken a grudge in him, she held herself back. Be-cause now that her fear for his life was extinguished, she feared losing him to his anger at her just as she had all this time they hadn't communicated.

So she left Ara to stand on his own two feet and in his own good time.

"You shouldn't overexert yourself," Nasser cautioned him. "The doctor said—"

Nasser's warning was cut short by Ara's scoff.

"I heard what the doctor said." Panting, he pulled his hands off the armrests of the wheelchair and stood with the teeniest of wobbles. He gave her a nod and another small smile, but he spoke to Nasser when he said, "I think just this once, the doctor will forgive me if I want to hug my sister without having her crouch to my level."

Anisa's bottom lip trembled as Ara opened his arms to her. In that instant, she knew that their relationship was on its way to healing and maybe even improving from what it was.

He hugged her tightly and whispered at her ear, "I missed you, baby sis."

Face buried in his shoulder, Anisa cried at that, and one loud sob that couldn't be completely muffled escaped. She bawled so hard she shook in his arms. When she finally settled down enough to draw back, her face wet from her teary display, Anisa could see that Ara hadn't remained unaffected either.

His eyes shone with unshed tears as he gave her another crooked smile.

"I missed you too," Anisa said.

More than you'll ever know...

Giving her another nod, his face lined with fatigue, he gazed at her with understanding. They might have stood like that, his arms still around her, if Ara hadn't suddenly gone heavy in her arms. Anisa cried out, nearly toppling down to the floor with Ara's body weight crushing her. Nasser came to her rescue.

Together, they eased Ara back down into his wheelchair.

Over her brother's head, she caught Nasser's eyes briefly, his nostrils flaring at her as he seemed to drink her in. And she hated that with one look he obliterated her upset with him and set her body alight with longing. Giving her head a shake, Anisa looked away. The only thing that would sting more than Nasser's abandonment was Ara discovering that there was more going on between her and Nasser than a simple protector-protectee relationship.

Now safely seated, Ara grunted, reminding her that he wasn't fully healed. That despite having made it home to her, her brother had a long journey to full recovery. It was enough for Anisa to temporarily set aside her friction with Nasser.

"Why didn't you tell me you were discharged?" Hooking a thumb at Nasser, she snapped, "Why didn't he?" She was upset because after he'd vowed that he would report to her the instant Ara had awoken, he'd reneged on his promise.

"Nasser doesn't hold any blame. I told him not to tell you."

Anisa frowned, more confused by all the secrecy. "Why not just tell me?" Then, because she had a sneaking suspicion, she amended sharply, "What aren't you telling me?"

Ara sighed, and somehow that peeved her more.

"I wanted to surprise you, that's all."

Well, he'd succeeded, but now that the joy of seeing him again had passed, it was replaced by a gnawing concern.

"The hospital did clear you to leave, didn't they?" It would be just like Ara to stubbornly check himself out. But he shook his head, allaying her fears that he'd left the professional care he had been receiving earlier than he ought to have.

"The doctor and I decided that I could recuperate at home once my tests came back with positive news."

"That's good," she murmured.

Ara flashed her another smile, the sight of it rejuvenat-

ing the warmth that was quelled by her ever-present fears. It
didn't last long, because Ara then frowned.

"I heard that an incident occurred in the city center, and
that you were almost harmed."

Anisa's jaw dropped, the whiplash switch of emotions con-
fusing her before her head cleared and anger stormed its way
to the front. She winged a glare at Nasser and hated how nonchalant he appeared under her baleful stare.

"He told you. Of course he did." She folded her arms.

"Again, Nasser was hired to do his job, Anisa. I asked him
to give me reports, and I think it's important. Otherwise I
can't protect you properly."

"Protection!" Anisa threw up her hands and laughed
mirthlessly, exasperated by these two men and tired of giving them no fight on the final say. "It's all about protection,
but neither of you can fully tell me *what* you're protecting me
from exactly." She looked between them, their silence backing her point up. They didn't trust her with whatever it was
they were up to, and it hurt beyond comprehension. "Well,
I'm tired of your protection. I don't want or need it."

Then, without looking back, she stormed out and past her
bedroom for the stairs, ignoring Ara calling her name, and
pretending her heart wasn't breaking that Nasser seemed to
not care whether she stayed or left.

"Is there something happening between you and my sister?"

Nasser ripped his narrowed eyes off the open doors to
Ara's study, where he'd only just watched Anisa tear out of
the room and had to kill his instinct to follow her. Not only
because he sensed that Anisa wasn't happy with him right
then, but now Ara was staring at him suspiciously after he
posed the question. It was the last thing Nasser expected to
happen, and the last subject he wished to discuss.

After nearly getting her killed.

He knew he'd hurt her by his sudden choice to pass her protection over to another, but it had to be done. In her presence, he allowed himself to get distracted, and that had nearly gotten her injured. Or far worse, *killed*.

Some might accuse him of exaggerating, but life was so fragile. Death could come from anywhere. Strike so suddenly that there was no protection from it. That was what had happened to Nuruddin. One second he was holding Nasser's hand and pulling him away from danger, and the next he was crumpling to the ground, dead long before medical aid could arrive.

That could have easily been Anisa a few days earlier. Then she would've died on his watch. Just the notion was enough to break his heart. He wasn't strong enough to protect her—and he didn't believe he'd ever be.

He'd done one final thing for her. Once he'd gotten news of Ara waking from his comatose state, he flew out of Hargeisa to Mogadishu immediately and saw to it personally that Anisa's brother returned home safely to her. He hadn't wanted her to get her hopes up, and so he'd left without saying a word to her, entrusting her safety and care to his reliable staff. Of course, she must have thought he had run away from her.

Rather than battle his fraught emotions, he capped the helplessness rising up in him and confronted Ara's inquiring gaze.

"Between us?" Nasser drawled, affecting nonchalance he didn't feel at all. "Besides professional courtesy, no."

Ara's eyebrows sprang up. "Oh. She seemed awfully upset with you."

Nasser pushed down the guilt that surged at being reminded that he caused any pain to her, and he smoothed his features so as to not reflect anything to confirm Ara's suspicions.

After assessing him for what felt like minutes, Ara nodded briskly. "I had to ask, you know."

"I understand." And he did. If their roles were flipped, he'd want to protect his kid sister too. Anisa might not realize it now, but she had people around her who would do a far better job than he when it came to safeguarding her. These feelings they had for each other would fade with time.

She'll forget me and move on, and it will be for the best.

He wished he could say the same, but as he had no mind to replace her, Nasser was prepared to mourn what he would lose out on when he left her. If only he was a different person...someone who could be enough for her. Needing a focus besides his self-pity, Nasser asked Ara the same thing he'd been asking him the moment he'd awoken from his coma.

"Do you have what I wanted?"

Rolling out from behind his desk to the seating area in his office, Ara motioned for Nasser to take a seat across from him. He didn't speak until Nasser was seated and at eye level with him. "I do. The list is in an encrypted file. Your IT team at my company has the key as they built encryption software for it."

"Forward me the file."

"I already did earlier, on our flight out of Mogadishu," Ara said.

Nasser stood hastily and snapped up his tablet from Ara's desk. He hadn't had time to clear everything off since he'd temporarily taken over his office. It worked to his benefit just then, because within minutes, he had made calls to his team for the decryption code and had access to the very file Ara mentioned.

The names of the culprits who'd had a hand in Nuruddin's death stared him in the face. He'd dreamed of this day for so very long, and now Nasser had a hard time believing what he was looking at. He stopped scrolling, one name in particular having jumped out at him from his tablet's glowing screen.

"Sharmarke." He looked up at Ara, scowling. "Your father-in-law's involved."

"I typed the list, didn't I? I'm aware of what names are on there." Ara sighed, sounding and looking more fatigued by the second. "It's a disappointing revelation at most. I didn't expect it to be true, but I confirmed it. Sharmarke was one of the government officials who sanctioned the attack at the protest rally that killed your brother, Nasser."

He regarded the list again. "Where is he now?"

"Before I tell you, humor me for a moment. Is vengeance still the path you want to walk?"

What kind of question was that? Everything Nasser had done after the day he lost Nuruddin had led him to that moment. Even if he wanted to walk away, he didn't know if any other path was open to him.

That's a lie, and you know it.

Nasser breathed deeply as an image crystallized in his mind. It was of Anisa in his arms, both of them smiling and lost in a happiness of their own making. But just as quickly as he thought of her, he relinquished the futile dream. Being with Anisa was impossible for him. And without her, he had no choice but to fulfill his plot for justice.

Realizing Ara awaited a response, Nasser demanded, "It is. Now tell me where Sharmarke is."

"He's under house arrest currently, while I secure the evidence that will put him away. But if this is the path you're still determined to be on, then go, take your revenge. Either way, it concludes this business of ours."

As Nasser strode out of Ara's study, he recognized that though this *business* with Ara might have ended, that he wasn't quite finished. He had one more stop before he finally sought the revenge he'd wanted.

He only prayed that she didn't turn him out, especially as it could be the last time Nasser saw or spoke to Anisa ever again.

Not long after she marched out of Ara's office in protest at how delicately her brother and Nasser were treating her, a knock on her door had Anisa scrambling out of bed and straightening her hijab. She paused to check her reflection, dashing away the fresh tears streaking down her cheeks and clearing her throat of the sadness that clogged it before she opened her bedroom door.

Nasser stood a respectable distance away, his face as inscrutable as his thoughts and feelings.

"What do you want?" she grumped.

"May I come in?"

"No, because I was just headed out," she snapped, stepping past the threshold and closing the door behind her. The thought of being trapped with him in her bedroom had her heart palpitating wildly. If they were going to have a conversation, she would have the choice of a setting.

She led him down to the kitchen, where she microwaved herself a bowl of buttery popcorn. Grabbing her snack, she then headed for the family room, parked herself in front of the excessively large wall-mounted television, and flipped through movies until she settled on a chilling horror film. Not her usual go-to genre, but her dark mood called for something bloodier. And as terror and chaos played out on the TV and she munched on her popcorn, Anisa could almost pretend every part of her wasn't finely attuned to Nasser's presence so close to her.

Almost.

Because try as she might, she was very aware of him. It irked her, but it was the truth. Rather than calming down, with every passing second Anisa grew more agitated. The movie hadn't even played for a full five minutes when Anisa snatched up the remote, pressed Pause, and lanced Nasser with a glare.

"Are you just going to stand there?" she asked, feeling more waspish now that she was looking at him.

"I'm not staying, Anisa. I only came to tell you that I'm leaving."

She rolled her eyes and scoffed, "Why tell me when you've already left before without saying a word?"

He had the nerve to sigh. "It's because I'm done working with your brother."

"You mean you're done protecting me." She curled her lips into a sneer. It was either that or give in to the tears that began sparking at the corners of her eyes. And she was tired of hiding from these emotions she always seemed to feel around him, needing this off her chest more than anything.

Anisa set her popcorn down on the sofa beside her so it wouldn't impede her from standing, marching right up to him and poking a finger at his face. "It was a heartless move to leave without telling me you were going."

"Heartless?" Nasser's face grew stormier in a blink.

The swift change in him should've been warning enough for her to back off, but she only had a fleeting few seconds of caution before he acted. Faster than she could evade him, he ensnared her wrists and hauled her into him. Though suddenly pressed flush to Nasser, Anisa didn't resist. She was too shocked by his quick actions to process what had happened.

"Is it heartless of me to want to find the people who are responsible for my brother's death? *Punish* them so that they never inflict the damage they did to my family on anyone else?"

He pushed his face closer to hers with every word. By the end of it, he encompassed her whole field of vision.

"No, I'm not heartless to want to seek vengeance on those

who hurt me and my family." Their chests were nearly touching now, and his flinty gaze roved lower down her face to where she had drawn her bottom lip between her teeth. She saw a muscle twitch along his jaw, and his brow creased that much more. Now his thumbs stroked tenderly along the sensitive part of her inner wrist. "Not heartless," he murmured, as if he had to convince himself more than her.

And then, just as she seriously thought that he'd kiss her—

He let her go abruptly.

Gawking at him, Anisa touched her wrists and swayed in place at the sudden loss of his touch.

Nasser raked a hand over his short black curls, his palm snapping around the back of his neck. He rolled his shoulders, a strained look crossing his face. "The reason I'm leaving is that your brother promised me something in exchange for your protection. I wanted the names of the people who'd had a hand in killing my brother. Not the men who pulled the trigger, but those that hid behind their bureaucratic titles and public offices.

"When Nuruddin was killed, *I* was accused of his death. Do you know what it's like to be labeled a criminal and a monster and be locked up falsely? To be a scapegoat for the politicians who killed my brother? Then to be forced into the military by those same politicians who only hoped that I would be killed in the line of duty somewhere and make their lives easier?"

He stared at her with hellfire in his eyes. "I didn't die though. And now I want what I've always wanted since my brother was murdered. I want vengeance. Justice. I want to right wrongs, and I intend to do so." Then, seeing his head turn toward the exit from the family room, Anisa rushed around him and blocked his escape.

She stopped shy of throwing out her arms dramatically, instead trying to use her words to calm him. "There has to be another way." Anisa gazed at him pleadingly and clung to the hope that she could dissuade him from leaving on some violent mission to avenge his late brother.

"Anisa, you can't stop me."

She knew that she couldn't.

But I can try.

"So, what do you plan to do when you find these responsible parties?"

Nasser gave her a look that chilled her blood. From that one glance, she inferred that he meant to take his ultimate revenge.

Panicked, Anisa breached his space, pushed up on her toes and got up in his face.

"You can't do what you're thinking, Nasser. It won't bring Nuruddin back. And I'm certain he wouldn't want you killing yourself with all this guilt. Because your brother's death isn't your fault."

"*Because* of me, my parents had to bury their son prematurely. *My* mistake killed my brother. *Mine.*"

"Is that how you feel, Nasser, or is that what your parents told you?" And when he didn't respond, Anisa kept on, her hope that she was getting through to him cemented when his brows furrowed with consideration. "Maybe they feel different than you do. Maybe they never blamed you, and all they want is for you to be happy and free of this burden of responsibility for your brother's passing."

The longer Nasser remained quiet, the more hopeful she was that she'd saved him from making a life-altering mistake.

But she came crashing down to reality when he cleared his face of any emotion, locking her out of his thoughts and feelings.

"And what if your parents' death wasn't an accident? What if you knew the names of the people who killed them?"

Anisa reared back from him as though he had dealt her

a physical blow. His cruel words certainly packed the same punch, leaving her ridden with senselessness. And when she finally did feel something, it was abject disappointment in him for stooping so low and using her parents' deaths to make a point about why he had to fulfill his revenge plot.

A part of her knew that he was doing this on purpose to force her into pushing him away.

But she was too tired to call him out on it. So she didn't. "I can't stop you, can I?" she said sadly.

"You're better off letting me go," he replied.

Tightening her lips to keep herself from sobbing, Anisa moved aside and watched helplessly as Nasser breezed past her.

Since meeting him, she'd always accepted that they'd eventually go their separate ways. But she hadn't realized until that instant just how difficult it would be to allow him to walk away from her again. Anisa wanted to be enraged with him, yet all she felt was heartache. For him. For his brother. For his family.

For us.

Or what they could have been had Nasser not chosen his revenge over her.

CHAPTER TWELVE

SINCE LEAVING BERBERA nearly a week ago, Nasser didn't feel as strongly motivated by his mission of vengeance.

It started when he'd followed the address Ara had given him to the remote home that imprisoned Sharmarke. Nasser sat across from the evil man and stared him in the eye with the knowledge that he'd played a role in delivering Nuruddin to an early grave and then sending Nasser to prison along with other innocent protestors. He imagined throttling him many times, reaching over the table that separated them and choking him before the guards Ara had stationed outside the plain one-room house heard the mischief and caught on to what was taking place right under their noses.

But the more he looked at the old, tired man sitting hunched and in a rumpled suit across from him, the less anger he felt. If anything, he pitied him for the poor choices he'd made, and seeing the hopelessness in his eyes was as satisfying as watching the life go out of him at his hands. Nasser left him alive and as well as anyone could be while housebound and with the only freedom they could look forward to being the prison that awaited them.

Not even bothering to pursue the other names on the list Ara gave him, he'd then flown straight to Hargeisa, where his parents lived after having moved from Djibouti a long time ago, and where he had grown up along with Nuruddin. He'd dropped in and surprised them. His mother nearly collapsed from joy, and even his stoic father had smiled tearfully and hugged him for longer than usual. It had been a long time since he'd visited, worried every time he did that the love they had for him would change to hatred and blame. He wouldn't fault them if they did resent him.

Now, after a few days spent in the comfort of his family, he traveled to the place he had visited only once before.

He stood over his brother's grave and the stone covering the hole that was Nuruddin's final resting place. Nasser crouched and traced the etching in the stone, spelling out Nuruddin's full name and his birthdate and death date. The only other time he'd been here was right after he had been freed from prison and forced to sign up for military service. And he'd only come because his parents compelled him to; he hadn't wanted to confront his guilt immediately.

So he imagined it had come as a shock to them when he'd asked to visit Nuruddin.

Standing behind him now, his parents watched as Nasser pressed his palm in the center of the sun-warmed stone.

"I missed the chance to see him properly buried." He stood and looked back at his parents, his heart aching. "I suppose it's divine punishment." Unable to hold their gazes for this next part, he cast his burning eyes down to Nuruddin's grave and said what he hadn't been able to tell them for all these years. "It's my fault he died."

His mother gasped, the sound followed by her hurrying over to him and taking his face into her hands. "Look at me, Nasser. You are not responsible for what happened."

"We don't blame you. How could we when you're all we have left?" His father came up to them, his hand gripping and squeezing Nasser's shoulder.

Kissing his cheeks, his mother took his hands and pressed them to her chest. "You're our pride and joy. We miss Nuruddin, of course, but it doesn't diminish what we feel for you. We'll always love you, Nasser, and we'll always love your brother, too."

Blinking back tears, Nasser hung his head, taking in their words and recognizing the peace that came with them. For so long he'd bottled what he had been feeling for fear and shame that he'd only bring more pain to his parents. He'd even kept the truth of Nuruddin's death from them to spare them.

But now, as they held him and reaffirmed their love for him, Nasser fought past the lump in his throat and told them everything.

About how Nuruddin tried to save him. And how he'd been gunned down right in front of Nasser.

The crooked government officials who'd been behind Nuruddin's death had spun the media coverage of the violent use of force at the rally as having been necessary. They painted the peaceful protestors as rebels. They had then told Nasser's parents that they should be grateful their son had only been forcefully conscripted into the military.

It all came tumbling out of him. When the full truth was aired, he sighed long and hard, an oppressive weight he hadn't recognized shifting off him.

His parents shared a look when he finished speaking. Then his father nodded solemnly. "We know." And before Nasser could ask how, his mother explained.

"We heard from the others who escaped the protest." She named a friend of Nuruddin's and then said, "He came to visit us about a year after you'd left to board at the military academy, and he told us everything about that awful day. About what you and Nuruddin both suffered."

"Why didn't you tell me that you knew?" Nasser asked once his shock passed.

"It was a decision your mother and I made. We didn't see a reason to open up an old wound. What happened to your brother…" his father trailed off, blinking suspiciously "…

was terrible. But we still had you, and we only wished to do right by you."

They wanted to spare *his* feelings. Nasser couldn't believe what he was hearing, considering he'd invested all this energy trying to protect them from the truth of Nuruddin's death.

When in reality they've been doing the exact same thing for me.

Suddenly an urge to laugh struck him hard, so he did.

He threw his head back from the laughter. Wiping at his eyes as his humor wound down, he noticed his parents traded worried looks.

"I'm fine," he reassured them. "I only just remembered something funny."

He chuckled again at how silly he'd been all these years. Not once had he even thought that his parents would want to protect him too, in their own way. Now that he knew better, Nasser stared at them through new eyes.

"Thank you." He embraced them both, smiling down at them. "I'm sorry that I haven't been around very much, but that'll change now. I promise you."

As they bade Nuruddin farewell and walked down the dusty hill to where Nasser had parked his truck, his mother leaned into him and said, "Although we love seeing you, your father and I were surprised by your sudden visit."

His father interjected then, "I thought you said we weren't going to ask him."

His mother flapped a hand dismissively. "I changed my mind," she said, to which his father clucked his tongue.

Nasser smiled at their lighthearted banter, wondering how he could have ever allowed his misplaced guilt to get him to stay away from them.

"We just want to know if anything's wrong, Nasser," his mother told him. "Anything that might have brought you home to us."

"Nothing's wrong," he replied. As to why he'd come for a visit, Nasser thought of Anisa. She had planted the seed for him to go see his parents—for him to open up about his feelings to them. If he had anyone to thank for this peaceful bubble he was wrapped up in now, it was her.

But he couldn't see her.

Not after the way he'd ended things.

"A friend advised that I should visit you."

"Oh? We'll have to thank this friend of yours one day then," his mother said with a loving pat to his arm.

Then, instead of waxing poetic about how Anisa was amusingly stubborn, beautiful, creative, and easy to talk to, he regaled them with the adventures he'd shared with her. From the lemur who decided to do its business on his shoulder, to the handline fishing they'd done on the beach together. Though they were memories he would treasure forever, Nasser didn't want them to remain as only memories.

He certainly didn't want those memories to be the only pieces he had of her.

I love her, he thought, so very naturally.

He loved her and he'd messed up what might have become a really good thing with her. And all for what? Because he'd believed that he couldn't protect her. Nasser scoffed inwardly, surprised that he hadn't seen she never needed his protection—at least not in the way he imagined. And that just like his parents had tried to protect him, Anisa had done so in her own way. She'd attempted to shield him from seeking out the revenge that would ultimately have only ended up hurting him. Somehow she had known that his vengeance wouldn't give him the pleasure he once believed it might.

Nasser shook his head, disgusted with himself.

But he stopped there, not beating himself up about it any longer, his mind already spinning as he thought of what he could do to win her back.

* * *

Nasser leaving again shouldn't have been new to Anisa, but it felt different the second time.

Because I know he's not coming back.

He'd said so himself before he left her. Before he had gone off to chase after his so-called idea of justice for his brother.

She wasn't important enough to him, obviously. And yet here she was, giving him way more thought than he deserved.

Deciding that staying busy would get her to move forward, Anisa turned back to her writing. She'd also extended her stay in Berbera, not yet ready to leave Ara, even though she was still upset with him for crossing a line and trying to exert his control over her. Ara was the reason that Nasser came into her life, after all. Her brother was partly to blame for this heartbreak she was nursing. The other part was solely on her. Even before learning that Nasser had only protected her to get information from Ara for his mission of revenge, she'd known deep down that Nasser was the last man she should fall in love with.

Because it was love.

Still young and new, but powerful enough to leave her staring off into space while quietly fretting for his safety.

What if he does something stupid and gets himself hurt?

She'd already had to handle Ara just being out of the woods. Anisa couldn't bear the thought of another person she cared about getting hurt.

As the days passed, her anxiety only doubled down and injected its poison into her dreams. The nightmares she'd once had of being run over by speeding motorboats and drowning along with her parents had turned into terror for Nasser's well-being. She started sleeping less and less, avoiding her bed for fear that her bad dreams would somehow be self-fulfilling.

In an effort to keep from falling asleep, she alternated between writing, watching films and TV shows, and pacing the halls at night. She might have walked the grounds outside and stretched her legs had she not figured the guards would report to Ara about her night wanderings. The last thing she wanted was to give him a reason to hover over her more.

And since she couldn't go outside as easily as she would have liked, Anisa settled for getting some fresh air up on the rooftop terrace.

She hadn't gone up there until Nasser had left, not having a reason to explore before then. But now that she had, she could see why Ara had paid for it to be built when he'd remodeled their childhood home. It was beautiful up there, the spacious seating area around a firepit and the touches of greenery seamlessly melding beauty with comfort and luxury.

Once she discovered how peaceful it was, Anisa began going up to the terrace to calm herself.

That night was no different.

She hoped for a quiet moment to herself. Instead, she came to a fast stop when she saw that she wasn't alone.

Ara stood a few feet from her, his wheelchair nowhere in sight but a cane within arm's reach. The only reason he hadn't noticed her was that he had his back to her and his hand raised, his cell phone pressed to his ear. It was hard to tell who he was talking to as she could barely catch what he said in his deep, murmuring tone. The words she did hear didn't make sense.

"Let's talk later... No, not now... This isn't the time..."

Though she couldn't hear the other side of the conversation, Anisa gleaned from Ara's tense posturing that it wasn't a chat he was happy to be having.

She was only now recalling that Nasser had told her Ara liked the terrace most. Apparently even being wheelchair-bound in his condition wasn't enough to stop her brother from coming upstairs. And now his cane made perfect sense since a stairway connected the terrace to the house's lower floors.

Silently cursing herself for forgetting, she immediately started backing away from him. As curious as she was about who the caller was and what the call was about that had Ara sounding so flustered, Anisa didn't think he'd appreciate her listening in on him. Before she could tiptoe away without him ever knowing she'd been there, Ara suddenly pulled the phone down from his ear and turned, his eyes landing on her.

"Anisa," he said, sounding as surprised as he appeared. Then he frowned. "What are you doing up here so late?"

She resisted poking her tongue out at him, her humiliation at looking like she'd been eavesdropping disappearing in a puff of smoke and replaced by her annoyance.

"I could ask you the same question." She crossed her arms.

He shook his head. "As I'm sure you just heard, I was taking a phone call."

She narrowed her eyes. "I barely heard anything. And if I had known you were up here, I wouldn't have disturbed you."

"Did I accuse you of disturbing me?"

Anisa harrumphed, not knowing why he'd reduced her to feeling like a little kid again with one lightly scolding remark. How was it that after four years of being her own person, and of not having to rely on Ara, she hadn't shed this keen need for his approval?

It heaped more irritation onto her already sour mood. And since she didn't think she had anything nice to say, she turned away and only stopped at the sound of her name.

"Anisa, wait." The sound of Ara's cane tap-tap-tapping on the terrace's stone flooring came up behind her. "We should have a talk, shouldn't we? A proper one. It's been years, after all."

Her arms still folded, she faced him and nodded quickly, knowing that this day would have eventually come. The fact that they hadn't spoken for so very long was the elephant in the room.

"There's something I've been meaning to say. Something I should have said the moment I saw you again." He took a deep breath and then said, "I'm sorry, Anisa."

Anisa blinked fast, at first certain she hadn't heard him correctly, and then feeling tears forming already when Ara had barely spoken.

"I apologize for not having ended our silence earlier. It was childish of me. No, it was downright *wrong*. When I awoke in the hospital, I thought of you first." Ara's lips twitched up, a small smile wiping the signs of strain from his features.

It had to be taking much of his effort to stand upright when he still wasn't feeling all that well. Knowing that he was pushing through his discomfort for her had Anisa's bottom lip trembling and her heart throbbing with compassion. She would've opened her mouth to stop him so he could rest, but Ara jutted his chin upwards in determination, propped both hands over his cane and held himself as tall as he could in his still-recovering state.

"I thought that I wouldn't see you again, and it put these past years without you in my life into perspective. Anisa, I don't expect your forgiveness, but I'm asking—no, *hoping* that you'll let me earn your trust back as your brother. Please."

She wiped at her eyes at his proposal, sniffled loudly and laughed. "Great. You've made me cry."

Ara laughed with her. And just like that, the tension between them evaporated.

Still wiping at her eyes, Anisa said, "I'm sorry, too. I could have picked up the phone and given you a call. I was too stubborn."

"Must be a family trait," he teased. Then he eased back on his cane and gestured for her to join him on the terrace. Standing at the very edge of the rooftop deck and looking out over their home city, Ara told her, "I'm glad you're home. It doesn't feel as lonely with you here."

"Lonely? You shouldn't let your wife hear you say that. Speaking of, where is she, and when do I get to meet her finally? Her name's Zaynab, right?" It was really all Anisa knew of his wife. Besides that she was raised by her mother primarily in the UK after her parents divorced. Sharmarke had remarried a long time ago, and he hadn't spoken of Zaynab, not until he'd messaged Anisa with the news that Ara had married his daughter and they had become real family through marriage.

"I still can't believe you're married," she remarked, snorting then. "I hope she knew what she was getting into."

"We're actually getting divorced."

Anisa goggled at him. "Divorced? Why?"

"It's complicated, but you might as well know." Then he told her Adeero Sharmarke was involved in the deadly assault at the protest that killed Nasser's brother, Nuruddin.

Anisa dropped onto one of the cushioned benches nearby, shocked to her core by this turn of events. "I can't believe Adeero Sharmarke would do that."

Ara's sigh was long-suffering. It made her wonder how long he'd kept this information to himself. She knew it had to be a while judging by the way he sounded more fatigued than he had seconds earlier.

"Ten months ago, I reached out to Nasser because I liked what I was hearing about his company's security services. We got to talking, and I learned he lost his brother at a protest rally in Hargeisa years ago. I knew that Sharmarke worked in government around that time in the city, but whenever I tried broaching the subject with him, he would casually dismiss me.

"That was my first red flag. So, I did the research without Sharmarke's help. And what you're feeling was how I felt when I first started looking into the protest for Nasser. The more I dug into the government files I could get my hands on, the more I noticed Sharmarke's name alongside other crooked politicians, and the more I'd hoped it wasn't true—that there was some mistake somewhere, and he wasn't involved. But he was one of several who had signed off on the use of deadly force at the protest. Though he hadn't killed Nasser's brother outright himself, he might as well have."

His brows furrowed in consternation. "I had a choice then. Conceal the truth…or try and accept that Adeero Sharmarke wasn't who we believed him to be. I chose acceptance, and part of that meant telling Nasser the truth."

As soon as the words were out of his mouth, Anisa sucked in a sharp inhale, and her spine went ramrod-straight. "*That's* why Nasser left. You let him go after Sharmarke. What if he gets hurt?"

What if he dies?

Ara sat down beside her, a look of relief briefly streaking over his face as he stretched his legs out and set his cane aside.

"Given what he does for a living, I feel confident that Nasser can protect himself," Ara said, but taking her hand and rubbing her knuckles in comfort when her worry for Nasser didn't fade. "It's Sharmarke I'm more concerned about, but I've stationed men to keep Nasser from doing too much damage."

"Ara," Anisa whispered, her whole face itching with the urge to cry anew.

"As much as Sharmarke might deserve it, I won't let Nasser make the mistake of killing a man and tainting his soul."

Full of gratitude, but unable to put it into words around the big lump in her throat, she curled into Ara's side. He wrapped his arm around her shoulders, embracing her as best as he could with his healing wounds. It reminded her of when she was younger, after their parents died, and Anisa would wake from one of her night terrors. Never too far away, Ara would show up and comfort her until the terrifying feeling of loneliness vanished. Until she remembered that she wasn't ever alone, not so long as she and Ara had each other.

Anisa thought they were finished with all the soul-baring, but when she peeled back from Ara to wipe her eyes, she froze at the troubling frown on his face.

"There's something else. It regards *Hooyo* and *Aabo*."

She pushed up onto her feet, suddenly feeling like she needed to go for the longest run of her life—but she settled for pacing in front of Ara and feeling his eyes follow her carefully.

"What about them?" she asked, wringing her hands.

"It's about how they died."

For the next several minutes, Ara turned her world upside down. He told her that their parents hadn't died in an accident but were murdered in cold blood. Anisa sobbed through most of it, horrified that someone had torn their family apart purposefully. And that she'd nearly died along with their parents. By the end, Anisa scrubbed at her face, her eyes feeling raw.

She now understood why Ara had tried to protect her all this time. Why he'd made their home one big fortress. Why he'd sent Nasser to her. He wanted to safeguard her from the monsters who had killed their mom and dad.

"I wish you'd told me earlier," she said. "It hurts even more knowing that you suffered by yourself, and I couldn't protect you like you protected me." Anisa hugged him then, squeezing Ara tightly. "Thank you. For thinking of me, putting me before you, and just being my family."

When she began to let him go, Anisa felt Ara's arms tightening around her, quietly indicating he didn't want to release her just yet.

"Anisa, you just being with me now is enough to protect

me from feeling like I'll drown in my sorrow." He slowly released her then, smiling at her, his eyes dark with unshed tears.

"Did they find who…?" Anisa couldn't bear to say *killed our parents*, but thankfully Ara understood her and answered with a slow, sad shake of his head.

"That's why I've been working with Nasser. After I learned of what had happened to his brother, I thought perhaps the same culprits were behind our parents' deaths."

"You thought Sharmarke did it?"

"I was wrong there, and I would say *thankfully*, but considering what he did to Nasser and his family, I don't think it would be appropriate."

Anisa nodded in agreement, her mind trailing now that Nasser had been mentioned. After everything Ara had revealed to her, it wasn't surprising that she'd been too preoccupied to think of anything or *anyone* else. But now Nasser was all she could think of again. And the subject of how her parents died reminded her of what Nasser had said to her in their last conversation a few days ago.

She'd thought Nasser's insinuation that her parents were killed was unusually cruel. Now she knew that he had only tried to warn her of the truth. Like Ara, Nasser had just been trying to protect her. And like Ara, all she'd done was push him away in fear that his secrets would cause friction between them. That because he was choosing to hide a part of himself away. He didn't trust her. So how could he care for her?

The truth was, she was still scared he could harm her. More so because Anisa knew she loved him.

But he hadn't hurt her thus far, and that had to count for something. At the very least, to spare herself from future regret, Anisa felt compelled to tell him the truth about her feelings for him.

She had all these wasted years of time lost with Ara to mourn. She wouldn't do the same thing with Nasser.

"I have to go," she suddenly announced, hugging her brother before bouncing up to her feet.

Ara gave her a confused look but said nothing and didn't stop her from hurrying away from him.

Anisa raced back to her bedroom, an idea forming in her mind. She rummaged through her luggage and pulled out Nasser's business card. He'd once told her that she could call the number on the card to verify his credentials. Now it might be the only way to get to him. It was perhaps pointless to try, but she wanted to, knowing that this was her last shot at making things right.

Her last chance at bringing Nasser back to her.

My last hope that he'll choose me.

CHAPTER THIRTEEN

WHEN NASSER RECEIVED a call from his main office and discovered from his executive secretary that Anisa had called and left a vague message asking to speak to him as soon as possible, he didn't know what to think except that the universe clearly wanted them to be together.

Not wanting to fumble it with her this time, he dropped everything overnight to drive out to Berbera from his parents' home in Hargeisa.

His mother and father weren't too happy with him for leaving, but they settled down once Nasser promised that he'd return.

"An important meeting came up, and I can't reschedule it," he had fibbed. He didn't want to let his parents in on anything if nothing would come of it. For all Nasser knew, she'd called for something mundane.

That was why he was going to see her.

If she was planning to shatter his heart, he wanted it to be in person. At least that way he could see her one last time.

It was fairly late at night when he'd left Hargeisa and even later by the time his truck's headlights beamed brightly on the steel gates to Anisa and Ara's family home.

The guards cleared him to pass through.

Ara was waiting for him in the foyer, sitting tall and confident in his wheelchair, his neutral expression not giving away how he felt about Nasser visiting so late and without forewarning.

"I didn't know we had an appointment," he said.

Nasser's mouth went dry. He'd been in such a rush to see Anisa that he hadn't given much thought to what to say to her overprotective older brother.

"We don't have an appointment." And before he was forced to think up a lie on the spot, a familiar voice he longed to hear came floating down from above them.

"I called him."

Nasser's heart gave a jolt as his head snapped up. Anisa came bounding down the stairs in fuzzy slippers, her oversized knit sweater and black loose-fit jeans giving her a homey look. She had her glasses on again, her eyes wide behind the hexagonal frames.

"You're here to see my sister."

"I am," Nasser said, his mouth drying because he had a hard time peeling his gaze off Anisa, and because Ara's hawkish stare seemed to assess him for any danger he might pose Anisa.

Still looking at Nasser unblinkingly, Ara asked Anisa, "Can we talk?"

They walked a little way from where he stood before speaking, and Ara, not seeming to care whether Nasser heard him or not, spoke loudly.

"Say the word and I'll send him away."

Nasser tensed at Ara's threat, his hands clenching into fists as he fought the urge to adjust his collar and relieve the heat slashing over the back of his neck.

The only thing that relaxed him was Anisa's laugh.

It has to be a good sign that she's in a humorous mood.

"Remember, I told you I called him," she said once her laughter subsided. "It would be rude if you sent him away."

"Are you sure?" he intoned.

Nasser was in awe that Anisa didn't wilt before Ara's drilling gaze.

She shook her head. "I know you're only trying to protect

me." Then, leaning down, she kissed Ara's cheek, hugged her brother, and pulled back from him. "I've got this though. I love you, but I promise I can protect myself too."

Ara's mouth opened, but whatever he said was too soft for Nasser to hear.

If he had to guess, he would say that Ara told Anisa he loved her too. It certainly would explain why Anisa came walking over to him with a smile full of her inner joy. Looking at her beautiful smiling face, he was struck by the instinct to take her into his arms and kiss her. And Nasser might have given in to the temptation if he hadn't noticed Ara watching them.

Returning his sharp look, Nasser tried to communicate that he wasn't here to harm Ara's sister, and that he wouldn't ever do anything to hurt her.

Not again.

After what felt like a long while, Ara bobbed his head once at Nasser and wheeled back. It seemed he'd been cleared to speak to Anisa. Still, even though Ara rolled away into another room and left them alone in the entrance hall, Nasser couldn't help but feel that he was being watched and tested.

One wrong move and I'm certain he'll drive me out.

Not only out of their home, but out of Anisa's life.

He didn't even care that he'd lose Ara's business. All he cared about in that moment was undoing the damage he'd caused to her impression of him.

"Do you want to go for a walk on the beach?" she asked.

"Yes," Nasser said quickly, feeling like he'd be able to talk more freely out of earshot of her brother.

Less than half an hour later, they were exiting his truck and navigating their way toward the dark waters of the ocean.

Anisa took off her sandals, dangling them from her hands as they fell into step.

Following suit, Nasser slipped off his socks and Italian

leather shoes, once again realizing he hadn't really dressed for their beach outing. But it only reminded him of how quickly he'd hurried to answer her summons. And how *desperately* he didn't want to ruin this opportunity she'd given him to fix the mistake he'd made with her.

He was admittedly nervous, but he wasn't going to squander this moment. Fortifying himself, he said, "My secretary informed me that you called. I only received the message a couple hours ago." Then, wanting to address how cold and insensitive he'd been the last time he saw her, Nasser blurted, "Truthfully? I didn't think I'd hear from you again."

"Are you upset that I called?"

Nasser couldn't help himself when she asked that. He reached out instinctively, taking her arm and gently drawing her to a standstill with him. Now facing each other, the light of a crescent moon barely casting shadows on the beach, he looked down into her eyes and unstuck his tongue from the roof of his mouth.

"Upset? How could I be upset when I wanted to see you?"

"Why?"

He breathed more shallowly, a pressure manifesting over his chest, right above his heart. "I didn't like what I said to you last time. It's haunted me since I left you. Because you were right. Vengeance wasn't the answer." He bared his soul, telling Anisa about the emptiness he'd felt upon facing one of his brother's killers, Sharmarke, and the warmth of being honest with his parents about Nuruddin. He needed her to know that he trusted her with everything. Every part of him could now be hers if she wanted it.

So it was worrying that she moved back from him, forcing his hand to fall off her arm.

She then hugged herself and stared at him, her eyes owlish behind her glasses and full of wariness.

He didn't blame her for being leery of him after he'd gone

from hot to cold and back in a span of days. Only now he knew that the feverish heat she'd inspired in him would never let him go—and he didn't want it to.

Not ever.

"Anisa," he said, holding his ground and giving her the space she clearly needed. "I would have come back even if you hadn't left the message. I was planning how I would do it." He had gone through several scenarios, from finding an excuse to have a meeting with Ara at his house to staging an encounter with her while pretending to do updates to Ara's home security features. "I was beginning to run out of plausible ideas to get a chance to speak with you, and then your message came through. I knew our meeting again was fated."

Anisa hugged her arms tighter before finally whispering, "I want to believe you. I do…"

"But you can't," he finished for her.

She sighed. "It's just that I don't want to hope and get hurt again."

Nasser was stricken by her words. All his effort to protect her hadn't taken into account that he'd been the reason she was hurting so badly right now.

Maybe that was why he skipped everything he'd planned to tell her and leaped to the crux of why he had driven at ungodly speeds to close the distance between them and see her again. "I love you."

When she stared at him, her eyes doubling in size and her lips parting in awe, Nasser repeated it for her.

"I'm in love with you, Anisa, and that's why I'm here."

He loved her?

Anisa wouldn't have trusted her own ears if she didn't see for herself that his eyes shone with the proof. He looked at her as though she was all that mattered. Not his vengeance or his secrets or his driving need to protect her. Just her.

"I know that I've hurt you, but if it's any reassurance, I hurt myself even more," he continued, uncharacteristically breathless. From the moment she came down the stairs and rescued him from Ara's interrogation, Anisa had sensed a change in him. And she could hear it for herself and see it in the way Nasser's chest rose and fell quickly. His words rushed out of him like he couldn't speak fast enough to capture all that he felt.

Naturally Anisa's qualms slowly and surely vanished, one by one, leaving her with a restlessness to go to him.

But she held back, knowing that if she went to him right then, she wouldn't be able to say what was on her mind. Following his sweet confession of love for her, it was the hardest thing to stand apart from him, and he only made it more difficult when his face darkened with heartbreaking disappointment.

"The reason I called you, Nasser, was because I didn't like how we ended things either. I shouldn't have let you walk away, even if at the time I thought that was what you needed." She gulped, nervousness pricking at her. "It was the same with Ara. I pushed him away because I believed it was what he wanted, and I was wrong. It was like you told me. He didn't call or message me for all that time because he was scared that I'd reject him."

"You two mended things then," Nasser said with a nod and smile. "Good."

"I'm glad that you and your parents managed to talk, too." She could see that speaking to his family had been good for him. The haunted look in his eyes the last time she saw him was gone. "I guess we both learned that we should be honest about our feelings with those we love."

"And what about us? Where do we stand now?" he asked softly.

Nasser had given her everything she had once asked of

him. The sheer honesty and openness, and above all else the complete trust in her. Anisa didn't need to think about it, quietly inching forward then, her bare feet gliding over the sand to him, her toes digging in when she stood before him with very little space between them.

"I think," she began, her heart thumping in her ears, "that we're far better than before."

Nasser responded by taking the hand she wasn't holding her sandals with and running his thumb over her knuckles.

Anisa leaned into him then, her cheek pressing into his chest, and feeling his chin settle over her head. He let go of her hand and embraced her. The cozy warmth suffusing her heart and spreading out from her core changed into a fiery need in the blink of an eye. Gripping the front of his shirt and turning her blushing face up to him, she said, "I also think that we can stand a whole lot closer."

His deep, throaty laugh thrummed through her, his mirth becoming her own.

"Odd," he said then, his face closing in on hers. Their lips brushed softly as he murmured against her mouth, "I was thinking the exact same thing."

Anisa didn't know if it was her long anticipation or the relief that he loved her that weakened her legs more. Thankfully, Nasser stabilized her and allowed Anisa to deepen their kiss. He returned her passion with just as much enthusiasm. When they came up for air, she gasped, "I love you," her face flushing with the embarrassing realization that she hadn't told him before.

But with twinkling eyes, Nasser merely said, "I know, Anisa. I know."

EPILOGUE

A year later

ANISA WAGGLED HER fingers at Darya and their other friends, smiling widely at their appreciative noises when the sunlight sparkled off her new and now most treasured piece of jewelry. The engagement ring was not the first beautiful gift Nasser had given her, and frankly, it wasn't even her favorite.

No, that was reserved for the cheap but pretty phone chain Nasser had given to her a year ago, shortly after he'd declared his love to her and she had returned his feelings. The chain had replaced the one she'd broken when they first met. Nasser had bought it while they'd been in Nosy Be for the jazz festival—he just hadn't told her.

Still, as much as she adored the phone chain, she couldn't stop staring at or touching the engagement ring. Even now, she found herself stroking the diamond lovingly, to the amusement of Darya, who nudged her with a grin.

"So, tell me, are you more in love with the gorgeous ring or the equally gorgeous man?"

Anisa looked up, her eyes easily finding Nasser in the crowd of their friends and family. He was looking at her, too, somehow holding a conversation with her brother and sharing a secret smile with her from afar.

"The man. Definitely the man," Anisa said to Darya.

How was it that she fell more in love with him with each

passing day? And she knew Nasser felt the same about her, constantly letting her in on how grouchy he became when work pulled him away from her—or her work kept them apart for some time. It happened more now that she'd quit her job as a production assistant, moved back to Berbera permanently, finished her script, secured a film agent, and successfully pitched her idea to a small but growing production company. Anisa still had a way to go before she saw her creativity come to life on-screen, but she was several steps closer, and just happy that she was finally doing what she always wanted to do for a career.

Nasser was busy, too, expanding his business and extending his services to those who might not have the money and means to afford what his wealthier clientele could access. He even began recruiting young men who had left the military in Somaliland and were looking for a good job to provide for their families. It meant that he was looking into opening an office in Hargeisa, nearer to her and the life they wanted to build together.

Now that they had a wedding to plan, Anisa was all the happier that he'd gone down the path that he had with his career.

In that way, they had that much more to celebrate than just announcing their engagement to all their loved ones.

Anisa cast him another look and saw him gesture to her to follow him. He excused himself from Ara and the other people he was speaking to and walked away.

She trailed after him, muffling a yelp when his hand shot out from around a quiet corner and drew her into his hard chest.

He tipped her chin up and gave her a sweet, toe-curling peck on the mouth.

"Stop," she chided, lightly swatting him and looking

around for any eyes on them. "What will my brother, your parents and all our other guests think if they catch us?"

"That we should skip this engagement and turn the congratulatory party into a wedding."

She poked at his chest gently. "Don't tease me like that—I'm already stressing about planning a wedding in a year. The thought of doing it in one day…" She mockingly shuddered at his implied deadline, biting back a soft moan when his hands framed her hips and pulled her harder into him. "Keep that up and you'll have us married this second if my brother and your parents have their way. Anything to prevent a scandal."

"I'm bargaining on it," he said with a smug smile before he stole another kiss from her.

He finally let her go when their names were called. Before the search party discovered them and set off gossiping tongues about premarital escapades, Nasser offered her his elbow like a gentleman and guided her back to their guests. They did the rounds, greeting and thanking everyone. Anisa had worried most about Nasser's parents, but his mother and father were more than welcoming. Pleased by the news their son was getting married, they'd practically adopted her the instant he'd introduced them. She'd gained a form of surrogate parents in them.

"I hope my mother and father aren't being too pushy," Nasser said to her when he had her alone next, only this time it was out in the open so that neither of them would be as easily tempted to sneak kisses and prolonged touches.

"Pushy?" Anisa wrinkled her nose and shook her head immediately. "No way! I think they had a good idea about potentially looking into a guest space for them once we're married and moved into our new home."

"Let's table that. I'm not ready to share you just yet." Nasser's laughter rumbled through her as he pulled her closer against him. When she tried to push him away, he only held her tighter, breathing into her ear, "Don't worry. No one's looking, so let me hold you a little longer."

After that she didn't have the heart to try to wriggle free, not that she ever really wanted to in the first place.

When Anisa did finally pull back enough to look around, she realized with a start that someone was missing. "Where's Ara?"

Darya was within earshot, and she turned to them and pointed toward the exit. "I just saw your brother walk out. There was a woman with him." She went on to describe the woman. Nasser told Anisa, "That sounds like Zaynab. His wife."

"Soon to be ex-wife," Anisa reminded him, keeping her voice low so as to not generate a rumor. Ara was already dealing with the finalization of his divorce. Zaynab seemed like a nice person, but Anisa didn't know what to think of her in light of the impending marital dissolution. All she'd seen was Ara's quiet torment. She wasn't sure if it was because he felt like he owed Zaynab something after her father, Sharmarke, was officially sentenced to prison for the cover-up of Nasser's brother Nuruddin's death and other political corruption schemes, or if Ara truly cared about her.

"Should we go after him?" she asked Nasser.

He frowned, shaking his head slowly. "We could, but he's an adult, Anisa. If he wanted our help, I'm sure he would have asked us."

She knew Nasser was right. It was just that she felt as though Ara could use her help for once.

Reading her mind, Nasser gave her a hug. She melted into his arms, blushing when she caught the stares of some of their guests who had noticed their lengthy embrace.

"Nasser, everyone's beginning to look at us," she remarked, trying to pull back, only to feel his arms cage around her tighter.

"Let them stare. All they're seeing anyways is a man who is hopelessly and perpetually smitten with his lovely new fiancée."

Anisa smiled brightly, seeing his logic for herself. Then, closing her eyes, she held him to her heart, where Nasser was and always would be, and where she knew without a doubt that he held her too.

* * * * *

If you enjoyed this story,
check out these other great reads from
Hana Sheik:

The Baby Swap That Bound Them
Forbidden Kisses with Her Millionaire Boss
Temptation in Istanbul

All available now!

COMING SOON!

We really hope you enjoyed reading this book.
If you're looking for more romance
be sure to head to the shops when
new books are available on

Thursday 26th September

MILLS & BOON®

Coming next month

ALWAYS THE BRIDESMAID
Ally Blake

'Are you serious? You will actually be a pretend best man at the wedding of a person you do not know, for me?'

Shut up, Charlie! Just say thank you, then, maybe have him swear a blood pact.

By then Beau had pushed his chair back, and also stood. He tossed his napkin to the table and said, 'It seems so.'

Charlie felt as if a pair of hands grabbed her by the waist, lifted her from her chair and propelled her around the table then, for suddenly she was leaning over Beau, flinging her arms around his neck and hugging the life out of him.

Her body a comma curled into his. The heat of him burning through her clothes, till his heart beat in syncopation with her own.

Her inner monologue cleared its throat, waking her from the heady fog. And she pulled away, pushed more like. Once clear, she tugged at her t-shirt, and attempted a smile.

'Thank-you,' she managed. 'I mean it, Beau. This will be life-changing.'

In a good way for once, she hoped with all her might.

Continue reading
ALWAYS THE BRIDESMAID
Ally Blake

Available next month
millsandboon.co.uk

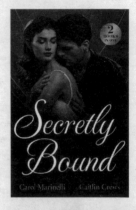
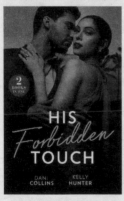
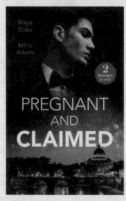

LET'S TALK

Romance

For exclusive extracts, competitions and special offers, find us online:

f MillsandBoon

X @MillsandBoon

⊙ @MillsandBoonUK

♪ @MillsandBoonUK

Get in touch on 01413 063 232

Afterglow Books is a trend-led, trope-filled list of books with diverse, authentic and relatable characters, a wide array of voices and representations, plus real world trials and tribulations. Featuring all the tropes you could possibly want (think small-town settings, fake relationships, grumpy vs sunshine, enemies to lovers) and all with a generous dose of spice in every story.

♪ @millsandboonuk

📷 @millsandboonuk

afterglowbooks.co.uk

#AfterglowBooks

For all the latest book news, exclusive content and giveaways scan the QR code below to sign up to the Afterglow newsletter:

SCAN ME

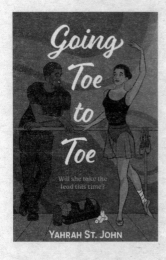

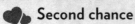
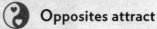
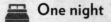
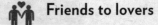

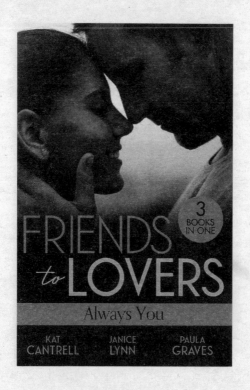

OUT NOW!

Available at
millsandboon.co.uk

MILLS & BOON